Dear Reader,

The first time I read the novel that is now in your hands, I had to go for a walk. I couldn't stop thinking about Sarah and her deeply observant revelations, Minah struggling with the expectations that come with being the eldest daughter, and sweet Esther, so lonely in her pursuit of goodness. Each holding onto their broken bonds of sisterhood.

The women in this novel—their observations, reflections, shame, and desires—are the driving force behind this story of morally questionable fortune-seeking. You may recognize your own pain and anxieties in a universal theme: no matter how high-minded, personal or creative, our dreams always seem to come with a sticker price. What do we have to pay in order to achieve what we seek? What are we willing to give up? Even forgiveness, that most elusive of priceless transformations, comes with a cost.

While *Sisters K* certainly delves into dark places (it is inspired by Dostoyevsky, after all), I cherish the comfort and catharsis I find in its singular moments: strawberries dipped in sugar; a poignant response from a thoughtful student; haircuts on kitchen chairs; cold opalescent skies; the kindness of neighbors; a message finally received. These moments stay with me with all the lyrical tenderness and power of a Mitski melody. Between the sisters there is harsh sarcasm and sharply cutting remarks, a hot priest and unanticipated twists—all of which I think lovers of *Brothers* will find delight in.

Maureen's work is an illumination of all that writhes in the dark corners of the soul. It has been a privilege to be her editor and an honor to introduce you to her masterful debut. Each sisters' transformation through their harrowing ordeal transformed me in turn. May they transform you.

Sincerely,

Allison Miriam Smith
Editor

The Sisters K

A Novel

Maureen Sun

THE UNNAMED PRESS
LOS ANGELES, CA

AN UNNAMED PRESS BOOK

Copyright © 2024 by Maureen Sun

Published in North America by the Unnamed Press.

www.unnamedpress.com

Unnamed Press, and the colophon, are registered trademarks of Unnamed Media LLC.

Hardcover ISBN: 978-1-961884-06-9

This book is a work of fiction. Names, characters, places and incidents are wholly fictional or are used fictitiously. Any resemblance to actual events or persons, living or dead, is entirely coincidental.

Cover artwork: Reclining Woman by Henry Moore
Cover design and typeset by Jaya Nicely

Manufactured in the United States of America

Distributed by Publishers Group West

First Edition

Divided tongues, as of fire, appeared among them,
and a tongue rested on each of them.

—Acts 2:3

Contents

Part 5

Part 6

The Sisters K

Part 1

For do you not sometimes dream that you can sing whatever note you like,
and run up and down the whole scale, like the angels on Jacob's ladder?
I sometimes dream that even now.

—Isak Dinesen, "The Deluge at Norderney"

1

The daughters

The sisters Minah, Sarah, and Esther shared the same father but were not full-blooded siblings. And though they each considered the same woman their mother, they were not raised by the same women.

No one could or would tell Minah, the eldest, much about the woman who gave birth to her and, as their father claimed, abandoned her to return to Korea when she was one or two—the facts were never clear. He said that after her mother abandoned her he had no choice but to send Minah back to Korea to be with his brother's family. Minah couldn't remember them, only the day of her return to Los Angeles. She disembarked clutching at a flight attendant on a day in high summer and met Jeonghee, her new stepmother. Above and beyond them stretched the vast, impressive ceiling and endless corridors and dazzling wall-to-wall windows of LAX, where the infrastructure seemed to be protecting everyone from the heavens crushing them on all sides.

"There she is," Eugene indicated indifferently, already turning to leave the terminal. Jeonghee took Minah's hand. At Jeonghee's side, Minah could see only her stepmother's belly, which was protruding with child.

Jeonghee was happy to find that her stepdaughter, contrary to reports from Eugene and her brother-in-law, was attentive and affectionate. She was lonely in America, in her small minimally furnished house, in a suburb she could not locate on a map, knowing only that it was an hour outside LA. At first she'd been impressed by her freshly painted new home, one of a row of cottage-like houses with front yards presenting trimmed bushes and pruned trees. It soon became a place of confinement. She knew no one apart from her husband, who was away all day, and was afraid to venture outside alone. Minah became her solace and only friend.

Minah, just learning to speak in complex sentences, never left her new mother's side. "Let's have breakfast," Jeonghee said every morning. "You spilled cereal on the floor." "Let's have lunch." "Let's watch TV." "You can have a snack." "You can play in the backyard while I cook." But Minah didn't want to leave her, so Jeonghee continued to talk. "I'm going to make rice porridge for us. You have to cook the rice for a long, long time. Do you want something else?"

"Let's have a rest," she said often, because her calves were swollen and her back ached.

She began to talk about herself. "I'm going to wash my hair today. I need to learn to drive. Your father said he'd teach me. After I learn I can take us to the hair salon. I don't feel right with my hair like this. I feel like I can't leave the house. We can both get our hair done at the salon. That would be exciting, wouldn't it?"

"Yes, yes!" Minah exclaimed.

At the table, between bites, Jeonghee said quietly, "Strawberries dipped in sugar might be my favorite thing. We can have them all the time, if we want, did you know that? You can always find strawberries here even if they're not in season. We should be happy about that. We should always think of good things."

Minah chewed and nodded. She was happy with Jeonghee. For a few minutes they ate in silence.

Jeonghee said dreamily, "I wonder what your mother was like."

Minah stopped chewing. "My mother?"

She'd believed a mother was a person to acquire and that she did, at last, possess a very good one.

"Let's finish the strawberries," Jeonghee said quickly. "Your father's going to bring some melons tonight. He doesn't like strawberries, so they're just for us."

Jeonghee didn't talk to Minah around her husband. When Eugene was home she treated Minah coolly, like a nuisance, and waited on him. Minah, far from being displeased, felt she had a secret relationship with Jeonghee. Eugene managed his dry-cleaning business from early morning to early evening and sometimes didn't return home until late at night. Her bond with Jeonghee made the true, secret life of the household, which her father merely visited, where she and Jeonghee existed in their love.

On the nights when Minah heard Jeonghee wailing, screaming, pleading in the bedroom with her father, she covered her head with a pillow and repeated some of the things Jeonghee had said to her and her alone, including her insistence that Minah never approach the master bedroom.

Jeonghee went into labor during the seventh month of her pregnancy and returned from the hospital without a baby. Within months she was pregnant again with Sarah.

Jeonghee was only one of the many women and girls who would look after the sisters.

During her convalescence and second pregnancy, Jeonghee rarely left her room. Eugene hired a series of babysitters for Minah. Tanya, Erica, Brie, Jennifer, and Jenny were teenagers who quit within weeks. Gail was the exception. She was tough and duplicitous and had no qualms shutting Minah in her room, a chair under the knob to her door, while she met her friends in the yard. She didn't even mind Eugene's leering at first, thinking she could turn his prurience to her advantage. But Eugene fired her after discovering the boys lurking in the alley behind the house.

"Fucking Oriental perv," she screamed from the street before getting in her car.

"You don't need a babysitter anymore," Eugene decided. Minah was sitting rigid on the sofa, her fists so tight they were turning white.

The other girls left their own traces, having introduced Minah to bubble-gum, clear nail polish, and the phenomenon of crying, not out of personal grief, but for the plight of a person on the screen.

Jeonghee, too, sometimes cried now when they watched TV. They were watching a western that bored Minah. A man with flaring nostrils and heavy jowls whom Minah found faintly repellant was holding his hat to his chest and gazing into the eyes of a woman touching her apron to the corner of her eye.

She asked her mother if she was sad. Jeonghee wiped her tears and said nothing, which not only hurt but frustrated Minah. With high-pitched petulance she asked, in English, "Are you really feeling sad?"

Jeonghee got up and returned to her bedroom. She didn't talk to Minah anymore except as she did in the very beginning. "Let's eat lunch." "Let's watch TV." She referred to herself only to say, "I'm tired. I'm going back to sleep."

They brought Sarah home.

Eugene was beaming. "Your mother did very well," he said to Minah.

Jeonghee was very pale. Around her, vivid flowers were blooming in red and fuchsia, gold and mauve, their petals like the waves of a fever. That morning, Eugene had rushed out to purchase three bouquets for her. She looked at them without, it seemed to Minah, registering that they were something out of the ordinary and crept toward the bedroom leaning on Eugene.

But Jeonghee had noticed the flowers: the gorgeous, gaudy colors seemed to mock her, and she resolved to see right through them.

Eugene had also brought home a crate of her favorite Asian pears and boxes of tangerines, apples, and strawberries. Jeonghee loved fruit. He bought her slippers and scented soap, a soft pink robe and hand cream that could also be applied, he said proudly, to her stretch marks. He was proud to know this detail about women's bodies. He neglected to buy supplies for the baby, apart from diapers, but Minah's cradle was still in the garage. At Jeonghee's request he bought soft blankets, bottles, nipples, and formula for Sarah.

Once his second daughter was brought home, Minah, for him, became morally illegitimate. With Sarah's birth, he grew besotted with Jeonghee's frailty, sublimely different from his first wife's willfulness. Though Minah bore his name and blood, he decided that Sarah was his true firstborn. Minah's mother had chosen her daughter's name for its resonance with Korean syllabics; Eugene chose "Sarah" himself, the Anglophone name of the well-bred Korean girls in whose company he was determined she would belong and whom she would excel in every way. She would be raised with greater devotion and privilege than Minah. The beautiful meekness of her mother assured him that Sarah would grow to be a more prepossessing woman than Minah or Minah's mother.

He was forgetful; he was wildly self-absorbed. He was also sentimental, and though he would often neglect Sarah, confusing his satisfaction with her as his offspring with fulfillment of her needs, the memory of her first weeks at home—when he felt passionate love for his wife and love and pride in his second daughter—became a sentimental touchstone for the rest of his life.

Two years would pass before Esther was born. It was Jeonghee who decided on her name, taken from one of the nurses in her ward, a somewhat surly and intimidating woman who Jeonghee sensed was the same age as herself, but whose broad, bony face, with red-rimmed nose and faded blue eyes, appeared ten years older. Jeonghee timorously assented with cowed nods and pounding heart to all the orders Esther barked at her about caring for the baby and caring for herself. When Esther left, and she was alone behind her partition, she realized the nurse had jolted her awake after months of thoroughgoing enervation. There was no trace of compassion in the nurse's attitude. Her hard bristling energy aroused envy in Jeonghee, who dreamt of being emptied out, unburdened of herself, the ever-present consciousness that weighted her like water in a drowning body.

Eugene was less excited about Esther's birth, if only because it seemed a repetition of Sarah's. His feelings, in this vein, were already spent.

For the first years of Esther's life, Jeonghee confined herself once more to her bedroom, holding and nursing her infant in bed, using Esther as a shield against Eugene, who was enraged by his wife's uselessness. But he would not strike a baby. When he accepted that she was indeed ill, he charged Minah with the care of her sisters after school, when he was away from home. But Minah wandered elsewhere with her peers, and Esther began to spend most of her time at the next-door neighbors'. In the afternoons, only Sarah was at home.

Eugene's schedule was increasingly irregular; he might be away for two or twelve hours of the day, or even a few days and nights. Apart from his dry-cleaning business, with which the children were familiar, he was involved in real estate ventures and unknown investments he often discussed on the phone. What the children, usually Sarah, overheard was sinister and obscure. They heard their father warmly greeting his associates, sharing smugly in crude, casual jokes about girls, women, white people, and Black people, spewing vicious curses on anyone who complicated their plans with frightening vitality. There was a world the daughters could not see, peopled with men like their father.

Their father was himself sinister and obscure. He yelled at them, he slapped them and knocked their heads and threatened worse beatings and brutal privation. His anger they recognized and understood; they heard it at school and saw it on TV. More unsettling was his laughter, the grin and glee with which he patted the girls on the shoulder after they'd picked up the shoes, bowls, or toys he'd thrown at them, the gentle chuckle with which he pointed out the shards at their feet.

He took them once to visit Jeonghee at the hospital. She was sleeping. Her lips were white and cracked; saliva, thick as glue, trailed down her chin. When a nurse entered, Sarah turned away from her mother and searched the woman's face for guidance. Minah alone expressed sorrow and began to cry.

Eugene pulled Minah into an embrace. The gesture was so gratifying, his giddy excitement overflowed. He was eager to prolong his performance and elicit admiration from the nurse.

"*I try to help them, but I think this is a bad idea, but I think maybe they want their mommy,*" he said in awkward English, stroking Minah's arm as she sobbed.

The nurse, uncomprehending, didn't respond. She was watching Esther, who crept up to their mother to wipe the drool, then stared at her own wet finger. Esther shifted her gaze from her finger to Minah, and she, too, began to cry.

After their father dropped them off at home, Minah locked herself in the bathroom.

She was thirteen. Over the course of Jeonghee's decline, her independence and stubbornness came to bitter fruition. Her father's rages drove her to tears, but even his threats and beatings could never induce her to clean the house or cook or help Sarah with her homework. She smoked in the alley, stole makeup from the drugstore, and stayed with friends in their homes whenever she could.

Finally, when it was clear that Jeonghee's surgery had failed, their father capitulated. He hired an elderly Korean widow to cook for them and a young Mexican woman, Carla, to clean the house on weekends. He also called upon Carla sporadically, when he was away till very late or gone overnight, to look after the children. But she herself was so young, only nineteen, extremely shy and especially awkward in English, that she provided little companionship for the sisters. Minah and Sarah were already accustomed to relying upon themselves; Esther demanded to be allowed to go next door. Carla mostly watched TV and nervously gestured for the older girls to join her, which they sometimes did, as long as she agreed to change the channel.

Between their mother's first hospitalization and the introduction of the *ajumma* and Carla, Eugene made weekly shopping trips to the supermarket and Target or Costco with Sarah. It was a bewildering ritual for her. He asked her what they should eat, what she and her sisters needed for school. She was seven and wasn't sure, and so for months until the *ajumma* prepared their dinners, the fridge was stocked with dozens of hot dogs and cartons of spoiling milk, and Minah had little to wear apart from a sparkling sweatshirt and a T-shirt laminated with the faces of a boy band she loathed.

Sarah rarely spoke in her father's presence or even conversed with her sisters. On her expeditions with her father she mostly pointed at things or said a mix of simple English and Korean: "markers," "shoes," "this." He held her hand and grinned and said she was much better than Minah, better even than Esther. He could tell: Sarah was smart and well-behaved, a good girl, his favorite child. He liked that she rarely whined or cried and asked him to buy notebooks in which she said she was writing stories. Esther was good but weak, badly made. She had cried through more nights and thrown more tantrums as an infant and toddler than either her or Minah.

Every week he told Sarah he was growing rich. He was saving all his wealth for the future. If she continued to be good, it would be hers.

❧

Eugene was impulsive, but this did not mean he was not analytical, not reflec-tive. It gave him a terrible thrill—he knew it was terrible, this frisson—to possess insight into other people, especially his daughters; to wield knowledge with which he might shape and deceive, tease and possess. And so, as long as his daughters lived with him, he was apt to sit and stare at them in silence, scrutinizing for a few minutes, longer, before returning to the pleasurable maelstrom of his more thoughtless actions and unfiltered reactions.

It was the only time he was so still. The sisters could not forget he was there; they adapted to his gaze, learning to detect the looming and disappear-ance of another consciousness at their backs. They learned, too, to pretend they did not notice or care, except when he entered their room, always without knocking, as they were changing. When this happened, they either ran from the room with their clothes at their chests or pulled them on with such urgency they might rush out without noticing that their necks were con-stricted within the taut band of a sleeve. He didn't stop them from leaving, though sometimes they heard him give a surly growl about the requirements of a father to surveil the morality of his daughters. Other times he simply laughed at their skittishness.

"I like to watch them, observe their characters," Eugene once said to the *ajumma* who dropped their meals off once a week.

When he focused his malice and hunger upon Minah, she could feel herself burning under the hot light of his cold heart, like the suspects she saw interrogated on TV writhing under the glare of supercharged overhead lights. The interrogator across the table and his invisible colleagues, protected by the one-way glass, wanted a confession, but what did her father want? She understood he wanted more than the completion of chores and general com-pliance. Perhaps he, too, wanted a confession, but it would be the admission to something of which she was innocent. She hated him and could not think of herself as guilty in any way before him.

When he was raging at her, she sensed dimly her father was experiencing pleasure and that this pleasure gave him life. She found no relief in the calculated lapses of rage, when he, ever grinning, gave her a twenty and said, "One day you'll understand."

She was too young to understand that he wanted her to want his love. He wanted to change her so that she would want it. He wanted her to suffer from this want; he wanted her to suffer.

She wanted to do anything to get away from his heartless wants, his pleasure. At such moments she thought of the woman who'd given birth to her. She realized, with the unbearable despair of a much younger child lost on an empty street, that her first mother, too, had been desperate to escape.

They were alike, she and this unknown woman, except that her mother had succeeded where she could not—not for a while.

2

The neighbors

It was by coincidence that a Russian family came to live next door to Eugene's, the only other immigrant household in that quarter of the middle- to lower-middle-class white neighborhood.

Anna first encountered Sarah and Esther when Misha, her three-year-old grandson, drawn to the sounds of the sisters in their yard, wedged his pacifier between the planks of the wooden fence concealing them from view.

The two sisters were making mud pies. Sarah topped hers with grass she said was mint chocolate and was foisting it on Esther to eat, pressing it into her chin. Esther shook her head and started shrieking. When Anna opened the back gate, fearing that the girls had tried to dislodge the pacifier and embedded their hands with splinters, she didn't understand at first what she saw. Esther's face, limbs, and round bare belly were smeared with mud. It was drizzling. One of the safety pins of her diaper had come undone.

Sarah glared moodily at Anna before lowering her eyes.

Anna closed the gate. She reminded herself that Minah, the girl with heavily lined coltish eyes she would see slipping back home through the alley after dark, also belonged to the household. She remembered the times she'd seen Sarah through the window sitting alone in the front yard, seemingly absorbed in knocking a stick against the front steps. The childish sobs and screams erupting at all hours next door had provoked greater irritation than alarm. In these hazy images of her ignorance, the children were content in their innocence and ordinary in their unhappiness.

She found herself knocking at her neighbors' door and introducing herself to Jeonghee, who appeared wrapped in the robe gifted by Eugene long ago, now threadbare and nearly white. She had planned to confront the girls' mother with their neglect; she hadn't known she would offer to look after the two younger children at her own home, for her own benefit, she explained, so that her grandson would have company. Jeonghee was at first frightened by the stranger, as she was more and more by most people, and even confused by Anna as a specimen, a white woman with broken English. She had trouble grasping what Anna was saying. Anna's tone was pressing and impersonal, as if she were not speaking of children but steps to repair a faulty power line upon which they both depended.

Then Jeonghee understood. Without consulting Eugene, she agreed to let Esther spend the day with Anna and Misha. She even smiled, not because of the offer, but for her gratitude to the dignified older woman for not re-proaching her, not making any reference, as far as she could tell, to the state of her children.

She had a flash of Esther's namesake. She wanted to care again, but she cared less for her children than she wanted to care for them. She wanted to care for her most helpless child. The memory of caring, of loving, shuddered through her.

Sarah, however, had to stay with her. Eugene was in the habit of talking to Sarah when he returned home. He whispered to her about his business affairs, smirking at Jeonghee as he lowered his voice just enough so that his wife couldn't hear. As a threat to his wife he loudly asked Sarah whether she liked her packed lunches. He wanted her to practice the piano in his presence, to prove she was making progress. When he was unhappy with her, for lack of improvement, for backtalk and sullen silence, he locked her outdoors, either in the front or backyard. At first he allowed her to take a

pencil and a notebook with her; eventually he saw this as a counterproduc-
tive indulgence. Over time Sarah stopped responding to these expulsions
with the hysterical fear and despair that had seized her in the beginning,
especially after dark. She remained in a trance while outside, sitting quietly,
pulling up grass, wholly given over to doing nothing, whittling herself
down to nothing.

Esther continued to fuss and throw tantrums when she returned from
the neighbors', to which Eugene might respond with pinches or screams
until Jeonghee took her away and carried her back and forth in the garage.
She directed all her energy into nurturing and protecting Esther. In her
heart she had already ceded Sarah to her father.

Minah was allowed to do as she wanted. When her friends learned to drive
she began to leave the neighborhood, often spending the night with them.

Eugene didn't discover that Esther was regularly at the neighbors' for
several weeks. At first he was furious, thinking that the previous tenants, a
couple who twice called the police to report a domestic disturbance, were
now trying to take away his children. When he learned about Anna, he
knocked at her door one afternoon with a bottle of wine and the simpering,
conspiratorial grin he burnished for new people he wanted to win over.

Anna's daughter, Katya, Misha's mother, answered the door. She was
rarely home; it was her day off. She liked the little girl she sometimes came
across in her living room but hadn't given much thought to the girl's family.
She took a step back before catching herself. Here was a goblin, a compact
man with large yellowing teeth stooping in an ingratiating attitude. She
recognized his grin and ironic laughing eyes as the same kind of menacing
sneer she used to regularly receive as a young woman from strange men.
She was horrified by his blotchy, shriveled, simian-like right hand. Even if
she'd known it was scarred from a burn and further damaged from regular
exposure to dry-cleaning chemicals, his hand, attached to the rest of him,
would have struck her as an emblem of evil. In it, Eugene was holding a bottle
of wine.

She pushed herself to accept it. She forced herself to smile. It was a blessing for Esther that she did.

When Sarah was sent next door to retrieve her sister, she went in anticipation of hearing music. In the evening Anna often played the piano or listened to cassettes of classical music as Esther and Misha played on the floor. Sometimes Katya came home early from work and drifted brightly through the house singing softly as she cooked, drank wine, complained about her clients at the salon, teased and kissed Misha and Esther.

Sarah was told by her father not to linger at the neighbors', but after her mother died she was loath to remain home alone. She'd grown used to her mother shut up in the master bedroom, emerging only to ignore her; she had found reassurance in the bare fact of her mother's physical nearness. With her mother absolutely gone, she told herself she was not being disobedient by spending an hour, a couple of hours, waiting for her sister, since the cassette player at home was broken and her piano teacher wanted her to listen to music on her own.

She came to love Anna's home, to sit on the sofa with one of the books on the coffee table Anna had strategically left out for her, discounted books on impressionism and Greek myths, the Bible, and a few Penguin classics. She liked to enter and walk down the long rug, faded and intricate with arabesques, to the living room, where small, unremarkable paintings of dark trees and bright fruit hung on the walls. One tall lamp had pale tassels hanging from its cream-colored shade; another, on a grainy wooden side table, had a bulging glazed ceramic base glowing with broad rings of red and blue. This was a home with details. Sarah waited on the deep brown velour sofa and realized she did not remember, at that moment, the color of the sofa at home, except that it was pale, with a pattern; she could not remember whether it was softer or firmer than the one she was on. She had the impression that this room, unlike her living room at home, would never be forgotten. Even if the family moved and threw out the things that made its ineffable atmosphere—the lamps, the sofa, the paintings—and themselves forgot this place, some trace of it would survive in the material world. For if most rooms were like mere photocopies, this space possessed the third dimension of accretions of a layered, worked, and reworked painting.

In both this household and Sarah's the furnishings testified to the contingencies of thrift. But to be in her own house, to move through the yard, the common areas, the bedroom in which she had a twin bed and Esther and Minah shared a bunk bed, was to be hopelessly caught up with the roving eye of an utterly mindless camera. At home her own vision was suppressed, forced to become one with this relentless recording, with these cadences of movement and respite, confinement and escape.

Anna told Sarah she should bring her homework and work at the dining table; Misha and Esther always took so long to eat their snacks, finish their games, and practice their scales with her. She said, in a quiet, affectless voice, "They are so slow, and you do nothing." Sarah couldn't tell if Anna was aware of the comfort she took in watching the younger children, if she was inviting her to be a part of her home; or if she was judging Sarah for her idleness or even her longing, which was stronger than her shame at wanting to stay.

Anna occasionally asked her to show what she'd learned from her music lessons, but she always refused with a hard shake of the head. She preferred to remain silent and watch Misha and Esther flanking Anna on the piano bench, by turns cheering or squirming in boredom when Anna performed the simple pieces she wanted them to learn. She liked to watch Anna's face alternately grow more severe or soften as she played, sometimes humming under her breath.

The pieces were simple and yet so polished and profound and clear, minor floating miracles of form, texture, and feeling, each note falling like heavy drops on her body before dissolving completely into chambers within herself that were as equally mysterious, and perishable, as the music. They evoked deep envy and longing in Sarah, and she did not yet know what name to give these feelings or what exactly caused them. She would associate this troubling stirring of emotion with this setting for a long time. Many years later, she understood why she declined to sit at the bench and play herself, though she was rightly confident that she had more innate talent for music than either Misha or Esther or even Anna. She nibbled on crackers and cookies and thought hard about Anna, who was not open or expressive but reserved in speech and her gestures of affection, even with her grandson. Anna, like the room, had layers—unknown depths of wisdom and will, of power—that she could not measure. Sarah was ever anxious that Anna was watching her and forming judgments; she was afraid of Anna and avoided being physically close to her. Anna, like a witch, might smell the fear and unwholesome loneliness that festered at the core of her resentment, budding arrogance, and envy. She was afraid, too, that there was something about herself that would corrupt the tableau of the three on the bench that gave her such a strange feeling of peace. And so she refrained, though she longed to impress Anna, from filling the room with the pieces by Mozart and Chopin that she knew by heart.

But she could not hold back, at the end of a windy afternoon, after watching Misha throw a tantrum over a canceled trip to the pool, from whispering fiercely to Esther as they were gathering their things to a recording of Bach: "This song is in A minor. Did you know that?"

From the muffled music from next door, Anna had known Sarah was musically talented. She did not know Sarah had perfect pitch.

Sarah won several regional piano competitions. She was also a very good student. When she was fourteen, Anna convinced Eugene to send her to a private boarding school in the Northeast.

By then, Minah was living in Seoul. After high school she'd persuaded Eugene to pay for a summer of Korean language school and decided to stay.

Eugene was beginning to drink in the evening. Long a teetotaler—he wanted to have the advantage, he'd told Sarah when she was young, over those who drank—Eugene started phoning Sarah at school in Massachusetts while drunk. During rambling monologues that took place, with the time difference, around midnight, he revealed that he'd hired the most expensive piano teacher in the area for her because of an unspoken wager with a business partner that Sarah would outperform the partner's daughter. She had succeeded magnificently, and for that he was beaming with pride these days. He was delighted, too, that a few Korean parents who patronized the dry-cleaning business had grudgingly congratulated him for his daughter's admission to a prestigious school. That spiteful, sparkling joy of recognition spurred him to spread the news at the Chinese restaurant favored by the community, where he roamed amid the dining tables like an oily maître d', first asking the diners after their own children, rowdy and unhappy, lively and happy, and so vividly imperfect to their parents at that moment. He retreated from time to time to drink alone at his table; after a few beers he wandered the dining hall as if he were the guest of honor, stopping at tables to boast of Sarah's accomplishments even as the fathers interrupted their quarrels with their spouses to tell him they'd had enough. The restaurant fell silent when one man pushed him away. To their collective relief and disgust, Eugene bowed, wiped his eyes, and thanked the man for reminding him to be humble.

The following Sunday he attended the local Korean church, where, laughing, he thanked the Lord for his blessings while dropping several twenties into the collection basket and gorged himself at the potluck following the sermon.

"They want to know: How did a man like this manage this success?" he howled with glee. "I know they hate me, and why they hate me, but I can't help it. I am what I am, and that's what makes them so angry! And now they can't even say I'm a bad father!"

He would alternately call Anna a witch for parting him from so much money for Sarah's tuition and chuckle with gratitude to her for relieving him of the burden of his youngest daughter. He admitted he'd grown so negligent in his duties toward Esther that he was now giving Anna and Katya cash in hand to pay for Esther's clothes and school supplies.

"Without you here, I'm a bad father to your sister. When you're here, I'm better," he said with a treacly fondness that stoked Sarah's revulsion.

When she listened to her father's Korean, Sarah understood the basic sense of his words without always grasping their precise denotations. The first time he cursed Anna, she knew he was describing her as strange and unnatural, and remembered her old uneasiness before her neighbor. She had herself called Anna a witch in her mind, over and over, like an apotropaic chant, to conceal her secret self from Anna's detection, to protect herself from Anna's judgment. Eugene rambled, and Sarah's heart trembled, then thrashed in the prison of her chest. Misha, Esther, and Minah, too, when sent with Sarah to retrieve their sister, were relaxed with the cool but gracious old woman. Only she, Sarah, was compelled to protect herself from Anna's unusual power to detect the black egg in the thick, wild nest of the perceptible person. What did it mean that she shared the same impression of Anna as her father? It must mean that though she embodied a scrambled iteration of both her mother and father, she was, in essence, a repetition of him alone.

Anna must have known this before her.

Without a word, she hung up the phone. She'd never hung up on her father before, though endlessly tempted on each call. She was always afraid he would stop paying her tuition.

She stared out the window and heard her roommate talking to someone in the hall.

She was sure her father would continue talking for a while.

To Sarah's surprise, Esther began to call her every week.

"We're learning about history. A lot of it is where you are. Have you seen the Liberty Bell?"

"That's in Pennsylvania, not here."

"Oh." Esther never seemed embarrassed, even when her sister condescended. "But you've seen other things, like where there was a war, right? I know there were lots of Native Americans. We studied Thanksgiving. Misha says math is better. He really wants to grow his hair long like his friend Luke, but Baba won't let him. She said if he never cut his hair it wouldn't get very long anyway because it's so curly. He almost started crying. She asked me if you're okay."

"Did Anna tell you to call me?"

"No. I asked her if I could call you. She told me to call you last week but I forgot. Is it okay if I wear the clothes you left, like your blue dress?"

"No."

"Okay," she said brightly. "I have to eat now. Bye."

Esther talked as freely as she had when she was younger, six, seven, and Sarah was still living at home. She used to talk as if she expected Sarah to listen and respond, even when Sarah turned her back or told her to shut up. Minah, when she was home, was much more affectionate with Esther. She always nodded and smiled as her youngest sister babbled about the foods she liked, other children at school, the puzzling phenomena of personal taste and personality.

Sarah realized, after hanging up after Esther's second call, that Esther was about eight when she stopped talking to her, their father, even to Minah, except for practical communications. For the past few years, when Esther was at home and not next door, she was silent, though when she rose and dressed and ate her cereal her face was ever bright and cheerful. Now that Sarah was away, Esther was talking to her again. She didn't know why.

The memory of Esther's reticent years hurt her. She felt a quick wrenching pang. She took a deep breath and kicked her clothes into the closet and slammed the door, and the pang didn't recur. The memory melted away.

When Esther first began calling, Sarah would say she couldn't talk or responded with her usual annoyance and condescension toward her younger sister. As the weeks passed, Sarah found herself unburdening herself, usually to complain about everything she had to do, everything frustrating about her peers or teachers—she hated their fake goodwill, their privilege and smugness, their sheltered obtuseness. Afterward, she was embarrassed and got off the phone as quickly as possible.

On Sarah's first return home from boarding school, Esther rarely addressed her sister, as if nothing had changed between them since Sarah had first left. Sarah was confused and felt an echo of the pang that Esther's first calls provoked. Then she told herself: Nothing really happened. That's how it is. And again, the pang disappeared.

3
Little sister

Esther's calls to Sarah became less frequent until they stopped her last year of boarding school.

Esther called her older sister for the first time in a year, during Sarah's first term in college, to tell her that their father had brought a woman home to live with them.

Soojin, who went by Sue to those who didn't speak Korean, was twenty-three, a former waitress at a barbecue restaurant in Koreatown where she met Eugene. She'd arrived in the U.S. only two years ago.

"He says we're going to move to a bigger and nicer house for Sue."

Sarah said nothing.

"You'll have your own room."

"It doesn't matter. I'm not coming back anymore."

"But he says if you don't come over the break he won't send you any more money."

"I don't care. I can take out a loan now."

"Why would you do that?" Esther's voice was pained.

"What do you think? Because I'd rather go into debt than see him or his disgusting mistress."

"It won't be that bad. I'll be here, too."

"I don't know," Sarah said at last. "I'll see."

She knew she would do nearly anything to avoid the debts other students were amassing, debts that determined for them which career paths they'd pursue—how they'd occupy themselves for life. Yet here she was, deceiving herself, if only privately, on the phone with her sister.

When Sarah emerged from the terminal, Eugene was chatting on his new cell phone, laughing and lighthearted. He was still talking when he took her suitcase. She followed him at a distance to the parking lot. With a promise to his interlocutor of greater financial returns to come, he hung up in the car, where Sarah sat in the back, and talked about the new house. She was conscious then that her Korean, which had deteriorated steadily since the early years of her fluency, had grown weaker still. She recognized her father's circumscribed vocabulary, but comprehension was no longer automatic and required attention. A few phrases, some unknown nouns she supposed described features of the house, were sounds without meaning, like useless tendons in a dying muscle.

Still, she felt her father's undeniable expressiveness, the disquieting vigor of his coarse language reaching out to her through the cloud of ambiguity. "*They feel shame,*" he said of other Koreans with good-for-nothing children who, compared with him, lived in squalor. And no more forceful words were imaginable. The poems she loved could make her heart beat harder; they channeled something unsayable into words. They revealed something of the mysterious energies of the world. Was this, too, eloquence?

She regarded the back of her father's neck with disgust. No. Poetry must exclude those things that made him what he was.

Their new home was on the other side of town in a neighborhood rapidly constructed in the past year that had replaced acres of dusty bungalows. The houses were wide, high facades of stucco in ocher and ivory, coral and pale lemon, all flanked by palm trees, a few featuring fountains. The streets bore Italianate names: Calabria, Bergamo, Bernini. As they drove through its streets, the neighborhood seemed to materialize magically for Sarah; the magic had less to do with the surprising rapidity with which it had been erected than the powerful resilience, in different places, in various transformations, of what she wanted to avoid.

Her father proudly opened the front door. "Go ahead," he said. "Take a look around."

The front room—the sitting room, Sarah supposed it was called, remembering her novels—was nearly as large as the whole of their former house. She approached the sculpted mahogany armchairs around a marble-topped coffee table. "*Italian*," Eugene said in English. He followed her down the hall along the cool, mirrorlike surfaces of marble tiles that captured a gauzy web of soft, warm colors—peach, beige, blush pink—against a dense clouded white, like the fingers of a sunset in an overcast sky. He noted they were also Italian. In the dining room an imposing cabinet displaying cups in glass and crystal overlooked a long table lined with cushioned chairs. A large-screen TV facing a tastefully weathered leather sofa dominated the family room.

The pièce de résistance for Eugene was the grand piano, the long curve of its rim stately and beautiful, the raised lid like a frozen wing. She approached to see it was collecting dust in its hammers and strings. She told her father she practiced the piano diligently at school and wanted to take a break during her stay; in fact she had given up playing after starting college. She saw no point; she would not be a musician.

Her father trailed behind her like a third eye. In their past home Sarah often felt she was followed by a camera against her will. She felt once more that she had no will, no way to reject the circumstances that renewed themselves wherever she found herself. The things within these walls were so powerful and cold. As she took in the new household, each object triumphantly reaffirmed a reality that refused to take her in. She did not belong here any more than she did in the house in which she'd grown up. "Italian," he'd said, and Italy was as distant as the clan of Korean students she'd known in grade school was alienating. Some socialized with her out of pity, others out of curiosity or a precocious schadenfreude in her blotted image in their community. Their parents dissociated themselves from her father, openly scorning him behind his back and before her eyes in the school parking lot, in the aisles of the Korean grocery store.

In the reception after the class performance of *Macbeth*, in which she played the vanishing role of the gentlewoman, they patted her white bonnet and listed his offenses, so that she should know what was proper, what was wrong. All her life she'd known this double estrangement, her second-generation identity and alienation from those with whom she shared far more distant forebearers. There was no one like her father.

She knew he was still watching her as she looked out into the yard, where a young palm tree was lifting its long fronds and crimson rosebushes with sharp, dark leaves were shivering in the breeze.

Upstairs, in the last room at the end of the hall, Sarah met Esther. She and Sue were folding towels, and Sue was giggling.

"Little sister!" Sue cried out in English at the sight of Sarah. She seized her in a tight rocking embrace.

No one would touch the glasses or crystal in the cabinet or eat at the long dining table; no one sat on the mahogany armchairs or played the grand piano.

Sarah told her father she was staying only for the three days leading up to Christmas. She explained that flights the day of the holiday were significantly cheaper, and he patted her on the back for her economizing. He gave her $300 in cash and told her to do with it as she wished, after which he returned to the leather sofa to watch TV with Sue. He kept his hand on her thigh, squeezing from time to time.

When Sue got up to get him a drink he slapped her behind, and she shrieked happily. "Like the first time we met," she said. Sarah rushed to her new room, where she cloistered herself for most of her visit. She intuited correctly that it reproduced the showroom of an upscale furniture store that imagined carved wood painted a blinding white the appropriate material for a girl's quarters. She threw herself onto the violet bedspread.

From there, Sarah would hear Esther talking to Sue from various corners of the house, helping her with chores. When she came down for meals Sarah came across Sue mopping the floor, dusting, and wiping windows, wearing a ruffled silk blouse. The blouse was a recent gift from Eugene she would wear the length of Sarah's stay. She's like a child who won't take off her princess costume, Sarah thought.

They ate take-out burgers and fried chicken, rice, and store-bought Korean condiments, Sarah and Esther at the kitchen counter, Eugene and Sue in front of the TV. They drank out of mugs and plastic cups that had survived a decade of carelessness and violence.

In the bathroom she shared with Esther, Sarah found a box of pads under the sink beside the toilet paper. A profoundly sad tenderness for her sister filtered through her. She hoped Anna or Katya had been there for her when she first got her period. She bitterly remembered having no one she wanted to consult, checking hourly to see if the bleeding had truly ended or might start up again until she feigned a stomachache during class, went to the school nurse, and asked, as if in passing, whether she needed a pad if she hadn't bled for two days. She wondered if Esther knew how to use tampons, if Eugene forbade her to use them as he had Sarah when he'd guessed that it was she and not Minah using the products whose wrappers filled the wastebasket. "No one will want to marry you if you do," he'd said, peering at her as if her susceptibility to spinsterhood could be detected in the grain of her skin. She'd willingly complied while living with him because she'd once overheard Jeonghee warn Minah gravely, "Never use them. They're very, very dangerous." She understood only now that Jeonghee, like their father with herself, had not been concerned for Minah's health.

The bathroom was designed like a professional dressing room, with bulbs framing the length and sides of the mirror. She gazed at herself for a long time and remarked how soft her face looked in this lighting. She laid her hand flat on the marble counter, as if searching for a low pulse buried within its cool mass.

She was lying on her bed with an unopened book when Esther knocked at her door.

Seeing her in the doorway, Sarah was sure that Esther was now at least as tall as her. Esther's body was developing to resemble her own. Their shoulders, their proportions, the length of their limbs were echoed in the other's.

Esther sat at the foot of the bed. She looked at her sister with an expression that struck Sarah as expressionless. Her eyes were at once blank and inquisitive, like those of a dumb animal with sharp instincts.

She said quietly, "Sue's English isn't very good, but it's getting better fast. She says she's learning a lot from me."

Sarah snapped upright. "She seems crazy and totally childish. I never thought it could get worse with him. And now this. And how can he afford all this, this house, the piano, on top of my tuition? Is it just from being a cheapskate all these years? Is he going into debt for her?"

"I'm not sure."

"What about you? What are you going to do?" She knew her questions were cruel. But she didn't want to stop herself, she wanted her sister to shake off her animal strangeness, to become again the human entrenched in the same unhappiness as herself.

"What do you mean?"

"You don't have Anna and Misha next door anymore. You should go to boarding school, like me. You should get away from here. You should get away from him as soon as you can."

"I didn't tell you. I applied to your school and didn't get in. He said it was the only place he'd send me. So I'm staying here."

Sarah parted her lips but said nothing.

"It's all right," Esther said. "Sue's all right, and he doesn't hurt me."

Esther's cheeks were still round and full with baby fat. Sarah had suffered from acne since she was twelve; Esther's skin was clear and smooth. Her hair was silky, her eyes lively and bright. Sarah couldn't tell whether Esther was beautiful, as she appeared to her at this moment. Sarah lacked both the distance that would make her objective and the love that could infuse her vision and render her sister perpetually graceful and appealing. But she could tell that Esther was what most parents wanted for their children: Esther was healthy, and if not happy, then sympathetic, kind, whatever it was that people meant when they said their children were good.

The sight of Esther's strange, lovely face in this room made her nauseated with despair. She thought of Esther in this house without Anna or Katya, and without Misha, who was closer to Esther and more like a sibling than Sarah would ever be. She thought about herself, she who had never had a person like Anna in her life, and a lump formed in her throat.

"I want to be alone," she said.

She spent the afternoon of Christmas Eve at the movies and had lunch in a diner. For dinner Eugene took Esther and Sarah to the Chinese restaurant of their youth without Soojin, who, to Sarah's tremendous relief, was forced to stay behind. She was no doubt still bawling and raging in the master bedroom, where Sarah thought she'd heard Eugene repeating, his tone traveling from amused superiority to violent exasperation, "There are limits."

Sarah returned to college. Esther rarely called. When she did her tone was remote, her questions practical: "What did we do with those old raincoats?" "Do you remember if I'm allergic to penicillin?" Or, more disturbing, but delivered in an equally pragmatic tone, "Dad hasn't been home in three days, have you heard from him?"

From time to time, Sarah thought of her younger sister and told herself Esther, like a typical teen, no doubt had an active and absorbing social life. She did not want to admit her fear that Esther, her sweet and vulnerable younger sister, had given up on her. She didn't dare call Esther herself.

On the few occasions she imagined Esther at home with their father, she felt a pain that she treated like a cramp, discomfort to be countered with stoicism. But it was not the thought of Esther unhappy and lonely that gave her pain. Esther was beginning to flicker in her thoughts like a figure in a blurry silent film, her appearance more like a disappearance, a testament to her vanishing. Esther herself was not lost: Sarah was losing Esther as she went through her life merely flickering with awareness of her sister.

In the college library she came across a review of a book by a woman who had grown up under an oppressive government in a faraway land. "The writer compares living in her native country with having sex with a man you loathe." In her dorm at her computer, she found herself typing out variations on the line, which had already sunk deep into her consciousness.

Living in that country is is like having sex with a man you loathe.
Living in that house was like surviving as a hostage in enemy country.
Living under his roof was like preparing to be married off to another man you fear and loathe.
No longer living under him but knowing you carry him with you is to find you have never left home.
No longer living under him or near him but knowing that he came from this world is to learn the world itself is like the home you left behind.

Her own words, spilling out of her and coalescing like mercury, like a shimmering toxin, stunned her.

Did she not have a life and a future of her own?

And there he was again, and there she was, hunched on the floor of the master bedroom in their first home, with him facing her, crouching, a couple feet away. He leaned in and held his face within inches of hers.

When she was still a young child, he would send her out of the house to punish her. When she was older, nine, ten—old enough, he said, to understand what he wanted of her—he ordered her to come to his room, where her mother was always in bed. It started when they learned that Jeonghee was not merely depressed, as Minah said, or lazy, as Eugene declared, but terminally ill. Sarah would enter the room where she sometimes caught a glimpse of her mother's face before she turned to the wall.

Jeonghee had lost the animating sensitivity that once made it a pleasure for her children to look at her face and address her. Her eyes had become dark, lusterless coins in a waxy face where the rest of her fine features seemed to be melting away. The bags under her eyes were remarkably purple and puffy, as if she were storing unexpressed tears, wrapped in a vulnerable membrane, on her face. The slackness of the forehead and cheeks trickled down to the cavern of the dark mouth, the lips that rarely parted for nourishment and produced no sound.

"If I was a bad man," Eugene said to Sarah after summoning her, "I would punish your mother for falling apart like this."

She looked down at her hands as he paced the room, sat down on the bed beside the unresponsive body of his wife, got up, and, bending and craning, peered into her downcast face.

"I thought she was a good woman, I thought she'd be a good mother. But she's *lazy*, she's *no good*. She's not even a woman anymore.

"Now you're turning out like her."

He was sick of her mother, of her sisters. He worked so hard for them, and when he came home he felt nothing but disgust and rage. It was enough to kill him. To kill him. He'd put his hope in her; she alone carried the flame. And she extinguished it through her own laziness, her stupidity, that *ugly* mean look she always wore these days. She was supposed to be beautiful. This endless encounter was like amber, and a fragment of her was forever preserved in these scenes outside the flow of time. Why couldn't he have sweetness and beauty in his life? He worked harder for it than anyone he knew. "If I was a bad man, I would punish you and your sisters. I would beat you like my father beat me. But I've never laid a finger on you, have I?"

It wasn't true. He didn't knock Sarah or Esther on the head anymore, but Sarah didn't know he surreptitiously grabbed Minah by her hair or ears, pushed her into the wall, twisted her arm. She didn't know either that after the three police visits prompted by calls in the night from their former neighbors, her father had received warnings that were sufficiently alarming to make him refrain from drawn-out beatings. It was true he'd never given any of them a beating as a ceremonial punishment. He didn't hit them repeatedly, compulsively, only haphazardly, impulsively. This was why he believed he'd never truly beaten them before. With a revelatory shudder Sarah saw him as he saw himself. He was not a man who hurt his children, though plenty of Koreans did, even though he was full of righteous anger. He didn't even beat his wife anymore.

Besides, from Jeonghee he learned that beatings were ultimately fruitless. He needed to do more than simply express his anger through physical violence, which resulted merely in fear without understanding. He couldn't be alone with this anger, these passions. He needed to justify them; to instruct her and his favorite child.

If he didn't uproot and destroy the bad seed inside her, she would never marry. How could she? Was she destined to become a worthless slut like her older sister? Like Minah's mother, who was no better than a dog? God, he was tired. He worked like a dog. He towered above her; he loomed over her; he tilted his face to inspect her face. He was in the grip of something—what was it? She was in its grip, too. She was paralyzed, mesmerized. She hated him with every particle of life in her. It was her life, not his. She tried to retreat and play dead, to hide her life in the dark folds of her buzzing brain, which held thoughts he could not know; in her pounding chest, which clenched and pounded with her own passions; in the deepest recesses of her immature, dangerously permeable person. She hated every cell of his being and every last thing emanating from it; she hated the air around him, which was also the air around her. Yet this thing that gripped both of them—it did not seem entirely personal. It was alive in him, it passed and disseminated through him, and it was taking hold in her. So she must split herself in two, her body in the room, and the self to which she must hold fast, the self she would detach from the world in which he was chuffing on her like a bull. She was already trying to dress like a slut, folding up the cuffs of her shorts like that. At her age, it was disgusting. Astonishing. Disgusting. What was it within her that dishonored the good mind he'd bequeathed her, that slept and wouldn't wake? Why did he toil for her? He was kneeling now before her, as if to show that what she misunderstood as punishment was in fact an appeal. Why was he cursed with all the bitches in this house? Why didn't she see? She did not see.

Even if she'd wanted to speak, she wouldn't have been capable. Acid was rising from her pith, burning her throat; its walls were closing. From now on, the very words emerging from the darkness in the pit of her would be corrupted and strange. They would never make sense in the enlightened world far beyond her home, where the air was limpid and clean. It would never be possible for her not to be impure.

He patted Jeonghee's lower body, which was buried under a heavy quilt. "Your mother is sick, and you don't think to comfort her, to be the best daughter you can for her."

Jeonghee stirred.

With time, Jeonghee did more than nod in implied agreement. She raised herself on her bed and made her own pronouncements of what was wrong with her firstborn. Her dull eyes became glassy, shining with pleasure at the evisceration. "She doesn't appreciate what she has. She's spoiled. She's a brat." Jeonghee flashed on her daughter the eyes of one possessed. She was avid for a reckoning she herself would never receive; she would settle for violence, for punishment of any being in any form. "She has everything she could want and all she does is complain. She wants more toys—she's too old for them! She wants to spend money on useless things like her rich friends. She doesn't want to study—she just wants to watch TV and play outside and go to hell like her older sister. She doesn't deserve any of it!"

It didn't take long for Jeonghee's vitriol to exhaust her. But instead of collapsing into bed, she would drag herself out of the room. Eugene, in an eerily kind voice, encouraged her to return to bed. She ignored him and shut the door behind her with a careful meekness that confusedly telegraphed remorse and the exhaustion of gratification, and collapsed on the living room sofa with a weak animal wail. From beyond the terrible threshold, Sarah never failed to shiver with horror at the sound, despite the wall she had mentally erected between herself and her mother.

Before he allowed her to go, he required her to embrace him.

She was at her desk in college, but she was not lost in the past. No, she felt as if the part of her that had been trapped in amber was suddenly, with the crack of a hammer, exposed to the air and revived, like a miraculously twitching wing of a prehistoric fly.

She wrote more:

Having lived under him for so long, I've been trained to disappear, to give in to all the terrible men of the world.
Having lived under him for so long, I'm prepared to do anything to protect myself from now on.

She wondered at what came out of her. Her life was so much better now. She had some friends, and she loved being a student. What others told her was true: Your life is better than the lives of too many to count. When she looked around her, at the reality of her dorm room with her own desk, her own bed, her own books, these ordinary, tangible marvels in her life seemed to protect her from the violence shimmering on the horizon like pale buildings in smog.

She had never had a boyfriend, and she wanted one, but her life was not bad.

It was her own, now.

Minah returned to the U.S. not long after Sarah met Sue.

During Sarah's last year at college, Esther called for the first time in a year to tell her that Minah was now in Massachusetts studying for a law degree.

"Really?" Sarah said with sardonic skepticism. "I would never have expected that. I didn't know she even had a college degree. Didn't she drop out of community college? I thought you told me that."

She rarely thought of her older sister anymore. When she did, she vacillated between indifference and disdain. Growing up, she'd regarded Minah as one more source of resentment in her life. Minah could be cruel, savaging Sarah's appearance, calling her not by her name but "Daddy's girl" for weeks on end. Minah had always been antagonistic toward Sarah, whereas she seemed to cherish Esther.

"She didn't drop out. She transferred to a real university." Esther explained how Minah had, over the years, taught English in Seoul while taking courses online and in person at American colleges with campuses in Seoul. She then returned to LA and enrolled in a community college. After a year she transferred to a four-year college before starting law school.

"I'm going to stay around here for college, but at least you two will be closer," Esther said.

Sarah said nothing. It made her deeply uneasy, even haunted, to think of Minah within visiting distance and to know that Esther was speaking to their older sister regularly.

"I'm not sure she'd want to see me," Sarah said, affecting hostility she did not, at the moment, feel.

"She does. She asked me to tell you she was near."

"Well, maybe I'll see her then," Sarah said, now affecting coolness to quiet the turbulent feelings within.

Sarah began to see Minah every few months.

Esther went to Santa Cruz for college. Midway through her second year, she dropped out and never returned.

Part 2

The difference between poetry and rhetoric
is being ready to kill
yourself
instead of your children.

—Audre Lorde, "Power"

1
The dinner

The original message from Esther was locked somewhere in the ether. Sarah would never read it or even make a serious attempt to access it, though for a long time afterward she would imagine what it contained.

She was still trying to enter her work email account—the server insisted it didn't recognize her—when she received a message from Esther in her personal account, which she used less frequently.

> Why haven't you written back? Are you not using your other email anymore?
> Can I stay with you?
> Love,
> Esther

Sarah was confused and not a little alarmed by the last question and thought she should read the first message before replying. She called the IT department at the college where she was teaching and learned her account had been suspended. It was true that she'd just been told she wouldn't be rehired for the next term, but the semester had just started. Was her entire inbox lost then? she asked indignantly. How was she supposed to communicate with her students? How was she supposed to do her job?

As the technician nervously promised to do everything he could to re-instate her account, she felt a rising tide of relief. She would be spared all the hurtful reminders about deadlines intended for faculty returning in the spring term. "It's all right," she said with sudden gentleness. She would share her personal email with her students and do without it.

In her following message, Esther explained she was flying to New York next week. Their father had relocated to one of his properties in Englewood, less than an hour from Sarah, and intended to stay long term. He'd decided the best doctors for his condition were in New York. He said he wanted to be closer to Sarah—and Esther did, too.

That's most of it, the email ended, and Sarah thought she could hear something more, a tone of uncertainty, even self-consciousness; the faintest note of regret. She intuited there was more to the original message, and for a moment she considered calling the technician back to say she'd changed her mind.

But she didn't want to call again. She wanted to stick by her decision to give up on those messages for good.

Sarah knew their father was ailing, but she was convinced he was grossly exaggerating his illness. She'd continued avoiding most contact with him apart from occasional calls over the past year, as she had for years. She was reasonably independent and no longer vulnerable to threats of withdrawn support, as she was in college. But she was not financially stable, and when she received large deposits of cash in her account, often without any notice from her father, she did not object.

She was still staring at the first email she'd received from Esther when she felt her underarms grow damp. She was not going to worry about her father's health. But it was much harder to ignore Esther's request for a place to stay.

She'd seen Esther once in twelve years, the last time they were at their father's together, when he was still living with Sue. Then, for years after Esther left college abruptly, no one but Misha heard from her. Sarah gathered from him when he reached out that Esther was moving around the country, living on the last tuition check their father had sent her directly. "She says she's fine," Misha told her, and that was enough for Sarah to stop thinking of her sister for months until she felt duty bound to contact him again for an update or send another email that would go unanswered.

When the tuition money ran out after a couple years, Esther stayed with friends, housesat for others, and took a few jobs that pained Sarah to hear about: as a a sales rep for a cell phone hut in a strip mall parking lot outside LA, as a waitress at a hotel on an island in South Carolina.

When Sarah was honest with herself, she knew she was less concerned about Esther's welfare than she was pained by guilt or shame—she didn't know which. When Misha gave broad outlines and minor details about Esther's circumstances—the parking lot shack at night, the hostel in San Francisco, the hotel restaurant overlooking a boardwalk—she felt a panic-tinged pain. She imagined the first sparks of friendship in the hostel, the popular boardwalk from which one could see the water, and she knew she was incapable of existing in the world as her sister did. There was a murky fundamental wrongness to her that Esther somehow threw into relief. After hanging up the phone, Sarah thought of her sister alone with their father and Sue while she was at college. She saw her carrying that aloneness with her as she waited on tables with rude white families, as she presented cell phone features to morons and jerks in a soul-crushingly ugly strip mall. Then the pain felt like guilt, a singe of remorse for not being the responsible sibling who encouraged her younger sister to return to school, for not even remembering the name of the island where Esther worked.

Or was she ashamed of not feeling guilty?

She never asked Misha or Esther herself for further details of her life, but she thought often about what Esther was doing, imagining the details for herself.

She tried now to picture living with her sister and saw herself growing exasperated and even cruel within days. Her life was bad at the moment.

The walls of her apartment barely contained the shameful fug of her bitterness and depression, and no one else must breathe it.

She decided to put off answering Esther until her dinner with Minah tomorrow.

※

After law school Minah moved to New York, where she and Sarah began to meet once or twice a month for dinner in Koreatown.

They met a few blocks from Penn Station after Sarah had finished her teaching in the city for the day and before she took the train back to New Jersey. Her days were long; it became rare for her to do anything for pleasure in the city other than dine with her sister.

For three years now she commuted to the city at least twice a week to teach at two, sometimes three colleges, uptown and downtown. The pay was bad, a few thousand without benefits for each demanding course. The commute was over two hours door to door, and her position as an adjunct was steadily demoralizing, but she'd found her life manageable until recently.

The commute was no longer simply draining; it, too, became demeaning, reminding her afresh at every wearisome stop that she'd remained in Princeton, a town she'd never liked, for her ex-boyfriend. She'd finished her doctorate before Victor and stayed on in their cheap apartment as she watched her peers accept stable teaching jobs around the country or move to New York. For a student town, Princeton was bewilderingly lifeless. The quaint-from-a-distance main street housed mediocre, overpriced restaurants and prestige labels beyond the reach of most students. The only bar where it was easy to hear yourself talk had shut down, to be replaced by another ice-cream parlor; there were already three within blocks of one another in this place of sleepy, sterile charm. To pursue her ambitions, and then a serious relationship with Victor, she passed eight years of the prime of her life here. He had gone to Italy for a language course in June and returned in July to say he was leaving her, he was in love.

Her apartment on the outskirts of campus was a small two-bedroom bungalow, one of many in a complex rapidly erected as an army barracks in the fifties or sixties. No one planned for them to be inhabited for so many decades; they had little insulation from the cold or from the sounds of conversation or sex or chairs scraping the floor next door. But the shabby student complex was affordable and housed an intimate community of impromptu gatherings and unlocked doors you could knock to borrow sugar or soap. Without Victor, Sarah withdrew absolutely from community life. The neighbors she knew, she knew through him, and she never doubted they liked him and had merely accepted her. After the breakup, the apartment was nothing more than what it was, an unreliable shelter of paper-thin walls.

Victor was living rent-free with his new girlfriend and agreed to pay half the rent until the lease was up in May next year. Even if she wanted to stay past then, she couldn't, since she was no longer a student. She thought of moving every day but knew of no other realistic option. She was going to lose her one solid gig at a college that nearly exclusively employed part-time lecturers and had no other work lined up for the spring term.

Esther's message temporarily interrupted the familiar circuits of Sarah's embittered thoughts—about Victor's infidelity, her penury and lack of prospects, the general misery of her fate—and replaced them with irritable questions about her sister's visit. Why was she asking her and not Minah for a place to stay? Minah's beautiful Chelsea apartment was a short trip over the river to their father's condo in New Jersey. And Esther was closer to Minah than to her. So why was Esther preparing to impose herself on her?

The next morning she woke to a single question that supplanted the others. She wanted to know what Esther had written in her original message.

On her walk to the station and on the train to the city, the letter began to write itself in her head: I want us to speak frankly to each other. Is it really okay if I stay with you?

I want to tell you what happened when I dropped out of your life. I've wanted to talk to you for a long time. Things should be different between us. I know you better than you think, and I care about you. I don't blame you for your coldness, your hardness . . .

Esther was kind, but there was no reason to expect such generous and sentimental words from her. The imaginary email embarrassed Sarah. But it continued to write itself as she stared out the train window and remembered her equally embarrassing, mendacious dreams.

Throughout her life she'd had vivid, mostly bad dreams. She dreamt she could fly, but she was trapped in a long corridor with low ceilings where the villains inevitably caught her by her ankle. She dreamt she had no body; she dreamt she was naked, she was late, she was in lust. Sometimes a beautiful thing happened: she was swimming in a deep river, in a cloud of silver fish. They were ordinary dreams, and yet they were visceral and accurate. They depicted what lived in her depths.

These days her dreams were dishonest. Instead of translating her inner life into symbols, they distorted reality to meet her most pathetic desires. Only dreamers of deep-seated bad faith fulfilled their wishes in sleep and thus desecrated the potential beauty and force of the inner life, like kings who richly rewarded coarse flatterers as their kingdoms crumbled around them. She was becoming one of them now. She dreamt of men she wanted and others she didn't wanting her; of enemies mourning her death, and encomiums for brilliant accomplishments that would always elude her in her waking life. Esther came to her, weeping with joy, beaming with love for her.

Sometimes Esther was hurt or in danger and Sarah saved her. In her real life she knew she'd never done anything to help her.

On the subway to Koreatown after her class, she resolved to be straightforward with Minah: You're more in a position to help Esther than I am now. You've always been closer. She should stay with you. But her resolve crumbled when an obvious fact occurred to her for the first time: Minah's apartment was a studio; Sarah had a spare room that was once Victor's study.

Minah was seated at the restaurant bar talking to an Asian man in a suit hovering over a glass of red wine. She'd told Sarah she wanted to introduce her to her new boyfriend soon, but not that it would be this night, and Sarah was deeply annoyed.

For the past couple years, Minah had introduced Sarah to whomever she was dating at the time at one of their Koreatown dinners. The tradition started when she announced with remarkable forthrightness her intention to marry and start a family with a wealthy, preferably Christian Korean American. Sarah's role was to give a favorable impression of their family, which her education consistently did. In exchange, her meal was free since the boyfriend always paid.

The man with Minah noticed Sarah first. Behind him, Minah's eyes met Sarah's with what seemed at first a hard, supercilious glance, then became in the next instant a nearly opaque expression of vulnerability, a barely perceptible appeal for help. Sarah had never seen her sister so anxious to impress a man. When the man turned back to Minah, she was smiling, no doubt pretending the smile was continuous from Sarah to him.

When Sarah reached the bar, he said, "You have the same way of entering a room."

They followed the hostess to the barbecue table he'd reserved. Sarah was trying to remember his name.

"Paul was free tonight, and he's been wanting to meet you for a while," Minah said.

Sarah learned they'd met through friends at church, just as Michael, Paul's romantic predecessor, had met Minah.

"But not my church. It was at my friend's daughter's baptism," Minah inserted briskly. "It was my first time at a Catholic church." It was her way of telling Sarah that Paul was meaningfully different from Michael.

But to Sarah, Paul resembled Michael, and not only physically. They were the same type: tending toward stout, the rounded limbs wrapped in satiny cotton sleeves; not quite tall, but tall enough to want to incline his head down to Sarah while addressing her. Their hair was cropped short, and they wore tasteful office clothing: dark slacks, buttoned wrists. Paul's slightly wide face was certainly different from those of the men who preceded him. But because he, too, seemed thoroughly dull, incurious, and, by consequence, uninteresting, his features, like theirs, appeared generic despite their distinctness, suggesting sensory functions rather than sensuousness.

By the end of the evening, Sarah would realize that Paul was not nearly as dull as she assumed. She would notice that beneath his impassive features, each fiber of him was tense and controlled, and unlike Michael's, his dark eyes could be quick and responsive.

He said, his voice clear and hearty, "I guess I should tell you more about myself. I'm thirty-six, I work in finance. I haven't been in New York that long. Before New York I worked in DC, after Georgetown. I grew up in Maryland with Korean parents and one Vietnamese grandparent, my grandfather. I like good conversation and good food, but I should probably go on a diet. I was raised Catholic and I still belong to the Church." He added warmly, "I want you to know about me. And I like to be direct when it's important."

"All right," Sarah said with a note of indifference. She stopped the waiter and ordered a glass of wine.

"You're family," he said in another jovial burst, before his tone plateaued to somberness. "Not just an old friend. This is a meeting of families. It's important to me."

"Okay, but I'm Minah's sister, not her mother," Sarah said, suppressing a tremor of irritation.

He blinked ironically. "Right."

There was an unexpected pressure in the word. Their eyes locked, and Sarah understood he knew more about their family history than others before him. He'd expected her to assume maternal watchfulness over her sister since their mother was dead. Her casual reference to their mother offended him. His conservatism, the very idea that he was marrying a family and not an individual, disturbed her.

At first seeing Paul, Sarah saw the same bodily envelope she'd encountered in dull, forgettable Michael. To watch and hear Paul speak was to witness a different soul working its unmistakable way through the density of ordinary, pliable flesh.

Minah smiled as if she didn't know what was happening. She said, "Our mother was very gentle and very quiet. She didn't play that role."

"That role?" Paul echoed questioningly.

"She wasn't judgmental. She didn't micromanage us or scold us even when we did something bad. She never wanted anyone to feel bad or uncomfortable. She was just so gentle and very kind."

She continued to wear an expression of gentle affability as she spoke, but there was a cool undertone to her words: an understated declaration of her authority at the table, her intention to make her disrespectful sister and her overbearing lover come to an understanding.

Minah, too, like Paul, had unremarkable features. In isolation, abstracted from the others, they were ordinary. Her eyes were a little narrow, her lips a little thin; and she was beautiful, the most beautiful of the three sisters. Sarah couldn't remember a time when Minah wasn't beautiful to her. To her, everything was always right and good in Minah's face. For the first time she saw how someone else could see her sister not only as sculpturally beautiful but alluring.

"She was loving," Minah continued calmly, shaking off with each word the last of the vulnerability Sarah initially perceived, "and that's why she's my real mother."

At this, Sarah turned to Minah at her side, but Minah and Paul were looking intently at each other.

Minah hadn't wanted her other boyfriends to know about her confused upbringing. They were by and large conventional-minded nitwits in finance who wanted a nice woman with a proper family who would in turn raise a nice, proper family. And Minah wanted the same—no, she longed for it, she lusted for it in a way her unimaginative exes could not. It didn't even matter to her if she didn't love her spouse as long as she respected him. He would figure less as an individual than part of a luminous pattern in a life of shared commitments and community, an ethnically Korean community. They would have children, and for the children they must have plenty of money to make a beautiful home and future.

"You want a rich man, that I understand. But why a Korean?" Sarah had asked, to which Minah replied, pensive and enigmatic, "After living in Korea, I started to feel Korean."

She was unabashedly candid about her goals to Sarah, and so the lackluster slideshow of suitors over the past years hadn't surprised her. But Minah's honesty with Paul was surprising. Perhaps she even loved him.

He must be the one, Sarah thought. She was beginning to resent Minah for not preparing her for this dinner. She wanted to help Minah, but not if it meant enduring the company of a self-righteous man who was ready to judge her.

Minah broke off her gaze and said, lightly teasing, "Paul, Sarah's here to spend some time with you, not refuse you or give me away. She's not old-fashioned like you."

"Right," he said again. He faced Sarah with a rigid smile he was trying to wrest into meekness. A door was creaking open to an anteroom, but it was one Sarah saw no point in entering.

He said he was impressed with what he knew about her, she was so accomplished. He knew so little about literature, though he did like to read. Maybe she could give him some recommendations . . .

Boredom, Sarah realized, had at least the happy effect of draining the life out of her ill will.

Paul dominated the table talk with the same officious self-importance with which he took over the grilling of meat, dropping morsels on Sarah's plate even after she said she was full. "You need it more than me," he said with confidence, which both mystified and provoked her for his obscure, prying assumption about herself. He recounted, point by point, the eventful plot of a novel about a plucky and precocious child she wouldn't have wanted to read even if he hadn't spoiled it so painstakingly; he summarized articles about the benefits of exercise for one's mental health and longevity. He was an enraging masculine type familiar to Sarah from common experiences spanning her nearly thirty years of consciousness, but it had been a while since she'd had to suffer so much bloviating in such close quarters for an extended stretch of time.

She avoided meeting Paul's eyes, brushing her gaze over his chin, his collar, Minah's smooth jawline. Barely puncturing her boredom from time to time was the sense that Paul, who was trying to catch her eye, was discerning and subtle even if his conversation was not.

"What do you think about yoga?" he asked Sarah. "The article was about low-key exercise like walking and gardening, but it mentioned low-key yoga, too. Do you do it, too?"

"Not really. I've tried it, but it's not for me."

"Why not?"

"I don't like the whole lifestyle ethos of it."

"Hmm," he said, in the same dubious tone with which he'd ironized his affirmative "right." "Minah's thinking of teaching yoga in a women's prison, you know."

Sarah snapped back to attention. She could not picture her sister in altruistic engagement with convicted criminals any more than she could imagine her shaving off her long, carefully tended hair. Her first thought was simply dismissive: Minah was too ignorant to have an inkling of how awful prisons were and just wanted to impress Paul. It was rapidly contravened by her more nuanced and judicious recognition that Minah was certainly not without intelligence. She simply chose to behave as if she were, if it was opportune.

"I didn't even know you did yoga," Sarah said.

"Don't you remember when I was talking about becoming a yoga teacher? Like everyone, I fantasized about leaving my office job to teach yoga, but after I changed firms and I liked my job better, I forgot about it. I guess it was a long time ago, around the time you moved to Jersey. You were pretty stressed that year. I was, too. If it wasn't for yoga, I don't know what I would have done."

It was a white lie of the kind Minah often told her boyfriends. Sarah was certain the conversation had never taken place.

"That's true," Sarah said. "That year was a blur. But tell me more."

"It's been so long since I've done it regularly, I'd have to put in a lot more time. But I'm thinking about it."

"You mean, why would she do it in a prison," Paul said. He was reverting to the frank, vaguely confrontational tone of their initial contretemps, which Sarah unexpectedly now found refreshing.

"Yes."

"Because—you can explain yourself," he said to Minah.

"I know it sounds really strange at first—yoga, which is all about peace and relaxation and self-care, in a place where you're not free, and you're not supposed to be at peace with yourself. But that's why it makes sense. It's what you need when you can't breathe."

"I can see that," Sarah said.

"It would take a lot of time and work, but it would be worth it." There were programs to help troubled youth that she'd been considering, but she was more drawn to teaching women in prisons. Women suffered in ways that men didn't, she said, giving Paul a bright smile that Sarah found distasteful. They might even be said to suffer more, and so were in greater need of relieving that suffering.

"I think it's a great idea," he said.

Sarah mused that Paul was probably a creepy religious hypocrite who liked preaching abstinence and fidelity and watching women do yoga. She was equally disdainful of Minah's glib feminism, though she wasn't sure whether Minah actually believed her cant about women's suffering, just as she couldn't tell whether her sister was truly convinced that their mother's gentleness, when she was gentle, flowed from the pure source of kindheartedness and not from her brokenness. In any case, she was sure that prison yoga was no more than an idle fantasy of personal goodness.

"That sounds great," Sarah said, and smiled.

Outside the restaurant Minah hugged Sarah as Paul flagged down a taxi. "Thank you," she whispered.

Paul rushed back and clasped Sarah's hand. "So good to meet you," he said. "Let's do this again."

The car pulled away, and Sarah headed to Penn station. She found herself in a state of disquiet, fluttering with harried thoughts like moths trapped in a bottle. The lights were on everywhere and the sidewalks were crowded, as usual, with people in their twenties and thirties speaking fluent Korean. Many of them were likely solidly bicultural, having spent at least a few early formative years in Korea or embedded in a Koreatown, or more straightforwardly Korean, raised in Korea and merely passing through New York. How many of them were like her sister, who chose a trajectory from West to East as a young adult with bad Korean? Although Minah could now pass as a native speaker, when Sarah thought of her this way she began to hallucinate subtle American accents in the Korean flowing around her.

In the bustling departure hall she joined one of the many clusters of evening commuters staring at the monitors. She didn't understand the connection between Minah's conventional self-fashioning and her return to the language and tribe of her youth. It must have been in Seoul that Minah decided to cultivate the simple, genial persona she assumed full-time now, convincing herself that convention was neither stultifying nor punishing, but simply gave a universal form to the fulfillment of basic dreams. Drop by drop, the disturbing, amazing energy of her youth was leached out from her. Did Minah believe she would be happiest with another Korean simply because she was ethnically Korean, and a fundament of convention was to belong to a homogenous community? Was her return to her roots actually a drive to triumph over her father by producing a Korean family that would, unlike his, flourish under care and love—or a perverse, pathetic, not-quite-conscious wish to meet her terrible father's approval by accepting his people as hers at last? Sarah wanted to think Minah was trying to redeem her heritage and divorce it from their father by forging a happy, normal family of her own. But she didn't think she'd ever know what was true, precisely because she didn't think Minah knew herself. Minah, in choosing convention, was also spurning serious introspection and attempting to suppress her own intelligence.

Though she had little respect for Minah's marital ambitions, she found herself looking forward to the dinners and the cheerful, amusing dissections that usually followed at their favorite frozen yogurt shop in Koreatown. Minah would tell her boyfriend after dinner she'd rejoin him later, she and Sarah needed to catch up. They would choose a spot close to the front counter, and the spread of candied cherries, chocolate chips, and pink mochi was at once garish and weirdly comforting under the overhead lights that made everything as bright and abstract as a cartoon. Minah would grow garrulous as she listed the pros and cons of a lasting union with the boyfriend and ask Sarah for her opinion. Sarah would open with the caveat that she and Minah were very different before expounding her thoughts on his suitability to Minah's great project. Minah was impressed by the way Sarah could weave minute observations about an offhand comment about his brother, who was clearly more successful than him, or repainting his office two years in a row, this time in entirely neutral tones, with broader insights about human nature to produce what seemed less like a prediction than a scientific hypothesis.

Minah might then fall into a thoughtful silence, which she once interrupted by saying, "You've always been good at watching people."

Sarah stiffened. The comment sounded an unpleasantly personal note. Though she'd developed a greater affection toward her sister in the past year than ever before, she didn't want to talk about their past or herself in any depth. With her sister she wanted companionship and comfort, not the candid explorations of intimacy and vulnerability.

She hoped Minah would notice she was beginning to withdraw. But Minah persisted: "You're really sure you don't want children? With Victor or anyone else?"

"Yes."

"We really are different," Minah said with a quiet, quizzical sigh before returning to the subject at hand.

Minah generally referred to their past with an attitude of blasé resignation, as if it were bad form to do otherwise. When Sarah wondered aloud whether she got tired easily because she took after Jeonghee, Minah replied simply, "Probably not. She was seriously depressed and terminally ill. I don't think you're either," and recommended drinking more water.

The personal note in their warm banter was rare. Yet after Sarah's initial reluctance to a reunion after Minah's return to the U.S., she accepted Minah's overtures and eventually sought her sister out over the years precisely because she wanted to *see* it—the changed past. She wanted to behold its transformation in her sister by the light of day. She wanted to feel again, in her sister's company, the vitality of her own self in time.

By the time of their reunion, Sarah had ceased to hate her sister with the passion of an injured child, though at the thought of Minah she was dismissive. She was disdainful of her for the rough habits and rude language she remembered so well. She was not only disdainful but acutely embarrassed by the memory of Minah's outbursts, the demonstrations of such violent, fruitless emotions. She accepted Minah's invitation to coffee out of curiosity that compensated for her attenuated sense of family duty.

The very sight of Minah seated at the café was unutterably moving. As they talked Minah revealed her changed self to be poised, polite, and well-spoken. For Sarah it was like seeing Lazarus ordering coffee, checking his phone, carelessly scratching at his head of freshly trimmed hair. It was much more than the resurrection of the past: in the blink of an eye, the past had fructified into an unimagined form; a spectacular, ordinary body.

The past with all its pain was suddenly pulsing warmly in her, too; it lit them both up from within. The pain, too, was changing. It was mysterious and beautiful, like the organic luminescence of uncanny life in the awful black depths of the sea.

Sarah still could not say to herself whether she loved Minah. But she felt loyal to this ineffable pathos, this extraordinary sense of both her sister's resilience and her own inner life when they were together. She judged Minah for her passion for convention and, at first, for her tendency to talk of men as if they were dog breeds and not people. But her feeling of loyalty soon overrode what she came to consider the petty moralism of the privileged. If Minah was selfish, she was not selfish in the truly objectionable way that deeply cherished children so often were. She had self-respect, but not the kind of self-love that governed these children as they grew up. This love of self they interpreted as loving goodwill for others, for which the world's privileges and love were their due. This was the true, original selfishness, the outrageous belief that one was owed love, when Sarah and Minah knew that no one was owed it, no one could even ask for it. Decency might be a requisite, but love was always arbitrary, always a gift.

Minah might talk about men as if they were dogs, but she was, after all, planning to breed with one of them.

She was a pragmatic diplomat with reality and, like Sarah, was well-versed in the truths of suffering and sadism and selfishness. The sisters were like veterans of enemy armies long dissolved: at last indifferent to the original cause of conflict, they were forever bound by the experience of war, which they alone knew, as they navigated the strangely diminished dimensions of civilian life. This, Sarah reflected on her rattling train, might be why she appreciated the postprandial anatomies of whomever Minah was dating at the time. She didn't approve of Minah's dreams, but in supporting her pursuit of them, she was validating her sister's vision of a future after a past that had made both sisters doubt the purpose and potential of their marred lives.

She wanted to help Minah. Even more, she wanted the will to do something for her. Unlike her sister, she had no vision of a future for herself. She'd once wanted to be a scholar whose work would reveal the realities of the human animal to itself, the meaning of its art and the mechanics of its being. She'd wanted to know herself and teach others how to do the same. Ambition and passion had since waned into weary longing. She was not unaware of this, but she could not lift herself out of her waking slumber.

She often carried an image of herself in her mind as she went about her life. She longed to touch that self, to pinch her, slap her, move her in some way so she would change her life. That self was always out of reach. Her body in the world was both burdensome and inaccessible, and her mind was trapped within it.

The train car started to smell of deep-fried foods and their confluent farts. A mostly silent couple with two small, tired children were having their dinner; farther down, some teenage boys, raucous and jolly, were talking very excitedly about the upcoming talent show at their high school. They were bristling with life, entangled with one another like overgrown brush, entangling her with them. One of them suddenly leapt in the air, and in the ensuing uproar of laughter Sarah caught a spark of their warmth. She decided against changing cars.

She had a premonition about Paul she didn't understand. She recalled the odd disjunction between his insipid talk and his acute darting eyes. She began to suspect he'd nattered on over dinner because it was his way of drawing attention away from his scrutiny of his girlfriend's sister.

When the train pulled into Princeton and she stepped out into the freshness of the night, Sarah's premonition crystallized into certainty. Paul was the first of Minah's men to perceive that, though the sisters might not be close, they were complicit.

2

The news

The morning before she was to see her father, Minah decided she would try to pray in the mornings.

Since joining a church ten years ago in Seoul, she'd thought of prayer as sacred words to repeat and reaffirm, best practiced with others at church. When she prayed alone at home, she rapidly recited a common prayer before bed. She wanted now to try to pray thoughtfully, every day, in her own words, and her head was clearest in the morning.

It was Paul who made her question and care whether she was praying well. When Paul spent the night with her, he prayed in silence before bed, his back turned to her. She was never more attracted to prayer than she was then, as she tried to imagine what he was communicating to God.

She was certain he wasn't reciting a prayer and tried and failed to imagine his original words as she lay by his side. In her frustrated longing, one thing grew clearer: she could not imagine herself similarly opening herself to God. She enjoyed the communal practices of religion; she liked to attend church, to pray and do good works as a group, and especially to sing in unison and feel her voice rising bold and clear from her sternum into the shared sacralized air. In her first attempts to pray like Paul, alone, she tried to recapture the pleasure of speaking and singing in unison with her fellow parishioners. She thought of how easy it was to talk freely to her friends and even to Sarah, but the things she shared with them were matters too paltry for prayer. The more she tried to pray on her own, the more unnatural it felt, and in her frustration she recalled the stories of saints who encountered the Word long before they understood or embodied it. The thought of their ultimate conversion did not inspire her, but led to another realization: conversion, too, was beyond the reach of her imagination, because she was not certain she believed in God.

She was told and told herself that there could be no pretending before the divine. Instead of questioning her own sincerity, she'd allowed herself the consolations of the fallacy that she was a person of faith and thus had nothing to reveal in prayer, because she couldn't help but share everything of herself with God. It was the trial of not knowing Paul's prayers that made her see that up until now, she assumed she was a believer because she wanted to be one.

She wanted to be with someone who was. Her deepening passion for Paul inspired her not only to pray like him, but to hope to believe like him, and thus make herself more desirable to him. According to the unconscious theology of her passion, she would gain access to his words, and perhaps even his faith, when she offered her own up in prayer. After all, wouldn't they share the same interlocutor?

She sat at the side of her bed, lowered her head, and clasped her hands.

"I am going to see my father tomorrow. I can't even remember the last time I saw him. Or even talked to him."

She paused.

"I just realized something. I'm thirty-four now. I've lived without him for half my life." She paused again before uttering, "Today is the first day of the rest of your life."

The cliché fell from her lips without intent, but there was an ironic echo to it that seemed meaningful to her.

"No regrets."

She found herself trying out more sayings, more clichés, to see if they felt any more or less pertinent to her. They were like driftwood floating past, either a lifeline to cling to or a burnt plank from someone else's distant fire. She didn't know which: therein sounded the irony.

"You're always hardest on yourself."

"God helps those who help themselves."

"Love will set you free."

"Love the one you're with."

"The truth will set you free."

From a tote bag on a pleasant-looking woman she'd seen in the subway, she remembered: "Be kinder than necessary."

"Many hands make light work."

Her mind drifted. Tomorrow would be doubly momentous: not only was she going to see her long-estranged father; her sisters, too, would be together in the same room for the first time since she left home at seventeen.

Her sisters had their own common phrases. "Whatever," Sarah often said. "What does he know?" When she was tired of defending her point, she said, "Never mind. What do I know?"

Esther, too, spoke in negations. "I'm not sure," she said. "I don't know." In her case, though, she wasn't shrugging with cynical indifference or throwing up her hands in exasperation like Sarah. The nothingness in Esther's responses was ambiguous, like hands raised in defenselessness, or defiance; like bare hands meekly or daringly extended toward a strange dog. When she said "I don't know," the words were simultaneously a tender appeal for Minah's empathy and a challenge to her to uncover the matter for herself. That was, at least, how they sounded on the phone. She had not seen Esther in many years.

She found it achingly difficult to talk to her youngest sister, whom she'd ardently adored growing up. Esther as a child was so sweet and pretty and happy and bright. To Minah's continuing surprise, she was now closer to Sarah, whose dull, dour face she'd disliked so intensely when they lived together under their father. Though Minah knew Sarah disapproved of much about her, she also realized Sarah disliked and mentally condescended to most everyone. Sarah's misanthropic temperament, however, did not make her more cruel or even impolite than others, only more sensitive to human weakness and meanness, Minah thought. Sarah could be trusted to comport herself reasonably when dining with a boyfriend even Minah found ineffably unpalatable and, just as importantly, to tell her with perfect bluntness afterward that he was categorically awful. Whereas Minah was not sure Esther understood any longer the norms of social intercourse.

She no longer understood her youngest sister. She did not understand why Esther dropped out of college when their father was paying for it, and when she asked, she was puzzled to the point of trepidation when Esther said, "I still don't know." When she entreated her sister not to waste her life, Esther replied quietly but emphatically she was trying her best and ended the call. She was afraid Esther had grown irrevocably strange, and her fear compounded the distance established by a decade apart. In recent years, as she began to dream of starting her own family, she tried to call or at least email her sister monthly, even setting up a reminder on her computer calendar. She was motivated not only out of a painful memory of love for Esther as a child, but out of guilty superstition that if she lapsed in her communications Esther would become entirely unrecognizable. Or worse: her own children might become strange to her in the future.

And so, though she had divulged to Paul, in a first with any boyfriend, the unhappiness of her childhood and youth, she had yet to mention that Esther was staying with Sarah for the foreseeable future.

She was supposed to meet Sarah at Port Authority tomorrow afternoon so they could take a bus together to Englewood, where their father was living in an apartment building he owned. From what the two sisters could gather, over the past twenty years he'd invested in real estate in both California and the Northeast, usually in areas on the fringes of Korean communities. Neither Sarah nor Minah knew the extent of their father's holdings.

Minah learned about the property in North Jersey only when Esther called her a few days after her dinner with Sarah and Paul. It was an un-seasonally warm fall afternoon and Minah was texting with a friend from church about plans for a picnic in Central Park. She considered letting the call go to voicemail, but the afternoon was bright, her friend eager to meet Paul, and she wanted to be generous to her sister.

"Hi, Minah. It's Esther."

"Esther. Hi. How are you?"

"I have to tell you Dad's moved to New Jersey to be closer to his doctors in New York. He said he wants to see you. He wanted me to tell you."

The languorous pleasure of the day and its promise of mirth withered in an instant.

"I don't think I want to see him."

"That's up to you." Even when Esther spoke mildly, as she did now, her voice imparted a tensile strength.

"I thought you didn't talk to him anymore," Minah said, but this wasn't true. She was aware Sarah talked to him occasionally, and from her she knew Esther did, too. The truth was that when she thought of Eugene she couldn't stand to think of him as he was now, living in the present, keeping up a feeble correspondence with her sisters, and growing old. He was fixed in the past with his specific, obscene acts of cruelty: his pleasure in throw-ing her clothes in his unflushed toilet, his way of gripping her wrist or her nape with his scarred claw of a hand when no one else could see. He was his rotting teeth, the horror of his physical presence. She wanted these timeless things that defined him to remain buried in the past.

"I talk to him sometimes. He put me on a family cell phone plan and calls me sometimes. He asked me to tell you and Sarah his news. He's moved not just for the doctors but to see us again before he dies. He wants to see us all together in his place in Englewood, so I'm flying over and staying with Sarah. He said he knew you and Sarah wouldn't bother to visit him even on his deathbed if it required a plane ticket. I think he does want to see us all together. He says he's going to die soon. I wanted to tell you all this, like he asked. That's all. I don't mean to tell you what to do."

The news was all the more disquieting conveyed in Esther's measured mezzo, the timbre of which Minah had come to associate with forces she could neither shape nor grasp.

Esther said, "I tried to tell Sarah, but I'm not sure she understands."

"Is she not picking up her phone again? She does that sometimes."

"She didn't reply to my email. I mean she won't understand unless I tell her in person. Maybe not. I don't know. But I think so."

Minah still didn't see what it was Sarah didn't yet understand, but she refrained from asking. As she did on most calls with Esther, she decided to push through the routine questions of concern and formulas of care and end the call. Like a telemarketer terrified she might have stumbled upon a demented woman living alone, she told herself she could hang up after persisting with the survey she felt duty bound to conduct.

"Do the doctors say he doesn't have much time?"

"He says one thing and then another. I think he's gotten different opinions."

"What does he have?"

"I don't know. He won't say. I just know he's had lots of tests. I meant Sarah will think he's lying to get her attention. I don't think she'll believe him until I see her and talk to her like I've talked to him. Or until she sees him."

"But he is probably lying if he won't tell you what he has." The memory of horror was fading and reason returned to her. "He's hiding something. Why would he move all this way for better doctors? That doesn't make sense. There aren't any good doctors in LA?"

"I don't think he's lying about being sick. And it doesn't matter. It doesn't matter to me. It still means something, even if he's lying," Esther said with a firmness that quickly collapsed into a faint quaver. "I still want to know what he wants to tell us. It might matter differently for you."

These last words would have sounded like a judgment from any other mouth, but from Esther, who had developed a kind of tone deafness, they were literally intended. She was not judging her sister for doubting their father, but asking Minah to respect her own desire to speak to him, just as she would accept Minah's refusal to meet their father. This was the meaning Minah rapidly gleaned. After their call she would, as she now habitually did, bury the impossible question of the meaning of what Esther meant to say.

Minah wanted to ask, What is it you want to know? Instead she softened her voice to say she expected to see Esther during her visit, that she missed her very much. As reason regained her mind, the memory of love repossessed her heart. She wanted to ask Esther how she was. But that involved the question of what she was doing with her life, and she didn't want to antagonize her sister if she'd lapsed once more into wandering about with sad, scattered people—drifters, losers . . . She cringed to think of Esther in such company—and to feel them within grasp of her, through her sister.

"I'll see you. Soon. I miss you very much," Esther said with unmistakable tenderness that brought tears to Minah's eyes. She had once found it easy to understand her sister.

"I'll come see him," Minah found herself saying, "if you're there."

"Okay. I love you."

Esther hung up before Minah could say, Take care.

She felt both lost, swallowed in darkness, and exposed to dangerously harsh light.

She often had the unsettling sense that Esther could hear her moods and thoughts through the same radio waves that delivered their voices. Esther probably knew she made her oldest sister ill at ease. In her rare moments of unflinching self-reflection, Minah told herself Esther wasn't oblivious or strange at all. She was using this diagnosis to conceal the desolate truth from herself. Her sister wasn't tone-deaf. For years now, Esther had chosen silence.

On the bus to Englewood with Sarah, she would insist that they try to intervene in their sister's life. How could they have let their little sister live like a drifter? How was Esther going to change her life? How could she herself have let Esther fade from her life?

She would pray for her youngest sister, starting now.

Minah took the bus alone.

Sarah sent an email that morning canceling their meeting at Port Authority: I decided to call in sick, so I won't be in New York after all. I'm not really sick, but I really, really couldn't face the commute and my students this morning, and they're going to fire me after this term anyway. Also Esther doesn't know the area and probably needs help getting to the apartment. I'll see you soon.

The bus stalled repeatedly in traffic until they crossed the bridge. In its fitful progress it relentlessly imposed on Minah the time to anticipate an imminent reunion with her father and Esther in the depressing company of strangers. The passengers included a few Chinese and a few Koreans, she guessed, of an older generation, carrying tied plastic bags and fake designer handbags. Young women who looked like they should have been in school and middle-aged men alike were playing games and watching videos on their phones. "Tell him that won't work," a gaunt white man was saying vehemently, "I didn't agree to that. That crook. Tell him that won't work." His vitriol was bottomless, he went on and on. His sallow skin was smooth but unusually lax, sagging from his beady hollowed, burning eyes. Vigorous and unafraid, he didn't seem old, but his body appeared wasted, as if he'd emerged from near starvation having lost not only muscle but control of his appetite for spite.

She felt unbearably susceptible to the man's roughness on the long bridge. The others were silent, staring out the window, hunched over their devices, too mindless to care or even notice his repulsiveness. She was tempted to shush him, but her irritation with him dwindled in proportion to her growing disgust with the other passengers in their impostures of life. When a man standing in the aisle started scratching aggressively at his crotch, their unaliveness rendered the act symbolic, collective. They coughed into their hands and reached for the bus pole. They allowed a woman to slump over without asking her where she wanted to get off.

Most descended shortly after entering New Jersey and melted into the bustling streets of the shopping districts. She was the only passenger left on the bus—even the sleeping woman had disappeared—as it skirted an affluent neighborhood of broad, trim lawns graced with upright elms and powerfully broad old oaks. The houses were all markedly distinct from one another, of varying styles, materials, and colors: painted wood and weathered brick, modern glass walls and Tudor gables. Her whole being, her sensibility and her spirit, vibrated with wistful awe at this setting of serene flourishing. Privacy, this enclave told her, was possible in any enclosed space, but self-expression was a privilege.

The tranquil houses gave way to a dry cleaner and a Chinese takeout and apartment complexes with empty pools. Then the bus was back in a commercial zone, and Minah saw she was alone with the driver. She approached the front and asked if they'd passed her stop. She knew her stop was one of the last but couldn't imagine it would be this far. The driver said nothing, the stony face in the rearview mirror registering no comprehension, betraying only hatred for her job. They passed by an isolated gas station and Minah began to panic. She was calling Sarah when the doors opened and the driver called out her stop.

She found herself in front of an office complex with a fountain. Before the empty rows of the parking lot, the fountain seemed surreal, like the proverbial falling tree in a forest, perpetually shooting upward and shimmering down for no reason, no person—except now, for her, and she was lost.

She heard Sarah answer her from the phone pressed into her palm.

"Where the hell am I?"

"I think you're at the right stop. Just follow the directions on your phone, it's a fifteen- or twenty-minute walk and then you're at the building."

"Why didn't you tell me it's in the middle of nowhere?"

"I didn't know. Esther figured out where it was and said it was easy to get to. She got us here, but I should've known not to trust her about it being easy. It took us over an hour with two transfers. I'll come down in fifteen and let you in."

Minah crossed a boulevard behind the complex, navigated a series of side streets, and took a shortcut through an alley with abandoned cardboard shelters, until she found herself at a small lot with about ten parking spaces, two of which were occupied by dumpsters. Sarah was smoking next to one of them.

"I don't think this is Englewood," Sarah said. "It's like when you look on Craigslist and the ad says Upper East Side for the Bronx."

The building was like an enormous graying cardboard box.

That bastard, Minah thought. Anger was singeing her heart; tears were simmering in her eyes. As cheap, as sick as ever.

"I told him I couldn't stay long," Sarah said in the elevator. Her eyes were bright with manic agitation, and she was speaking unusually quickly. "I said I was here to say hi and would come back soon. But Esther didn't want to leave till she saw you, and I didn't want to leave her here, it's too awful. He's lying in bed and says he's too tired to get up, and I can't tell if he's lying. I don't know what he's doing here. It's awful. It's like a nightmare."

They entered the apartment. At the sight of the living room, claustrophobia hit Minah like a wave. A TV screen on a massive console towered over a round dining table ringed with six chairs; the back of one of the chairs was leaning against an armchair, which faced a coffee table crammed into the angle of a sectional sofa. The sofa extended the length of the room and over half the far wall, which bore a single window. She could well imagine her father idling on the sofa, gleefully watching his daughters twisting and squeezing themselves into the dining chairs. He took such satisfaction in breaking them down, like a circus master whipping his wild animals until they leapt through the flaming hoop.

She was drawn to the window where, with one knee on the sofa, she looked out onto the barren plot behind the building. Rain was beginning to fall, mixing with the dirt into a muddy expanse. A dark bar of ragged clouds was hanging over a remote highway.

"Minah," Esther said. Minah hadn't noticed her in the open kitchen by the entrance.

They met by the dining table, pushing in one of its chairs. Esther embraced her.

A few freckles had formed on her nose. Her hair, which had once been like Minah's, long, straight, and black as onyx, was now cut above her shoulders, frazzled and choppy, dark but not quite black, glinting with strands of reddish copper. There were tiny, deep crinkles in the far corners of her warm, dark eyes, a depressed scar above her lip, a broken blood vessel on her cheek. Her cheeks were a little leaner; she smiled, and her teeth were still very white. Her lips were full, faintly pink and frosted with dead skin. Her face was luminous with happiness.

A moment passed, and another, and Minah couldn't help continuing to stare into her sister's face, to watch the white scar above her lip move with her smile. The finest lines were etched on her young forehead, under her eyes, in the dimples of her cheeks, which Minah read as hieroglyphics for long days of sun, cold wind, and dry air. But beneath the subtle filigree of lines, her complexion was healthy and bright, like dark honey in sunlight. She was beginning to resemble a paper lantern: delicate, radiant, and flammable.

Minah opened her mouth to speak but said nothing. She was digging in her mind for the right words and descending deeper and deeper, down to the utterances layered like geological strata under the pressure of so much time apart:

Did you have a good flight?

It's good to see you.

It's been too long.

It's amazing to see you.

Why have we waited to come together for him?

I'm sorry.

Your life has become so different from mine.

Let's sit down together.

I am sorry.

I'm still waiting.

"I'm sorry I'm late," she said at last.

"Let's go in," Esther said, moving toward the hall, at the end of which a door stood open.

He was lying on his side in a white undershirt, under a thick blanket.

Minah's breath caught in her throat. The memory of Jeonghee during her last years, suffering under the same blanket, was forever corrupted in an instant. His black trouser socks showed at the foot of the bed.

He did not look ill. He did not even look much older. A bald spot had appeared on his pate, and his face was thinner, but that was to be expected; he was at least seventy-five years old. Minah didn't know how old exactly.

He grinned when Minah entered the room.

Esther offered her sisters the armchair by the bed; after both Minah and Sarah declined, she took it herself. Sarah leaned against the wall between the bed and the door, and Minah stood by the window, which she saw overlooked the dumpsters. She knew he'd followed her with his eyes as she crossed the room. He smirked when she looked his way again.

He began speaking in Korean, which Minah alone among the sisters understood fluently, and inserted phrases in English, as had become an entrenched habit with time.

"You all wanted to leave me. Now here I am." He coughed and rose to drink some water. "Esther, give me your hand."

She pushed the chair closer to his bed and complied.

"Sarah, I know you don't want to be here." He cast a scornful glance at Sarah, then turned to Esther. Though his words were addressed to Sarah, he continued talking at Esther and patting her hand. "Sarah, I know you don't like me. You don't have love for me. But that's okay with me. Most days it's okay with me. I tried my best. *I try my best. But you don't care I try, but I know, I know I try. And now I am here. Your father.* Your daddy."

He coughed again and laughed.

"You went across the country to get away from me. And now see where we are. I'm here with you. See how sad and sick I am. I'm your father. My *lungs* aren't working anymore. I'm dying. *I die!*" He sighed. "*Even the best, best doctor say I live one year. If I am lucky, two.* But I've never been *lucky*. Not with three wretched girls to raise. I raised you all alone, and it killed me! Now I'm dying, and you're letting me die alone.

"Sarah, you've been smoking. I can smell it from here. What a disgusting girl. You're the reason why I'm sick. You're the reason why *Daddy have cancer. You know,* I'm only here for you. Esther would have visited me if I'd stayed in LA, but you, no. *I must come here for you!* And I used to be so proud of you! Esther is *nice* but hopeless. She's hopeless. You were the best and smartest, but how can I be proud if you *do not care, you do not love me*? I want to know. I'm dying and I can't even rest because now I know you, my daughter, do not have a good heart. Say something. Answer me, I'm begging you! *Say to me, explain to me!*"

He cleared his throat and hacked into his cup. Minah had nearly forgotten this repugnant lifelong habit. She had a flashback of the assorted cups and mugs in their kitchen sink, half full of water, milk, Coke, all with gobs of phlegm curdled at the bottom or floating on top.

Sarah said nothing. She was staring out the door. Minah looked to Sarah's backside and felt her suffering.

"*There's nothing to say*," Minah said fiercely in Korean.

Only Esther did not seem overwhelmed. She was focusing on Eugene's hand with a perturbed, preoccupied expression.

Eugene laughed softly and sighed. He pulled his hand away from Esther to address Sarah and Minah in both word and attitude.

"You think I came here to see your miserable faces! I came here to be with someone who cares for me. I have a son!"

He lifted himself upright, and a triumphant rictus hardened on his face when Sarah turned to him at last with wide eyes.

"After today, I don't want to see you again. I don't need you. *My son take care of me.*"

Minah gaped at their father's claim. She wondered whether her sisters had processed it; she immediately suspected it was a lie. But she was less astonished by his outrageous lie than her own shock. How had she not prepared herself for the pure barbarity and faithlessness of the man who could not resist, even now, the pleasure of tormenting his daughters?

Esther lifted her intent gaze to their father. As if in response, he said, "Okay, he's not really my son. But he's a good kid, and I've cared for him like a father. I've supported him. I am his father. Now he's a doctor. A very smart doctor. And he's taking care of me now. He has for months because he's a good son. I've been here for months but I didn't tell you because you don't care about me. I see you still don't care about me. But he does. He's a *good boy* with a good heart. He's gifted and handsome and he'll be rich. None of you useless bitches knows how to make any money. Even if I gave you my money you'd still live like trash. I've given up on you. All three of you. If only he was my trueborn son! It doesn't matter, he's still better than any of you. That's why he's going to be my heir. I won't give any of you anything. And I have so much to give . . ." He chuckled and cleared his throat. "You worthless girls, you don't deserve anything from me. Nothing! You're *trash* compared to him! But . . . but no, I say that because I feel so sad, because you don't love me. I know, Sarah, *Daddy knows*. I've been a terrible father to you and I'll always regret it." He pressed his face into his pillow and moaned.

It was him. It electrified him to incite rage, confusion, pain, and loathing. He was still himself, and he was at his most horrible as he lamented, with relish, the lonely crucible of his good intentions; the burden of his violent love.

The revulsion he roused in Minah was so potent it felt less like a rejection of his inhumanity, or an instinctive defense of her own fundamental decency, than an unbearable internal stew, a poison that was corroding her and making her less human.

She left the room and shut the door behind her.

She would later regret leaving. She would have to rely on her sisters' accounts of what followed, which she did not trust because of their imperfect comprehension of Korean.

She was about to turn down the hall back to the living room when she discovered the second bedroom facing Eugene's. Inside, she saw a replication of her childhood bedroom. The bunk bed she and Esther slept in as children, where she had spent long nights on top staring at the ceiling, stood beside Sarah's twin bed. Each was made up with their old bedding, Minah's with large red and white flowers against a pink background, Esther's and Sarah's a deep blue with green stripes. She recognized the dresser, the desk, the small bookcase. The bookcase was nearly empty except for a few school notebooks and titles in Korean, including a translation of *The Secret*, and a copy, in English, of *Gray's Anatomy*. This was where their furniture went after she left home and he moved into the well-appointed, airy house on the other side of town that Sarah, when pressed, had described to her.

Sarah had selected the bed sets on one of her shopping trips with Eugene. When Minah expressed a preference for the flowers that Sarah had probably intended for herself, she let Minah take the set for herself. It was a rare gesture, offered with her usual sullen face; what it signified Minah hadn't known.

The lamp on the nightstand had been left on. The pillow on the bottom bunk bore an indentation.

3
The class

"They're just kids. They're still figuring out the basics on their own. How to do their laundry, how everything on campus works. They're not ready to talk about these things."

Sarah was thinking about her interview with the chair of the English department three years ago. Around the seminar table, the students were composing a response to the day's reading.

It could be at once soothing and stimulating, like a purgative bath, to be in the midst of so much silent thinking. Thoughts were rising like gentle steam, carrying the temperature of the warm, organ-dark interiors in which they first began to churn.

She usually savored these rare moments in the classroom when she didn't have to think on her feet for the fifteen teenagers in the room. She drank coffee and reviewed her notes; she planned her dinner with Victor.

These days, bitter reflections filled her quiet moments like a miasma. She was one of the most recent part-time hires, but she was still stunned to be one of the first to be let go. She told herself she shouldn't be surprised Rachel was retaining instructors who were less qualified than her, mostly perpetually smiling young women who were less interested in teaching critical thinking than positive thinking through literature. After all, Rachel was herself a philistine. She talked of students not as if they were future scholars and citizens with responsibilities but infinitely precious half-wits. She valued niceness over truth.

At the interview Rachel said she was hiring to accommodate the largest incoming class in the college's history. Sarah later learned the college's new president had inconveniently asked the faculty after the acceptance letters went out what they most wanted her to do for them. What would make their jobs more fulfilling? They said: We want to teach less.

Their wish was granted. Their teaching load dropped from three to two classes a term. The third course was invariably the writing-intensive, and thus pedagogically demanding, seminars required of first-years, now predominantly taught by part-time lecturers with no contract. With all her hours in the classroom and out marking papers, replying to emails, preparing material, corresponding with deans about the one student she had each term in danger of failing, she estimated she was making less than minimum wage. She assumed the students were unaware they were being taught the college's hallmark interdisciplinary introduction to a liberal arts education by an exploited scholar-worker.

Rachel was satisfied with Sarah's credentials and, at first, enthusiastic about the class she was proposing on works about obscure and marginalized lives framed as ordinary or minor.

"How are they represented, why are they represented as they are," Sarah said in her best confident professional persona. "How do they resonate with the larger historical moment, with a greater collective. Those are some of the basic questions that I'd raise."

Rachel put down the syllabus and said, "I can see you have a lot to offer." She smiled intently for so long Sarah shifted uncomfortably in her seat. Her smile faded, and Sarah realized she'd wanted her to smile back. Rachel took up the syllabus again. "*Madame Bovary*, wonderful! And Freud, I guess that works . . . But . . . have you taught *Open City* before?"

"No, but I'd like to try."

"You do know how it ends?"

"Yes, I do," Sarah said with a touch of coldness. Of course she knew how it ended.

"I'm not sure it's appropriate for a first-year course."

"Because . . . ?"

"I just don't think the students are ready to talk about rape in that way. They're just kids. They're still figuring out the basics on their own. How to do their laundry, how everything on campus works. They're not ready to talk about these things."

"But they have to talk about rape and consent during their orientation, don't they? And it's all over TV and the internet. And I see that a lot of instructors are teaching *Hymn to Demeter*. That's about abduction, rape, incest, genocide, every literal and symbolic death you can think of," Sarah said, attempting a gently knowing smile.

"Well, I'm very dubious about *Open City*. It's your course, but I really think you should reconsider it. And why don't you add some lighter texts? They'd help your students feel more engaged."

Rachel was friendly when they ran into each other, but Sarah was convinced it was her unwillingness to drop the offending title from her syllabus that had marked her early on as difficult and worse: indifferent to innocence, insensitive to the veritable children whom Sarah saw in the halls basking in Rachel's smile.

Sarah remembered the photos in Rachel's office of herself with her husband and children and with colleagues and friends. Of course Rachel had many more meaningful relationships than her. She was friendless now without Victor. She'd moved in with him because she thought he was good for her, and she'd thought this was love. Victor was mild-mannered and reassuring; with him, wrapped in the gauze of his calm inoffensiveness, she was more acceptable to others. After their breakup she understood that he'd been drawn to all the qualities in her his friends disliked: her coolness and apartness, which attracted his romanticism; the flavor of her acidity, which no longer amused him and began to leave a sour aftertaste after a year under the same roof. He left her for someone like himself, affable and meek. Katie was white, and her father was a professor of Italian in the Midwest. Sarah couldn't deny she was likable and kind.

Her problem might be that she had a ponderously idealized notion of friendship. It was supposed to be easy, a habitual exchange of affects: an exchange of pleasantries and small kindnesses, the sharing of interests and a sense of common courtesy. She wanted friendship to be a forged bond, un-contaminated by sex, in which she could bare and build her soul. But this, as she'd always known, was rare and unrealistic, and she did not feel she could bare her soul to the few she called her friends. She tried and failed to insert herself into the vast interlacing networks of friendship that made the legible world.

She was waiting for her students to respond to the conclusion of *Open City*. Throughout the novel told from his first-person perspective, the narrator Julius trains his discerning eye and ear on the people encountered during his peregrinations in New York, Brussels, and Lagos, while revealing little about himself. His voice is aloof, his reflections empathetic and unerringly intelligent. His own relationships are without deep intimacy, as he gradu-ally reveals despite himself. In the penultimate chapter he is confronted by a woman, the younger sister of a childhood friend in Lagos, with the hour, ever seared in her mind, when he forced himself on her. He never mentions her again.

Nearly all the reviews she'd read were by men who thought this late disclosure was aesthetically awkward or simply described Julius as a keen ob-server of cosmopolitan life, making no reference to the crime or the sinister symptoms of self-inflicted moral damage haunting the entire narrative. Her question for her students was: How does the revelation of Julius's crime affect your understanding of the novel?

It wasn't lost on Sarah as she watched one student write with their head down in the crook of their arm, like a small child, that she resembled Julius. She was a hypocrite.

She was preparing to talk to the students about the ways the narration of this initially sympathetic character implicated them, the readers, in his crime. It was easy and no doubt satisfying to denounce this fictional character without considering the consequences of exclusionary judgment. But a community is composed of brothers and sisters, some of whom will commit crimes, and no community will survive if it not only denounces the crime but renounces the criminal. Judgment requires one person, who can choose to remain aloof; rehabilitation requires that the innocent and the guilty alike understand their ties to each other. Julius, at the age of fourteen, violated someone he should have treated as a sister. Before committing his crime, his own body was brutally abused by a teacher. Now, an only child become an adult, he has dreams of a younger sister.

Sarah had dreamt of Esther only last night. At this coincidence of life and art she was both humiliated and defiant. She knew it was a cliché of hypocrisy to insist that the ideals you extolled were not applicable to your unique situation. But her experience was, truly, different. She judged her father. She wanted him to disappear forever.

She told the class to wrap up what they were writing. The classroom silence was becoming suffocating.

She wanted her father to suffer. She wanted Minah to suffer, too. Minah had been so unkind to her as a child. She was older than Sarah, she should have loved her the way she loved Esther, but instead she made Sarah unhappier than she would have been without her. She even wanted her students to suffer. Rose, with her private school education and gleaming new phone and laptop, who judged in her abject essay that Emma Bovary's "real problem" was her "materialistic bad attitude." Amina, who disagreed: the problem was that Emma didn't even try to love her husband.

They had fallen under the illusions of a reverse narcissism according to which others should be capable of the goodness they saw at the core of their own souls, or else those others were to be judged. And they had perfect faith in the inviolability of their own souls, which circumstance would never touch. To have a soul was to see good and evil as distinct and absolute. To denounce evil made them feel good—it felt good to be good.

She saw Amina checking her phone under the table. The thought came to Sarah as clearly as if she'd uttered it aloud: May you find yourself trapped one day and be judged for it.

May my father suffer for what he has done to me.

May he suffer.

May he understand the evil of his nature and everything my sisters and I suffered and still suffer under him before he dies.

May this understanding make him suffer more than he can bear.

The students were thirteen girls, or young women, one nonbinary person, and one boy, or young man. Each year on the first day of class there were about five men, most of whom dropped out after Sarah said the first part of the course would be devoted to representations of women at home.

She asked them to share what they'd written. There was always at least one or two beats of silence before anyone volunteered to speak. The pause was a polite custom whose meaning was: I'll speak only if you don't want to.

"It made me rethink everything," Piper said, "what he did to Moji."

"His rape of Moji," Sarah said. She was always the first to say the word "rape."

"I felt like I read the book for nothing," Genevieve said.

"Why? Say more."

"I felt like everything he said before was a lie, and I just read a book by a liar and a coward."

"Let's keep in mind that the narrator is not the author. The author created a character named Julius, and he's showing us how a rapist can only forget his crime if he loses his own humanity."

"I know what you mean," said Alex to Genevieve. "I felt like the book was a total waste."

"But did you feel," Sarah said, "before learning about the crime, that you could identify with him? I know I did. I felt like I was walking with him in these cities—I *liked* walking with him. So many of his thoughts on the people he met and the places he explored were sympathetic to me."

"What?" Mia asked softly, though with visible alarm. She was a particularly thoughtful student. Her slouching figure snapped into a startled line. Did her teacher just admit to identifying with a rapist?

Sarah gave them her prepared reading of the book. She started by reaffirming that the crime was egregious and not to be diminished and concluded with reflections on the difficult and necessary demands of community. She spoke in a tone of moral seriousness that drew its force from her private turmoil, which she presented as a righteous passion for restorative justice. Some of the students who had nodded their heads in approval of Genevieve's wholesale rejection of the book now looked distressingly confused.

There was more note-taking, and Sarah wondered what they were writing. She spent the rest of the session going over the requirements for their second essay.

She knew she would receive, once again, one or two papers whose main argument was that Julius was an evil sociopath.

Minah was waiting for Sarah on the steps of the library. She looked formidably sleek in her dark trench coat and tall black boots, but the air of sophistication was undercut by her pacing, the occasional outward glance that betrayed inner turbulence.

Minah had never visited Sarah on campus before. For a moment, even after Sarah recognized her, her sister didn't seem like someone she knew personally. She didn't seem to fall into any category—friend or acquaintance, colleague or neighbor—of her social life. At the sight of her, Sarah had the sudden dizzying impression that she didn't know where Minah came from, what she was doing there, what she wanted from her.

It took just an instant to remember. Minah had called her that morning insisting that they meet.

"What happened at Dad's after I left?"

"He cursed you. He kept raging. That's all."

"Did he mention his son again?"

"No."

"Nothing more about leaving everything to his son?"

"No."

"Doesn't it bother you at all that he just told us we have a brother he's hidden from us all our lives? Why do you sound like you don't even care?"

"Because he's been telling me since I can remember that he wished I were a boy, a son worth all his disgusting devotion," Sarah said with rising resentment for having to revisit unhappiness to placate her sister. "And that was when he was in a good mood. He's been threatening to disown me since I was eight and didn't even know what that meant. So no, nothing he said was new to me. Anyway, what do I care if he does have a son? He's not a part of my life, even if he exists, and I don't want our father part of my life, either."

"We have to meet," Minah said.

Sarah didn't want to go to the campus café and risk being overheard by her students. Minah offered to pay for lunch at a pricier restaurant down the street rarely frequented by undergraduates.

Sarah read the scattered patrons as a Scandinavian family of tourists, a professor with her graduate student, visiting parents waiting for their children to finish their last class. A confusing, familiar sense of mixed relief flowed through her, like strong wine sprinkled heavily with cork. The restaurant had been a packed success for several months, but the crowds faded away as the complimentary bread got staler and the steak au poivre too gristly to chew. What remained were the pretentious French bistro-style chairs, the expensive, generic lack of taste. Here, Sarah felt less like a struggling adjunct, more like a properly salaried adult. But she didn't like the place, and she couldn't think of anywhere else to go.

She was about to take the booth seat when Minah brushed past her and sat down.

"Paul's invited you to a service followed by lunch some weekend," Minah said briskly.

"That's nice. No thank you."

"Please come. It would mean a lot to me."

"I'll go to another dinner but not a service. It's not just that I'm not religious. I'm anti-religious. And services sound really boring."

"This is really important," Minah said severely. "Paul knows you're not religious and has already guessed you look down on religion. He doesn't care. He still really wants to talk to you, get to know you. Please do it. Please."

"I don't like being bored."

"Do it for me. Okay? Okay?"

"What's wrong with you?"

"What kind of question is that?"

"Why are you so worked up?"

"You know what I do for a living, right?"

"You're a lawyer," Sarah said, drawing out the statement with a sigh.

"You don't even know what kind of law I practice, do you?"

"No. Tell me."

"I work in wills and trusts."

"Okay," she said, intoning it as a facetious question. She could feel herself playing the part of the sarcastic, bratty sister. She was annoying herself, but she was also enjoying the role.

"So I know how inheritance laws work in different states. Are you listening or reading the dessert menu?"

"I'm listening, okay? You need to calm down."

"Listen. Listen! I believe he's dying. And I believe he has a son. An illegitimate son, living in New Jersey right now. He said his son is a doctor, remember? I found a medical book dedicated to his son, in Korean. I was looking through the other room when you two were still with him. Dad's a liar, but I believe him. You know him. He's outrageous. He's unbeliev-able. That's why I believe this. So listen. In any state an illegitimate child can make a claim on their mother's estate. Maternal inheritance is common because maternity is easy to establish. But paternal inheritance is a gray area. In California—"

"What did he write?" Sarah asked softly, humbled. "In the book?"

"'To my son.' In Korean. That was all."

"Oh."

"Listen. In California, if there's no will, it's very hard for an illegitimate child to make a claim on a father's estate, even if he can prove through a DNA test he's a biological son. The father has to have made some public acknowledgment of paternity before his death. And what 'public acknowl-edgment' means is open to interpretation in the courts. In intestate practice it's been very hard for illegitimate children to inherit part of an estate with-out being recognized. If Eugene is a resident of California when he dies and doesn't have a will, everything goes to the three of us. The son wouldn't have any chance of challenging the will. Any competent lawyer would have told Eugene this. Even if he does have a will that gives everything to the son—which some courts would deem a public acknowledgment—we could contest the will and would have a very good chance of each receiving a quarter of the estate. I know California courts want all acknowledged biological children, legitimated by marriage or not, to share the estate, even if one of them is omitted from the will.

"But in New Jersey, the law is different. And if Eugene did arrive a few months ago, he could qualify as a resident before the end of the year. It's one of the few states where an illegitimate biological child can actually con-test a will as long as he can prove that he had a relationship of some kind with the deceased during the deceased's lifetime. 'Public acknowledgment' is less important than proof of any kind of relationship with the biological father, and a postmortem DNA test would be accepted in court. Do you understand what I'm saying?"

Sarah was beginning to understand the source of Minah's agitation, but there remained something else marring a complete illumination of the situation. She experienced it as a cataract, a painless yet oppressive impediment to reality. Sarah's concern was different from her sister's. Her vehemently sexist father had a son whom he'd concealed from her and her sisters all their lives. All her life, she'd had a brother growing up somewhere out in the world. What was it she'd written once in college . . . *No longer living under him or near him but knowing that he came from this world is to learn the world itself is like the home you left behind.*

She shook her head. She didn't want to think about the nebulous existential implications of her brother's existence. Minah's preoccupation was something tangible: it was financial. "So he wasn't lying. He was threatening our inheritance. That's what you're saying. But everything you're saying about state laws seems irrelevant. So what if he said he was leaving everything to his son? Either he has a will that we can't change or he doesn't, in which case it seems unlikely we'd have any influence over him."

"You don't get it. You still don't understand him. He was inviting us to persuade him to write it or change it. What else did he say after I left?"

"Nothing, I don't know, I don't remember. He was rambling."

She remembered feeling spellbound in that room, like a character in a book encountering her fate; like a character in a movie who loses all sense of self-preservation and does not flee but lingers to see if the one before her will indeed kill her. It was as if what was happening was not her life, but a story whose ending she needed to know. Yes—she, too, believed he was dying. She'd felt it in the room, in his uncharacteristic desire for Esther's hand. And she understood why he wanted Minah present. He'd wanted Minah there to translate in case Sarah didn't understand the awful outpour of his dying heart.

"Do you at least see what's he's doing? And what we have to do?"

"No. Just tell me."

"We have to make sure he writes a will that names us as the sole beneficiaries. The most his son can do then is claim a quarter of the estate. Fine.

We couldn't do anything about it if he collected enough evidence that Dad acted like a father toward him or played any role in his life—that all, by the way, with a DNA test, would pretty much guarantee that he'd have a claim after Dad dies, with or without a will. But if Dad doesn't name us and gives everything to his son—then, strange as it sounds, *we* would be in the weaker position. Weaker than the illegitimate son would be if he was omitted from the will but had evidence of a relationship with the deceased. *We* would have to contest the will, and I know from practice that New Jersey is more likely to respect the will as the sacred intention of the deceased than the claims of the justly or unjustly omitted children."

"I don't understand. Why would we be in a weaker position?"

"The law often doesn't make sense, especially in practice. In this case, it built upon existing tradition and lacked the imagination to anticipate a situation like this. We're in danger of losing all claim to the estate to the son's advantage if Dad writes a will that cuts us out. As he's already threatened, in so many words. Even if he doesn't name the son in a will that omits us, the son could reasonably inherit at least a fraction of the estate, if not everything. I know this, I've seen jaw-dropping, blood-boiling cases like this before. I can name a few sexist old judges off the top of my head who would hand half of the estate over to the son if Dad wrote a will that didn't name either us or the son as beneficiaries but gave everything to some society for the reunification of Korea, as he once told me he wanted to do. The judge would say he had to respect Dad's implied wish to deny the legitimate children—the daughters—an inheritance. He'd say that omitting us, whether in so many words or not, must be respected since legally recognized children are expected to inherit. He'd argue that an illegitimate son couldn't be denied in the same way: Eugene couldn't be said to have *expressly* omitted the illegitimate son, even if the son wasn't mentioned in the will, because unrecognized children aren't expected to inherit from their father. Their father, not their mother. Do you follow me? It could happen."

"Do you think Eugene is that clever? That imaginative himself?"

"I think he's the devil and can imagine anything."

Sarah had never heard Minah speak so articulately or so vigorously before. Her forceful intelligence seemed to clarify to Sarah, who was ever steeped in murky subjectivity, the ways of the hard real world. But as Minah continued to explain, Sarah couldn't shake the estranging sense that they were talking about pure fictions. Human law was an obscure web of arbitrary constructions in which Minah was attempting to entangle her. She had never thought of Minah as either imaginative or analytical and was impressed and surprised she'd thought this matter through so thoroughly. Minah was drawing her into a predicament that featured all the vivid detail and emotion of a paranoid fantasy.

As a child Sarah had enjoyed elaborating minutely detailed fantasies of escape from her father until the requirements of a realistic fabrication became depressingly overwhelming. The means of escape without money: How far could she travel with a heavy bag? How long until she was found and returned home? The likelihood of finding loving and enlightened parents—white parents existing in a world apart from the everyday indignities and alienation and violence her family knew, whose energies were devoted to culture and pleasure—who wouldn't prefer unblemished children of their own. The possibility of escaping what compelled escape: everyone said she looked like her father. They said the eyes, but her eyes were rounder and brighter; they scrutinized her further and said not the eyes themselves but something in the cast of the eyes under those dark brows. She feared and knew they saw, in the interplay of her features, the quickening of her father's blood. Even the mouth that was undeniably her mother's, full and slightly pouting, was like a pale ruby set in her father's crown . . . The fantasies themselves became a labyrinth, ultimately reinforcing the very conditions of confinement to which they were apparently opposed.

"But . . ." Sarah said, shaking free of her memories to face a situation that seemed no less vague and ungovernable.

"But what?"

"He's already said he doesn't even want us back. He said that after you left. He doesn't want to see us again. How can we convince him of anything?"

"Sometimes I can't tell whether you're really smart or really stupid. Esther's with him right now. He's already asked her to move in with him and look after him."

"Fuck you and don't call me stupid. I didn't know that. I knew Esther went back today, but I didn't know he asked her to stay with him."

"Okay. I'm sorry. I'm just under a lot of stress now. I take it back."

"I thought today's visit would be the last, or one of the last times before she wanders off again. She says he has an aide. So I assumed he didn't want or need us around. To be honest I didn't want to think about it. I have a lot else to think about now," Sarah concluded irascibly.

"I understand," Minah countervailed with cool politeness edged with impatience.

"She said no, right? She told you she wouldn't live with him."

"She didn't say."

Sarah was finding it hard to think. What was it that was nagging her now? "Okay. What if Dad dies in New Jersey and wants to leave everything to Planned Parenthood and the World Wildlife Fund?"

"Then we'd get nothing, not the three of us or the son. Unless we all try to contest it. But neither state is likely to challenge the written will in that case."

"I think he's more likely to do that after trying to have us compete like reality TV contestants for his money. Knowing the whole time that none of us would get anything for our pathetic efforts. Why should we play this game you think he's proposing?"

"I don't think that will happen. And I know the money would help all of us. I'll speak for myself now. I need the money. I need to have a better life. You don't want children. I do." She was addressing Sarah in a different register now, no longer pressing and overwrought, but desperate, gentle, and profoundly weary. "I want a clean house for them. I want to feed them organic food and dress them in nice clothes and walk them every morning to a good school in my neighborhood. That doesn't make me greedy. I make money, but all of it goes to my student loans and my apartment.

"You're asking yourself why I left the serviceable apartment I shared with a nice roommate in Inwood and got a renovated studio in Chelsea overlooking the High Line. You don't know how hard it is to find a good man in New York. Everywhere you turn there are ten beautiful, intelligent women for one eligible bachelor, a guy with a good income who's still a selfish little boy at heart. They date you, sleep with you a few times, then leave you for one of the other women they're already sleeping with who might have more money and a better job but somehow less brains and character and even looks than you. But she's happier. People are drawn to happiness. Happiness brings good fortune, not the other way around. I moved to a better place and bought a whole new wardrobe as soon as I figured that out. It didn't take long before I was being pursued by half a dozen men, including one who dumped me after a one-night stand but started calling again. He started thinking of me as promising wife material after I changed my life.

"But I didn't do it just for the men. The clothes and apartment and nice sheets and vases with fresh flowers make me happier. Even if you're not feeling good one day, living in a beautiful place makes you feel like you've stepped out of a painting. Some of the veneer of the beautiful and pleasant things rubs off on you, even when you're waiting in line at a CVS, where one guy tried to pick me up. It's not the monetary value of the lifestyle that makes you desirable. It's that so much of it isn't necessary to live. The flowers and the view that make you feel you're human and not a caged animal.

"I want to have children who are radiant and happy like the women I can't compete with, not without the luster and advantage of these things I can't really afford. I want them to grow up safe and spoiled with enough childhood happiness stored inside them to last them their whole lives. You must have met people in your life who could never imagine what we've grown up with. They tell you, 'You must be exaggerating, your father only did what he thought was best for you.' I want my children to be like those people. Their happiness is the most beautiful in the world. It's beautiful and ridiculous and priceless, like a Fabergé egg. You might find them absurd, but you could never bring yourself to damage one because it *is* priceless. Because the world is more beautiful with them than without. You will never convince me that what we suffered has given us greater wisdom or humanity. None of it was worth it.

"You've probably asked yourself before today why I can't marry for love. I will love any children I have more than my husband. I know that already. So I'm not going to marry for love. I'm going to arrange a marriage for myself with a suitable partner and hope I fall in love, but if I don't at least my children will have a decent father who will provide for us. I want to have a better life. I want to create a good life. That's how I'm going to live.

"Last question: Do I love Paul? I don't know. But I like him more than any other boyfriend I've had yet, and he wants the same things in life as me. I respect him and I want to be with him. He wants educated children with good values. And I suspect he's willing to be as ruthless as me in giving them the best life. He wants intelligent children, and he finds you intelligent. He wants children gifted like you, and that's why he wants to get to know you. I know that. He's somewhat intrigued by you. I know that, too. If you think I'm jealous you haven't understood anything I've said. I need you to come to church and have lunch with us. Please," she said, and the request was a fist gently brought to rest on the table.

"Okay," Sarah said with a gulp. Again, she felt humbled: she did not know she could be so moved by her sister. For as long as Minah spoke, Sarah was mesmerized by her forthrightness, by the melding of pathos and fierceness in the delineation of her worldly dreams.

"And I need you, with Esther, to make sure the three of us are named the beneficiaries of the estate in a legal will. You could make him convert to decency on his deathbed. He hates me, but he's loyal to you despite what he says and however you might feel about him. We can't do anything if his son is granted a quarter, but at least each of us will have a quarter then. I don't think it doesn't matter what we do. It matters more than anything now."

"I still don't understand," Sarah said. The coffee in her empty stomach was beginning to make her feel lightly panicked; she woke from the spell of Minah's confessional. "You're acting as if you can't live without his money. I'd like more money, too, but I've accepted long ago that Dad's unreliable and can't be depended on for anything. You know, he once called me at college drunk and weeping saying he wanted to build an orphanage in Seoul in his name. He's more likely to make a grand gesture like that, which would also be a middle finger to us, than divide his estate fairly in three. Or four. I admit he's given me money over the years. Not often. He'd do it without my asking. I'd check my account to see if I could pay my credit card and find a cash deposit anywhere between a few hundred and a few thousand dollars. Of course the money was useful. I got a warm winter coat and went to Berlin for the first time and bought lots of books. But they weren't regular payments and they weren't amounts to change your life. I don't understand why you're suddenly acting like his money is indispensable. You've been living without it for long enough. So have I. We've both grown up knowing we can't rely on him."

Minah swallowed hard. Her eyes flashed with exasperation. "I know you don't care as much about money as me. But you need money, too. You're not with Victor anymore. You don't have a full-time job. What if you don't get one next year, either?"

Sarah flushed with shame at being confronted so starkly with her failures. Then shame gave way to anger at her sister.

Minah didn't stop. "I don't understand why you don't understand. I sometimes think you have no understanding of money or class. That's the problem. Dad paid for your college. I have debts. Serious debts from law school and more. A lot more."

Sarah could feel her anger mounting steadily, deep within her. She didn't want to help her sister, much less listen to her anymore. She might even want to hurt her. "But what makes you think his money will change your life? As far as we know he hasn't even paid off the mortgage on the house in California. I never understood how he paid for it. Or do you want to inherit that shithole we just visited?"

"You are so naive. Are you really that naive?" Minah was not only contemptuous but offended by Sarah's inability to see. "He's worth over ten million. I think as much as twelve."

"What?" Sarah gave a faint gasp.

"How do you think he bought so much property and real estate? That shithole's just one of his places. By borrowing off his dingy little strip mall dry-cleaning business? After the accident with his hand he met some ambulance chaser and sued the company or the distributor of the chemicals. I was too young to understand all the details, but I heard all the phone calls. I saw letters from the lawyer. Somehow he got millions for it and then made millions more. You don't remember all those phone calls day in and day out from brokers and property managers? The only thing of value he bought and used is the house, but his assets in California and New Jersey and his investments are worth much, much more."

"What if he gives everything to just one of us?" Sarah said suddenly, surprising herself.

"What?"

"What if he gives everything to Esther?"

"Or to you."

"Yes. Or to me."

"That's out of my hands. All I could say to you, in that case, is that the chance of having his money is the only reason why I haven't murdered him yet. Only that money will let me live in peace."

Minah took a final sip of her coffee, dabbed her mauve-tinted lips with her napkin, and pushed her cup to the side of the table. These were not ordinary actions but performances for Sarah. They were imperious gestures that expressed the poetry of her charismatic unhappiness and the drama of her willfulness: the poetry and drama of her life concentrated, in that moment, in the hand that held steady. See, she was saying through them, this power and poetry is invisible, but it's there, even when my hand doesn't tremble and the cup doesn't break.

"If he leaves everything to one of you I will contest it. That's all."

"If he leaves everything to me I will share it with you and Esther. Evenly."

Even as she uttered it, her imagination was branching out wildly like snaking green vines. She might inherit everything and travel the world. She could refuse to give Minah anything but an insulting token of their father's wealth. She would have the security to be magnanimous in both currency and deed—if she was financially stable, she knew she would be kinder. She would regain the power to envision a future.

"Good." Minah signaled for the check.

Outside, the imminent rain made the air feel like chilled velvet. Minah held the collar of her coat close to her throat, like a woman in a photograph. Across the way a brown-skinned woman was pushing a stroller and holding the hand of a white child toddling beside her, and a man walking a stout dog with a joyful trot quickened his pace to overtake them. A woman, likely Korean, was wrapping flowers in plastic sheathes in front of a bodega. A young woman in sweats entered the store, and the next instant her arm extended from within, like the magical movement of a puppet, to open the door for the woman with the stroller and child. Sarah didn't know whether she was still in a world in which Minah was not grasping and insensitive but righteous and strong.

"I'll tell Paul you'll come to the service. Let's do it soon." Minah's voice softened as she made a last request: "Paul doesn't know about my debts. He's guessed I have student loans. He doesn't know about my credit card debt. It goes without saying you can't tell him anything I told you today."

"Of course."

They walked toward the subway, both a little abashed by the strange and unexpected intimacy of the last hour. They got on the same train and sat down beside each other, and the awkwardness was still there.

As she was waiting at Penn Station, Sarah received a text from Esther: I was going to make dinner for us but now I don't know when I'll be back.

The station was drearier than usual. Furiously moving bodies appeared on the verge of internal collapse, like insects that emerged, mated, and died within the span of a day. She needed to pee; the line for the women's restroom stretched into the waiting room, where more homeless people were huddled on the benches, more tourists were fascinated or disgusted by the degradation, more regular commuters were not only resigned but inured to the purgatorial setting. Armed guards in camouflage were toting guns the length of their arms; they looked to be the only ones laughing and fraternizing in the whole of the station. They were accompanied by German shepherds with glassy eyes. Like many working in the stores or waiting for their train, the dogs were at once lifeless and alert, projecting a strangely menacing sense of fragility.

The fetid airlessness of the underground arena was thick with the threat of outburst and abuse; Sarah felt herself swallowing it with the tasteless packaged food she regularly bought on her way home. She perceived all these things now more acutely because of her charged hour with Minah. She felt her anger, but she wasn't sure if it was still directed at her sister.

The train pulled out of the dark cave of the tunnel into an expanse of wild reeds thriving in a dark marsh. A concrete bridge lofted above them and curved through the mist and steel-gray sky. The mist made the sunless sky opalescent, mysterious and beautiful above the wasted landscape.

She set down to marking the in-class responses. They were usually either more nuanced or starker and more assertive than any comments made by the writer in class.

We know that rape is unforgivable in the twenty-first century. But does Cole? Julius is a monster.

Alex was proving to be the kind of small-minded moralist who was also a bad reader, though she thought of herself as a left-leaning intellectual activist. Sarah shuddered to think of the abuses she would unleash in a re-education camp.

Each morning before the seminar Sarah spent at least five minutes at the photocopiers, where she often found herself rereading a summary of goals and concerns for teachers of critical writing tacked above the machines. One of its conclusions was that "18- to 21-year-olds have difficulty appreciating context and how it shapes meaning." But she could perfectly well imagine her students having the same blinkered responses in ten or thirty years, with fully developed prefrontal cortexes. They were at this very moment invisibly flowing like tributaries to the sea of power-hungry hypocrites and ruthlessly stupid purists steadily sinking the world in their cruelty.

She wondered whether she would have responded like Alex at her age. When she was younger she, too, was a moralist, but she was also full of self-doubt and curiosity and inclined to credit her teachers with superior insight. She admitted to herself that she took pleasure in causing Alex and Genevieve discomfort while undermining their narrow opinions. Was she not unlike the ugly moral crusader who, in her shameless egotism, makes no effort to inspire goodness but revels in provocations that lead not only to discomfort but the most dangerous defensiveness?

She returned to her work. Not all the responses to the book were so obtuse.

I didn't understand why Julius would admit to something so awful and then never mention it again. It's like he totally forgot about it and wanted to forget it. Reading the end made me nervous. Are there things I've forgotten?

The question touched her like a cool cloth on her nape. Lina rarely spoke up and always forgot to add her name to her work.

The train was lumbering past the urban stretches whose specific features she could never remember. She was fated to watch the sequence of electrical wires, parking lots, warehouses, rows of blank-faced condos, again and again, without their ever making a lasting impression on her. There were houses, but she never saw people. The soccer fields were empty and muddy.

Minah's urgent voice was echoing in her mind more stridently. She remembered distant times when they were both in exile from home, either expulsed or repulsed by their father, lingering in the neighborhood after dark. Once they were by the public pool, where they encountered Minah's neighborhood frenemies, mainly white teens who never really accepted her despite what they all recognized as her superior spirit. Minah joined them in climbing the gates and swimming in her underwear. One of the girls yelled at Sarah to get undressed, too. "You have nothing to hide, you're too flat chested," she'd said, and giggled viciously. Minah exhibited not a modicum of protectiveness or affinity with her sister and dove underwater, her rippling figure a world away.

How could Minah not have understood the sacrifice she was asking of Sarah? Her sisters were to persuade their father to write a will favorable to them all by taking care of him. He couldn't stand Minah, and he preferred Sarah to Esther. And so she must be the one to serve him. She must be the one to make his dying easier.

Closer to Princeton, she started to recognize what she was seeing: a strip mall with a mediocre Thai restaurant she'd once tried with Victor on a dismal drive back from New York; a signless gyro joint—you could see the enormous rotisserie from afar—right off the highway with parking for two cars only; a long series of tire vendors. Then the train rushed past the acres of trees buffering the wealthy university town from these unvarnished places.

Her father was dying. She wanted to believe in an afterlife. But hell couldn't exist without justice, and justice wasn't possible when the wrongdoer could never understand his sins. Her father was insulated in his essential evil. As if innocent, he was protected from his guilt.

Hell was as factitious as the novel she'd just defended, which said that criminals suffered the self-inflicted dehumanization of violating another's humanity. How many rapists suffered not at all for their crime?

She hated the idea of poetic justice. She scorned the poets of beauty and truth who preached among themselves the ineluctability of justice, the redemption of art. Poetic justice was Dante's hell, where suicides woke to find themselves embodying the trees from which they'd hanged themselves, condemned to speechlessness until someone broke off a piece of their bark: in their oozing words of blood, she read the perverse promise of paradise, the power of poetic words to change the story of the sinner and sufferer alike. But there was no poetry in the suffering the violator could never know.

There was no hell. There was only a purgatory in this world for the select few who learned what they were and what they had done. That was the only kind of justice that existed. It punished only the seekers of truth: those who tried to understand themselves.

Part 3

Even though you're dying, you think. Even though you're dying, you listen.

—Kim Hyesoon, "Commute"

1

Esther at home

Esther was waiting for her father to answer.

He was still clearing his throat. He was struggling to clear more than the usual mucus he normally expelled with a few vigorous grunts. He was straining and in pain; her heart quickened at the difference she could hear in him. She heard guttural, muscular scraping in his throat; she could almost hear the clenching of his stomach, his ribs, his neck, as sweat, too, was squeezed from pores on his forehead.

At last he spat into a mug and looked up with malign satisfaction. "Here. Look here. *Look.* Blood. Blood in my lungs."

He shook the mug before her. The yellow-brown jelly quivered and, with it, a greenish syrupy swirl of digestive fluids and foamy spit, but there was no blood.

"This is why I don't eat anymore. If I eat more, I make more of this. I feed it. It eats. *I don't eat.*"

"When is the aide returning? The woman who was here yesterday. When is she coming back?"

"*I don't want. Edwin want her, not me.*"

"Edwin. Edwin is my brother."

His characteristic Cheshire cat grin was just beginning to spread when his face drooped. He was too tired. "Yes," he said. He turned away from her.

"When will Edwin be here?"

"Soon. Tonight," he said weakly. "Let me sleep."

In the fridge she found a half dozen prepared Korean meals of kimchi fried rice and noodles and stews. She heated the noodles and stood eating at the counter with a fork and staring out the window toward the highway. She was absorbed in the memory of the widow who came every week when they were children to deliver home-cooked meals. She would return from Anna's to find the widow and her father at the dining table. Her father would order her and Sarah and Minah, if she was home, to greet the widow and sit on the sofa. As they sat—it happened so often they might be bored or ashamed, annoyed or burning with murderous fantasies—he lamented his life with them. When he wasn't looking, bent over holding his head in his hands or gesturing toward the offspring of his misfortune, the widow threw him a glance of contempt. When he looked to her for affirmation, she nodded sympathetically. Lifting her chin, she seemed to assess the girls from a loftier perspective of righteous disapproval. "Your life is hard," she would say, glaring at Esther.

It was always Esther she glared at. Esther in turn would gaze at the widow while Sarah and Minah stared at the carpet, pretending they were elsewhere, imagining their father's demise, dreaming of a crush. She was unhappily perplexed by the widow: who she was and why she was listening to their father were grave puzzles for her. The longer she stared, the more the widow disliked her and the deeper Esther's perplexity grew.

She had nearly finished the greasy noodles when Eugene called out. "Esther! Bring me a Coke!"

She was about to open the freezer when she found herself gulping and breathing hard. She was not conscious of any anxiety or fear and wondered at this involuntary response. She poured herself more water and emptied the glass and felt calmer. Then she cracked a few cubes from the ice tray into one of the sippy cups in the dish rack and filled it with Coke. It was the cups drying in a neat row that had first signaled to her that someone was looking after her father.

In his room, he reached for her hand. "Come here," he said gently.

She had the impression he was completing the smile he'd attempted earlier, that neither his mind nor his body retained any memory of the painful episode of coughing and hacking.

"You still haven't grown up, have you?" He patted her hand. "I want to tell you that *I forgive you* for stealing my money. I sent you money for college, and you stole it from me. Do you understand what you did? *You understand?*"

"Yes, that's true," she said. She wished she could speak Korean. In English, he spoke even more vehemently, as if through volume he could break free of the limits of his vocabulary. Or did she imagine he was louder in English because of her limited Korean? She heard the same intensity and dissonance in his native language. Piercing through the loud flapping of fervor was a needy, needling note like metal scraping metal: the self-pitying clawing of the ego for attention and pleasure and power, on and on, for more. It made Minah and Sarah feel they were chomping on iron.

It made Esther feel stronger and bolder. She didn't know why she listened all the more attentively when she heard it. She knew only that she had never feared or hated her father as her sisters had and did.

She didn't want to think she was like those who found him magnetic despite themselves and came to enjoy the spectacle of his indecency. They formed a mere handful, but they existed: customers at the dry-cleaning business, Korean and also white parents at their school, the widow who cooked for them, and the mailman at their second, upgraded home. Originally turned off by his insinuating grin, they appreciated it when they realized they, too, could say whatever they wanted about the physical appearance of neighbors and teachers, the unsavoriness of the Vietnamese, the immorality of American culture. With each encounter, they found themselves reminded of all the ways in which they were stressed, slighted, discontent with their lot, and they wanted to act as he did, without shame. The more corrosive their discontent, the less odious he became. They began to approve of him despite themselves; they did not, as they might have claimed they would, cut him off. They exchanged looks with other parents who said he was scum, then had lively talks with him in the school parking lot, unburdening themselves of a part of their indefinable anger. With him, their anger, their feelings, were not merely justifiable; they were more reasonable than the truth.

The widow lived alone and received little money or attention from her only child, who lived an hour away. She returned every week and listened with an undeniable frisson of complicit pleasure as Eugene sadistically criticized his daughters in his buffoonish performance as a beleaguered single father.

What was the source of his crude appeal? Did it come from the same source as the strange vitality that glowed behind his memorable grin? Sarah and Minah sensed this vitality but did not want to recognize it as anything else but his boundless loathsomeness; they did not want to recognize any further human motive or connection between it and the qualities they accepted as human. But Esther perceived a relation between his energy and the fervor, ingenuity, charisma, dedication, and generosity she'd encountered in more noble characters. If she suggested the affinity to her sisters, they would no doubt deem it sacrilege, a desecration of any understanding of goodness or beauty. For Esther, as her hand rested in their father's, his vitality appeared as a mysterious capacity that could take manifold expressions—and she was drawn to this mystery, in him and in others.

The strident note of cruel need in Eugene's voice struck a corresponding chord in her that filled her with clarity and courage, like a bell flooding a plaza with its rousing peals. She, like the widow, was somehow emboldened by this sound. Yet they were nonetheless differently attuned, and she could not say why.

This was yet another thing she wanted to talk about with Sarah.

Her father started to pat her hand then gripped it, increasing his pressure until he was squeezing and straining to remain steady as he fixed his shining gaze on her.

"Stop that," she said coolly.

He chuckled to himself, pinched her hand, and dropped it. "*You tell me the truth now.*"

"All right."

He extended his hand again, but she kept her own in her lap.

"*You are sneaky. Very sneaky. You say, Daddy, I love college, Daddy, I need money for to stay in college, and you take my money. And now you have nothing. You have nothing.*" He was nearly shouting. He chuckled again and lowered his voice. "*You are sneaky. But! You don't have nothing now. No money, nothing. I am sneaky. I know. But I don't have nothing. I have some-thing. I have much.*"

"I stole because I didn't want to stay in college and I didn't want to return to you. And you didn't want me to return, either. I knew you didn't need the money. And I know you aren't really upset about it," she said matter-of-factly.

His face hardened with suspicion. "*What you do when you have no more money? Huh? What you do? You have nothing. How you get money then? You like a slut, eh? What you do? Tell me!*"

"If I was a prostitute, you might understand why."

His expression remained hard, but she saw a shadow flitting across his eyes. She knew he didn't understand this conditional; her face to him was like a window darkened to outsiders in daylight. Though he hadn't under-stood the sense of what she said, it suggested to him something devious and offensive. He was a volatile man of unhampered drives who considered the implicit request to wrestle with complexity a suspicious aberration of life and, most insidiously, a threat to his vigor.

She was thinking of how she might break down the thought and make it accessible to him when his voice rose again. "I don't care what you do with yourself," he said. He turned to lie on his back. "It doesn't matter at all to me anymore. I felt so much shame over you, I cried at night. Did you know that?" His voice was gentle again. "*I cry when I think of you. I call Anna, I* ask, 'Where is my daughter?' And she doesn't say. My own daughter. She say she don't know." He turned his face away.

"It's true. I don't think she knew."

He didn't respond.

"Will I meet Edwin? I want to know when I should come to be with you. I need to arrange things with him."

"No. Edwin doesn't meet you. Go now."

She didn't move.

"Go!" he shouted, turning back now with his face contorted in a snarl. "Go now! You don't meet Edwin. You will not meet Edwin. He is my son. You are not my daughter."

Esther returned to her sister's in a trance as she brooded over her father's parting words. Why was this judgment, one among so many accusations and insults he'd hurled at her over her life, echoing without fading in her ears? As the malicious words repeated, she wondered, too, why she was saddened rather than wounded or enraged, as her sisters would be, when Eugene spoke to her with the intent to wound and enrage.

The living room was dark and Sarah was shut in her room. She didn't emerge to greet her.

Esther sighed. She was tired of her sister avoiding her. She had arrived over a week ago, and so far Sarah mostly confined herself to her bedroom. Each morning Sarah reacted to their encounter in the living room or kitchen of the cramped apartment as if it were an awkward chance meeting on a city street. She complained ostentatiously about how she'd barely made any headway in the pile of papers she had to grade, and when she returned in the evening she said she'd eaten after her class and wasn't hungry, though Esther could hear her in the kitchen late at night.

"Help yourself to anything there is," she said again and again, her voice unnaturally pitched, her eyes both wide and evasive in her flustered gestures of hospitality. There was very little in the kitchen, and so Esther, herself mildly embarrassed by Sarah's strained behavior, walked the mile and a half to the grocery store. She returned to Sarah's with enough staples to last them more than a week and was met with another show of lightly veiled distress edged with irritation. "I would have gone with you," Sarah said, and both understood that she meant something else: I wish I felt comfortable enough with you to have gone with you, to eat and cook with you, to stay up and talk with you, but since I don't, I am unhappy with you here, and all I can offer you is this wish.

Esther reminded herself of this moment, this wish, as she made dinner for them. She cooked canned black beans with garlic and added dry crumbles of the goat cheese she found in the back of a refrigerator drawer. She wasn't hungry herself; it would be easier to go straight to bed. But she wanted to clarify the wish for her sister, make it feel more palpable and real. When she did, it would come true. She knew she would sleep better when it came true.

Patience would not serve her any longer with Sarah. She'd slept under many shared roofs and was experienced in clearing the air of fraught feeling. With small, solid gestures she could change unhappy silence to wordless warmth. She did housework—cooking, laundry, tidying—or introduced from outside something usually simple and conventional, a bunch of wildflowers, a bar of chocolate.

She tried, too, to cut through dreary silence or empty exchanges by talking herself. Though she had grown more reticent over the years, she sometimes thought few things made her happier than speaking well. Her remarks and stories and reflections were not always eloquent or even coherent, but when she was moved to talk she gave her company a sense of being addressed specifically. She spoke unassumingly, with an attitude of respectful kindness that was, despite the directness of her attention, aloof rather than personal in tone. In this peacefully impersonal distance her company found themselves, too, wanting to talk in ways that gilded their words with intention. At times, it also inspired them to make their rapport more personal than not.

But it could be easier to talk to someone you barely knew than your own sister. She could not guess what would develop if she tried to talk to Sarah. There was no impersonal distance between them; everything she said was personal for Sarah. That was at once the difficulty and the reward.

When the sisters were younger, and Eugene dropped them off at a new place, Esther found solace in Minah's stubborn, defiant courage. It was she whom Esther wanted to be near in the fast-food joint of a highway rest stop, where Eugene would leave them for the afternoon so Minah felt she had no choice but to look after her sisters, or the dingy waiting room of a lawyer's office in Koreatown, where they were driven directly from school one day and abandoned for hours for no reason any of them could fathom. She clung to Minah, whom she could feel reasserting her strength from one moment to the next. But she looked to Sarah—silent, self-effacing, taking in their surroundings with eyes darting here and there—to assess the danger and meaning of where they found themselves. Even now, she could look to Sarah's profile as she washed dishes, or gazed out the window on the train to their father's, and sense the transaction of thoughts—about her chores and the problem of cleanliness, her wounds and the impossibility of forgiveness, her meals and the problem of fatigue, her work and her life—pouring back and forth between her sister and the soapy sponge, her sister and the landscape, replenishing the opaque insensate material of the world with a little life. In her endless thinking, Esther saw a flicker of purpose. She was waiting to see what shape the purpose would take.

When Sarah took something seriously, her attention gave it new life. Esther wanted to share things with her sister, to have them live in her sister's mind, so that she, too, could take on another life.

She knocked at Sarah's door and told her she'd made something to eat.

≈

Emerging from her room, Sarah was startled to see the back of Esther's seated form in the middle of the living room, facing the sofa and the blank wall. Then she realized Esther was sitting on Victor's former desk chair, which she must have brought in from the room she was staying in, Victor's former study, and placed in front of the coffee table now laid out with food and drink. Since Victor had taken the dining table and the armchair, there had been no place where she and Esther could sit facing each other until now.

Sarah was aware that the breakup had left her furnishings sadly inadequate, but it was only now, confronted with the unexpectedly moving and melancholy sight of Esther's back against the hard chair, in the dim light of the one standing lamp in the corner, her double-socked feet on the frigid warped tiles of particleboard Victor had denuded of a beautiful, well-worn rug, that she was hit with the consciousness of herself as a person who lived in this unaccommodating, unloved place and chose, from day to day, not to make any manageable changes but to stubbornly adapt by blinding herself to it. Things were growing less real to her every day.

She sat down on the sofa and looked down at the meal ruefully. "I'm sorry," she said, "but I don't think I can eat this. I'm not very hungry."

She got up and returned with two plastic cups, a can of tonic water, and a frosted bottle of vodka.

"I don't drink a lot, but I've had a bad week."

Esther promptly collected the food, stored it in the fridge, and poured herself a drink. "I'm actually not hungry, either," she said, settling back in the chair.

Sarah thought of inviting her to share the sofa, then decided against it. She wanted space.

They drank and Sarah smoked in silence.

"I can smoke outside if it bothers you," she said.

"No, it's fine."

"Have you been warm enough at night? I know it gets cold in here. That's why I take such long hot showers. Hot water is included in the rent but not electricity."

"I've been okay."

"But you can use the space heater if you need it. Just not too high or too long. It gets expensive." Sarah had the feeling Esther was about to speak. "All right," she said. "Tell me what's going on with Dad." With her unapologetically blunt tone she wanted to forestall any sentimental appeal or passive-aggressive attempt to induce guilt over their father. At the same time she knew, in a deeper, slower-moving chamber of her consciousness, that Esther would not have voiced either. But she continued to speak as if Esther was someone who would.

"He has an aide. I think his son—Edwin—also comes by sometimes. I know he's not well. I think he has cancer. I don't know how far it's progressed or even what kind of cancer it is. I don't know just how bad he is. It's hard to tell."

Sarah made a small grunting noise of disdain. "Because he's a liar." But the effort at disdainful irony quickly crumbled before the towering fact of his dying. After a pause she muttered, "So he does have a son."

"I think so."

"Minah thinks . . ." She recoiled unexpectedly at sharing Minah's suspicions with Esther, then rallied herself to overcome this resistance. "She thinks this son, Edwin, is trying to get Dad's money for himself."

"I don't know anything about that," Esther said. She did not appear at all moved by this idea.

"So is he dying?"

"I don't know. But I think he's at least in danger of dying."

"So what *have* you learned from visiting him?" she said irritably, before quickly adding, "Sorry. I don't mean to take this out on you." She spoke more softly, though her voice still carried a vein of spite.

"What have I learned? There is an aide who comes by. Edwin also comes by. Dad wouldn't tell me how often they do. He's starting radiation therapy,

or he might have already started it. Or he thinks he's going to have to start it. I didn't understand everything he said in Korean and he wouldn't explain things to me. He says he doesn't need our help, but he's also asked me to stay with him for the time being."

"You're not considering it, are you?"

"I'd rather stay here," Esther said quietly.

At this, Sarah felt herself riven between anger and remorse. She was already resentful of Esther's request for an extended stay when she'd made it so clear—yes, she'd wanted to make it clear—that she wanted to be alone; she flushed at the absolute lack of grievance at her inhospitality, the substantial absence of resentment that made Esther's words as cool and pure as water. Was she correct in reading Esther's preference as a pathetic, tender hope to be closer to her? She rapidly reproached herself for polluting perception with desire. She had done the same when imagining Esther's missing message as full of tenderness toward her.

She couldn't say how long she'd been lost in the unhappy, sticky tangle of her thoughts when Esther spoke again: "Do you think people are more alike than not?"

"What?"

"Do you think people have more in common than not?"

"I don't know. Why are you asking?"

"I kept thinking of this when I was with Dad this afternoon."

"I don't know," Sarah said again. Then, wanting to hang on to this different conversational thread, though it held no interest for her, so that she might pull herself out of her herself, she asked, "Why did you think of this?"

"I think about it a lot, actually. I've thought about it a lot, at different times and places. Today, I was thinking about the old woman who used to cook for us. She didn't mind listening to Dad. And I don't mind being with him nearly as much as you. Which I understand. I did more when we were kids, but now . . . I started wondering if I'm like her. How we're different. How exactly."

"You're nothing like that hateful old hag," Sarah responded decisively.

"I was also wondering about what you and I have in common. How much we're alike or not, in ways we don't know, or I don't know."

"Hard to say." Sarah gulped down her drink. She did not think she and her younger sister bore even much of a physical resemblance. She realized she did not, in general, think about her sister's interiority except as Esther's thoughts might touch on herself. With these simple reflections, this unremarkable but nonetheless surprising evidence of Esther's mental life, she, too, began to wonder how much she and her sister shared that went unseen.

Esther smiled. "Do you remember how I used to beg you to take me to the puppet shows in the park? Misha refused to go, and Anna didn't want to take me. She said I was too old for them."

"I think Misha outgrew them before you." Sarah had also thought Esther immature, at ten, to be crowding ecstatically before the diminutive stage, a head taller than the children around her. She remembered pulling Esther to the back and her following without protest, so overwhelming was her joy to be anywhere within viewing distance of the imminent spectacle. Even for a child she had a marked capacity to lose herself in plays and shows and the stories Anna and Misha told her. She was a sweet and lively child who could fill a room with her light and also disappear into herself for long stretches. Facing her now, Sarah noticed how much Esther had faded. She still had a kind face with a quiet alertness to her expression and her movements, but she had lost much of her old radiance.

"I liked the stories—they were all about princesses, remember?—but I liked being in the audience just as much. That's what I realized when I started going to plays and movies on my own . . . I didn't really start doing that until I was alone. You know, after I dropped out of college."

Sarah was afraid to look up. She cleared her throat and lit another cigarette. She did want to know more about that time of Esther's life, but she didn't want to hear it from Esther herself. The familiar feeling of shame or

guilt flared to life when they were alone together. She felt its flame leap up and lick her insides now.

"I had a lot of time on my hands," Esther continued. Sarah was still looking to the side, wondering whether Esther was looking at her. "Up until then, whenever I went out I was with someone. When I was in the theater alone, I started to wonder if the people around me were feeling the same things as me. I didn't have someone next to me to . . . to ground me, I guess, in a common feeling. I remember, when I watched the puppets, assuming everyone felt the way I did. Or not exactly the same way, but . . . that it felt good and exciting to watch something together."

She paused, and in the window of silence, as with those that followed, Sarah was surprised to feel the tension relax even as her senses were heightened and her heart beat briskly, like a runner acutely conscious of each fiber and breath of her body who feels herself freed by her exertions, floating with her swiftness.

She wanted to hear more from Esther.

"I used to believe other people could read your mind if they tried hard enough. Or even if they weren't trying, as long as they were close to you, physically near you. When Anna looked at me I was always sure she knew everything about me. When I was listening or watching with other people, I thought everyone's feelings and thoughts would get mixed up in the dark. That was it, that was what I loved about story time at school, too. And when I saw a good movie or a play—I still love any kind of play, with people or with puppets—I felt like I could express everything that's ever been in my heart. Inside my mouth is darkness, but when I open it, I'll be free."

As she relaxed into her heightened state, Sarah was aware of another feeling rising in herself, though she could not name it. She was touched by Esther's blended innocence and insight, how she fused them together in the searching candor of the moment.

"I remember you were spellbound by 'Rapunzel' in the park," Sarah found herself saying. "And afterward you were hurt when I said it was boring. You say you feel free when you watch a good play, but back then it didn't matter if the story was nonsense or the acting was terrible. You were always mesmerized. You had to believe in it, and you were upset when I didn't."

"Yes. I remember that. I still don't mind watching things that are bad. Not as much as some people."

"I can't," Sarah said, and the statement hung in the air like an affirmation of their essential difference. The picture of Esther's drifting years was suddenly no longer an enviable one of her meeting people and experiencing things Sarah would never know. Yes, she had envied Esther for knowing things she probably never would, even if it was spending a suite of empty days at bus stations and tacky restaurants. Even the dull people and difficult experiences of her drifting made Esther human in a way Sarah suspected she herself could never be. But what good would breadth of experience do her sister if she passed even more of her life passively watching the blurred spectacle of human dailiness, without being able to discern detail and meaning, and good and wrong, or good and better?

"Why don't you go back to school?" she said. "I don't understand why you left like that. You could have taken time off officially, you know. If you didn't like Santa Cruz you could have transferred. Why don't you find another school you'd like better and start there? I could even help you choose."

"I do want to go back to school. And you're right, I shouldn't have left the way I did. But I wasn't . . . I didn't care. I just wanted to leave. I felt like I would die if I didn't."

"Was it that bad? The place, the school, the people?"

"No. I liked it until the week I left . . . Can I tell you what happened? Why I left?"

"Sure."

"Have you ever been jealous before? Over someone you loved, or just wanted badly?"

"Yes," Sarah said, startled by the personal turn and even her own reply, which sounded to her ears as the first true word she'd uttered this evening. The next moment, she wanted to recant. The brave word was like a sword plunged into a forge, which she was astonished to see could melt.

"I left because I found my roommate having sex with someone I was in love with."

After a silence Sarah said softly, incredulously, "That's why?"

"I didn't even know him well. I'd seen him around and talked to him, and we were just becoming friends. That's all. But I was infatuated for months. I know jealousy is common. But no one ever told me it would make me feel like I was worthless, I was no one."

Esther's gaze was ever settled on her sister, clear, gentle, at times startlingly unselfconscious. But her body was less confident. Sarah realized she'd watched Esther's shoulders straighten and spread, droop and narrow, again and again, like a dog raising and lowering its ears out of alertness and fear, wanting and not wanting to know what it was hearing. One leg dangled over the floor, the other was tucked under her opposite thigh. She was wearing an almost overwhelmingly large hoodie over faded black leggings. Sarah caught herself. Esther looked like a child, a girl and not a woman. Why was it easy for Sarah to forget this, to treat her sister like one older than her years, older than herself?

Sarah wished she could tell her that the feeling of being destroyed was common. Then she did: "It happens to a lot of people."

When Victor told her about Katie, she was destroyed, and she wanted to destroy Victor and for Katie never to have existed. She'd wanted to die and to kill for something so simple, so unexceptional. But her jealousy had not pushed her to change her life so drastically. She could not imagine anyone else reacting as Esther had.

Esther said, "I keep trying to understand why it was so painful for me. So totally devastating. I was about to turn on the light when I realized they were together. I stood there and they didn't notice. And then I left. I heard sounds . . . I knew it was them. I knew even before I heard the sounds. It killed me. I just stared into the dark and it was like I wasn't there anymore. I couldn't believe I wasn't her. And she was herself, with him. And I wasn't supposed to be there, I was dead. But it also felt like I was too alive, there was too much of me there when I shouldn't have been alive at all—I know this sounds very dramatic."

"It does," Sarah said, "and doesn't. I mean . . . that's how it can be."

They drank in silence.

"What did you do then?"

She described, at first, what Sarah had just imagined: empty days amid people who were nothing to her, beginning in a hostel where she didn't talk to anyone and barely ate, staying in her room until she felt she was going mad. She spent one afternoon in a park, where a homeless man asked her for change, again and again, though she said nothing and wouldn't look him in the eye. He leaned into her intrusively but without aggression, as someone who from years of talking to himself had forgotten how to modify his voice and respect other bodies. He had forgotten what it was to be with other people. The encounter was so terrifying, she shut herself away again. But it couldn't have been long before she met a group from Spain that noticed her in the halls and the communal bathroom and invited her to join them for dinner in the kitchen. She didn't want to say no; she felt like she couldn't say no. Aurelia didn't want to travel on her own to see her cousin in Texas and asked Esther to accompany her. Esther was hollowed out—how could she do anything but follow her, and others after her?

"Did you see Anna and Katya?" Sarah asked a little timorously. She did not know what else to say.

"Anna?" Esther said quizzically. "No. They'd already moved to Toronto by then. But I was talking to Misha. We're still close."

She ended up back in LA, which was more desolating for her than the unknown places she'd seen with veritable strangers. "For a while, every day was like the day I ran away in a panic from the homeless man and cried alone in my room."

Sarah felt an ache at the hard reality of these bare words. At the same time, she felt an almost ecstatic anticipation building within her. She was going to talk at last about the essential things that exercised her daily with someone who would not judge her. With her peers she found she couldn't drop her attitude of cynical irony. She would talk freely now, with desperate honesty, with someone who was both intimate and alien to her, and thus might help her to reveal herself to herself.

"I was really lonely. But for a while in between school and LA, between those two periods, I felt good." Esther furrowed her brow and smiled. "What's funny is that I sold phones for a couple months. I bought maybe a dozen phones for other people over time, but for a while, when I didn't know anyone, I sold them." She laughed. She quit her job after seeing a HELP WANTED sign in a large clothing store where she quickly formed a rapport with Vicky, who would be her supervisor. Things began to change. She liked selling clothes, working near the dressing rooms and helping people find the styles that threw their features into relief and revealed their tastes and moods. She moved into Vicky's apartment and out of the place she was sharing with a college exchange student from Hong Kong who said he loved her.

"He was lonelier than me, so lonely he thought he loved me."

"Maybe he did."

"Maybe. I don't know. People say 'love' to mean so many things." She frowned meditatively. "Maybe that was part of my fortune. There were always people who wanted me to be with them. And I followed them all over the country."

"I've always wanted to disappear like you," Sarah said with an anguished excitement. "Or not disappear, but melt into a life that depended on other people. But I can't. I'm too afraid of the world. I don't belong in it. I don't belong in it or with other people. You met people who wanted you to be with them and who you wanted to be with, too. That's why you didn't want to say no. But if I did what you did—I wouldn't meet people I could be with. I'd meet people who wanted to use me or mistreat me, or people who bored and depressed me."

She had briefly hoped to free the words locked within her with Esther. But the things she said had the effect of confining her to herself. Once uttered, they became the pathetic facts of her limits.

"That happened to me, too. Why would you think it wouldn't?"

"I know, and I don't know: Why are we so different? Why can't I live with others and care about them like you?" She gave a tired laugh. "Actually, to be honest, I don't want to be with other people. That's fine. Because I'll admit it—I think I'm superior to them. I'm smarter. I've noticed more, suffered more, thought more deeply, than just about everyone I've met. I see through them. That's my problem."

"You are very intelligent," Esther said quietly. "You do notice more than most. But you don't see that I was afraid, too. I couldn't say no or yes. I did and didn't want to be with other people. Sometimes I still feel that way. But I'm not afraid anymore. Not like you are. Like you say you are."

Sarah sighed, and her sigh curdled into a groan. She wanted to laugh and scream. Talking to Esther was neither illuminating nor cathartic but a depressing confirmation of her bleakest ideas about herself. There was also something unsettling about Esther's role in this redundant insight that she did not understand. Her sister was a part of her and yet remained a stranger, like a new somatic condition, a ringing in the ear, whose provenance and significance were troublingly obscure.

She remembered then the dreams she'd been having about Esther since the message announcing her visit. Her dreams were on the whole delusional and self-serving, but these were not ones in which she saved her sister from harm. In them Esther was already hurt, and Sarah could do nothing but gnash her teeth and rage. These dreams were recurrences of those that had haunted her—she remembered them now—while Esther lived alone with their father and Soojin. She realized she had never truly worried about Esther during her time of rootlessness. The true danger had always been at home.

"You're not going to stay with him, are you?"

"Stay with Dad? No, I don't want to if I can stay with you."

"And if you stay here, what are you planning to do?"

"I want to help him, and I want to be close to you and Minah."

"You want to stay close to us and help him. I'm not sure you can do both."

Esther frowned. "But that's what I want to do. I don't understand."

Sarah herself had not understood why she'd claimed a contradiction. She was giving in to her bitterness like a sensualist, as an alcoholic did her drunkenness, and her bitterness, rising hot and caustic at that moment, convinced her not only that Esther was attempting the hopeless, but that she herself could not abide the attempt.

"The closer you get to him, the more you'll be hurting me. You'll be hurting Minah, too. You can't help him. He's beyond hope."

"How would I be hurting you and Minah?"

"By wasting your life on someone who gave you life only in the most grossly restricted biological sense and thereafter did nothing to help you flourish and much to poison your life and ours."

"He's dying. He might be beyond hope, but he's dying."

"Let him take care of himself."

"I want—I want to be useful. Is that so terrible? For years I've done this and that, here and there. I've had a few jobs, I've lived off what I took from him. I don't regret any of it. But most of the time I didn't feel useful. Even when I did what people call 'honest work,' I didn't feel like I needed to be there, I could have been anyone else. Now I'm back with my family, and no one can tell me it's no use to help a dying man. To help even him. Not even you can tell me it's truly useless. Because you don't believe it. I want to make his dying better."

"We shouldn't be the ones to help him!" Sarah felt herself growing animated again. "Esther, you have to think about yourself first. That means protecting yourself from him. He might be dying, but we've already seen that doesn't mean he's not trying to hurt us. His real sickness is his compulsion to manipulate us and punish us—to punish us for the fact that we are independent, uncontrollable beings. Female beings. Give up on him. Don't help him. Let him torture someone else. Save yourself."

"I want to help him, yes. But I'm not trying to save him. Only he can save himself. But I can help him live. And I am trying to save myself."

Sarah regarded Esther's kind, clear eyes, and despite her sister's expression of intelligent self-possession, she felt far older and wiser than her. "I was saying that I don't like people and they don't like me. Lame and sad complaints, I know. I know I sound like an old crank. But sometimes the most pathetic clichés and crusty old sayings are true. I want to trust people, but you can't trust them. You can't believe in people, Esther. You'll say people are individuals and each is a mix of good and bad, people are essentially good and institutions are bad, people are not evil but innocent in their wrongdoing . . . I've considered it all. Why don't I believe in people? Because of everything I've read and seen since childhood. And because they let us live with him. They saw how he was raising us and harming us, and still no one saved us. Of course we weren't the only ones. No one cares about other children. And now that I'm not a child—I know there is something about me that threatens good people. Repels them even. Repelled them even when I was a child . . . Even when we were children, what would have happened to us if we'd run away? Or told someone how miserable we were? Minah thought about it all the time. So did I. I told my first friends about our father, and they told me from the comfort of their happy homes that I couldn't give up on family, our father couldn't be that bad. I asked them to look into the void, a home without love, and they refused. No one cared because we weren't locked in literal cages. And even if our abuse had been sufficiently outrageous, we would have been controlled by bureaucrats and raised by foster parents who would also have abused us or neglected us. We'd have become prostitutes, addicts, and beggars. We would never have gotten an education. We've had to make our own escape. And we have, at last. People have only the inclination to protect their own, if even that. It's a fact of nature: we can muster only the strength to protect ourselves. He never protected us. He can't be one of us. I know you're a good person and you want to be good. But it's very hard to be saintly. All the saints were childless, you know. They had to give everything away. Don't give yourself away. You can still get an education. You can still do that for yourself."

"You, too," Esther said with unexpected urgent passion. "You can try to save yourself."

Anger leapt up in Sarah. This was Esther's response to her own effort to look after her? How condescending, she seethed, how sanctimonious . . . "The first step is freeing myself from cruel hopes and stupid ideals and malicious morals. That means freeing myself of people who hold them."

"Is that . . ." The frown, the distress distorting Esther's features, faded away. Her expression was clear, her face like cool, smooth stone, as she said, "Why are you angry with me?"

"You want to help him because you're good, you're better than me, and you want me to forgive him. I don't want to live with your example. I'm sorry, but I used to have dreams about you." Sarah wasn't sure how her apology related to her dreams, but the connection seemed meaningful. "I dreamt I couldn't protect you from him. I dreamt he was hurting you despite what you told me once, that he wasn't. I'd wake up moaning because I couldn't protect you. It doesn't matter if he never hurt you or raped you or abused you, he still marked us for all time. I'm still clawing my way away from him. How can I help him and forgive him? I couldn't bear it. You're like one of those sadistic moralists who want to burden the victims with the responsibility to forgive."

Again, she was speaking to Esther as if she were someone Sarah knew she was not, but she did not want to stop projecting; she wanted to unburden herself now, immediately, and she knew Esther would allow it. Besides, Esther was obscurely allied, as she saw it, with the opposing side: the side of an idealism that could not account for the real world, much less her own self.

"It's asking me to take the crumbs of myself I've scavenged from him and offer them to him. It's sadism to ask me to empathize with my own sadist. It's asking me to kill myself for his sake."

"Listen, please. I'm not asking you to forgive him or to empathize with him. I'm not. I'm not asking you to help him, either. How could I ask that of you? You would have every reason to hate me if I did. All I want . . . now, what I want, is the same thing I wanted when I called you in the past. When you were away, I wanted to hear from you. I wanted to share things with you. And I wanted you to remember you aren't just his daughter. I think you say this to yourself when you're alone, that you're nothing but his daughter. But you're my sister, too."

The words stopped Sarah's own. Her lips remained parted in silence for a long instant. Finally she said, "You're my sister, but I'm not sure I love you. I'm not sure I love anyone. But if someone hurt you I'd want to kill him. I'd want him to die in pain. And he has hurt you," she said vehemently. "He's hurt all of us."

Esther got up and sat beside her. Sarah was beginning to wilt from the tremendous strain of talking with unusual forthrightness. Esther placed her hand lightly on hers. "You're right. He's hurt all of us. But that doesn't mean . . . Even though I lived with you and grew up with you, I still don't know what you suffered. So how could I ask you to go to his side? I want to know . . . I know . . . you and Minah suffered in ways I didn't. And I've always known our mother gave me to Anna."

"The youngest child was given to the Church."

"What?"

"In Europe and in Asia, probably everywhere, families used to give the youngest child to the monastery," Sarah said blearily, sliding her hand away.

She was leaning away from Esther, resting her head inside the crook of her arm at the end of the sofa. "Because they couldn't marry them off or feed them. They couldn't care for them, at least not like they wanted. And it gave them credit in heaven."

"Yes, she gave me to Anna. And so . . . and so . . ." Tears rose within Esther; they did not fall, but her voice thickened, her words became craggy and bold. "I was afraid he would hit me, but I was never scared that he would maim me. I was never afraid he would violate me and destroy me. I think . . . that's why it hurt me so much to be jealous. I was jealous, but I also started to understand . . . I felt so ashamed. You wonder why we're different. I think all the time about the pain you were living through while I was at home with you. I ask myself why and how I got away without suffering as much as my sisters. How could I live with you without knowing what you knew?"

Esther paused, willing these words to imprint themselves on Sarah.

"You know how in old books and movies doctors would bleed patients to weaken the disease? Sometimes I have the feeling that you'd hurt yourself to protect yourself. I don't want you to cut yourself in a rage to make the disease bleed away. Do you see what I mean?"

"Yes. No. It doesn't matter." Sarah coughed and sat up. "I need to sleep."

At the threshold to her room she said, "I know I never did anything to help you," and shut the door.

Esther lay awake in the dark for hours. She heard Sarah using the bathroom in the middle of the night but did not hear her approach until she was leaning over her.

"She's wearing her coat," Esther heard Sarah say softly to herself.

Esther didn't remember falling asleep. When she woke at dawn, the space heater was on and the room was comfortably warm. While she was sleeping she must have thrown off the coat that she bought during a cold snap in South Carolina and wore in various drafty rooms on winter days and nights.

She thought of rooms like this, where she huddled in her coat and drank pots of tea and tried, a few nights when she couldn't sleep, to remember her mother. She remembered warmer weather and rooms where her friends and traveling companions from hotter climates shivered as she peeled off her layers. There were rooms in a sizzling landscape without air-conditioning where they walked around half clothed and asked one another about their stretch marks and birthmarks. They talked about where they carried their weight, their body hair and facial hair, their tattoos and scars.

2
The message

Dear Sarah,

I'm coming to visit you and Minah and our father. I hope you will let me stay with you.

And I want to tell you what happened when I dropped out of your life. I've wanted to talk to you for a long time. Things should be different between us. I know you better than you think, and I care about you.

I don't blame you for your coldness, your hardness. I still don't understand your silence. But I want you to forgive me for mine.

It's true: love isn't fair. It's unjust. You felt unloved. Why shouldn't you have felt unloved, though I loved you?

I haven't known how to reach you. I tried to. We're closer than you think, even though I still don't know what you suffered when we were together and what you're suffering now. I want to know. I want to know what I didn't know when I was living with you for so many years. How could I not know what was a part of me—and continue not to know?

I don't know why or how

How will I tell you

Your coldness, your hardness

Do you remember how we used to listen to Minah crying in the bathroom?
We listened together. We couldn't tear ourselves away. I kept listening because I didn't want her to be alone. You listened because you didn't want
to be alone. You said, "She's crying just because he threw out those ugly
jeans" "She's just upset because she can't go to New York with her friends."
You enjoyed hearing her cry. You enjoyed her pain because you, too, were
in pain. But even more, you enjoyed despising her for crying. Because you
never cried. You didn't scream or sing your favorite songs out loud like her.
You didn't cry. You locked yourself in the bathroom sometimes, but I knew
you weren't crying. You wanted to know if you were just as lonely in there
as you were outside, and you were. The same silence was in you there, too.

I am still trying to reach you. I am

The same silence

3

Three men

Sarah's voice cracked, and she stopped singing. She tried to whisper the rest of the refrain, but she'd already forgotten the words and couldn't find the printed lyrics. She imagined that her neighbors in the pew, even those behind her and before her, could detect the disappearance of her voice: the collectively generated sound waves were blocked as by a wall where she stood in body but not in the spirit of the song.

She mouthed the next verse, moving her lips with dumb helplessness like a dying fish.

She glanced at Paul. He was singing, not with notable gusto, but with calm, almost luminous confidence. She could make out his voice at each opening beat before it rose and softened and melded with the others.

She found it easy to memorize poetry and had read the Bible in its entirety, yet she couldn't retain these words, these epithets and shibboleths. *O Lord . . . glory to you . . . wash us in your love . . . the highest . . . sore with sorrow . . . he who comes.* They were formulas that meant nothing to her; they were like clouds stacked together to create fog.

She was alone with Paul. Minah had canceled with a text Sarah received while waiting on the steps of the church: Sorry don't think I can make it. Not feeling well again and need to catch up on sleep. I hope you get to know Paul and enjoy lunch. It's on him of course. Don't forget what I said before.

She rose and sang, kneeled and prayed, stood and listened and sat down again, growing restless all the while. Her spirits rose a little when she realized the priest was about to deliver the homily, the part of the service that most interested her: theology, interpretation, disputation.

The priest wore a white cassock and, over it, a deep purple chasuble with a gold pattern on the chest. He looked young, her age or not much older. He had a rangy figure and a narrow face with an intent, noble mien that reminded her of a greyhound. But unlike that smooth creature he had a thick head of auburn curls splayed outward from his skull, as if a mild electrical current had just passed through him. And unlike Paul, he didn't have good posture. His self-confidence was projected in his deep, unexpectedly assertive tone.

The subject of the homily was suicide. To the priest's regret, he hadn't addressed suicide during National Suicide Prevention Week, but it was never too late to address the misconceptions many parishioners had about those who ended their own lives. "I was still a student in divinity school when I met a woman in my parish who had lost her son years earlier to suicide. She was ashamed to speak of him—ashamed, I believe, even to speak of him to her priest—because she, like so many of us, had been taught that suicide is a grave and unforgivable sin. That God judges and damns all those who have taken their lives. That the despair of those who die by their own hand redoubles their sin, because they lacked the faith to accept the Lord and turned away from him toward death.

"This—is—false!"

His voice was both contentious and aggrieved. "No one knows what takes place in a person's soul in the moments—in the seconds—before their death. I told this grieving mother that we could not judge her son. I could not judge her son. Only our Father could do that. We could not assume that he was forever lost or that he had forsaken our Lord. No one knows what took place in the final milliseconds between him and God."

She glanced again at Paul. He was still gazing ahead. The expression of sanguine self-possession that had made him seem at once so solid and buoy-

ant while he was singing now, in this different context of the soul and its tor-
ments, made him appear distant and impervious. As he listened to the homily,
his face was less serene than blank. It was as if he had never had any thoughts
on the matter of the soul and its secrets at all.

She admitted to herself her bias against the self-satisfied religious type she
believed him to be. She knew, too, that gut feelings were often wrong, though
everyone everywhere cited them as heralds of truth. They were as fallible as
moods, as powerfully misleading as the mystical love she did not believe in
while those around her presumably did. But it was more than an instinct, it
was an intuition that told her Paul was complacent in his faith: that he had
faith in his faith. If there was bad faith, there were also better kinds of good
faith. His faith was strength, as he believed, but it was not the kind of strength
he believed it to be. It was the strength to forget, to insulate oneself and forge
ahead completely unhindered by the difficult work demanded of an ideal. He
lacked the strength to endure, to survive after breaking apart. He lacked the
strength Esther possessed.

The thought surprised her. She recalled Esther's face the evening of their
talk: life glimmered in her steady gaze, in the quality of self-possession that
came not from pride or even confidence, but from courage composed equally
of fear and a readiness to change and be changed. Sarah was not mistaken to
have thought of Esther as lusterless compared with her loquacious, spirited
childhood self. But she was wrong to think this change was a symptom of
disillusionment or weakness.

It was time for another hymn. She rose and mimed song, then began to sing
in a small, cracked voice, like someone humming alone while doing housework.
She felt herself flushing and sweating; she felt something akin to the hot un-
ease she'd long associated with being with Esther. But this emotion was shaded
differently. It was the strange exhilaration of voluntary vulnerability and exposure. Something in the homily had struck a nerve in her. This was how
she'd felt the few times she talked frankly and at length in therapy with the
one therapist she'd liked and saw regularly until her insurance policy changed.

Since then she attended therapeutic sessions with her psychiatrist a couple times a year, primarily to obtain the antidepressants that stabilized her so that, as her doctor put it, she had the stability to reflect upon her situation more lucidly. Sarah took her medication, which spurred her body to take care of itself, to get out of bed and feed herself and try to make a living. But she was not drawing upon that centering strength to undertake the painful, fruitful task of working through herself. She would not risk breaking apart.

With a therapist she came to appreciate, she spent the first sessions spinning a narrative of herself as an articulate, rational, even resilient person who, like so many others, just needed some outside support to figure out her life. She had no idea why she presented herself thus; she felt dishonest in the act of describing her past in this posture of eloquent thoughtfulness, but she couldn't stop herself. At one point this mild-mannered woman, always sheathed in an ugly dirt-brown shawl, said, "You are gifted. You can say anything you want to say." The largely silent session that followed was tense with embarrassment. But the walk home after the session and the evening alone were suffused with relief as sharp as joy. The memory of the tension drew her to the next session.

When Sarah started talking again, she said nothing that sounded extraordinary: "I am so tired in the morning. I'm neither sick nor well. I do feel better after I shower. I like the sound of water." Some things, though the experience was very painful to her, sounded self-pitying and painfully banal to her ears: "He locked me out of the house when it was dark. I was just a kid. I still feel shut out of my own life." And yet she would leave the office of this therapist she trusted feeling revived, even electrified. She was like an unknown actress who had just exited the stage after performing a powerful classic story: she was humanized, transfigured, her minor utterances woven into the dramatic fiber of life. Her shirt would be soaked in sweat.

Why was she feeling this way now?

Paul tapped her on the shoulder; he wanted to pass by. It was time for him to take Communion.

≈

"Lovely to meet you. Have a beautiful Sunday," Betty said, as she turned to leave the pew.

Betty had introduced herself to Sarah before the service began. She was an elegant, wizened Black woman in a navy dress with dark beads around the collar, accompanied by her stony-faced granddaughter, Trisha.

Sarah longed for fresh air. Without turning to Paul, she headed to the exit and bumped into Betty, who didn't flinch or turn around. Trisha did, with a frown to which Sarah addressed her apology, feeling embarrassed and confused at finding herself apologizing to Betty's sullen teenage proxy.

She pulled out a cigarette, then decided against lighting up as people continued to pool around her. She assumed the congregation, and especially Paul, probably didn't approve of smoking.

"Are you all right?"

She dropped the cigarette perched between her fingers. Paul leaned toward her, trying to study her face.

"Yes. Yes, why wouldn't I be?"

"Nothing." He looked away. She could tell he was a little concerned, as if he was beginning to doubt this afternoon would go well. He faced her again to say, "It's too bad Minah couldn't join us, but she must have told you she's sick. It sounds like a bad cold. I'm going to check on her later."

"She gets sick easily when she's overworked," Sarah said, vaguely hoping this sympathetic note would also present herself as humane.

They walked to the corner to find a cab to take them to the West Village, where he had a reservation for brunch. The cab took them back past the church, where worshippers were still massed in front of the entrance. She saw the priest in colloquy with one, solemnly nodding his head. She watched him clasp the man's hand with both of his.

Paul said, "I don't know that priest. He seems to have original ideas. I usually go to the Korean service. That's why I didn't know many people there, or I would have introduced you."

The restaurant was sunny and cheerful, with high windows framed by faded verdigris walls and tables and chairs of different shapes and sizes, all of a quaintly distressed, polished wood. Various mirrors with tarnished silver frames reflected the light. The clientele was more stylish and upscale than what she was used to. She took in silk pleated blouses and boots of the softest leather, designer handbags and priceless watches juxtaposed with faded joggers.

"I've never been here before," Paul said.

"Then why did you choose this place?"

"I wasn't sure what you'd like, so I asked Minah, and she said you'd like this place."

"That was nice of you." She could not think of why Minah would have recommended this place for her sake.

Then they had nothing to say, though she felt friendlier toward him.

They were seated.

He said, "Let's not be formal with each other anymore." His voice was unusually mild. "I'd like to get to know you and the rest of your family. And I want you to get to know me. I know Minah respects you very much. I'd like us to be open with each other, and I don't mind if you tell me exactly what you think of me, whatever that is. I can take it. We have to be honest with each other if we're going to be family."

"Okay." She had no intention of being wholly honest with him. At the same time, she felt she might betray herself; she wasn't used to someone speaking this candidly to her. She might be seduced by this candor to be herself transparent.

They studied the menu and ordered. He encouraged her to attend the service in Korean. At least part of the service would be translated or in English, and most of the hymns were in English. He could introduce her to his friends and Minah's.

"Why do you think Koreans are so religious?" she asked suddenly, surprising herself. "I mean, why are so many Koreans Christian?"

He was pleased with this gambit. "I have a lot of theories."

"In my experience Koreans are far more likely to not only go to church but to be true and fervent believers, more than any other Asian group I can think of. I've always wondered why."

"It's something I've wondered about, too. I think it has to do with a lot of things. Koreans were caught between China and Japan when the missionaries first arrived. The educated wrote and spoke in Chinese and studied the Chinese classics. They respected the Chinese, but they knew they were Korean." He looked again as he had while he was singing, bright, hopeful, engaged.

"Like the Russians in the nineteenth century. All the educated upper-class Russians spoke French. A lot of them had better French than Russian, which writers like Tolstoy hated. He wanted to be a Russian writer."

"Yes. Like them. I'm sure Koreans, like the Russians, wanted to be proud of their identity. But Korea was just a small peninsula hanging off China. And then there were the Japanese across the water, who Koreans still hate today."

"I don't think it's helpful to make sweeping statements like that. I still get white Americans asking me if I hate Japan."

"You're right. Not helpful. But you know what I mean." He said this last with a gushing, almost conspiratorial smile. Sarah sensed that for him, sharing these thoughts with another person had the feeling of an exciting mutual discovery.

"Yes. Continue. Tell me your theories." She was genuinely piqued, and sitting there, in that fashionable café-restaurant where she and Paul were the only non-whites, she did feel a connection to him as he spoke without any affectation of the questions close to his heart.

"So imagine a people caught between an overwhelming ancient power and enemies across the channel. They felt isolated. They were strict and devout Confucians, even more Confucian than the Chinese, in some ways. Confucianism is all about universal order and tradition and ancestry. It might have made them feel virtuous but also insecure about their own heritage. Their own language and culture. And that made them think of what they had that was theirs alone. They started thinking about their souls. They dreamt of another figure greater than their king or even the emperor, higher than any ancestor, who would recognize the lowest among them."

Minah had explicitly warned Sarah several times in both person and emphatic messages not to talk about their family with Paul except in general terms. She wanted to control what he knew about them. So Sarah refrained from mentioning the aunt who once stayed with her family overnight between flights from Boston to LA and onward to Seoul, at a time when her mother was beginning to spend both her days and nights in bed. Sarah would never see her aunt or anyone from her extended family again. The following week there were importunate phone calls between their mother and her sister, and her sister and their father, which ended with their father yelling at his in-law never to call again, and their mother taking the receiver from him and repeating, "Please don't call anymore . . ."

Before leaving, her aunt called Sarah to her and pressed a book into her hands.

"Your mother tells me you like to read. I like to read, too. This is for you. I translated this myself," she said in Korean that Sarah found easy to follow and surprisingly melodic to the ears. Until then, she had known Korean as a language of conflict and commands. "They're poems by a great, great writer named . . ."

It was a strange name Sarah couldn't retain. She lost the book and didn't think of it again until many years later in high school, when she heard the name pronounced by her English teacher. Her nervous system responded before her memory; she shivered and didn't understand why until she left the classroom. Her aunt had translated Seamus Heaney.

Their talk was paused by the arrival of their food. For a long moment they had trouble reviving their conversation.

"I think Koreans are like the Irish, too," Sarah offered at last, almost shyly. "Surrounded by water and colonized by neighbors more powerful than them. They're hard drinkers, and they're very passionate, always talking about emotions, especially anger and grief and resentment. I suppose they channeled those emotions and all their longing into spirituality. And Christianity would have been a more fitting outlet than Confucianism."

"Yes! That's the essence of it, my theory. Koreans understood better than those more powerful than them that there had to be something more. But on the other hand . . ."

"Yes?"

"I remember now, there was a visiting monk who told me that the first missionaries in Korea reported that Koreans didn't seem spiritually inclined at all. They had their shamans and superstitions, which they still have today, and they had Confucian ideas and rituals, but no coherent spiritual practice. Nothing explained to later missionaries why the Koreans had a genius for Christianity. That was his word, 'genius,' which confused me. And he explained that 'genius' can also mean 'spirit,' like the word 'genie.'"

"Yes. In a lot of Western languages the shared etymology between words for intellect or intelligence and spirit is more obvious."

"Ah, so you knew that already. I should have known."

To Sarah's mild embarrassment, she was truly flattered. She said, "You think that genius for Christianity has to do with the abasement the Koreans felt, their sense of inferiority."

"Yes, but not exactly. They had nothing. They felt they had nothing but a contradictory mix of religions and practices that didn't truly satisfy them or really come from them. They felt they were less than the Chinese and the Japanese. But they also believed that they in themselves were stronger than they seemed, stronger even than they believed, if that makes sense. They suffered because they didn't understand why they had nothing. Christ gave meaning to their suffering. I guess, in the end, my theory is totally simple."

She had always respected those teachers and classmates of hers who never lost sight of the fundamental questions when the rest of the class was flourishing complications or debating minutiae. It made her happy that Paul provided this most basic and elegant of interpretations; and it made her hope in her mind and feel in her body that fulfillment and meaning and right action could also be mysteriously simple—and life would not be so arduous after all.

They turned to their plates happily, with a feeling of accomplishment. After a few bites of her omelet, Sarah began to feel uneasy. The brie and the pancetta became a little hard to chew and swallow.

"That's also why Koreans are so passionate about justice," Paul said. "That's not unique to Koreans, but really raging over injustice—that's very Korean. Their existential calling, as a friend has said."

She considered this in silence while gulping her coffee. The familiar suspicion arose, that these characterizations might be innocuous and even hold a grain of truth, but might also be misleading. They were distortions mixed with insights. Who could say precisely why any one person, much less an entire people, developed as they did? And who knew whether a person did in fact hold true to what they professed to believe? Even in confession there must be an incalculable distance between the words tendered to the confessor and the intricate mesh of thought and desire, belief and misbelief, that they could never truly capture. She decided to suppress these doubts for now. She wanted to recapture the feeling of well-being.

"I have another question," she said.

"Shoot."

"Most Koreans in the US aren't Catholic. They're Protestant. Baptist or Methodist or . . . I don't really know the differences between the denominations, but it seems like they're much more inclined to Protestant evangelism than Catholicism. Why do you think that is? Why do you think your family is Catholic and not Protestant? I'm just assuming you were raised Catholic. Am I wrong?"

"No, you're not. It has to do with my Vietnamese grandfather. He was Catholic, and my grandmother converted for him. They raised my father to be Catholic. He was lapsed for a short time, then my mother returned him to the fold. So far in every generation someone has converted a spouse." He smiled. "Minah has said she'd convert if we get married. We haven't known each other long, but it's been long enough for me. Long enough to know I love her. I know she's what I want in life."

"If she feels the same, I hope you do marry," Sarah said quietly, embarrassed again by his frankness as well as her response. Only Esther spoke to her this way. She could feel his heart swell with gratitude and relief as he kept talking with greater energy.

"Being Catholic means more to me than being Methodist means to Minah. She's told me so herself. I only care that she believes in God, Christ, and the Church, any church, and she feels the same. I'm prepared to marry her as long as she promises to attend church with me, and for that it makes sense that she should convert."

Sarah nodded, though her misgivings had returned. She was ashamed of her family, but she didn't like the idea of Minah being swallowed into another.

"So yes, I'm Catholic because I was raised Catholic. Like my father, I've also strayed at times from practice. But I'm not as rigid as my mother, for example. I'm not anti-gay. I'm not opposed to birth control. Abortion, yes, but birth control is different. A lot of Catholics don't even understand the difference between abortion and birth control, medically. I'm not anti-science or progress. But I also think tradition is good. It connects you to your mother and father and connects them with your children. It's about honoring your bonds. The older I get, and I'm thirty-six now, the more I feel attached to my Catholic faith.

"To answer your other question: it's the conversion experience, and all the language of salvation and damnation, that attracted Koreans to evangelism. Koreans are radicals. Everything they do, they do to an extreme. That's why we have a reputation for being crazy. It's the Protestants, especially the evangelicals, who really tapped into the Korean temperament. I've been to Baptist services with my ex-girlfriend. You think Catholics are backward or intolerant? Try those really hard-core Baptists. Everything is literal with them. If it's in the Bible, it's black and white. It's the law. But at the same time nothing makes sense because everything is subjective. They turn the church into some kind of madhouse where everyone's crying and screaming and striking themselves on the chest. It actually scared me to see it. I once saw a shamanistic ritual outside Seoul, and I swear that service was more like shamanism or pagan witchcraft than any Christianity I could recognize. That's when I realized that you need family, tradition, structure, guidance. Not just whatever crazy spirit takes hold of you."

She'd sensed a lack, a complacency, in him during the sermon. He spoke now with a polemical urgency that she was inspired to meet. "Catholics have been great educators and scholars in the past. I respect that. But tradition for the sake of tradition, no. Power sticks to tradition and builds up like a residue. And families of all traditions are capable of erring dangerously and leading their innocent children astray, evangelical and Catholic and shamanistic alike. You are also succumbing to a dangerous literalism if you think God is your father and your family must be as one in faith. Didn't Christ choose his followers over his family? And his heavenly father— fathers of all faiths have abused women and their children and even offered them up to a god. Abraham was ready to violate the law against human sacrifice and murder his son for God. That doesn't sound like tradition. I know that's just one story in the Old Testament. But the overarching story of the New Testament is that God offered his only son as a sacrifice for the sins of the world. Why?"

"Because he loved the world."

"What kind of creator does that? What kind of father does that? That, too, is insanity. It's a lot more disturbing than a congregation in hair shirts collectively foaming at the mouth. The definition of tradition might be just that: sacrificing your children to your vision."

She was speaking a little too loudly. When she stopped, other voices surged to fill the void. Behind her, a woman was scraping her plate and talking to a friend about an upcoming vacation in Greece: "I'm still looking at hotels. I'm so excited. I've been wanting to do this my whole life."

As she was speaking, Sarah felt she was betraying Minah. But she hadn't been able to resist making the debate more provocative because she was beginning to like Paul. She'd wanted to be openhearted, to reveal at least a glimmer of herself to him. And she had: he heard in her words the personal message she did and did not mean to express, a truth that never ceases to astonish when draped in flesh. Your life has made you different from me.

Paul said gently, "I agree, education is important. And I respect your intellect and your profession. I really do. As for the rest—I'll have to think about it."

The gentleness in his voice felt like compassion for her past sufferings. She thought she even detected a humble acknowledgment of all he would never know of Sarah, of life, of God. She didn't think she believed in his humility, but she wanted to.

He was frowning meditatively at his plate. What was left of his eggs had grown cold, and he looked as if he didn't want it anymore.

Talk, she told herself.

"I wish there were a middle way between that kind of structure and that kind of subjectivism. That might appeal to me, if it existed," she said tentatively. "Hierarchical structures are always susceptible to abuses of power. Subjective individualism invites hysteria and narcissism and gross distortions of the truth. Both aspects have turned me off religion. And I don't trust faith. I'll never have unwavering faith in anything. That's also dangerous and frightening to me. Cults and fascism also demand absolute faith. I don't believe I'm particularly intelligent, but I could never give up what intelligence I have by placing absolute faith in any one thing. I don't believe reason will save the world, either. I just think . . . I don't know. I just wanted to say that Minah and I are very different. We're sisters, but we don't share the gene or the temperament that opens you to religion. I'm almost sorry for that. I've tried to imagine what it's like to have faith. And even though I feel like I can imagine conversion, I'll never have that experience. I'm not capable of it."

"We're more alike than you think," he responded with tender gravity. "If we weren't alike, we couldn't talk to each other. We're talking because we are alike. And if we are alike, one day you might believe. You might open yourself to God."

"And you might lose your faith."

He was startled by the logic of this reversal. "Yes," he said slowly. "Unlikely, but yes, that's true. I might be tested one day. If I am, I hope I would hold firm."

They finished their meal in a silence that was a continuation of his astonishment.

The waitress came by with the menu again to offer coffee or dessert. Sarah noticed for the first time bacon-wrapped dates stuffed with goat cheese listed under appetizers. Minah knew she loved them. She wondered if that was why her sister had chosen the place.

"Is Minah really going to teach yoga in prisons?"

He was handing his credit card to the waitress. "I don't know. I don't think so. I don't think she has the time for it now. She's still trying to make partner, you know, at her firm." He faced her again. "If we have children, I hope you'll teach our kids what you know," he said with the same sober tenderness that made her feel she should brush aside everything frustrating that came out of his mouth. Hadn't she learned by now that people were inconsistent? The views one avowed aloud were not necessarily a transparent window onto their more deeply ingrained qualities, those that shaped the nuances of sympathetic and callous human behavior alike.

Outside, Paul shook her hand, then said, "Hey, come here," and embraced her. "I'm so glad we got to do this."

He was going to take a cab to Minah's to check in on her and offered to drop Sarah off at Penn Station. She declined; she wanted to drink in more cool air. The day so far had been strange. She normally experienced happy occasions and infelicities alike as the outcome of fortune to be endured. Her life felt personal today, continuous with the person she was, and not something to which she must submit.

She checked her phone. There were several emails with questions from students, who were now writing to her personal address, and one email from Minah, asking her to call back with a report. She added that Esther was at their father's again: I don't like her spending that much time with him. It's not good for anyone to spend so much time alone with him.

Sarah walked toward the subway between hushed rows of town houses. Heels clacked and people laughed on their way past these homes whose silence seemed to absorb the footsteps and laughter. The brick facades shaded by trees protected the dramas within as she pondered her own. She was so often lonely. When she met someone she liked and got along with, she was always hopeful they would form a friendship in which the language in her head would evolve and emerge to become a brilliant common tongue. But with time she would hear herself tell herself clichés to rationalize what disturbed her about her friend. There was the amiable narcissist who was amazingly witty, and the liar who demonstrated rare compassion when Sarah was doing badly and went on to betray her confidence. There was the classmate who was so generous to her and shared her understanding of many books, and flippantly admitted to stealing cash and an antique ring from her feeble grandparents. There was the believer who knew so little about her and thought she should honor her father and yet another father above. As she negotiated friendship she weighed increasingly intolerable clichés. People are complicated; no one is perfect. You can't trust anyone but yourself. We owe so much to our families. Tradition has an important role in our lives.

She checked the time and saw she had a couple of unread text messages. One was from Victor, asking if he could come by to pick up the liquor he'd forgotten in the freezer. The other was from an unknown number: Hello is this Sarah Kim? This is Edwin Yoon. My father is Eugene Kim. I hope we can talk soon. Please give me a call.

She stood motionless until she caught the flicker of a curtain in the corner of her eye. Someone was wondering what she was doing outside their home.

She started walking, then stopped and called the number.

"Yes? Hello? Sarah?" She heard a swell of other voices in the background: "Did you fill out the forms?" "The restroom is past the cafeteria."

"Yes, this is Sarah. I got your message." Her voice was steady, but she felt her insides trembling.

"Great, let's meet up. Where are you now?" His voice was raised and rapid and jarringly casual.

"Now? Right now I'm in the city. New York City. I don't live here, but—"

"Where in the city?"

"The West Village."

"I'm not that far. Let's meet up now. I'll text you my address and you can give me a call when you arrive. I can step out for a few minutes. Does that work? I'll send it to you now."

She wasn't sure he heard her reply before hanging up. She started heading to the train that would take her to Penn Station. She didn't need to go out of her way to meet another presumptuous asshole. Like her father— their father—Edwin spoke to her as if she were an empty receptacle for his consciousness.

She was about to swipe her MetroCard at the subway turnstile when she hesitated. She was already identifying Edwin with her father. It was chilling to think of him making the same equivalence. She checked and saw that the address he'd given her was a hospital. Maybe he was rude because his mother was in urgent care. Maybe their father. She could not avoid her brother.

She started toward the hospital. She had no doubt she was headed toward a distressing encounter, but she was determined and eager to face it. Life was personal for her today. Her blood was warming, an unfamiliar energy was spreading through her. She had the courage to face her brother, though she was still too embarrassed to meet Esther's eyes after their one and only conversation a few weeks ago. Like Minah, Sarah was concerned that Esther was now spending long days and occasional nights at their father's. But she was also relieved when she returned home to find it empty. Before, she resented her sister's presence. Now she felt shy and inhibited with her, unable to respond to the words that were seared into her consciousness: "You're my sister," Esther had said, and more. Alone, she did her sister's laundry with her own, left her notes inviting her to leftovers, and bought her a new toothbrush.

She was walking rapidly and began to feel the weight of her bloated body; the ibuprofen she took that morning was wearing off. She tended to be more fraught, literally and emotionally, before her period. She worried she lacked the composure to judge her brother accurately.

She met her brother across from the hospital in the large plaza of a corporate tower of darkened glass. It was empty save for a few enormous sculptures of primary-toned red and blue balls and cones and some scattered café tables and chairs, the whole like an ill-advised inspiration by de Chirico. Edwin called her as she was hastening past.

"I think I see you," he said. "Stop and turn toward the red cone on your left."

He was wearing scrubs under his parka. Their father had a broad rounded face with flat features; the high-ridged bridge of Edwin's nose cleaved his chiseled cheekbones. There was something similar between father and son in the brow and the spacing of their eyes, the way their foreheads lifted when they looked up. Edwin's color was like Esther's, a browner shade than their father's. There was otherwise no other family resemblance that Sarah could immediately see.

She pulled a chair up to his. He was smoking a menthol cigarette. He stared into her face, unblinking, then threw his head back and stretched his arms. He groaned and smiled. "I smoke menthols because it's easier to cover the smell. I chew some peppermint gum and wash my hands after, and people really believe it's just gum and soap they're smelling."

He was behaving, Sarah thought, not as if she was his long-unknown sister but an old college roommate whom he once enjoyed lightly bullying.

"How did you know it was me?"

"I figured you'd be passing this spot to get to the hospital. I haven't seen a photo of you before. I just had a feeling it was you."

"You were looking for a Korean woman my age."

"No. It was more than that."

He didn't offer to explain, and she didn't want to know what he meant. "Are you a doctor?"

"I'm doing my residency." He stretched and groaned again and shook his head. "I'm sorry. I haven't slept in days. I'm really out of it. I just had an impulse to contact you and so I did it." The hard mockery of his eyes faded.

"Did he give you my number?" Sarah hesitated. "Our father."

"No. He doesn't want me to contact you or your sisters. I don't even know the name of your older sister. He just calls her . . ." He cleared his throat and gave a dry laugh, then shook his head with a solemn expression. "He calls her by a rude term, to tell you the truth."

"That doesn't surprise me." She was about to give him Minah's name but held back. "So how did you get my number?"

"He gave me your name and told me what you did, that you lived in Princeton and taught in the city. I knew he wouldn't tell me any more than that. So I googled you and scrolled and scrolled until I came across one of those sites that offers to give you information on a person if you pay. And I paid. I didn't know how else to get in touch with you."

"Why didn't you just email me? My email's online."

"I did email you. You never wrote back. I figured you didn't want to talk to me. Then I thought maybe you thought it was junk mail or overlooked it because I chose a stupid subject heading: 'Reaching out.' Like a political fundraiser or something."

He laughed with such vim he seemed a little deranged, and she wondered whether sleep deprivation might really be responsible for all that already made him so distasteful to her.

"I had problems with my account. It was accidentally shut down."

She most wanted to ask why he wanted to get in touch, but this seemed too aggressive a question. The next moment she found herself posing it: "Why did you want to meet?"

"Maybe because he doesn't want us to meet." He exhaled and coughed, then said meditatively, "I don't know why he didn't tell you about me before. Because he wanted to protect me? Protect you? I don't know."

His smile was gentle and tentative, like a meek but warm request for her to see themselves as siblings entwined in the predicament of a darkly enigmatic father. But as his smile brightened, the light in his face became both encouraging and amused, as if she were a child trying to help him with an adult task. The light gathered in his eyes, and she watched as the spark of condescension became the cynical pleasure of complicity. Yes, she was entwined with her brother. Not in their ignorance of their father's intentions, but in their inheritance of bad blood. Edwin was indeed their father's son.

She questioned herself; she knew she was primed to see him as a sinister reflection of her father. She said diffidently, for the sake of saying something, "You've been seeing him regularly."

"Yes. And I can tell you this," he said sternly, ruffling her with yet another rapid change of tone, "he is seriously ill. I'm the one who told him he had to get everything checked, including his prostate. A lot of GPs like his think it's a waste of time and money to do a PSA test every year. When he told me his back kept hurting and then he wasn't urinating as much—a man his age—I knew it was a possibility."

"What was a possibility?"

"Cancer. Prostate cancer. It's spread to his bones and now his lungs."

She didn't realize she was hunched over until he craned to peer into her face. "I see," he said. A couple minutes passed. "Do you want some water? I can get you some water across the street."

"No thanks," she said softly.

Her hands weren't trembling, but they seemed stiff and unwieldy as she pulled out a cigarette.

"Let me," he said. He cupped his hands around hers to light it.

A low voice came to her as his hands hovered over hers: Don't tell him anything. Don't say anything.

"I think I need to go home," she said. "I'll talk to you again later. I don't think I can talk more today. You understand."

"Hold on. Don't get up yet, you'll feel weak. It happens all the time in the waiting room."

She lowered her head again. His left hand was resting on his knee in front of her. "Are you married?" she asked.

"No. I was."

"Oh. Sorry. I just—"

"I wear the ring because it reassures my patients." He rubbed the back of his neck and gave a soft laugh. "They like to think of their doctors as family men. They think it makes you a better doctor to be married with kids. Like you value life more, or can't have values if you don't."

He cleared his throat.

"And I am," he said, unexpectedly forthright. "I am a family man."

4

The son and the whore

Edwin surprised himself by becoming a doctor.

He knew his mother had wanted to be a doctor, but he didn't look up to her. Nor had he gone out of his way to please her since he was a child. He never felt pressured to choose medicine or even to earn good grades. His mother might smack him on the head if he got a C or give him twenty dollars after a solid report card. These gestures he perceived as conventions of a role she agreed to assume, just as she tacitly agreed every morning to get dressed and participate in the economy by working as the regional manager of an Asian grocery chain.

"Your mom seems like a hard-ass," one of his high school friends had said after she stopped in the kitchen to retrieve the lunch she'd prepared for herself, adjusted the temperature of the fridge, set the timer on the rice cooker for Edwin's dinner, reminded him of which leftovers to eat, and shut the garage door behind her without a glance in their direction. She made these basic tasks and walking itself look like a precise and amazing practice, like hunting on horseback, requiring both physical endurance and infinitesimal mental calculations of factors beyond the ken of two self-indulgent teenage boys.

When she started as a cashier at the chain, she was quickly scorned by her coworkers as humorless and sexless. When she was promoted to management, they were deeply surprised to find her neither sparing with holiday bonuses nor reluctant to step in when their mother was in town. They confused affect with intention, warmth with virtue, assuming awkwardness was incompatible with fair-mindedness.

She was a sharp and fearless pragmatist who, at the cost of sleep and delicate sentiments, could have organized successful emergency relief missions for sprawling cities while intimidating every less-inspired worker into actualizing her vision. A perfect world for her was one in which all work was necessary and rational, virtuous and satisfying.

When she was young she thought she had a gift. Her sole wish was to make use of it and become a doctor. But she was poor and hadn't finished high school when she left Busan for San Jose, married to an abusive man. She divorced him within months of her arrival. The few eligible Korean men she met soon after wanted a woman with a clean past. Unlike many compatriots of her generation, she would not have hesitated to marry someone who wasn't Korean, but her English was still limited. Besides, she knew she was unsuited for marriage. She didn't have friends either in Korea or in the U.S. She knew she was unlikable.

She rarely had opportunities to practice English, and her struggles with the language convinced her that she was perhaps not so intelligent after all. She suspected, too, that her English would never be good because her simple, coarse Korean had molded her and now held her back. She could hear herself the country accent of the south risibly pronounced in her mouth.

She believed to become even a nurse she needed near-perfect fluency, and there was no one to assure her the words would come over time, in nursing school, with other students and teachers, and, further along, with everyone who peopled a hospital. She would learn.

She resigned herself to being a store manager. The same incapacity to comprehend hypocrisy or express nuance that led many to judge her as strange impressed others as touching, almost otherworldly. She didn't greet others in the morning or engage in small talk, but she spoke softly to the children in the store and offered them oranges and bought canned food for the stray cats in the alley. Sympathetic employees would address her warmly and speak to her with marked respect; they were otherwise uncertain of how to show her kindness.

Eugene first met her when the owner, a friend of one of his business partners, was consulting her about a shipment. Jeonghee was at home with their newborn, Sarah. He had received another cash payment from his legal settlement and was visiting the area to explore properties to invest in. He was in the mood to sing and asked the owner where they might go for karaoke that evening.

"I don't know, and I can't join you, I have to go home to my wife, but you might ask Ms. Yoon," he replied, gesturing with mischievous malice to a woman with a clipboard. He longed to tease her, to embarrass her—there was something not right about her as a woman—but he was by now dependent on her to run his business. With the chain expanding through Northern California, he wanted her to assume greater responsibilities as the regional manager.

Eugene was drawn to the challenge of seducing a woman without softness. He wanted to conquer the coil of energy within her, to see her broken like a bent wire hanger in sexual disarray.

She slept with him two or three times to get pregnant. She had, at last, a strong, steady income, and her most burning longing now was to raise a child. The father didn't matter to her. Though she did not know how to acknowledge the kindness of others, she sensed it, like subtle warmth on her skin, and wanted to channel her own kindness and longings into love for a child. At the center of her being was a bright clean flame. She did not know what to do with it, except to pass it on to a child.

When Jeonghee died after Edwin was born, Eugene tried to marry the mother of his son. He wanted to legitimize Edwin and for her to raise his daughters, and she refused. He planned to beat her, to rape her, to make her submit, and she, taking in his intentions when she opened the door, slammed it and called the police. For this he bore her unbegrudging respect. He loved to recount the story of that night to his acquaintances and to Edwin.

She barred him from the house until succumbing to his unceasing pleas by phone. How could she separate a father from his son? He visited at least twice a year, often more.

She gave Edwin all she could for a happy childhood. She provided stability, nourishing meals, and exciting games, schooldays using pencils she sharpened at night followed by playdates painfully arranged in English. She paid two married employees to look after him with their own children while she was at work. It was an arrangement that suited her and Edwin, who regarded the other boys as his cousins, until the family moved away, and he was deemed old enough to be home on his own.

At age eight or nine, Edwin learned another version of a story about himself and began to turn against his mother. There was no defining incident that established the script. It was disseminated in the air, on TV and bill-boards, in passing remarks from friends and questions from their parents about his mother and father, in school assignments about family trees. He couldn't be happy because happiness required a father, and his mother was powerless to change the universal storyline. She had divorced and conceived out of wedlock in a foreign country because she had an almost uncanny disregard, unnerving in others, for sclerotic common judgment. Now she found herself suffering the invisible compressions of convention, which were cruder and more irrational to her than the English language.

He was forgetting his Korean; he wanted to speak and be spoken to in English. She felt herself hacking away at what she wanted to say so that it would conform to speech that lacked the tactful indirectness of Korean, the modes of discourse that made talking easier because one was not merely a blunt agent or object—you did, I did, to you, for me—but a character woven into an ongoing narrative of social relations. Mother knows, Ms. Yoon must be tired, and, when appropriate, you can, I will. She could tell that her son's language was coarser than her Korean. Whatever, leave me alone, you're getting on my nerves.

Her love for Edwin was wild and tender. She continued to provide what stability she could and accepted, once again, that she lacked the abilities to make good on her dreams.

When she told him she'd once wanted to be a doctor, he associated this abandoned ambition with the core of loneliness in her; it fed into his embarrassment and contempt for her, which were redoubled with Eugene's visits to their home in Berkeley. Eugene grinned and gloated. He praised Edwin as handsome and smart and regularly gave both mother and son envelopes stuffed with cash. Edwin learned about the existence of his sisters from Eugene's cavils and curses about them, which were interwoven with gripes about expenses—private boarding school, an interior designer for his new home, property taxes in New Jersey—that only the wealthy could afford. Edwin resented his half siblings for living with their father and enjoying his prosperity. As he came to believe that the burden they placed on their father was not primarily financial but existential, he held himself innately superior to them. Surely their father would not be complaining about them if they were worth what he paid to support them.

His mother became friendlier with the workers who were growing old with her, but instead of feeling supported when they sympathized with the few plaints she dared voice about Edwin, she felt lonelier. They were just as powerless as her to change her son.

He went to college in LA and stayed there for medical school. It never ceased to give him a thrill to know something so literally visceral about a person without knowing them personally, without even talking to them. He could ignore everything a patient said and still know more than them about what was inside them. When this happened, he felt powerful and proud.

At his graduation from medical school his mother cried. He introduced her to his girlfriend. She was older than Edwin and already launched in a residency in dermatology at the university clinic. Meredith was fun and smart and had smooth skin and flaxen hair. She was one month pregnant and deeply moved by his mother's tears.

∞

They married in a civil ceremony.

He was halfway through his three-year residency in New York when his wife sued for divorce in LA after discovering nude photos he'd exchanged with a hospital receptionist.

She had a very good lawyer. To pay the awarded child support for the rest of their son's childhood, while she worked long hours and required paid childcare, Edwin would have to live like a cash-strapped student for another decade. His mother had paid for college and, having benefited from in-state tuition, agreed to pay his living expenses through medical school. He knew she could do no more.

"*You good-looking, you smart, handsome, you have good luck, like your daddy,*" his father had repeated over their irregular dinners while he was in college and medical school. He felt his luck turning when his father started calling to complain of physical ailments and apathetic doctors, and the prostate test he pushed Eugene to insist on confirmed cancer. He had intuited early on that for his father money did not represent the privileges of convenience or luxury so much as power, and he was correct in guessing that his father implicitly believed that power would save his life. So he arranged for him to see an oncologist at his hospital in New York who was neither renowned nor more experienced than those already caring for him in LA but was nonetheless—as he reminded his father again and again—in greater demand. This gratified Eugene immensely. He moved into the pied-à-terre he'd established in New Jersey long ago, where he stayed while checking on investments and, for a time, settled a mistress and her school-age son until she left to live with another man.

By the time Edwin picked his father up at Newark Airport, he had already filled out the insurance paperwork and hired an in-network home aide, Ruby, to stop by on days that he couldn't. He pronounced her competent and whispered in his father's ear that he should have better help, a fully licensed nurse or nurses who could more reliably keep abreast of his symptoms and manage his medication. He sighed, it was all so difficult with Medicare, such an impossible system, really designed to help the elderly survive rather than thrive. During a week of particularly acute fatigue and pain, Eugene gave him access to his financial papers. That was how he learned that his father was much wealthier than he had imagined.

He was about to hire a private nurse when he realized he would gain greater favor with his father if he cleaned and cared for him himself for a while. He told his supervisors about his father's condition and received a lighter, more flexible schedule, though this meant his residency might be extended. When he wasn't at the hospital, he was with his father. He napped in the break room and in the car service to Englewood, bringing with him the burgers or cake or the Korean meals his father craved that day. Once there, he cleared the floors littered with damp tissues and emptied the mugs full of sputum. He sorted the mail, vacuumed, and did the laundry. He loaded and emptied the dishwasher, had it repaired when it broke down, and scrubbed the toilet and bathroom floor with bleach. After dinner and Korean news on TV, of which he understood next to nothing, he passed out on one of the twin beds, sleeping so heavily he didn't always hear Eugene when he called out for a Coke with ice or wanted Edwin to inspect what he'd passed in the toilet. In the morning he made appointments with the urologist, oncologist, radiologist, and, when they learned the cancer had metastasized, the orthopedist and pulmonologist.

Edwin was invigorated by the new diagnosis. Despite his illegitimacy, which Eugene lamented as an unalterable and ugly fact of his identity, he was sure to inherit his father's fortune. He was the only one among his father's children to care for their father in his sickness, the only one, so Eugene told him, to even know of their father's cancer. Why bother to tell his sisters when they were so selfish and useless, such ungrateful and unnatural children? It was they who had made him sick unto death.

Edwin was soon worn out.

At first enthusiastic about full-time private help, Eugene abruptly changed his mind. "*No difference, same-same,*" he said. "*And one woman okay, not two. Ruby okay. No need for two because you are here. One woman, three times, two times in one week is okay.*" It couldn't be a question of money, of which Eugene had more than he could spend before he died. Edwin quietly cursed his father as they sat together before the TV. He didn't know how to work things in his favor without going mad any more than he could understand the newscasters droning on the screen he wanted to smash. His father had six months to a year, though no one could say for sure.

Eugene could pay for the most expensive round-the-clock care without touching his capital and still leave an immense fortune to his son. Edwin thought of the custom-tailored Italian suit Eugene paid for after his college graduation. As he was fitted, Eugene, clothed in a threadbare cotton shirt and polyester slacks, nodded with approval. Eugene wasn't really a miser. If he was living in an ugly apartment with irremediably sticky tiles and crooked cabinets, it was because he wouldn't find any pleasure in a well-appointed luxury apartment in Manhattan right now. He didn't care about ugliness or enjoy beauty. He spent money to provoke surprise and discomfort, display power and accrue indebtedness. He savored the strange juxtaposition of his vulgarity and the sophistication he could purchase.

Edwin imagined months on end of his father's disgusting dependence. He didn't think he could last much longer.

It dawned on Edwin that Eugene not only enjoyed his son's sacrifices, but enjoyed his son's abasement. He knew Edwin didn't understand the

Korean channel, which was why he wanted Edwin with him when he watched. He enjoyed the palpable restlessness at his side.

It was true: as Eugene watched Edwin clean the toilet, he did feel prouder of him than he did of his three wretched daughters. He respected Edwin for toiling without complaint to secure a generous inheritance. He was amused; he loved his son.

Money was power and dirt. It could also be alchemized into love.

When he wasn't sleeping, Eugene talked. He talked while eating and watching TV and resting, and Edwin listened. He rambled in English, slipping at times into Korean, about the disappointments of life, which invariably involved women.

"*They don't know how listen. Never listen! Your mommy don't listen, but she is strong. She is very strong. One time I try to make her listen, I want to make her listen to me, and she call the police. Police come and she say, 'Sorry, I think this man wants hurt me.' They say, 'Okay, good night.' She say to me, 'You be careful.* Don't touch me ever again! *You touch me, you never see your son again.' She know I have only girls. She knows I want a son. I say, 'Okay! Okay! You win. I don't touch you. I don't want to touch you. I want to see my son. I give you money, okay? I pay you to see my son, okay?' She like all women, they just want money. Your mommy a good woman.* She's a good woman. But—*she not really woman.* Not like a real woman should be. *My first wife is beautiful.* Very beautiful! *She's crazy. She wants to kill me, I try to kill her. If she don't run away, I kill her probably.* I had to shut her up. *She screaming, yelling. She holding a knife when I'm mad. Only bad woman leave her baby.* That girl is just like her mother! She thinks I'm her enemy. She made our house a war zone. *She think I am like enemy. She the worst* trashy bitch *of my daughters, like trash. The next wife is nice, good woman. Better than your mommy, better than* that lowborn bitch. I'll never forget her. She was so beautiful, so good and kind. When she died, I was all alone. She was the only one I loved. She made me feel beautiful things. *When she die, I am sorry. She leave me alone. You must listen. You do not trust bad women. You still have nice girlfriend?"*

Edwin had told his father that he wanted to marry a beautiful, intelligent woman who was also a doctor. That was all. If asked, he would say she was Korean. If it came down to it, he would ask a fellow Korean American resident to pose as a girlfriend. He knew his father would not look generously upon a short-lived marriage to a white American that had produced a mixed-race son. His mother warned him after meeting Meredith that Eugene, despite his flagrant transgressions from respectable convention, held others to a much higher, intolerant standard. Like other immigrants who rarely returned to Korea, he was like a living time capsule, preserving in his mind social norms and moral codes from the sixties and seventies that were, on the whole, frightfully regressive by mainstream American standards. They still believed, more than the Chinese, more than other Asians, in keeping Korean bloodlines pure. Not a day went by that she wasn't grateful to have left the country, she said, in one of the more personal remarks she'd made in years.

"Yes," Edwin replied. "We want to get married and have children. But we need to wait. We have to wait until we can save up, you know, for a good home for the children. We might have to wait several years, but it'll be worth it. She's wonderful. She's not like other girls. She'll be a wonderful mother."

"*Ruby, too,*" Eugene said, staring at the TV screen. "*She* lowborn trash, a real conceited bitch. *She don't know who she is. She think she is better than me. She don't know what she is supposed to be, what is work. She talk and talk to Esther and don't work, don't clean. Esther bad, too. You don't know.*" He chuckled maliciously. "*You don't know how bad she is, too. I know. I know what she do for money. She likes to be dirty. All women, even ladies, all women, same-same. You lucky, just one woman, Mommy, in your life. I always have minimum three. They no good. They don't love me.*

They don't love Daddy. Esther is a dirty slut *but she care for her daddy, she want to care for me. I know. But she no good. No good, dirty, dirty now. Sarah not dirty, but no good, no good now. She don't marry. She don't love her daddy.*"

Edwin broke into a sweat. Eugene had lied, of course. He had told at least one daughter, Esther, that he was sick. She, too, was now caring for him.

Eugene had always indicated to Edwin that the estrangement between the brother and sisters should remain permanent. He made it seem like a matter of potential cross-contamination between the two branches of his line: the sisters exposing their unworthiness to the brother, the brother sparing himself the shame of getting to know his sisters. Or the inverse situation was true: Eugene didn't want his bastard fraternizing with his legitimate children. But Edwin's whole being, his self-worth and self-knowledge, revolted against this thought. No. Eugene loved his son. He cherished the visits in Berkeley and the dinners with his handsome, intelligent son. Edwin knew this as firmly as he knew his mother was lonely and his father was dying.

But he had reason to be disappointed in himself. He was getting very good at reading his patients; his father was a trickier character to grasp. Once, when he was maybe seven, his father brought a live lobster and crab in separate boxes into the kitchen, waved Edwin over to watch, picked the crab up with tongs and dropped it in with the lobster. He should have known. He should have foreseen that Eugene voiced his true thoughts between the lines of his apparent words: Eugene wanted the siblings to meet. For years he'd asked Edwin and his mother whether she was seeing anyone, for love and companionship or sex. Even as a child Edwin sensed his father's wish to see his mother with a lover, perhaps interrupt them for a laugh. Eugene reveled in ugly surprises and provocations, awkward or turbulent scenes in which he could pry or play a role. Jealousy was not Eugene's weakness. It was prurience.

He was waiting to see how it would happen. Maybe Edwin would arrive early or late one day while Esther, Sarah, or the oldest sister was with him. Alone, in bed, he was surely licking his lips at the imminent confrontation.

Edwin wrote an email to Sarah. She was the only one of the three he could find online. He waited two days and could wait no longer; he paid to have her phone number. He couldn't simply wait to see what would happen.

He was unusually aloof during his hospital shift, he who was known for chatting garrulously, sometimes flirtatiously, with his patients. He worked mechanically while his sleepless thoughts evolved wildly, like spiders rupturing their sac, scurrying in all directions to spin their own intricate webs: I'll meet with her. I'll be natural. I have to see what she's like. See her and see what she wants. She doesn't have any money. Only the oldest one does, he says. But he doesn't like her. That's what he claims. What if that's also a lie. What's that saying—he's protesting too much when he talks about her mother, how much he hates her. He admires her. She was beautiful and sassy. She talked back and tried to murder him. He liked that. He might want to leave everything to her, because she's a bitch, because she's the only one who doesn't need it. She might be the only one who's told him to his face she hates him and wishes he'd drop dead. He might like that about her. He might like that and still give everything to Esther and Sarah. He keeps saying Esther's dirty, like she's some prostitute. Maybe he thinks it'd be funny to leave everything to someone filthier than him. I'm not going to let my son be dirty or dishonorable. He'll probably leave his money to Sarah. She's the most respectable, he says. She's the smartest, or he thought she was. She has her Ivy League degree and can't get a real job. He says he won't waste any more time or money on them. He doesn't mean it. I'm supposed to let him forget about me and my child? He never says what he means. He wants them to prove they love him. Right now. He wants us all to hustle for his money. He says he's lost hope in Sarah—that means he still thinks of her.

He's not going to let her fall apart. But she's not very attractive, she's the ugliest, he said, so she might not even marry well. She's ugly, but she's not dirty. Esther's the lost cause. Did she really steal his money and drop out of college? Am I supposed to turn him against them? Or do I pretend to be a good boy, a good brother who wants them all to reconcile? If they're visiting him, are they even on bad terms? I'm the fool here. I'm the victim. I'm cleaning up his shit, his literal shit, and he's not going to leave me anything. If I don't get anything from him I give everything I have to Meredith. I'm not going to have my son visit his father in some shithole apartment. What do I have to do? I have to play it cool. I have to be myself. He likes me. Remember that. He's always liked me even though I'm a bastard. He said bastards are a lost cause, but that doesn't mean he's not going to give me anything. He has to. He's going to leave me something. I'm not going to be some poor asshole whose son is ashamed of him. I just have to keep doing what I'm doing. I have to clean his shit and take him to the doctor. I have to be civil to my sisters, whatever they're like. I can't let them know what I want. I'll be myself, but I won't let them know the most important thing.

His thoughts ran manically, as if he were not thinking them, as if they were scrolling on a ticker tape, these lines he'd heard and recycled from elsewhere. *I'll be natural.* But if he acted as if he didn't know what he knew, he would surely disappoint his father, his father who loved him for his perspicacity. *He wants them to prove they love him.* Hadn't he already proved it to his father? Hadn't he slaved enough for him? *She's the most respectable.* When did his father ever think in terms of respectability? He was so tired, he was nauseated. *I'm not going to let my son be dirty or dishonorable.* The words repeating in his mind rang oddly, as if he'd developed a tin ear for his own thoughts. *Dirty, dishonorable . . .* These were not words he ordinarily reached for when he thought of raising and protecting his son. He couldn't have said whether he was thinking of his own son, channeling Eugene's wishes for Edwin, or giving voice to his own wish that Eugene provide for him.

Whatever plan of action he took must be subtle, he must not betray himself. Eugene disliked obvious sycophantism or machinations in others. He liked to be the sole actor in the room.

Edwin had no plan. For now, all he could do was see what his sisters were like. Then he might have an idea of what Eugene had planned for each of his children.

He never says what he means.

Am I supposed to turn him against them?

He might like that about her.

After meeting Sarah he returned to the hospital to complete his shift. The next morning he rushed to his father's to see Ruby before her shift ended.

He was deeply afraid she was going to quit before he could find a replacement. Once tolerant of her presence, Eugene was trying his best to push her to a breaking point. He loudly called her fat and lazy when she left the room. He demanded that she clean the toilet after using it. During Edwin's last visit, he was at his father's side when Eugene called out to Ruby. When she entered he locked eyes with her as he cleared his throat, spit into his cup, and held it out for her.

He ran into her in the hallway. "I hope today was better. I'm so sorry about him," he said breathlessly. "He's not in his right mind." He felt it was he who wasn't in his right mind. He hadn't slept for nearly two days.

"I get it," she said tonelessly. "I make sure I do my job." There was neither reproach nor indulgence in her voice.

On the counter he saw a note from Esther.

Edwin—

I don't know if our father has told you about us, your sisters. I'm Esther, the youngest. I don't know anything about you but your name and that you've been helping our father during his illness. I think we

should try to make a schedule so that someone is always with him,
Ruby or me or you or my sisters. He says he is dying. He says you are
a doctor, so you probably know better than me.
—Esther

She left her number and her email address.

He went in to see his father, who was sleeping. He thought he would try to sleep, too.

He opened the door to the second bedroom and saw a young woman sleeping. Her hair covered her face, the quilt the rest of her curled body.

He shut the door again and sat down on the sofa. He was tired to the bone. He toppled onto his side and sank into a deep, restless sleep, dreaming disjointed dreams he would forget, retaining only their throbbing rhythm when he woke.

He woke two hours later. He checked on his father, who was still sleeping. He opened the door to the room where he saw the woman he knew was Esther. She was sitting up in bed, drinking from a mug.

"I'm sorry," he said, affecting surprise. "I didn't know you were here. I'm, um, Edwin."

She was in jeans, wrapped in a dark woolen shawl. She looked like an ordinary, nondescript young woman. He'd expected someone who looked and acted like a beaten-down stray dog, scared, strange, aggressive, disheveled. Esther was the one his father said was dirty.

The next moment he did sense something feral about her. He waited for her to speak and thought she looked, with her blank opaque stare, less innocent than mindless, almost chillingly other.

"I'm Esther. I left you a note." Her voice was very clear and calm; the light of intelligence entered her eyes. Now she appeared to him perceptive and self-possessed, canny like a fox with its discerning slit pupils.

"I didn't mean to disturb you. I'm going to make some coffee. You can join me if you want."

He closed the door.

She joined him a minute later and asked if he would make some for her, too. It was all the time he needed to recover himself. His normally steady self-confidence was returning to him. He wasn't used to panicking. He liked talking, using his talents, meeting people, impressing and pleasing them. He experienced pleasure as a wash of self-affirmation. His mother had known him as an easy, happy small child.

He said, "This is a strange way to meet, don't you think?"

"Our father is a strange man."

He was struck again by the assured clarity of her tone, the resonant depth to the tenor of her voice, and felt a faint shiver of surprise at her response. It wasn't exactly strange, but it diverged from the beaten paths of his expectations. Sarah was more predictable. He'd known instinctively she would resist his brusqueness but ultimately let it sway her; he knew this right away, even on the phone. He would have to be a bit more attentive with Esther. He would have to be more delicate, though he could now see, in the natural light of the living room, the roughness of her appearance. Her hair was unbrushed, clumped in oily locks on her scalp; her skin and her lips were ashy.

"Yes," he said with a short, hearty laugh. "That's undeniable."

He laid out the coffee, sugar, and milk, and they sat down at the dining table.

He let a minute pass in silence; or was it she who ordained it? He wanted to appear diffident. He cleared his throat twice and drank from his mug. "I read your note when I arrived this morning. I should have thought of doing something like that myself. But our father—he told me he wasn't in touch with you. You know him, too, of course. You know him better than me. When I was growing up I saw him a few times a year at most. I've been getting to know him just these past few months."

"You met my sister Sarah yesterday. She was really surprised to hear from you."

He thought: So Esther and Sarah talk to each other.

"So now I've met you and Sarah, but I haven't met the firstborn."

"Minah."

"Yes, Minah. To tell you the truth, I didn't know her name till now."

"I can imagine that Dad kept a lot from you. From us, too."

"Yes," he said, dropping his voice to a more thoughtful register.

"He hasn't told us any details about his condition. I keep asking, and he just won't tell me, like it's a game. He's very childish. He says he doesn't have long to live, sometimes like it's a joke. But I have the feeling it isn't."

"That's true. It's not. I know the details. I'm a doctor and I've been taking him to see his doctors. He has prostate cancer and it's metastasized—it's spread—to his bones and lungs." He paused, waiting for the breathless shock he'd seen in Sarah, but there was only sadness in Esther's expression. "He isn't in a lot of pain yet, but I expect that to change. Soon. His back has gotten worse just this week. His doctors want to start radiation, but he says he doesn't want it, then changes his mind, then—"

"How much longer does he have?" she asked abruptly.

"It's hard to say. It all depends on what kind of treatment he gets and how he responds. It could be a few months or even a few years. It won't be— I'm sorry to say it won't be very long. It's metastasized. It's spread. Once that happens, you can't eliminate the cancer. But if we can keep the cancer from spreading too aggressively and shrink the tumor in the prostrate, he could hang on for a while. But I'm worried about his back. We had another scan last week and the tumor there is growing quickly, and the pain's getting worse. I'm surprised he's not in greater pain, to tell the truth." Edwin was in his element now. He was good at talking to families of patients. He felt himself relax.

"How long has he known?"

"Since the spring. He didn't want to worry you." The words came out reflexively; he had no clear idea of why his father had concealed his illness from his daughters for months. "But we didn't discover the cancer in his bones until August. He was in shock and denial for a while. Actually, I think he still is."

"You said he keeps changing his mind about radiation. Is there anything else he can do?"

"Yes. We all think he should start hormone therapy now and start chemo shortly after. We told him about the side effects and he said it wasn't worth it. Sometimes he says okay, he'll do it, then he backtracks the next hour. He's even canceled some appointments at the last minute. I can't drag him to the hospital if he doesn't want it. He's very stubborn. He's—I don't know how he is with you, but with me, he's always been kind of dramatic, almost larger than life. Do you know what I mean?"

"Yes, I do."

Why was he suddenly beset with the nagging feeling that he was a fake? He brushed it away and went on: "He's really resistant to the idea of hormone therapy, but that's the first line of action now. He thinks—he thinks it's emasculating. It works to lower testosterone. One of the possible side effects includes breast development, for example. Maybe part of him has accepted he's going to die and thinks he won't die with dignity if he doesn't really feel like a man. He wants to live the best he can for as long as he can. That's what I think is going on. Because he loves life."

It was as the words tumbled from his mouth that he understood why, despite Eugene's obvious indecency, he admired his father and saw him as strong, stronger than most, stronger certainly than his mother and even Meredith. He'd fallen in love with Meredith's boldness and ambition, her beautiful avidity for the things she'd staked out for herself in life: passionate love and professional accomplishment. She should have destroyed his belongings and clawed at him in a rage after discovering his affair, but no, she collapsed in sobs and told him to leave. Her appetite now was for little else but money.

Esther said, "He still feels deep down that he's going to live forever. It's denial, but it's not just coming from fear. He still feels he's going to live forever, and he feels it more than most people. For him it's a matter of wanting it enough. And he's strong. He's always been stubborn, and short-tempered, and strong."

Edwin wasn't sure what to think of this, but somehow her words made him feel inspired, though inspired to do what he couldn't say. He did know he wanted to keep talking to Esther. Like his father, he loved to talk to people. Unlike him, he particularly enjoyed conversations with intelligent and interesting women.

"You're probably right about the hormone treatment," Esther said. "He talked to me about chemo, but I think he was ashamed to mention the hormone treatment to me. Otherwise he might have told me what was happening. I'm glad he can talk to you about it."

"I'm glad I can help him."

"Why does someone who loves life refuse treatment?" she said with sudden vehemence. "He's not stupid. His denial seems somehow . . . mixed up with his shamelessness."

"What do you mean?" With this question he was also asking: What are you like? Because she seemed to think in ways that felt alien to him.

"I'm not sure. I mean . . . he's always had this shamelessness about him. It gives him life. It's like . . . he thinks if he's dying, he has to face his shame. If he's shameless, he'll keep living. He's chosen life because he loves life, as you say. He wants to be shameless and live. That's what I feel when I'm holding his hand."

She hung her head. She reminded Edwin, then, of a beaten-down dog, meek and incurably distressed.

"I've tried to talk to him about dying. I said if he is dying as he keeps saying, it's time to prepare."

His heart pattered rapidly as he inhaled. Was this a reference to a will? "Yes, it is."

"What do you tell patients who don't have much time?"

"If their family is there, we notify them first, usually because the patient is far gone and not entirely present. We tell them to prepare their goodbyes and remind them gently to get their affairs in order—to arrange for hospice care, for example, and any last will and testament."

She fixed her eyes on his unexpectedly. "You really do that—doctors really tell patients' families to prepare a will?"

"No, not in those words"—he was good at not flailing when it was crucial not to—"unless they ask what we mean. Which they do, if they're in shock. Usually they understand what we mean by goodbyes and having your affairs in order."

"I've already mentioned all of that to him. Or most of it." She gulped down her cold coffee. "I've never been very close to him. But I don't want him to die alone. Ruby coming by two or three times a week isn't enough. He wants to be with someone who knows him. Right now he's trying to live through us."

"I try my best," Edwin said proudly. "But I'm a doctor in training. I don't have that much time. I haven't slept well in weeks. But I'm trying." He immediately realized this was the wrong tactic, in case Esther insisted on spending more time with their father than he would. "And I want to do it. I want to be there for him. We finally have the chance to spend time together. I didn't have as much time with him as you. I was always a little envious, to be honest—you can understand that—but I didn't resent you, really I didn't. Okay, maybe a little, when I first learned about you, which wasn't until I was older, maybe fifteen. But please understand I need to see him as much as I can while he's still here. He's my father. He's becoming more of a father every time I see him."

"I understand," she said with gentle firmness, gazing at him with unabashed directness and frankness.

How was he to position himself with her? She was at once bold and forthright, even willful; susceptible and trusting, possibly weak. "So where do we go from here?"

"Tell me when you want to be here and we'll draw up a schedule. I'll consult my sisters, too. They're busier than me, they have jobs. I don't, so I can come by often, if need be."

"That sounds good. Thank you so much," he said deeply.

Fatigue crashed over him in a nauseating wave. Then he heard: "*Edwin! You come!*"

Edwin and Esther looked at each other.

"I don't think he knows I'm here," she said. "He fell asleep before he could tell me whether I should stay or go. He probably thinks I've left."

"I'll go see what he wants," he said.

Eugene wanted his shades pulled up, his mug replaced, another box of tissues, his laptop, a cold can of Coke with a straw.

"Esther's still here. I just met her," Edwin said as he stooped to pick up balled-up tissues and socks.

"*Tell her go home.*" His father didn't seem surprised, only aggravated.

In the living room Edwin found Esther tapping at her phone.

"He told me to tell you to go home. That might not be a bad idea. You should get some rest. The spare bed isn't that comfortable. Get some rest and we'll talk again soon."

"I can't go now. I just—"

"*Ed-win!*" Their father's voice carried a note of threat.

"I'll go see what he wants," Edwin said again.

"I'll come, too," Esther said anxiously, "in a sec. But my sister's downstairs."

"Okay" was all he could muster in the pressure of the moment. Why was Sarah here now?

In the master bedroom, Edwin cringed at the sight of their father's laptop, which must have slid off the quilt onto the floor.

"*It fall. You leave where it fall!*"

"I'm sorry, Dad. But look, it's working fine. It's not broken."

"*Esther here or no? She go or no?!*"

Edwin didn't think he'd ever seen his father so enraged, huffing like a bull with shining black eyes.

"She's leaving now," he said reassuringly.

But at that moment Esther entered the room. To Edwin's relief, Eugene focused his rage on her.

"*What you talk about with him? You say nothing to him! You don't talk to him! You don't say anything to me, to no one. I don't want* such a dirty lowborn slut creeping around here, corrupting my only son, bringing your dying father so much shame! You'd do anything for money. You think I don't know? I know what you were doing all that time. You think I'm stupid? You took my money, you wasted it on drugs and trash and who knows what else, and when you ran out you lived like a slut with men from all over, didn't you? That's what you learned from Soojin, isn't it? Or maybe you were teaching her how to be a whore? You made her betray me. You! What kind of girl does that to her father? What kind of piece of trash does that? My own daughter! Why isn't your older sister here? Why do I have to have you? I can't bear it anymore. Get out! Get out, you dirty whore!"

Esther left the room.

Edwin approached his father and gingerly patted his hand. Eugene was breathing heavily; he started to cough. "You shouldn't get worked up. Let me get your Coke," Edwin said gently. He wanted to catch Esther before she left.

He saw Esther at the end of the hallway. Her expression was bright with pain and alarm.

"I'm so sorry about that. He shouldn't speak to you like that. Whatever he said to you, you don't deserve it and he didn't mean it."

A voice came from the kitchen. "Of course he meant it." The voice was richly bitter, like overflowing beer. He turned to identify its source. "That was him talking. He meant every word."

She wasn't Sarah. She was the last of the three sisters, glowing with rage, glaring at him with a fury to match their father's.

"I didn't understand what he was saying," Edwin said. He was careful to sound more perplexed and concerned than curious.

The woman he knew was Minah was glaring into space now, as if she could see somewhere before her—there—their father's rot beginning to defile the physical world.

"He called her a whore."

5
Minah's skin

"I'm going to kill him," Minah said.

She was with Esther in a car to her apartment. She was still staring out into the middle distance, vaguely following the line of telephone poles and the blur of pedestrians. Occasionally she found herself seizing on details about to disappear from view: a flyer on a telephone pole either offering or seeking help, a stout woman with enormous hips crossing the street with a rolling suitcase, the bright headscarf of an old woman in a long black dress. Her being could not accept that these signs, these people, held no relation or clue to the hate that was consuming her. She could not believe that these symbols and figures of life could be so blankly innocent, entirely detached from her turmoil. Like a desert creature whose entire organism is attuned to the subtle signs of unseen water, she sought in these details something that would cool her and save her.

She had felt the same way about the tiles and walls of the bathroom that she'd stare at for hours when she locked herself in while living with Eugene. These details from the bustling world of the present were just as unbearably irrelevant to her life as the tiles, the walls of her childhood home—and her bitterness became too much to bear. She knew she should practice some self-control with the stranger at the wheel, but she could not stop the declaration, the first words she'd spoken since leaving Eugene's apartment. I'm going to kill him.

Esther touched her shoulder. She did not move to acknowledge it. Even that touch, from one of the few people in the world she loved, seemed cruelly alien to her inner life.

The familiar space of her studio reawakened Minah to her usual self, the one who planned carefully and worked hard for what she wanted and was, perhaps, on the cusp of acquiring it.

For all her tender love for Esther—the fervent love, she sometimes thought, that she'd once cherished for Jeonghee and transferred to her baby sister as their mother grew sick and mean—her only sincere motive in inviting Esther to stay the night was the same in meeting Sarah after her class: persuading her to persuade Eugene to leave his wealth to his three daughters, in equal shares. The urgency of this plan stirred back to life when she saw the dining table set for two with bulbous wineglasses and chopsticks on chopstick rests and soft, thick cloth napkins in porcelain rings.

At the same time, she felt a fleeting sense of unreality, as if these things of hers were also irremediably foreign.

"This is a beautiful room," Esther said.

"Thank you." The reply was not merely reflexive; Minah exhaled in relief at the simple remark, surprised at the level of gratitude she felt. She had, after all, spent hours cleaning the studio herself after firing her inexact cleaner. She vacuumed until her cream-colored rugs were warm and fluffy and scraped off the congealed grease on the top of the stove. She scrubbed at mildew and polished picture frames of her and Paul and her with her friends from church. With each vigorous back and forth of sponge and rag, she felt she was welcoming her sister to a clean, comfortable home in the way she should have years ago. She worked through the fever that had cyclically dissipated and stolen over her for over a week now.

She excused herself and sat on the toilet in the sparkling bathroom. She practiced deep rhythmic breathing and collected herself. Soon the sob of rage faded and grew distant, like the echo of a raging despair she knew in another life, an alternate universe in which she allowed herself to fall apart.

She sank briefly but deeply into the same dreamlike recollection of Esther as a child that had returned to her days earlier. For days she'd racked her memory for Esther's favorite Korean foods. All she could remember was Esther's singsong requests for blinis with sour cream, which had been followed by expressions of disbelief when both their mother and father ignored her. They often ignored her or simply yelled for her to leave them alone, but even Eugene rarely unleashed his temper on her. Jeonghee neglected Esther, but she protected her through this neglect. She made her complaints about Sarah, thus reinforcing her husband's passionate fixation on her first child. She gave him tacit permission to harass Minah, too—Minah who'd grown so troublesome—if only Esther was spared.

"What the hell is a blini, anyway?" Eugene had said, walking away while Esther explained. She gesticulated oddly, throwing up her hands and wringing them, miming various emotional clichés of delirious longing for lack of a better vocabulary. Minah vividly recalled Esther's response to their utter disregard: the rounded eyes and mouth of astonishment that only a happy child could produce at this fact of life, the limits of the real. Esther eventually settled for fish cakes and made balls out of her sticky rice, but she didn't sulk, no. Her bad moods were passing clouds; they left no lasting shadow. She could sob and scream as much as the next child, but she was adored, if not at home then next door. She was always expressive, never forced to dampen or distort her feelings.

Who was her sister now? Minah had disliked Sarah for so long partly because Sarah made her feel judged and wanting. Why was she now more comfortable with Sarah's captious cynicism than Esther's strangeness? She did not feel judged, not quite, when talking to Esther. But she did feel Esther was making an appeal or a demand for something she didn't have, even when she was simply thinking of her. Esther was still the child asking for something one didn't have or understand.

She flushed the toilet; the act felt symbolic. Neither she nor Esther was a child anymore.

When she emerged Esther was sitting at the dining table. She asked her if she was hungry.

"I'm really hungry," Esther said, quietly exigent.

Minah served bowls of rice and laid out fish cakes, seaweed, bean sprouts, and kimchi.

Esther asked for a fork.

"You don't know how to use chopsticks?" Minah said teasingly.

"No, I never really learned." She spoke with a trace of sadness.

"I'll teach you. Not now, but one of these days."

Esther chewed slowly, looking absorbed in the act, at once fleshy and ethereal.

Minah swallowed a mouthful of rice before setting down her chopsticks. "I'm not hungry. Just help yourself," she said. She summoned a warm, hospitable tone, but her voice sounded depressed and defeated to her own ears. Each time she was about to ask how Esther liked the various dishes, or politely break the silence by asking her sister what she liked to eat these days—by saying anything, really—she shut her mouth. She was afraid of hearing the same voice.

With her careful table manners, Esther seemed to take only small helpings. But within minutes, she had finished her bowl of rice along with the fish cakes and kimchi. She looked up from her empty bowl and smiled sweetly. Her smile expressed compassion for Minah's lingering distress, as well as satisfaction with her meal; in the sweetness of her smile, her bodily contentment and her compassion were one.

Consciously or not, Esther was always seeking eye contact. It did not seem entirely intentional to Minah, but another gesture of her sister's openness—her simplicity—which gave her the power to both discomfit and disarm. Minah remembered, almost felt again, Esther's touch on her shoulder in the car. This time, in memory, it affected her differently. Esther was someone who could puzzle and pain her. She was also someone who could purify silence.

"Would you like more?"

"No thank you. Maybe later." Esther paused. "Minah, why did you come to Dad's apartment? I thought we were meeting here."

Minah cleared her throat. "You said Dad was expecting Edwin, and you were hoping to meet him before leaving. I wanted to meet him, too, especially since Sarah didn't get a good impression of him. She must have told you that. I also wanted to see how Dad was treating you." Sarah had actually described Edwin to her as sinister, which had sufficiently alarmed Minah to send her to her father's that afternoon.

"I'm fine," Esther said adamantly. "I am."

Minah cleared her throat again. It was too soon to talk about what she most wanted to talk about. "I couldn't remember what foods you liked best, and I wanted to surprise you with your favorite. All I remember was how much you liked Russian food, but I wanted to give you Korean food, and I thought I remembered you liked fish cakes. I was right, wasn't I?"

"Yes, I love them. But why Korean food?"

"Why what?"

"Why did you want to give me Korean food?"

It was a harmless question. Wasn't it? But Minah was nonplussed. There was something provocative to it. The pattern of the past was about to repeat itself: uncertainty; discomfort to which Esther was either indifferent or oblivious; mounting resolution to end the conversation, to get out of the high-pitched wind and sink back into the warm waters of her life.

She would not let the pattern recur. "Because, silly, that's what we used to eat together. And I thought you might not have had the chance to eat Korean food in a while. I wanted to prepare it for you now that you're back."

Esther smiled. "I'm glad we have some time together. I've been wanting to thank you for what you did for me."

"Thank me for what?" Minah said. A feverish heat continued its throbbing and ebbing in her.

"For giving Misha the money to help me."

Minah had almost forgotten. She sent Misha money after he wrote in reply to one of her emails that Esther wanted to visit him and his family, especially Anna, who was too frail to travel, but didn't have the money for a plane ticket to Toronto. Minah continued to send him money during the months that Esther lived between his apartment in the city and the house in the suburbs where his mother lived with Anna.

"You don't have to thank me." She added dourly, "Misha wasn't supposed to tell you."

"I know. But it's hard for him to keep a secret. And I knew he couldn't afford to buy me winter boots himself."

Only now did it occur to Minah that she could have openly purchased the ticket herself. But she still believed she was not the one who could best help her sister. Her money had done more to bring Esther back into her life than her own presence and care could have accomplished.

She was still half lost in this thought when she asked, "How is Misha?"

"I'm not sure," Esther said. "I mean . . . I think Misha's fine." She bit her lower lip. "I haven't talked to him for a few weeks, actually. I've been busy, but . . . He wants me to live with him," she blurted out. "He wants us to be together. To get married and have children together. He says that's his dream." She looked to Minah, searching her face as if for an answer.

"And you're not happy about that?" Minah was trying to suppress a smile. She herself felt a pulse of joy at this unsurprising revelation. "When you . . . were traveling for a while, after you dropped out of school, you were hard to reach, so I'd ask him about you. I knew you confided in him in ways you didn't with me. His emails to me usually ended along the lines of 'Don't worry, I'm staying in touch with her. I'll make sure she's always safe.'"

"He's my best friend, and I love him like a brother," Esther said, unhappily forthright. "I could live with him for a long, long time if he needed me. But he doesn't need me."

"How do you know? Maybe he does."

All her life, Minah had cherished memories of Esther and Misha together in their delicious childishness. When she thought of having children, she thought of them dancing to Anna's performance of a solemn sonata as if it were a pop hit, or sleeping side by side on the sofa, Esther's round belly and silky limbs surprisingly warm to the touch when Minah gathered her in her arms to take her home. Her honeyed heat was the exhalation of an innocence that was not fragile but almost wild in its potent beauty.

Minah noted again Esther's changed skin: the very fine wrinkling around her eyes and on her forehead and whorled around her dimples, the freckling from overexposure to an intense, far-off sun. Thinking of Misha's love for Esther, she saw her sister almost as a painting: the discoloration and texture were like the fading and craquelure of an old painting of a young woman, despite which you could see that the face was tenderly observed and represented by the artist. Life and love were there, suffusing the sun damage on Esther's face, and Misha could see its layers and its light.

"How do you know?" Minah repeated.

"I know because I don't love him as a lover. How can he need me if I can only ever love him as a brother? How can he want to live with me and have my children if he knows—and he must know this, some part of him does—that I want to find love with someone else? It's too cruel."

"Cruel? Misha is sweet and loving. It's unfair to call him cruel."

"But it's not," Esther said in hot protest. "It's cruel to want someone to give up their desires for you. To want them to have a life that doesn't fit them. That's what he wants from me."

"What do you want?"

There—Minah could feel they had definitively crossed into the territory of the personal.

"I want a different love. I want to learn from love and discover love, not remain always in the love I have with Misha. I want sex with love. I've never had that before. And it's something I want."

Minah was speechless. She hadn't seen Esther grow up. In her mind, Esther, with her woman's body and prematurely weathered face, was none-theless a child, pure of heart.

"I know I might never have it. I don't know if you should wait for it or pursue it. But I want to be open to it. For so long I didn't want to touch anyone or have anyone touch me. I didn't want to think of myself as a sexual person. I thought I was a nobody, and for a while that was enough for me. I thought that was how I could be good . . ." The surge of confidence with which she'd declared her desires had ebbed just as precipitately to nothing. With each pause, she seemed to be trying to understand her own thoughts and pushing herself through her reticence to the right words. "For a long time I didn't really have a will of my own. I was usually with people who wanted me with them. They wanted to talk and for me to listen. And I did listen, and sometimes I wanted to listen forever. Other times I just wanted to be alone . . . One day I was with my friend's cousin, having coffee in his kitchen. He asked me if I'd ever been to Korea. I knew he wasn't going to say something rude, you know, like, 'What's the difference between Korean and Chinese people?' like a lot of ignorant people do when they talk to you. I felt like I knew him. Even though at the same time he seemed mysterious to me. He said, 'I want to travel the world, but I don't know how.' He said his mother loved K-pop and we laughed. He left and I didn't see him again."

She flushed. "Now I know I have my own will. I always did. And now I also know that it's good for other people, too, when you like your life. When you love life."

"Yes, it's good to be happy."

"Not just be happy. Love being alive."

"Love your life. Yes." Minah could feel Esther riding on a small wave of joy at affirming these freshly articulated thoughts; she felt the tempo of her own consciousness quicken as she listened.

Esther continued: "I love the feeling that life can give you, that you're going to live forever, even when you're unhappy . . . Because you're blessed to taste and see, every day. Like I . . . I love trees. And the sea. I love when you see and learn things . . . Even when you're miserable, you can learn what other people have done in their misery, with their misery. Noble things and awful things. Don't you feel when you learn something new—when you learned to read, for example, or discovered someone you know might be different, might be sweeter than you expected—don't you feel you might live forever? Not that you think you will. Just that you feel you will."

Minah thought, I like seeing Esther look happy. She looks happy now.

"Misha is my brother. I love him. But the way I love life—it pushes me to keep moving. I want to love other people, for now."

"You want more than spiritual love. You want sexual love."

"Yes. No." Esther was growing more excited, almost levitating in her chair as she poured herself a glass of wine. "What does it mean when people say that someone's very spiritual or very sexual? Everyone is spiritual and everyone is sexual. That's what I'm starting to believe, at least."

She was too embarrassed to continue.

Minah wondered if Esther could still be a virgin in her mid-twenties. The next moment she was certain that Esther must have slept with Misha and, as Minah herself did with her first lover, wondered why she was left unmoved. Immense tender pity washed over her for her youngest sister. It struck Minah again that she did not know her. Esther resembled at that moment nothing more than a shy wild animal observing a person at a fire, flinching from contact even as she was intensely drawn to this other warm body. For in revealing herself, Esther was trying hard to understand her sister. Esther's eagerness for love was indistinguishable from her irresistible curiosity in Minah's otherness, her sister's separate inner life.

Minah began quietly. "Sex with love is different. It's different with Paul—the man I'm seeing now—because I respect him. I know that sounds kind of lame. But it's true, and it's rare for me, at least, to find a man I really respect." She began to falter, as Esther had; she felt the pressure of Esther's attention and compelled herself to continue. "The best part of sex is to feel so close you're overpowered by another person. I don't mean dominated . . ." She didn't know how to clarify those moments when so many threads of desire and doubt were knotted together. "For me, at least. It's different for everyone, you know. I don't want you to end up thinking there's something wrong with you if you have a hard time finding amazing sex with love. A lot of insecure women I know think there's something wrong with them if they don't enjoy sex, or they tell themselves they're enjoying it with someone when they're not, not really. It's easy when you're young not to know what you're feeling."

As she spoke, she was needled by a sense of hypocrisy for repeating the advice she'd received in her twenties, which she'd considered irrelevant to her own experience. For an instant she recognized it—the consummate immersion in her own consciousness, whose nucleus was a place that words could not touch . . . the utterly engrossing sensation of being alive in the world, of being lost in her body, of being with a man she did not want and thought she wanted, and yet still believing that the plain wisdom of this counsel did not apply to her. She had a moment of vertigo at the thought of these words circulating through generations of women as hollow abstractions that took on meaning only when it was too late.

It was Minah's turn to feel embarrassed. She was used to talking about sex with her girlfriends, but Esther's patient, open face made her see her social self as painfully glib. And yet . . . it was refreshing, almost exciting, to be talking about sex and feelings and love with one who, she was certain, loved her deeply and was absorbing all that she said. If she kept talking, if she, too, pushed through something in herself, she might break through something similar with her sister.

"But sometimes I think my greatest pleasure is in feeling like I'm someone else or even something else. Maybe you meant something similar when you said everyone's spiritual and sexual. You'll laugh at me—no, you wouldn't laugh at me—you might just find this weird, but I think I feel most spiritual when I put on makeup or try on new clothes. I love beauty and feminine things, fashion and design and makeup and skin care. People like Sarah think I'm shallow for this. What does she think people want to do after a war? The women want to wear new dresses and paint their walls and give and receive flowers. She doesn't understand there are women who feel elevated and not demeaned by being feminine. It's not that I just want to look better, which does make me feel better. I love to feel that what I wear makes me different. No, not different—but that there's a part of me I didn't know was there before I put on that dress or that lipstick. It's another way of feeling you're not only you . . . or that I've taken something into myself that's changing me. I think women feel more. We can feel winds and colors and moods. It's because we're born lesser, and so we have to take in more of what's outside us. And that's what gives me pleasure. I love hot baths, I love how the steam empties me out and opens me up at the same time. Afterward I want to smell more, taste more, honey and fresh strawberries and mint. All those tastes and colors and smells—they make me feel kinder."

Minah stopped herself. She was disoriented; she hadn't intended to talk so much.

Esther responded enthusiastically. "That reminds me of something from my physics textbook from college. There was a picture of a ram's horn next to a seashell. The same shapes are everywhere in nature. It's physics. And so tree branches really are like veins and capillaries. I wish I could write poetry. Every time I see leafless tree branches in winter I think they're like arteries, veins, capillaries, reaching up to heaven. *The earth spreads under the skin of heaven . . . Heaven encloses the world like skin . . .* I've played with that line in my head for years now. Is that what you mean?"

"Yes! It is. And—you know, I'm just realizing this now—that's why I want to have children. It would be the greatest pleasure of my life to care for them and watch them grow. To *feel* them grow."

Again, Minah was puzzled at how she'd arrived at this remark. A shadow passed over her: the old, dizzying sensation that despite all her conscious wishes and visceral desires she didn't truly know what she wanted or who she was. Esther didn't seem to notice the fleeting shadow, and a darker wave of desolation passed through Minah.

"Do you sometimes feel like you don't know what you're thinking unless you explain your thoughts to someone else? I feel like I'm only understanding something about our family now, talking to you," Esther said excitedly. "All of us in our family, we have a strong appetite for life. We have a strong drive for more life. All of us have this restless spirit. I recognize it in Sarah, too. She wants to know everything. She's depressed now, but I know she'll come back to life. I know she will—she loves learning too much. And now I'm learning more about you. You're already so alive." Esther gave a radiant smile, which Minah tried to reflect back to her. "It's the one thing we all have in common with him. Our father. The more time I spend with him, the more I feel it. Our need, our passion, really, for more life."

Minah was doubly hurt now. "I don't want to think anything we have comes from him. Except our last name, which I will change when I marry."

"But still," Esther said tentatively. "He's a part of us."

"I refuse to believe that," Minah said in a flash. "I have nothing in common with him. I won't believe it. You have nothing in common with him, either. If you do, then part of you is evil and wrong." Minah would not be delicate with Esther if her sister was capable of uttering such a profanity: *He's a part of us.*

Esther parted and closed her lips.

"Esther, why did he call you a whore?"

Esther's eyes sparkled with distress.

"Why? And who's Soojin? What does she have to do with you?"

Esther breathed and swallowed hard. "Soojin is the woman who lived with us when you were in Korea. I mentioned her to you before, but I didn't tell you her name. I called her Sue. She left us after about six months. She left while he was away on one of his trips. He blames me for it. And it's true. I've never admitted this before, but I helped her leave. I gave her the couple thousand in cash he hid in his closet. And then I did use that tuition money to live on. So I have stolen from him."

Esther's obvious anguish incited not sympathy but anger in Minah. "*That's* why he called you a whore? That gives him the right to call you a whore?"

"I didn't say that."

"How can you bear to care for a man like that? How can you respect yourself so little to clean up after that monster?" Minah stood up, her palms pressed into the table. Then, as her anger cooled to distress, she sat down again.

"Whether we love him or hate him, however I feel about him, he's shaped my life. I want to help him. Why is it wrong to help someone, even someone so hateful? How can that be wrong?"

Minah caught the slightest tremor to Esther's words, which nonetheless rang with the clarity of will. They thrilled Minah with desperation. "It's not wrong, it's stupid. Because he's still hurting you. Why can't you see when something's hurting you? I sometimes think you've given up on your life. I do."

Minah saw her sister's eyes begin to shimmer with tears, but she could not hold back—she needed whatever was emerging to impress itself on Esther for good.

"You're being stupid. He's abusing you! You're not a child anymore. Why can't you look after yourself? He ruins everything he touches. He's hurting you. And you're degrading yourself by helping him! Why, why can't you see?" She realized she was standing again.

"Why? I don't know." Esther began to weep, turning her head to the side, inhaling and exhaling forcefully through her mouth. She made no motion to hide or wipe her tears or her snot as both trickled down her face. "Why are you talking like this?" Esther said at last, facing her.

Minah was frozen in place, still leaning over the table. She did not register the meaning of the words. She was stunned and frightened by the sudden intuition of another depth in Esther: unknown suffering and longing and knowledge, a vast foreign ocean in which Minah could neither stand nor orient herself.

Her heart felt like it, too, was frozen, clenched in an icy fist. Only her jaw moved slowly, as if she were trying to speak or scream underwater in a terrible dream. Why was she doing this to Esther? She didn't know.

Esther is someone I love. Someone I have always loved. She was so small when I first loved her. I've loved her longer than I've loved anyone. She is so tender and vulnerable. She is so sweet and strange. I am hurting her. I am hurting the only person I know I've loved.

The thoughts were stark and true, and none elucidated what was taking place in her now; none was commensurate with the rawness of her confused horror.

I am my father's daughter.

At this last, her heart unclenched and began pounding wildly in shame.

"I'm sorry. Esther, I'm sorry," she whispered. She edged close to her sister and touched her shoulder gently, then lowered herself and pressed her face into Esther's shoulder. It was surprisingly easy to give herself up to this gesture.

When Minah brushed her hair away from her own face, she felt her cheek was hot. Her fever had returned.

"I'm sorry. I don't know what came over me. I hate to see him or anyone saying such awful things to you. I'm sorry."

"That's all right," Esther said, her voice thick with the same thickness and wetness that made her snot and her tears. She picked up her napkin and dried her face.

Minah returned to her place. "Listen, I want you to meet Paul. The man I'm seeing. It hasn't been long, but we're very serious. We're talking about getting married. I want you to meet him. Will you do that for me?"

In her spiritual calculus, Minah offered Esther the privilege of this confidence as compensatory self-sacrifice for her cruel outburst. She wanted to be forgiven.

"Yes. Of course." Esther blew her nose and began clearing the table.

Minah prayed again for her sister that night, not on her knees, but in bed, half awake, her head on her pillow. On the eve of their reunion she had prayed for her sister's health and happiness. This time her wishes were more concrete: Lord, let Paul see only the goodness of Esther's heart. Let Esther understand I truly want the best for her and for me. Because Lord, I love her. I love her very much. Give me the strength . . . She ended her prayer, weak and feverish.

She turned out the light. She heard Esther turning on the sofa. *I want to help him. How can that be wrong?* Esther had this in common with Misha: both could turn the simplest statements into distillations of eloquence. "She's well," Misha would say to Minah on the phone. "She's happy." Esther and he possessed good hearts in bodies made both solid and buoyant with love. When they spoke, they spoke with the gravity and lightness of their whole being.

She rummaged in her bedside drawer for the last of her sedative cold medicine. *I will be a mother.* She'd been determined not to repeat the bad patterns of the past, and she'd failed again. She told herself to breathe deeply, to be mindful of her body: her fever, her frustration; the powerful, perhaps insuperable instinct to express her anger, to get it out of herself—to change something in the world with it, even if that change was realized as damage. In the past she'd regularly dismissed promising and self-absorbed ex-boyfriends alike, as well as scattered friends, for venial acts, reacting with disproportionate coldness or white rage. At the moment the passing thoughtlessness always felt monumental, like drops of water torture. After all, was not the lie one told a friend who needed a small favor essentially the same life-denying gesture as the hushed lie one told oneself when turning away from a hurt child? She knew this as well as she knew panic prickling up her spine, her breath trapped in her chest: people—those with whom she did and did not cross paths; people in the abstract who had more power than her—had turned away from her all her life. But now that she was going to have children she wanted to be more positive, more accepting. And she would become who she wanted to be.

She knew she held tremendous anger for her childhood. That was obvious enough. She talked about her anger with select friends, once with an ineffectual therapist, and a few times with her pastor. She told them she wanted to be cleansed of anger, to be clean of the past.

But in her secret heart she held faith in her anger. Because it was baked into her, which was the supreme injustice. Because she wanted to believe she was good, and if her anger was a part of her, wasn't it, too, good? She must believe in her own goodness, her pastor had told her, his voice so gentle and loving she could suppress the misgiving that these two justifications might be at odds. Injustice could not be good.

Her pastor told her she must also forgive, and she resolved to be forgiving; yet when she considered not only the wrongs done to her but those done to people she knew and didn't know—to her sisters, to women and children in places she couldn't locate on a map—she tasted again the nectarine sweetness of anger. It was not possible to be cured of anger in this world. Perhaps she would in the next.

She said a prayer she'd repeated for many nights now, her most soulful prayer, which flowed ceaselessly beneath her waking consciousness. She wanted children who would be a part of her, but they must not, would never, know the taste of anger. Only one badly hurt like herself, damaged like herself, should savor its sweetness.

She decided to take better care of herself; she would stop pushing herself to the point of sickness. She was tired of work. She would leave early tomorrow, if she could, and try to rest and recover once and for all. She was feeling her own body slip away from her, and she needed to remember it and care for it for the children to come.

She fell asleep.

Part 4

CORDELIA: You look terrible.

REGAN: I feel terrible.

CORDELIA: Why?

REGAN: Bad dreams.

CORDELIA: About what?

REGAN: About a filthy-faced woman who said that there'd been a rape. "A rape?" I asked. "When?" And she said, "A few minutes ago. Run!" And just as she said the word "run" another woman wearing a brown wig grabbed me and held me fast with weak fingers. She spoke of the things she would do to me, meditating on the pleasures. As she spoke, her wig would shift and I could see her real hair underneath, which was short and gray and caked with dandruff. She mentioned that there was a dump out back. "It would be a good place to serve you," she said. I knew my body would feel every imaginable horror. I stabbed a sharpened pencil into her hand, and there it stuck. She noticed it not. I said, "I stabbed a pencil into your hand," and she said, "You did, did you? Well, I haven't slept in three days and can't feel a thing." I screamed and struggled, and then woke up. I felt the relief that comes from finding your body safe in bed. And then I remembered that he is in the storm. It is happening to him. He is my father. It is happening to him and it will happen to me. Nothing can stop it.

—Young Jean Lee, *Lear*

1

The octopus

Sarah was preparing to cut Esther's hair.

Esther was sitting in a chair in the middle of the living room where Sarah had lain out newspapers. It was Sarah, eyeing her sister over coffee that morning, who had proposed the cut. Sarah got up on her toes—Esther was at least two inches taller—to examine Esther's scalp, then retrieved a clean towel and pressed it into her arms.

"You have to wash your hair first. You should wash and rinse twice. Your roots are really oily, and there are flakes and specks of dust in there. It's really gross. Wash your hair and leave the conditioner in while you scrub your back. Use my washcloth. It'll help with your bacne."

Sarah was about to advise her to shave her underarms but decided that would be going too far. Dirt and grease and the sour odor of the clothes Esther had worn and slept in at their father's for many days now—these, on the other hand, were nonnegotiable.

"You really need to wash your hair more regularly."

"But you never leave any hot water," Esther said sharply.

Sarah diverted her eyes and murmured an apology. She generally took long hot showers in the evening, and when Esther arrived she'd consciously kept up the habit, even prolonging them, as one of many passive-aggressive ways of telling her sister she didn't want her to stay. But their relationship was becoming a friendship, and she was embarrassed and contrite.

"That's all right," Esther said with a sigh, adding, in a subdued tone, "It's not your fault I usually forget to shower at Dad's. I'm too worried that he'll need me. When I don't show up right away he throws a fit. He's not doing well."

Sarah lowered her eyes. "I need to find the dustpan," she mumbled.

After her shower Esther added a bundle of clothes to Sarah's hamper and borrowed her sweats.

"I feel so much lighter," she said with a faint smile. Her whole figure seemed to exhale relief, but there remained a trace of deep fatigue in the weak curl of her smile.

Sarah tucked a towel around Esther's neck and began trimming the orange-gold split ends that popped like fireflies in the dark auburn mass of hair that had once been a silken cascade of inky black.

"How did your hair get like this?" she asked with an almost affronted tone.

Esther sighed quietly once more; as she exhaled, tender forbearance replaced annoyance. She knew Sarah did not yet know how to express care toward her except roughly.

"It was bleached three times a couple years ago. I don't think it ever recovered. Now that I think of it, it's barely grown since then."

"Why did you bleach it so much? Did you want to be blond?"

"I was staying with a friend, Zoya. Zoya wanted to be a hairdresser. That's what she said back then, but she's training to be a makeup artist now. She asked if she could color my hair. She wanted to make it ash blond. She bleached it three times over a month, and it was a pale ash blond for a while. She asked if she could try other colors, and she did silver and a very dark chocolate brown, then she bleached it again and made it lavender. It looked terrible each time. After that she decided she'd rather be a makeup artist instead. I was supposed to take better care of my hair. Condition it with oils, she said, but I never did that. I just washed it less often."

As she clipped, Sarah was constructing the scaffolding for this story in her mind. "You must have stayed with her a long time."

"About five months. We were both staying with her aunt. Her aunt liked us around."

"Where was this?"

"In South Carolina. Outside Charleston. By Cape Romain."

"Where you called me from."

"Yes." The next moment Esther said, "I wonder what you imagine about my life."

Sarah was alarmed at being perceived—at recognizing in herself at that moment, with Esther, a hard kernel of helplessly stupid disbelief that her sister's recent life was not as conventional as hers; that Esther had not chosen the path of advancement her older sisters were following even now. She tried to hide her stupidity, her lack of imagination, by focusing on the inessential. "No wonder your hair's such a mess. I'm still cutting off the split ends. There are so many I think I should just trim your hair all around shorter a couple inches. Okay?"

She grew absorbed in her task even as she began to mentally elaborate scenes from the period of Esther's life that she still struggled to comprehend. Over the past weeks when Esther was back during Ruby's shifts, Sarah and she had been talking more and more, about how they were feeling that day, what they were doing that week; about themselves and what and how they'd been doing over the last several years. The sleeping vegetable life of Esther's hair flowed through Sarah's fingers like the past itself. By some quiet miracle the past grew less mysterious as she smelled and smoothed and clipped its tips. She saw Esther baking under the sun at an unsheltered bus stop outside Houston. That was where she got her first sunburn. She, Aurelia, and Aurelia's boyfriend, Daniel, later drove down to Corpus Christi for his job interview at a hotel. On their return trip their car broke down. Esther walked a long way to get them food and water as Aurelia and Daniel said they'd wait with the car. But Aurelia was getting jealous; this generous friend turned possessive and petty around her boyfriend, and the couple drove off after getting help from a stranger, leaving Esther stranded until they returned hours later, their mouths greasy from burgers and fries. When Esther recovered from this second, more serious burn, she had freckles for the first time in her life.

Daniel and Aurelia's friends were more upset about Esther's burn than the couple. She left Aurelia and stayed with Nadia—or was it Nadine?—whom she'd met one night on the beach. What were Esther's last words to Aurelia? Sarah wanted to know. She would ask her later. She returned to Esther's travels. Esther followed two of Nadine's friends to the Badlands for a week. They were kind, two skinny teenage boys in love. For that week she was, as she told Sarah, like a timid stray dog, not because they treated her as an inferior; they treated her as someone silent and wounded, and gave her company despite or because of their exuberant love for each other, and she followed them shyly, gratefully, in the pull of this love. The boys went on to Montana without her, and she decided to head east alone after calling Nadine, who put her in touch with Zoya and Zoya's aunt. She traveled in an impromptu zigzag by train and bus, all the way to South Carolina. She imagined the islands off Charleston Nadine had described to her, the soft sand and dolphin-gray waters. She was always eavesdropping on her fellow travelers, she couldn't help it. "Please make those potatoes for me, you know I love them . . ." "They could tell something was wrong. Turns out the poor thing is deaf." Her most searing encounter from the time was with a young woman seated next to her on the bus muttering for the three hours of the trip, her head pressed hard against the window. "I want windows to shatter when I look at them, I can do it, I can make it rain broken glass. If I think hard enough I can make storms flood the streets and wash all the shit away. When men open their mouths to talk to me I'll force all the shit in the world down their throats. When they touch me their fingers will melt off their hands and their dicks will catch on fire. I want to see a woman murdering someone, ripping out his heart, wrapping his intestines around her wrists, sitting on his corpse smeared in blood and crying, I wish I could see this. I want to see it happening, I want to be her . . ."

Alone, Esther was sometimes scared in the motels with their motley keepers and cleaners and guests, who were leering and menacing, barely responsive and half alive, by turns polite and startlingly waspish. Mostly people did not notice her, or barely noticed her presence, or took cynical comfort in her glaring aloneness, as if they could siphon off her allotment of social power for themselves. Though Esther hadn't described her time alone so bleakly, this was what Sarah imagined. Sarah knew what it was to pass through the world alone. She was a diminutive, awkward, physically plain woman. When she ventured into the world, she was simultaneously shocked into lurid self-consciousness and silenced with every casually cruel encounter. Her un-whiteness coated her like a viscid membrane, rendering her at once extra visible as an object and invisible as a person as others tried to pick her up, taunt her, make use of her. Where are you really from? You could at least say something. Do you understand what I'm saying? You could smile.

Sarah inhaled the familiar wafts of fragrance from her shampoo. She tried to follow the thread of goodness that wove in and out of Esther's fragmented narrative. She pictured Nadine looking upon Esther and her burns, seeing her as nothing more than a person with burns in need of a better shelter. There were people who did not see Esther as anything but a human body on its own, and talked to her and gave her extra fries in restaurants and told her to avoid certain streets after dark, sometimes chiding her for traveling alone, other times asking her why she was on her own. Sometimes they talked about themselves for a long time, as if the quality of her silence was a soft, warm wine that helped wash down the pieces of story stuck in their throats like meaty knots of sinew. "I have a daughter who likes to travel like you. But it's not for me. We're different in other ways, too." A few times there was someone who invited her into their circle out of kindness, or out of the same curiosity and longing for otherness that ushered Esther to that bar, late-night diner, hotel buffet, or public park noisy with birthday parties and barbecues, where the glittering greenness of grass in the sun was like a shared dream. Afterward, Esther called or wrote Misha and told him where she was and where she was headed. She told Sarah about the friends she made, some of whom invited here into their homes. People and places were confused in Sarah's mind, but she could not forget the Ecuadorian woman whose son had eloped with a Korean American who wanted to practice talking with Esther before meeting her daughter-in-law. Sarah thought of the woman claiming descent from Scottish rebels whose daughter, adopted from Korea, no longer spoke to her. This woman wanted Esther to tell her what to do. Sarah was at first offended, then haunted by their ignorance. She wanted to ask Esther what she told them, but something pulled her back each time. The answer would become clearer than any words the longer she lived with her sister.

Sarah saw Esther walking in cities with the same backpack she carried to their father's, lingering in restaurants where she was out of place in her jeans and hoodie, ordering roasted peppers and risotto. She spent a good deal of the money intended for her tuition on donations and tickets for music, any kind of music, bluegrass, chamber music, church choirs; for operas, one traveling circus, and plays. They were a way of being with people. Even in the worst performances there was always something salvable: an atmosphere replete with giddy excitement; the touching awkwardness of an inexperienced actor rediscovering their body on the stage; a perfect line conveyed in a warbling voice. *O our lives' sweetness* . . . One had only to watch and listen for it.

Sarah could not remember a time she did not feel shame like a gland excreting the hormones that turned her away from other people. Esther knew shame differently. It did not compel her to withdraw or spurn, judge or hurt. She did not see herself apart. She saw the potential and endurance of shame and pain everywhere. She would never escape it; she would not try. It made her not only more compassionate and patient but bold, so that she did not cower when she was harassed, ignored, stared at for appearing so alone. Shame was the crux of her shameless fearlessness, just as impatience to create something good, to have goodness in her own life, simmered in the flow of her patience with the dull, the irritable and irritating, the spiteful and the cruel.

Esther was at rest stops making a meal of potato chips and doughnuts, drinking out of her thermos and refilling it at drinking fountains studded with chewing gum. She was reading local signboards, asking the waitress for directions, feeding stray cats, walking miles to reach the farmers market for a crisp apple, resting on a bench in the town square as the bells tolled noon. This was Esther in the prime of her youth, unconcerned with her health or her appearance, attuned only to the restless feeling of life within her. No, that wasn't true. Esther wanted to be healthy, to sleep and eat well and for her sister to do the same. Nor was she unconcerned with how she looked. Sarah had caught Esther totally absorbed in her reflection at least twice. Sarah sifted through the dark, uneven strands of Esther's hair for the dead ends, the rare tangles and white hairs. In that seeking, she began to understand the tender tolerance and omnivorous curiosity and quietly propulsive hunger with which Esther attended to people and things like her hair, her face, her sisters, and her father.

Yes. There was an essential hunger in Esther that Sarah was just starting to recognize, a hunger that was like willfulness. It had sent her far from home. It guided her when their father extended his hand from his sick bed and she took it without recoiling, as her sisters did at the very sight of him reaching for their touch. She attracted so little attention herself from a distance, among other people, but when you were alone with her, she wanted to do and be something for you.

She wanted to be as ordinary and creative as light.

She wanted to suffer the weather and be the sun.

Sarah satisfied herself that she'd cut off the split ends, combed Esther's damp hair until it became a sheet of darkness with mahogany ripples, and trimmed all around to make the length as even as possible. They were steeped in intimate silence for so long that Sarah was startled when she herself spoke: "There. It's already shining, your hair. It's finally breathing."

Esther was visibly thrumming with high spirits as she hurriedly packed her backpack. "You're right, it looks so much better now," she said as she glanced in the bathroom mirror one more time.

"When will you be back?" Sarah had a subtle impression of playing a role—a tiny prick of intuition told her that something in her was changing—as she asked this question.

"I don't know. It depends on Edwin's schedule."

"All right. Let me know when you're heading back here. And send me an update. About him."

Let her go to him, Sarah told herself as she locked the door behind Esther.

Minah was waiting for her brother at the deli across from the plaza where he had met Sarah the week before.

She'd called in sick to work the day before and was preparing to leave for her office when, in quick succession, she got a text from Sarah asking if she could give Minah's number to their brother—Minah said yes—and a text from Edwin asking if they could meet. She readily, gleefully called in sick again.

She was losing her once tenacious hold on her job. In the beginning, she'd worked relentlessly, with a ferocity bordering on masochism. She'd had more billable hours than almost every other new associate. She had far fewer hours now and found it hard to care. When she reflected on her indifference, it warmed into gratification that was not unlike the pleasure of stealing as a teenager. It, too, shared in the slippery pleasures of glorious escape and defiant harm.

She had been an associate for years now. She was still young, but she was never going to be promoted to partner. She could feel it in the greetings and small talk exchanged with her colleagues and especially the head of her department. Once enthusiastic, they had atrophied into forced formulas, a double language in which the perfunctory "Hey, how's it going, how's work going, how's the new client?" was to be understood as a sign of disappointment.

When, five years ago, she got the call with the news that the firm wanted her, the man who was now her boss had told her, with a frankness she'd appreciated, "There were other candidates with stronger résumés, more relevant experience. But I was impressed with your interview, and I wanted to give you a chance. The other partners didn't. I like to take risks. You're quick, you're sharp. You present very well. You have a lot further to go than the other candidates. We're excited to see how you're going to grow on our team." In retrospect, she found his attitude paternalistic and the reference to her appearance inappropriate. When he said "Hey, how's it going, how's work?" with a caustic glance at her open-toed shoes, he was telling her she'd let him down. She burned to tell him she didn't care, though the urge belied her own ambivalence. It was in the office that she both cared and suffered most.

She heard rumors—had she heard them, or had she just interpreted random mumblings from here and there?—that they were planning to replace some of the associates with fresh hires from higher-ranked law schools. "You can hire anyone from anywhere these days, high and low," she'd heard one of the partners say.

She had to hold on to her job until she married Paul and got pregnant. He said he wanted her to work. He was a modern man, he said. But he also believed in the bond of a mother and her child, and when the time came—presumably not before then—he would support her preference to stay at home past any maternity leave.

His tender reassurances issued from his confidence in her fiscal and moral integrity. He would not want her if he knew how badly she'd managed her money. Her credit card interest had already eclipsed her monthly payment on her massive student loans. He would deem her irresponsible and even dishonest, certainly a bad role model for her children. Like her boss, he would judge her weaker than she first appeared. Paul took her to exquisite restaurants and bought her jewelry and leather gloves, scented hand cream and perfume, artisanal olive oil and chocolates. But would he understand the desperate urges to console herself with similar purchases during those lonely years when she struggled for her college degree?

Her father's ill-gotten money would make her whole. She was waiting for her brother to make sure that no member of her family would hinder her from having the family she dreamt of daily.

She needed to know, for one, about Edwin's own household. Sarah, stupidly, hadn't bothered to ask. Sarah reported that he'd described himself as a "family man" but hadn't asked him about his wife or any offspring. "I thought it was his way of saying he was going to take care of Dad," she'd said glumly to Minah, to which Minah responded with frenzied disbelief:

"You spend your life reading and writing and you don't understand plain English? Do you know what this means for us? Sweet little grandchildren are a lot more appealing than three fucked-up grown women. Especially if they're boys. You asked Edwin if he was married and he said he was a family man. 'Family man' means he's devoted to his wife and kids."

"Not necessarily," Sarah said with a whiny defensiveness she hoped would conceal her lie.

"Okay, I see your point," Minah forced herself to say. She needed Sarah on her side.

Minah recalled the other week when she reminded her sister that she, Sarah, also needed a lot of money, and very soon, in order to find another place to live. With the same appalling pitch of self-pity Sarah had pleaded, "Don't remind me, I don't want to think about it! I'm not going to think about it right now. I don't need to think about that right now." Exchanges like this persuaded Minah that Sarah was ultimately unreliable. For all her intelligence, there was an aspect of childish helplessness to her, an almost voluptuously self-indulgent powerlessness that warped her common sense and was less tragic than pathetic, precisely because she had given herself up to it.

So it was up to Minah to do what was necessary for her and her sisters. This was what Paul loved best about her: her will.

When Minah saw Edwin for the second time as he approached her table, she noticed as she hadn't before that he was good-looking. He smiled, and his smile was winning.

It was so different from the annoying hand-wringing and solicitous spinelessness he displayed at their father's. "I'm sorry," he kept saying. "I'm so sorry, I don't know what's gotten into him." Which had to be bullshit. She thought, My family is pathetic. Sarah's pathetic, this newfound brother is pathetic. And Esther—Esther was, too, though not because she was weak. She was strong, and with pathetic wrongheadedness she was wasting her time and strength on their brute of a father.

Edwin didn't look weak or hapless now. When he sat down, she was acutely aware of his physical nearness, this unfamiliar being of shared origin. Even if he did not appear or even act similar to her, something within his opaque flesh had to be the same as hers: the sinus congestion, the body odor that changed with alcohol, a taste for pears . . .

"Minah, thanks for meeting me here. Especially . Especially since you must be busy yourself. You're a lawyer, I hear."

"Yes. And you're a doctor."

"That's right. The doctor and the lawyer. Our Korean father should be proud," he said, his smile now warmly ironic.

"He's not. He's not proud of me."

"He's not proud of me, either. Already you and I have a few things in common. We're second-generation overachievers with an unimpressed father. I'm glad at least one of you understands."

She picked up at once on this subtle way of distinguishing her from her sisters to suggest a certain connection. "Understands what?"

"I'm going to get a coffee. Can I get you anything?"

She wanted a coffee, too. When he came back, he was transformed once more, his demeanor almost meekly sincere. He began speaking in a tone of fond familiarity, as if the three-minute break was an ellipsis that compressed and made real the time they might have spent together if they'd learned of each other long ago.

"He seems proud of Sarah. He seems to run hot and cold over Esther. What happened last time was awful. But he accepts her in his way. And I won't insult you by lying, I know your relationship with him is particularly strained. That's what I meant. I'm glad at least one of my three sisters knows what it's like not to have his approval."

Sarah had failed to extract important information from him; she would not be as useless as her. She would not use the same tone of shy candor he was inviting her to share. Simply and directly, she said, "What is your relationship with him like? If it's so strained, why did he secretly arrange to follow you to the East Coast and have you care for him without telling any of us he was even sick for months? It seems like you have not just his approval but his trust."

He smiled yet more warmly, as if he understood and even sympathized with her distrust. He took off his scarf, and she saw the collar of his scrubs under his fleece. "That doesn't mean he's proud of me. And he only trusts me for my medical advice because his first doctor in LA was incompetent, and I found him another who discovered his cancer. After that he decided he didn't trust any doctor I didn't know personally and came out here. He moved all the way here and not too long after we learned he has stage IV prostate cancer. We can probably extend his life, but we can't cure him. All that trouble to learn there's no real hope. And for that I'm pretty sure he's starting to distrust me, or at least resent me."

His expression sobered. Minah felt herself relax a little at this plausible admission of Eugene's frustration. She even felt slightly sorry for her brother.

She glanced down at the table; his hands were around his paper cup, and she saw his wedding ring. In a studied tone of conciliatory thoughtfulness, she said, "Maybe he did it to be closer to Sarah. He's most attached to her, even though she never visits him. Maybe he thought if he was nearby she wouldn't have any more excuses."

"That's true. It wasn't a convenient move, but maybe it helped him, psychologically, to face his illness here." Edwin was annoyed with himself; this same thought had occurred to him before, and he had nonetheless been brash with Sarah. An instinct to treat her as a rival had overpowered him. It was easy to submit to it when Sarah herself was weak, easily overwhelmed by an overbearing man. She, too, had submitted to what came naturally.

"So what's going to happen now?"

Her voice was deep and clear. Her eyes were carefully lined. From the narrow sleeves of her classic navy blazer emerged thin wrists and long fingers with manicured tips. Minah, Edwin thought, had a worldly elegance—and, most likely, worldly ambitions—her sisters entirely lacked.

"They want him on hormone therapy and then both radiation and chemo. The last scan showed a tumor forming in his back and the cancer just beginning to spread to his lungs." He cleared his throat; it was a habit he'd developed at the hospital, a way of saying to the patient's family, Words fail me. "The lungs aren't symptomatic yet. But a tumor in the spine can be excruciatingly painful. And the tumor in his prostate is still growing. But he's resisting the hormone therapy, though that's the first line of treatment." He described their father's maddening changeability, his regular concession to and refusal of treatment. "He'll calm down, and even apologize, and tell me he agrees to the whole treatment plan, only to wake up the next morning and refuse and rage again, accusing me of trying to turn him into a woman—the hormone treatment reduces male hormones and can have feminizing side effects. He refuses chemo because he thinks we'll trick him, inject him with estrogen and call it chemotherapy. He's even suspicious of the painkillers. He knows they're addictive and says he hates junkies and refuses to become one. He says he needs to keep his head clear. He's strong enough—for now—to endure the pain. He's been taking massive amounts of ibuprofen and acetaminophen, but it's not enough for the back pain. Which is already bad." He paused meaningfully. "One thing is clear, though. He needs more care than Esther and I can provide him, but he refuses to hire anyone else, apart from Ruby. And he treats her badly. I think he wants her to quit. He wants her to quit so he can demand more from us. And we're already exhausted, me and Esther."

"Do you have children?" Minah inserted her question bluntly. She was vexed by this mention of Esther. He was an interloper stating in so many words that he was not only a full member of this nuclear family but one of the privileged two caring for their father. It didn't matter that neither Minah nor Sarah wanted to spend any time in Eugene's company; the privilege was in the opportunity to influence the dying man of wealth.

Edwin straightened in his seat. He decided to return to an approach of directness and brevity. "Yes."

"A boy? A girl? Only one, I'm guessing, at your age? By the way, how old are you? If you don't mind my asking."

"A boy. Just one. Born last year. I'm twenty-eight."

"You're divorced, and he's with his mother?"

"Yes."

They looked at each other unabashedly. She hadn't, like him, ever pretended to be meek. She knew he would not pretend to be meek anymore. She knew because she recognized his mind—it was like hers. She knew in the pit of her stomach and by the army of nerves on the surface of her skin that their bodies were related; and they both knew a more profound, electric likeness lived in the mysterious collusion of matter and mind.

It was in acknowledgment of this mutual recognition that Edwin volunteered to make himself vulnerable. "His name is Christopher. Our father doesn't know about him."

"You don't want him to know?"

"Not now. Because of the divorce. He wouldn't approve. You know he's a hypocrite," he said with a low snarl of resentment.

He was admitting, at last, that her suspicions were true. He and she were alike not only in the way they were made and the way that they thought, but in what they were trying to acquire for themselves.

"He'll never fully approve of me because I'm illegitimate. It means something to him, marriage and legitimacy. As it does to a lot of hypocrites."

"I'm practically illegitimate in his eyes. He might have told you about my mother. Who isn't Esther and Sarah's mother."

"Yes. I figured that out from his ramblings. But he was married to her."

This might be the moment to pose the question she'd prepared even before agreeing to a meeting. "Do you feel like he's a father to you? I know he's your biological father. But do you feel that you're his son in every sense?"

"I'm not sure how to answer that. Do you feel like you're his daughter in every sense?"

"Yes."

He hadn't expected this answer. They fell silent again and exchanged another long look.

She felt as if she were in a movie, in a scene where you expected the characters, seated across from each other as she and Edwin were, to fall in love or expose a momentous secret. The longer they were together, the more you could feel the sheer cumulative weight of your anticipation exerting pressure on the screen. The revelation might be a cliché, but it was always satisfying nonetheless. Who didn't want to fall in love, to have their deepest selves at last revealed; to be changed, to be saved? By virtue of the unnerving, exhilarating presence so close to you, your self-consciousness became a shared consciousness. You were compelled to tell the truth, which no longer seemed quite obvious, because the truth grew stranger and more oblique the longer you remained in the presence of this other.

This must be why, Minah thought, Sarah read so many novels.

"In law school," Minah said, "we read a case about child visitation rights that went all the way to the Supreme Court. A man, I'll call him Michael, had an affair with a married woman, say Mary, living with her husband, Joe something. After Mary gave birth to a girl, she left her husband and moved in with Michael. Michael raised the girl, he was her father, for three years. A paternity test later proved that Michael was also the girl's biological father. Mary and Michael split up, and she moved back in with Joe, whom she'd never actually divorced. Joe didn't want Michael around. He didn't want Michael to see the little girl anymore. So Michael sued. He was suing to have the right to visit his own daughter, a girl he'd raised for three years."

"Am I supposed to guess the outcome?"

"You can."

"He was denied the right."

"Yes."

"Because he wasn't married to Mary, the mother."

"Yes. A man on the court, Scalia, wrote the ruling that basically declared legal paternity sacrosanct in our society. It supersedes the raw tribalism of biological paternity. Most importantly, a child can only have one father and one mother."

"Do you agree with the outcome?"

"No. No, I don't. A parent is the one who raised you. I don't consider my biological mother my mother. I don't remember her. Esther and Sarah's mother raised me."

"You're saying your father is not really my father."

"I'm saying that paternity is not as straightforward as one might think."

"Is that little girl illegitimate, according to the law?"

"No. Because her mother remained married, even when she was living with another man."

"And according to you?"

"I wanted more than anything, when I was a kid, to learn that my father was not my father. I couldn't stand to be his progeny. His genes were like a disease. I could leave home, but I carried his disease with me. I even fantasized about being white, having normal white parents and friends and boyfriends. But the white people I met before I started high school let me down. Some were mean and selfish, some were nice, but even the nice ones didn't understand anything I tried to tell them about myself. I also hung out with the mean kids, I felt some solidarity with them. But they turned on me again and again, the Korean girl, because they needed to feel superior to someone else. Finally I started leaving my neighborhood for high school and I met other Asians, a lot of them also unhappy, but funny, sympathetic, smart. They understood me. They were humane. Most of them, at least. And I realized that some of the Asian kids I hated in elementary school were just as unhappy as me. Well, almost." She smiled ironically. "So I knew being Korean wasn't bad in itself. I learned that Koreans are people, too. Isn't that amazing? It's amazing how much racism I'd internalized. So much self-loathing. That's why I went to Korea after high school, to stop hating myself and learn more about myself. I learned to speak Korean. I learned more about my family. But I still wanted more than anything not to be his child.

"On the day we discussed that Supreme Court case in class, there was a visiting scholar who said that a psychologist testified against Michael. He said a child would grow up confused with two fathers. She'd receive mixed messages because there should only be one man to tell her what to do. It's what psychologists call the 'law of the father.' It doesn't matter who your biological father is. What matters is which man has power over you. The one who judges you and punishes you. That's not the way he put it, but that's what he meant. Since then I've made an uneasy peace with the fact that my father is my father. According to the law, he is my father."

He suppressed the urge to ask, Why are you telling me this? What are you trying to say? He was surprised by how moved he was by her recollection, but he was suspicious of his sympathy. He was intrigued and confused. He perceived in her a sincere desire to share something deeply personal with him, to touch him and create a bond, as well as another intention to use the power of intimacy to her advantage.

"White people aren't all that bad. And a lot of them have pretty fucked-up families, too. You must have grown up in a nice neighborhood. My neighbors weren't white." He shrugged and grinned. "But what do you think we should do about his care—your legal father, my biological father, that is."

"Whatever he wants to do. It's his prerogative. You and his doctors have already laid out the facts of his prognosis for him."

"All right. But I'm not talking about his medical treatment. I'm talking about his day-to-day or, really, hourly care. Because he shouldn't be alone. He gets lightheaded and has trouble walking sometimes because of the back pain. I've been helping him go to the bathroom. But I can't keep up this schedule," he said calmly. "I've been spending maybe fifty or more hours with him a week. That does include nights when I've been sleeping, but you don't sleep well when he's in the next room. Esther's been there about fifty hours a week herself lately. It's not something we can keep up."

Minah smiled darkly at her brother's move. "As you know, our father and I don't get along. I've visited him twice since his move and both times he told me never to return."

"He says that to Esther, too, you know."

"He means it with me. Otherwise I would gladly lighten Esther's burden. And yours. Sarah will be done with her teaching soon, so I expect she'll do her part during her winter break. But there's not much I can do right now for him. I know that lets me off the hook. And I know this is easy to say, but I wish, I really wish, I were in a position to help a father I loved. The only thing I can suggest is that you and Esther and Sarah hire extra help, with or without his permission. If you offer enough money you'll find someone willing to put up with even him. And we both know he has the money."

There was no other practical matter to discuss. There was nothing else to say, now that she had said the unsayable. But neither wanted to leave, not yet.

Edwin said, "Sometimes I think personalities began as experiments. An evolutionary experiment. Dogs, rats, even octopuses have personalities. Even a creature with three hearts and blue blood can be shy, bold, social, aggressive, curious . . . Why should people, let alone animals, have such different personalities? I think it's because you never know which qualities will end up saving your life. Nature favors the bold if they don't die from hurling themselves into battle or trying poisonous fruits. The timid homebodies will survive longer as long as they find an adequate source of vitamin D, but even then they need to find a mate."

She raised her eyebrows quizzically.

"I've met all three of my sisters now and talked to each of you. You're all quite different. Sometimes you wonder why nature made some siblings so different."

"How are we different?" The question escaped her. She was annoyed with herself for letting him know she wanted to know what he thought of them, of her.

"The main difference between Sarah and Esther—for me, in my limited experience with them—is that Esther speaks her mind and Sarah doesn't."

"With me Sarah speaks pretty freely. She has no problem criticizing me," Minah said with an affected hint of boastful nonchalance: she, too, found the times Sarah clearly left thoughts unsaid irritating or unsettling.

"With you, sure. But she's also pretty guarded. She was with me. She's polite but not forthcoming. Whereas Esther, I thought it would be hard to talk to her, but it wasn't at all. I felt sort of awkward meeting her the way I did, by accident, at your dad's—our dad's—place, but she has a way of making you trust her. Trust her, but without feeling entirely at ease. Do you know what I mean?"

"Yes. Yes, I do."

"I find myself talking about octopuses with you, but I don't know whether to trust you. Why is that?"

Minah pursed her lips slightly. "I can't tell you whether or not to trust me. I could, but it wouldn't mean anything. You'll have to judge for yourself. And I can't say why you don't feel you can trust me."

"We've been honest with each for the past hour. You really don't know?"

"How can I know what of everything I've said or done, consciously or not, has had that effect on you?"

"It's simple. You don't trust me. You don't want to let me into your family. You might like me personally, but that's not enough for you."

She raised her brow.

"I want you to meet my son one day. You're his aunt by blood."

She broke her steady reciprocal gaze to gulp down her cold coffee.

"You asked me whether I really feel like his son. I really feel like your brother, your family. Already. If you asked me to do something for you, I'd do it. Because we're family."

"It's easy to speak hypothetically about favors in the abstract," she said with the same forceful rapidity with which she tried to intimidate her legal opponents. After a moment she said, "I'm sorry. That was rude."

He made an impromptu calculation. It was best to end it now, to highlight the contrast between her suspicion and his professed dedication to his sisters. "I should get to work now." He gently cupped her wrist. "I'm glad we met, Minah."

From within the deli, she watched his back as he jaywalked and rushed to the hospital.

Edwin found his twenty-hour shift passed by more quickly than usual. The excitement of his meeting with Minah had carried over into his work, giving him confidence when he was with patients, occupying his mind when he was filling out paperwork and washing his hands.

When he emerged from the hospital, exhaustion hit him all at once. A sense of bleakness flooded his depleted system.

He stepped out to the corner to hail a cab and froze. Why hadn't he realized what Minah was telling him? *According to the law, he is my father.*

When their father was dead, the law would be on her side. She and her sisters would inherit everything.

But his father had a will. Hadn't he been talking of changing it? "*They do nothing for me. Why I give them money?*" Eugene had yet to openly consider leaving his son anything. When he mentioned his wealth to Edwin, he did so with a knowing grin. He would sigh and say, "*But who know? Maybe I give them. Maybe Esther, she helps me. Sarah, she is busy now. She will help. Maybe. We will see.*" He studied his son with laughing eyes, baiting him to lapse from his role of filial devotion and betray the crass core of his motives. Edwin never did. But he was exhausted, he was growing desperate. During his last visit to his father's he had rested his forehead against the front door for five minutes, more, before entering.

He was still standing in place at the intersection. A cab slowed down at the corner and sped on. A woman paused at the sight of him. Then, as she took in his sculpted face and broad shoulders, she dropped her initial curiosity in his mysterious absorption and looked him over again, this time appraisingly. She moved on.

He laughed out loud. Minah was afraid: either their father didn't have a will, or he had one in which she was cut out. She might not be close to her sisters, but there was no trace of mistrust in her attitude toward them. The tension was between her and him.

So it was possible there was no will, and their father's references to money was a sign that he was preparing to draw one up soon.

If Minah, as a lawyer, knew beyond a shadow of doubt he had no claim to their father's fortune, she would have told him so plainly, no doubt with great satisfaction. Instead, she'd tried to intimidate him with her knowledge of the law. And he had learned that paternity was "not as straightforward" as one might think.

He didn't fall into bed when he got home. He emailed a friendly colleague at the hospital who was engaged to a lawyer and asked her for her fiancé's number.

2
The cell

The three sisters were eating dinner with their father at his apartment. He had decided the seating: Sarah would sit across from him, Esther to his right, with easy access to the kitchen, and Minah to the left, nearly trapped between the wall and table. The two empty chairs were wedged between Sarah and Esther, and Sarah and Minah.

He was subdued today, saying little, neither shouting nor swearing or even grunting or glowering. He addressed Sarah exclusively. He cast quick glances now and then at her sisters, mostly indifferent, slightly annoyed, as if they were strangers at the next table in a crowded restaurant. Otherwise he focused solely on his food and on Sarah.

He was wearing a blue button-down shirt and the dark polyester slacks he wore daily when he was healthy and had put on for the occasion. They were wrinkled; Esther would later tell them Edwin had helped him get dressed the night before, and he'd slept and lain in bed in his good clothes for nearly a full day. He spoke very slowly in Korean, careful to use only words he thought Sarah would understand. He spoke gently, as if to a small child, though she could not recall him speaking to her in the same tone during her childhood.

It was probably because he had finally started radiation. He was, at last, feeling thoroughly weak in both body and spirit.

"Do you remember when your mother used to make this soup for you on your birthday? It's a tradition. An important Korean tradition. You have it on your birthday and when you have a baby, because it's good for new mothers. Remember that when you have your own children. There's no real reason for us to have it now, except that I was thinking of you on your first birthday. Or maybe it was your third, my memory's getting confused these days. No, it was your first. For a long time whenever we gave you something new to eat you made such an unhappy face. And you were always spitting up your food. You were so small. I was so worried you weren't growing quickly.

"But then, one day, on your birthday, you had a sip of this soup, and you opened your eyes wide, like this"—he raised his eyebrows comically high—"as if you couldn't believe such deliciousness was possible. You stretched out your arms and even your little fingers out like this." He extended a grasping hand toward her, from which she reflexively withdrew, though the table was wide between them. "You reached for the bowl and cried because you wanted more. We were both laughing, your mother and I. I told your mother to step aside, and I spoon-fed you an entire bowl myself."

He had called Sarah importuning her to bring seaweed soup from the best Korean take-out restaurant she knew, along with anything else she might want, for dinner. "To eat together, *like family*," he said. He would reimburse her in cash.

"Okay. I'll come," Sarah said tonelessly. "Do you want Esther and Minah to come?"

"*Only if you want. But you must come. I know you busy-busy all the time, but you must come.*"

He dissolved into a weak but steady trickle of thanks and praise for her good heart. Then, with more self-pity than anger, he accused her of abandoning him to Esther, who was a simpleton, and to Edwin, who only pretended to have patience and love for his dying father.

"*Only you help me,*" he said. He released a sob and hung up.

He could not mean what he said in English; she had not visited since he announced to her and her sisters that he was dying. He meant: Only you can help me as I need. I want your help only. His voice was nakedly fearful and aggrieved. She bit her lip hard. His pitiful gratitude, his weakness, and even his suffering were like tentacles squeezing and probing to find a way to her heart.

It was only the second time she'd answered his call since his move to be closer to her. The first time, she found herself picking up as if mesmerized when she saw his number appear. She had just met her brother. Family life was changing: it was an albatross, and now the albatross was part of a story that might be a mystery. But his rants about Ruby and his doctors merely returned her to the sordid banality of his reality. There was no mystery to the fact that her gross father had slept with women like Sue and had another child who'd inherited his creepiness. Thereafter she generally ignored his calls and deleted the messages he left several times a week and called him only on Thursdays, at home after her last class, with a vodka tonic at hand. If he had something important to say before then, she would learn through Esther.

She'd answered his call this time because she'd had a vivid nightmare about him. Again, she picked up as if in thrall to a greater imperative. She wanted to understand the meaning of her dream.

In it she found herself in an unknown room with her father. He was grinning at her from the bed, his nakedness only partly concealed by the sheets. When she looked down, she, too, was naked. In looking at her own nakedness, she knew that this had begun a long time ago. But what was *this*? It might have been initiated with violence, but in the dream she had no memory of any physical violence or even physical contact. She was certain only that she was forced to be completely naked before him while he remained minimally, crucially concealed. When he was covered, he remained more powerful, more human than her; yet somehow the threat of exposing himself also granted him more power. This was not the violation of unwanted penetration or touch. It was nakedness she was forced to reveal. Yet there was no revelation.

In the dream she tried to remember when, in the ancient history of her childhood, she had been appallingly passive enough to submit her body to him. In submission she had been complicit in the voiding of her own personhood to become an extension of him. Returning his gaze from the bed, she knew he had done this to Esther, too. When she began screaming, it was at the thought that he had done this—he was doing this—to Esther.

She woke from the vivid black-and-white dream less distraught than stunned.

She tried to analyze the dream.

The therapist she missed once asked her bluntly if he had violated her. And her being was flooded with the sickeningly sweet certainty that he hadn't, the sweetness cut with the horror of having to contemplate the subject at all. Had he ever touched her, he would have destroyed her utterly. She wasn't strong as some survivors were. She would never have pursued a challenging career, or tried to build a life with a lover, or retained the instinct to protect her body from harm. Even her egregious sense of injury would not permit her to conceive of herself as a victim of the most invasive bodily violation.

But she did not have to have been touched or raped by her father to know the pleasure he took in holding power over women. It was true what people said: sex is everywhere, even where it isn't. He had always wanted consummate control of her. He wanted her broken before him, and she was. As a child, and even now. And so she was still caught in the matrix of his lust.

She knew she was not complicit in his abuse. What irrational part of her thought that she was, and why? That was the damaged part of her speaking.

It was the part that made her an extension of him, even if he had never touched her.

His love, what he presented as love, was in fact another form of a lifelong desire to use her, shame her—to feel alive at her expense. His tenderness reached her as an obscene transgression. It boiled in her stomach like bad wine.

Her most consuming longing was to be purified of him.

Over dinner she had struggled to make herself swallow most of the broth, to chew most of the seaweed, to refuse the instinctive connection her body made between the good, warm, fragrant meal and her father's body and grasping love. She refused it, and yet the awful connection asserted itself. As he imitated her infantile delight, her innocent wonder and joy—revived, transposed—became his tenderness, and his tenderness was continuous with the horror she felt as she lifted, then lowered her spoon.

After dinner, to Sarah's profound relief, their father asked Esther to accompany him back to his room. His back pain was making it difficult to walk, and since he refused to use his walker, he required someone to lean on.

Esther was used to helping him and knew how to do it. But Sarah knew he hadn't asked her because she didn't want to offer her support. She knew he knew; she also knew he wanted, today, to accommodate her.

When Esther returned from his bedroom, she asked Sarah to return the next morning. "Edwin can't come until Thursday, and Ruby's not working here anymore," Esther said. Her eyes were lowered. "The agency is sending a replacement on Monday."

Sarah didn't ask Esther why Ruby wasn't returning.

When Esther looked up, her face gave Sarah a jolt. Sarah had never perceived a grain of bitterness in Esther before. She had seen melancholy, frustration, and fear in her face, but not bitterness. Esther was sensitive but resilient, like a child; she was pure, an innocent who was supposed to wake each morning renewed.

"I'll be back tomorrow morning," Sarah said. "I'll pack some things so I can stay for a few days. Until Monday."

"Okay," Esther said faintly. She turned to spend another night in the second bedroom.

Minah and Sarah left together. They were silent going down the hall and taking the elevator and waiting for their respective ride shares. Sarah felt that something was happening to them. Something had changed with the dinner.

They complained of the cold and asked each other about their work. Sarah admitted that she was technically on winter break. "But I have to finish grading final papers and assign grades," she emphasized, "which is actually hard to do."

She wanted to defend herself from Minah's anticipated charges of neglecting the problem of the will. But Minah simply said, "Please remember."

On the train Sarah kept thinking of Esther's expression, though she tried not to. It was cold on the train; she had to keep her overcoat on. The car was so quiet she was surprised to hear the conductor ask someone to remove their feet from the seat. Everyone was falling asleep. She had thought she was alone.

It was bitterness, or at least the beginning of bitterness and not just fatigue, she read on Esther's face. It resembled fatigue because it was bitterness without rancor, a bitterness like a weighted blanket that made you want to sleep.

How long had it been now? Sarah was ashamed to realize Esther had devoted herself to their father for months now. Not weeks, as she kept thinking. When Sarah and Esther overlapped at Sarah's, usually for a few hours in the late afternoon, Sarah asked how their father was, not out of compassion but out of fear she would be required to do something for him soon. She'd stopped telling Esther to limit her time with him, and not only because Esther was committed to his care. She was only too relieved not to do what Esther was willing to do and too eager to put what she did out of her mind.

When Sarah discovered Russian novels in her youth, she'd told herself that suffering would make her better because it would make her wiser. But even Esther, who was already better than her, could not tolerate caring for their father for so long.

And yet, life produced beautiful novels and philosophy and art; survivors who, defying her imagination, became brilliant teachers, activists, resilient mothers; Esther as she was the evening they talked confidentially for so long, an evening that Sarah stored like a gem in the vault of her mind. Suffering could lead to wisdom and grace; it could bear fruit. But the fruit ripened and rotted in the blink of an eye. The fruits of suffering withered from long suffering.

At her father's apartment the next morning she found Esther drinking tea and toasting bread for her daily peanut butter topped with strawberry jam. Their father was sleeping. She was wearing leggings Sarah had forgotten about and an expensive-looking cashmere sweater Minah had given her.

"He slept through most of the night," Esther said. "But I had trouble sleeping anyway. I don't know why."

Sarah volunteered to take over for the rest of the day. She would work in the other room until he woke up.

She sat on the lower bunk with her back to the wall. She had three dozen papers to mark and grade. She swore she wouldn't spend more than fifteen minutes on each; she'd lost her job, and her work didn't matter anymore. But she ended up challenging interpretations, marking infelicities, and suggesting new lines of thought for much longer. She found it irresistible, the chance to argue and critique, as if she were unveiling another text between the lines of the original. In the cases of weak essays, it was the truer text.

She'd finished with just one paper when Esther entered and said, "That's the bed Edwin usually sleeps in." Esther climbed into the other twin bed, Sarah's own childhood bed. "I'm going to try to sleep."

She told Sarah to give him his oxycodone if he asked for it. The medication was new, intended for the breakthrough back pain that resisted the prescription doses of ibuprofen and acetaminophen he took regularly. A voracious tumor was pressing against his spine. Surprisingly, he rarely requested it.

Esther said faintly, "He's finally agreed to the hormone treatment. He doesn't seem to be in denial anymore." Her voice quavered a little. She turned on her side, away from Sarah. "He's not trying to be defiant anymore. He's agreed. But we'll see. I don't know . . ."

A thought pricked Sarah: her indifference to their father's health was affecting Esther. Sarah's fiercely maintained distance between herself and their father was, in unseen ways, making Esther's efforts to care for him more difficult, as if Esther herself had to surmount that bitter distance each time she reached out to him.

It wasn't long before Esther's breathing deepened in a solid rhythm.

She took her computer to work in the living room. She stared out the window, onto the empty dirt acres where plastic bags drifted like dire, dazed seabirds.

She heard her father calling for Esther. She hesitated, then went to her father herself.

"Ah, *you here*," he said softly. He switched to Korean. "Where's Esther?"

"She's sleeping."

"Ah." He closed his eyes, breathing shallowly through his mouth.

"Do you need something? I heard you calling for Esther."

"What? No, I don't need anything. I just didn't know where Esther was. I thought I heard her leaving."

"No. She's just sleeping now."

"Ah, *okay*."

She remained standing, watching him as he lay breathing through his mouth, occasionally licking his lips, white with dead skin. What was so remarkable or awful about him now? He was weak. He was an old man dying of a common disease. He loomed in her memory and imagination as a singularly terrible figure. Now, before her eyes, neither a memory nor a phantasm, he existed as a failing body. He was passing from the realm of emotion, where dimensions were always grand, to the cold diminishment of the ordinary, the real. He couldn't hurt her as he'd hurt her before.

At this thought, she smiled to herself.

Her father stirred. She took an involuntary step back.

"Come here," he said, indicating the chair drawn up to the bed.

She pulled the chair farther back and sat down.

"Give me your hand." He extended his right arm.

She hesitated, then slowly moved her hand toward his outstretched palm. She gasped when he seized her wrist with his right hand, pulled her closer to him, and swung his left over his side to press it against the hand in his grip, palm to palm.

"See?" he said. "Our hands are the same. That's because we are the same."

He was holding her wrist with his damaged right hand to press her own against his unscarred left palm. He overturned her palm and held it beside his left.

She knew his eyes were searching for her eyes, but she kept them fixed on the sight of their hands. The longer she stared, the more harmless and uncanny they seemed, the palms round like sand dollars, the fingers like the thick arms of starfish.

"I see your mother in you. I loved her very much. All the good things I felt, all the best feelings I had, I felt through her. She taught me love. I haven't been the same since she died.

"I see myself in you, too. I always have, since you were a child. I wanted a boy, of course. I wanted one very badly. But when you were born, I wasn't disappointed the way I was with Minah or Esther when they were born. I didn't feel much for them. I don't know why. But I did with you. Because when I saw you, I knew right away you were my child. I didn't feel that with them. That's why it didn't matter to me, in the end, that you were a girl. You don't understand because you don't have children yet. It's not true that all children are the same. You were my child. You were just as good as a boy. You always have been. You were like me, and you were like your mother, and I loved your mother. I wanted Esther to be the same, but she isn't. Only you."

Her discomfort, her disgust, was suspended. She was spellbound and struggling to resist. She felt as she had when he called her to ask her for a special dinner, and as she used to feel when Esther was still a child and called her during her years at boarding school to say hello and prattle about this and that. Sarah answered not to hear what her father or her sister had to tell her or even to learn how they were. She wanted to see how she would feel. On those calls, upon hearing the first syllables of that voice, her organism would light up with pain, with fear, with tenderness and fear, with the kind of vital stress that clarified the flotsam of her subjectivity. She wanted that clarity to burn her confusion, her doubts, her bad faith, away.

She was very good at distorting what she didn't want to admit and denying what she didn't want to confront. And yet a part of her was ever drawn to the siren song of annihilating knowledge, of self-knowledge that could sunder the foundations of what you are. It was truth and not mendacity that was eerie and dangerous. Lies and especially evasions, small and great, were what kept her afloat and adrift. The mysterious choice was to approach the abyss, to be wholly vulnerable and alone, as she felt, for a single instant, before she heard the voice of her father, of her sister.

It was he who first pulled his hand away. He was tired and could not keep it raised any longer.

"Did your mother ever tell you I was sick when she was pregnant with you? No, she couldn't have told you. You were too young when she died. Before you, there was another baby that died. I didn't get sick when she was pregnant with the first baby the way I did when she was carrying you. Every day, for one, two months, I threw up. I went to the doctor, who told me that sometimes a father can get the same sickness as their wives, at the same time. It's rare, but it happens. That was how deep my feeling was for you. I still feel it."

As if his love were asserting itself as stronger than its vessel, he began to cough uncontrollably. He turned onto his other side, away from her, wheezing, coughing, hacking.

He turned back and reached for her hand again, and noticed her hesitation before offering it. "*It's okay, it's okay. You don't want. I understand. But I want tell you now what is very important. You must understand. I change . . .*" She did not understand the word, which he said in Korean. "*I change it. You and Minah and Esther, you are together. I don't want people say I am bad daddy. But now—who care? I die.*" His tone darkened. "*So I change it. You are three my children and Edwin, but you are not the same. I know. I am not a bad daddy. You remember what I say now. Edwin comes tonight. You come back tomorrow noontime. You go now, okay?*"

He settled onto his back and closed his eyes.

Sarah entered the second bedroom and sat on the lower bunk, gazing at Esther's sleeping form. She felt dazed. When Esther stirred and spoke from the depths of her quilt, she gasped as she had at her father's touch.

"Do you remember Sue? The woman who used to live with me and Dad?"

"Yes. Barely. Why?"

"She left not long after you met her."

Sarah waited for Esther to continue. She blinked hard and shook her head lightly, to try to break out of her strange mood. "What about her?"

"I helped her leave when Dad was on one of his trips. I gave her money to leave. A lot. From the cash he always had stashed in his closet. She didn't have any money."

"Or so she said. She was a gold digger. Why else would she be with him?"

"Sure. She admitted it. She also said he was fun. But he never gave her cash. He gave her things. And she was getting unhappy and wanted to leave.

Do you think it was wrong to give her the money?" Her voice was rich with anguish.

"No. If she wanted to leave, I'm glad you helped her."

Esther raised herself to a sitting position, gazing ahead as if she hadn't heard Sarah. "In the beginning she was very affectionate with me. She called me little sister. *Dongsang.* You know that after you left Eugene started spending a lot of time away from home. So Sue and I ended up spending a lot of time together. We cooked and ate together and watched TV. We also spent a lot of time cleaning. Eugene ordered her to clean the entire house on her own, but I helped her. She'd say, 'I only see the spots in the mirror because you show me,' and laugh and smile at her reflection. She was very cheerful, on the whole. She liked being herself. We'd scrub the stove, and she'd talk about things she found beautiful or imagined to be beautiful, like a dress she saw on an actress or a pair of shoes. Paris, Hawaii, colorful birds. I taught her the word 'toucan.' She sometimes sang a tune she made up: *Toucan, you can, who can?* She could be really idiotic.

"She liked to pat my cheeks and call me 'sweetie.' One day she told me a story of how she lost a precious pair of earrings. She said each was a beautiful sparkling diamond encircled by tiny sapphires. We were cleaning the bathroom, and she blew onto the mirror and drew the diamond with her forefinger and used her long pinkie nail to draw the tiny blue studs.

"She said she was stopped on her way to work by a white cop for no reason. She couldn't find her license, and so the cop arrested her. When she got to the station she kept crying hysterically. The cop got really mad and accused her of being drunk. Then she slapped him. He said, 'I'm taking you in. Your life is over.' At the jail she was sent to a closet with a female cop and ordered to strip. She didn't care about the cheap dress she was wearing for work, but she was already worried about her earrings. They were a parting gift from her mother when she left Korea. The cop took them and put them in her pocket, then put on plastic gloves. She stuck her hands into her vagina and forced her to bend over and spread her cheeks. 'To check for more trea-

232 / MAUREEN SUN

sure,' Sue told me she said. Afterward she was left in a cell with a dozen other miserable women. She was there for three days before they released her without explanation. She didn't say all this in her own words, but she tried to say something like it. She gestured to her genitals and cried."

"Oh my god. That's—"

"It was a lie. She was never arrested. Something like that happened to one of the other waitresses where she was working when she met Dad. One day when she was ranting about how much she hated working with them, Dad said, 'They picked on you because they're not as pretty as you. And don't get mad at Yooyoung. Poor girl, she's not right in the head after what happened to her with the police.' I asked him what happened to her, and in broad strokes he told me the same story, without the most graphic details. Except he said Yooyoung was arrested because of mistaken identity. A woman with her name was wanted for fraud. The way Sue looked at me, I knew Yooyoung had confided in her and told her everything. She considered me an enemy after that day. She yanked my hair so hard it hurt to straighten my neck. Once when I was in my room she put a chair under the doorknob so I wouldn't know where or how long she'd been gone while Dad was away. I bunched up my sheets to pee on, I didn't know what else to do. She didn't understand I wouldn't tell him. She couldn't understand that people weren't all like her. Instead of patting my cheek, she started pinching them so hard she left bruises.

"I've thought of her so often over the years. I try to understand her and her lies. Why did I give her the money? Dad knows something happened between me and Sue. He's been asking me why I sent her away. He says she was basically a dumb whore, a slut—I know the word now in Korean. It's almost as if he feels protective of her now. He said when he met her she was sharing a tiny room with two other restaurant workers who hated her. So where did I expect her to go? Did I feel threatened by her? Did I see myself in her? His words were: '*You don't like her? You, you are like her.*'"

"What did you do when she pinched your cheeks?"

"I told her to stop," Esther said, her features bunched in bemusement. She finally turned to face her sister. "What else?"

"Oh."

"When he insulted me before I didn't feel it the same way. I was strong. Stronger. I knew what I was doing, caring for him, and I wanted to do it. But it hurts me now. I would rather care for a stranger."

"I know what you mean."

Esther continued to speak urgently, with rising anguish. "When I was traveling I went to churches sometimes. I was lonely and I didn't have anything else to do. They always talked about loving your neighbor. Love your neighbor as you love yourself. But I didn't love myself. How could I love myself in the way they meant? I cared about myself, but I didn't know myself. I don't know what I'm capable of. Why am I strong sometimes and not others? I don't know every corner of my soul. I don't always know what my body is doing. I don't know my neighbors, either. Have you ever talked to anyone here? Sometimes in the elevator I see this sad man who seems to work night shifts. When he gets near me what looked like sadness feels more like anger. Toward me. But what do I know about him? He's a stranger to me. You, too. You and Minah. Sometimes I think I've reached you, but often I don't know. Or I'm wrong. Parts of you will always be mysterious to me, even though I love you more than I love myself. Do you think that's what it really means? The commandment?"

Sarah had never seen Esther so overwrought. She racked her memory, and the only images that came to her were of Esther throwing a tantrum as a child. "Mean what? I don't understand. I think it means to care for others as you care for yourself. Love in the Bible can be either *caritas* or—"

"Does it really mean love even those who are strangers to you, just as you are unknown to yourself? And those you love can be unknown to you?"

"I don't know. I'll think about it. But I can't say." Sarah felt her heart pounding.

Esther touched her cheek with the flat of her hand. "My face feels hot," she said quietly. Her eyes were shining.

234 / MAUREEN SUN

"Are you feeling sick?" Sarah tried to sound gentle. She wanted Esther to be as she herself knew her: gracious, perceptive, and, yes, strong. Esther was solid like a tuning fork that could nonetheless transmit something other-worldly with a touch. With that touch, she could produce an ethereal note that was consonant with what was inside Sarah. With the kindness of her silences and the hair she left in the shower, the freshness and force of her words and the small details of her housekeeping—the apples in a bowl on the table, the mirror wiped clear for the first time in months—Esther made Sarah feel real. Sarah was beginning to feel like a real, compelling body amid real people and things—if she touched them, they would move; she would give them life. She was just beginning to sense the possibilities of her life.

Sarah did not want Esther to drift away from her, to be as strange and otherworldly as Sarah had once imagined her. Now here Esther was ranting about neighbors and her sisters as strangers. She did not want Esther to suffer. The thought of Esther growing apart and being alone and suffering made Sarah desperate. For the first time in her life, she was possessed by the certainty that she loved her younger sister. The conviction made her weak with panic.

"No," Esther said. "I'm just feeling . . . Do you ever try so hard to stay up you can't sleep? That's how I've felt, on and off, for days now."

"Let me make you some tea."

Esther didn't seem to hear her. "Will you stay here with Dad until the new aide comes on Monday? Will you do that for me? And I'll stay in Princeton. I'd like to be alone until then. It would help me. It would help me a lot."

"Yes. Yes, of course. But we'd already planned on that, remember? That's why I went back home to get some things. But I almost forgot, Edwin's coming tonight, not tomorrow. That's what Dad told me. So we'll leave together tonight and I'll come back tomorrow."

"I must have gotten the days mixed up," Esther said, her misery weighing down her quiet syllables.

UNCORRECTED REVIEW COPY — NOT FOR SALE

It was Wednesday. Sarah had imagined the two of them together at their father's for a long weekend. The prospect of being alone with him for three whole days was so painful she felt a yet stronger tug of desperation.

"I understand," she said.

❧

Sarah and Esther returned to Princeton. For dinner they had Chinese takeout; Esther ordered not only a main dish of noodles but soup and spring rolls and a side of bok choy. She paid for their food with cash from their father.

As they ate they watched TV on Sarah's laptop, one episode after another.

Esther went to bed early, and Sarah stayed up until two to finish marking her papers.

The next morning Sarah took the train to New York to drop the papers off and clean out her office and to meet Minah.

She did nothing but stare out the window on the train. She didn't feel like herself. It didn't help that she was waking most nights clenching her muscles. When she called her psychiatrist for a refill of her antidepressants with an additional request for a few Xanax, her doctor, though agreeing reluctantly given the "family circumstances," told her that these recurring symptoms were just as likely to be an indication that she needed more physical exercise.

"You can't take care of your mind without taking care of your body," her doctor had said, to Sarah's extreme annoyance. How was twenty minutes on the elliptical supposed to alleviate the existential crisis of her abusive father's dying? But she feared, not for the first time, that there might be truth to her doctor's admonition. If there was truth to it, there would be nothing meaningful to extract like a nugget from the polluted waters of her soul. Maybe what Esther and I need, she thought wryly, is just to eat and sleep better and do yoga with Minah.

The very idea of teaching yoga in prison had disgusted her. How could you teach people forced into cages to focus on their breath and let go of their rage? Without being observant, she had always felt a greater affinity for the religions of the Book. The people of the Book understood the terror and beauty of poetry and appeals in the wilderness, of testaments and laws, of anger. That emotion and breath were given to you as life itself.

Yet she could not, not at that moment as the sun struck the prismatic river outside the window, think of a practice to which she would rather commit herself if she were locked in an empty cell. To chant words of a language you didn't know, to breathe in and out, out, out . . .

The halls of her department building were vacant. She unlocked the main office to leave the final papers in her mailbox. In her own office she packed her folders and books, then left. It was painfully desolate to leave the place she had worked for years without any ceremony.

Has anything really changed between now and then? she asked herself as she and Minah sat down in the same restaurant of their first reckoning with Eugene's fortune.

"Tell me what's going on," Minah said sternly.

"I have no idea whether he has a will or, if he does, what's in it." Sarah knew it was a misguided, even absurd sense of delicacy that inhibited her from speaking of money gained by their father's death over the phone. But somehow she felt that in person, face-to-face with Minah, their presence— their presence together—would justify their intentions and absolve them of their greed.

"Okay." A look of resignation washed over Minah.

"He was talking about his will," Sarah said with sudden bright breath-lessness.

"What?"

"I just realized. He was talking about his will yesterday. I thought he was just rambling. He'd been rambling in Korean about our mother, then he switched to English. He switches to English when he wants to emphasize something because he thinks I don't understand any Korean at all. I think he switched to talk about his will. He used a word in Korean I didn't understand. And I admit I was distracted. I've been having trouble focusing lately. But the word must have been 'will.' He said he was going to change it."

"Tell me exactly what he said."

"That's the thing. He didn't make much sense in English. I didn't even bother to understand him at first. But it makes sense now."

"Tell me exactly what he said."

"I can't remember exactly."

"Do you remember the Korean word he used?"

Sarah concentrated. "It sounded like . . . *you won.*"

Minah took a deep breath. "Yes. That means 'will.'"

They both paused, as if to pay respect to the weight of the moment.

"Go on."

"Let me think. After that he kept saying 'I change it,' to mean he's going to change it."

"Okay. So he has one now that he's going to change. Did he tell you how it stands now and how he's going to change it?"

Sarah focused again. "Let me think . . . he said—he said . . . he said he didn't want people to say he was a bad father. But he didn't care anymore. So he was changing the will. He said—he said that the three of us and Edwin were different. And so we'd be treated differently."

Minah turned pale. They sat in silence.

"You're sure," she said at last, her voice hoarse.

"That's how I remember it."

"Tell me exactly what he said. His own words. Not your translation. His own words."

"He said, '*I change it*'—the *you won* . . .'" She lowered and closed her eyes. She pronounced each word with slow emphasis, as if they were scattered coins she was picking up from the floor: "'*I change it. You and Minah and Esther. And Edwin. You are together. I am not a bad daddy. But now—who care? I die.'"* She gasped for air. "I don't remember his exact words. I can't. I just remember what I thought he meant."

She thought, in fact, that given more time to reflect she could produce a fairly accurate reproduction of what Eugene had said; she had always had an excellent verbal memory. But she could not stand to put herself in his place for another syllable.

"He thinks he deserves better care from all his children, which he hasn't gotten. So he's going to change the will to benefit those who have helped. Maybe Esther. But probably Edwin." Minah's words were a rustle of rapid reasoning, but at the name of her brother, she choked back a sob.

"Edwin was acting different," Sarah said meditatively. "When I saw him yesterday, at Dad's."

Minah perked up.

"He was acting like . . ."

"Yes?"

"He was more self-righteous. That was it. He seemed like an arrogant schemer to me before. But this time, he acted like I had offended him. He said, 'I'm his son. I need to see him regularly.'"

Minah broke into a cynical smile. "That's because he believes his own lies. Just like Dad. He believes in his fucking performance."

She sank her face into her hands, frightening Sarah.

"Okay," Minah said, now leaning in toward her sister. "We have to pull ourselves together. There must be something we can do. We have everything to lose. You said on the phone you were going back today to take care of him. Without Esther. You'll be alone with him for a couple days. You have to convince him not to change the will. Appeal to him. You need the money for a chance to save your career. Didn't you tell me you have to publish more if you're going to have a shot at a good job? You need the money to write. And for the family you plan on having. Things have changed for our generation. It's not enough to work hard and get an education. You need an inheritance to get ahead. It's not the America he used to know. Tell him that. He might understand that. Tell him the status of his grandchildren lies in the balance."

"Don't you think he'll be offended if I just come out and beg him for his money?"

"No. And besides, we have nothing to lose." Minah shook her head. "I don't understand. You're his favorite. I can't believe he'd write you out like this. Was he angry or bitter when he told you this?"

"Not angry. Maybe bitter. Depressed. Defeated, maybe."

Minah's paleness transformed from sallow to luminous. "He wants you to change his mind. Don't you see that? He's not going to change the will unless you spend more time with him. That's all he wants. He's being manipulative. But even I don't blame him for that now. Esther says he's doing worse. He knows he's dying. And he loves you most."

"Stop saying that!" Sarah whispered ferociously.

Minah's bright eyes widened in surprise. "Okay. Okay. I'm sorry."

"I have to go now. To look after our father," Sarah said gruffly.

She got up, keeping her head down, and put on her coat. She glanced at her sister, whose expression was now that of wide-eyed alarm, and left.

"Fuck the train," Sarah said under her breath once outside. She would pay for a car service.

"You having a good day?" the driver asked.

"Fine," she said. She did not feel like talking with a stranger, and the powerfully cloying air freshener hanging from his rearview mirror already made her feel he was invading her allotted space in his car. Then she started worrying he'd give her a bad rating. "And you?" she added lamely.

"Good, good," he said, and that was all.

On the drive, as she stared out the window, her sister's expression returned to her. She'd wanted to shout in Minah's face: I don't care if he leaves the money to you or me or the local animal shelter. He can do what he wants. You want *me* to care for him. You want me to ask someone I loathe to hand his fortune over to me. To beg him.

Why hadn't she? She was sick of Minah's needy desperation. She could feel it even when they weren't together; the very sight of Minah's texts on her phone asking with faux blandness, How's it going? Do you still have a lot of work? oppressed her.

Yet the flares of resentment and irritation always smoothed out quickly. Images of the same soothing scene would come to her like a soft breeze. They appeared to her in the days after Minah declared their father was worth at least $10 million. It was a shock to hear a concrete figure affixed to his wealth, which had long figured in her mind as images of the house in California: the artisanal Italian furniture, the piano, the garden.

After their meeting she had a dream of the place that remained with her like a vivid memory. The house was empty, airy. The piano was rigid with silence. She stepped slowly across the marble tiles veined in peach and blush pink. At first the house was eerie: its emptiness was the haunted aftermath of the violence she and her sisters had known. But the longer she lingered, the more the house and all its objects seemed to be responding to her foot-steps, awakening, like the rousing of souls long deadened by despair. The piano was lifting the wing of its lid, preparing to waft full, ripe notes into the air. She opened the sliding door to the garden. White and red and violet flowers were glowing in the twilight. She shivered with pleasure at the promise of transformative rage—the fierce vindication of things degraded by her father's touch.

She agreed with Minah. They would not be wrong in using their father's money to compensate for what couldn't be atoned. They could not let their brother diminish the material consolation they were due. It was her due: her father had promised when she was a child that she would inherit his wealth. Each of the sisters had a moral and natural claim to his fortune, but she was the only one burdened with the insuperable bond of his favor.

The car was caught in traffic. LUXURY APARTMENTS FOR RENT—the banner hung across a dark building giving directly onto the highway. When you looked closely, some windows were curtained, others unobstructed and offering vague outlines of boxes and empty halls.

She whipped her face from the back passenger window toward the windshield so abruptly she was barely aware of what she was doing. She faced the sun striking down hard on the hood of the car, blanching the sky, fading the asphalt, glossing the droning cars around her. She was caught in the burning glow of a snapshot taken from elsewhere, an unseen heavenly eye; all of them on the highway were glowing like things unlike themselves, like pale stars hanging in an afternoon sky. There were words for this moment: epiphanic, mystical. But she did not feel transcendent or illumined, changed or charged. It was a dazzling instant in which the infinity of all possible worlds existed; and when the moment was over, she knew she was nothing more than what she was before. There was no new bond between herself and other people, certainly not this driver, who was talking in what sounded like Haitian Creole on his Bluetooth. In this world she was headed to her father's with the ulterior motive of an inheritance, dreaming of a beautiful place to call home.

When she had experiences like this, she was sometimes prompted to write them down. When she made an attempt to do so, she was dogged by the sense that she was not merely coarsening but distorting the many-shaded thing she wanted to express; that, though she tried hard to cleave to the unique asymmetry of the experience, her recorded thoughts were essentially the elaboration of thoughts she had read about elsewhere. She had never been able to write honestly about her life. The only thing she knew truly when she tried to write about herself was that she wanted to be another person.

She was losing out on something by not fleshing out to herself, in some way, what she glimpsed at such moments. It was something she could not name, and it was slipping through her fingers like sand.

3
The message

I know you better than you think, and I care about you. You didn't do wrong.

You weren't wrong.

You and Minah and I are together. But who cares?

Your cheek

4
Three women

Esther had just taken a very long hot shower. She was alone at Sarah's. She would be alone for the next three days.

She was lying on the sofa. She was tired—she was tired of thinking of people. She didn't want to think about anyone for a long time. Not her father; or Sarah, Minah, or Edwin; or even the faces of her past. Her whole person ached at the thought of her family. One by one, she was extinguishing these oppressively personal and expressive characters from her mind. She wanted to think of the sea, mountains by the sea, like those she knew in California. No. She wanted to think of places she had never been but would, she passionately hoped, one day.

How sweet it was to hope for something for herself, in the future, in a place without anyone she knew. Blue-black waves, the smell of the sea, the sound of tides; and beyond the shore, the sound of a stream, the smell of sap, and silence. No one would be there. Not anyone she knew. Wasn't this vision more real, in some ways, than even the people around her who, trapped in themselves, polluted the air with their deceptions and their demands?

She started to wonder about people she did not know. She began to think about Ruby.

When Esther thought of Ruby caring for her father, she pictured her poise, her endurance. And she recalled cracks in her dignified posture and needle-thin, needle-sharp glimmers of resentment . . .

At their first meeting at Eugene's, Esther observed Ruby for an hour tending to her father, preparing food, drink, and medicine, and cleaning. Esther asked questions about Eugene's habits and needs. Did the medicine need to be taken with food? Should he be pressured to eat when he lacked appetite? Ruby answered carefully. She was gentle without warmth, efficient and professional, until minutes had passed and she said with a flash of impatience, "I have to go now. I have to be at my own home."

When Ruby entered the apartment the next day, Esther was in the living room. She thought she could feel in that instant a tremor of giddy delight shoot through Ruby at the sight of her. Ruby took off her coat, put away her own prepared meals, pulled out her thermos of coffee, and sat beside Esther on the sofa, smiling, her movements light and precise, unlike the stolid gestures of duty she'd performed the day before. In the startling glassy brightness of her smile, Esther recognized the hard shine of loneliness.

Ruby's dark eyes widened. "It's nice to see you here. Are you leaving or staying? You look like you're settling in with your mug there."

"I'm staying," Esther decided.

"That's nice to hear. It'll help me. It's hard to do a night shift alone. If you're bad, you just sleep. I never sleep on the job, even with patients who usually sleep through the night. I'm alone, but I'm not alone. But if you're staying, I really won't be alone."

"Is that the hardest part of the night shift for you? Staying up?"

"No." Ruby's face transformed once more, sad and thoughtful, as if she were arriving at an unhappy truth about herself.

Esther waited, then said, "I spend most of my nights at my sister's. I find it hard to sleep, too, when you're in the home of someone you don't know well."

Another smile bloomed on Ruby's face. How isolated Ruby must be, Esther thought, to glow with such pleasure at this minor confidence about her relationship with Sarah. At her father's, Ruby was alone with his temper, his flatulence, the fug of his gross self-satisfaction, his malice. What kind of life did she have outside, in the world?

"When I was much younger, but older than you are now," Ruby said warmly, "I'd just started this job. I wanted to be a good aide, and I tried to talk to my patients. I thought it would make them feel better. I asked them about their day, their family. Their hobbies and passions. I asked them about their children. I talked about mine, and they gave me parenting advice." The warmth was leeching from her face. "And sooner or later they gave me their philosophy of life. They said life is family. Life is a struggle. Life is a struggle for love. Or, if they were without family to help them, without anyone, they said the same, but negatively. Life is nothing without family or love. Those were the patients who talked to me. There were those who didn't. Who don't. Like your father."

With "father," that look of smoldering melancholy returned, filling the mask of her features like smoke bottled in glass. Esther recognized its resemblance to the faces of those blank-faced, half-feral children, tired and wary of the world, glaring at her like wizened stray cats when she passed them trailing glassy-eyed parents in grocery aisles, fighting with other children on neighborhood sidewalks. Of older loners at bus stops and secondhand stores with a childlike senility to them, their minds so desperate for the generative touch of others that when they began to talk, they spoke without filter, like dying trees scattering countless seeds as far as the wind will take them. The next instant, self-consciousness might shut them down in response to the slightest hint of discomfort in their interlocutor. Esther knew this vulnerability. Ever since her father's devastating decision to leave the house next door to Anna's family, Esther had grown to find the ready confidences of the lonely moving and deliriously sweet, like half-rotted apples in a field. She wanted to listen, to elicit the seeds she believed any and all, stunted and thriving, bitter and contented alike, would release if she attended long enough, if they wanted to speak truthfully . . . She'd had many painful encounters with desperate men and women who clung to her, figuratively and once literally, to deliver a babbling monologue of confessions confused with delusions and desires.

She learned to avoid or at least delay the defensive silences in those who hungered for real contact. She developed the grace to listen in such a way that the speaker wanted to do more than unburden themselves, wanted to converse so that their words themselves would not wither in isolation. They might mingle with another's, echo meaningfully in the ear of another.

Esther said, "Even with those you don't talk to, do you sometimes feel yourself growing close to them, just by being near them for so many hours at a time?"

"There was a woman who didn't speak English. She was very delicate. She had white hair like a soft cloud all around her small, wrinkled face. Her daughter was kind and loving, and I tried to brush her hair the way her daughter brushed her hair and to hold a glass to her lips the way her daughter did. She would touch my hand to thank me. I never felt close to her. I was afraid of hurting her when I touched her or even when she touched me."

"Right now I'm living with my sister Sarah. I hadn't seen her in so many years when I moved in with her a couple weeks ago. I thought we'd grow close quickly from living together. The way you hear children at summer camp and soldiers in training and traveling performers grow close, because they eat the same food and sleep in the same rooms after working together all day. They begin to talk and smell the same. They can't help but feel close. I thought—I hoped—living together would make us close, though even as children we weren't close. I was wrong."

"I made the same mistake," Ruby said solemnly. "I thought sleeping in the same house would make me feel compassion even for the most difficult patients. I sleep nearby and feed them, bathe them, clothe them. I hear them talk to their friends and family. I hear them mutter under their breath and cry and whisper in their sleep. But the ones born with sickness in their heart, the ones who make you doubt your god—it's hard. Sometimes it's very hard. You seem very intelligent. Very sensitive. I don't meet many people like you." Ruby's eyes glimmered. "I've been thinking about this for a long time. Nearly all my life, because I'm old now. It's a mystery that you can live with someone and not feel something for them. You can even raise a child you don't understand." She paused. "With my son, you see the open sky, an open field. But with my daughter, there were thorns and weeds between us. My own rose. Something in me was not nurturing her. It was giving life to something else."

They heard a loud groan.

"Let me check on your father," she said hastily.

On her return Esther perceived with a pang the deep chagrin Ruby felt for having revealed so much of herself. From then on, when she overlapped with Esther at the apartment, the contrast between her short-lived volubility and her new formal reticence created a palpable chill, like a misted window in winter. Her froideur was the pitiful pride of the shamed. Esther had first recognized it, as a child, in Sarah.

Ruby was professional. At the end of her shift she gave Esther careful summaries based on written notes on her father's appetite, bathroom usage, hours of sleep and wakefulness, pain levels and painkiller consumption, and sometimes his mood, which was usually described with a brief line: "He's moody today." "He's moodier than usual." During these updates she would not meet Esther's eyes. Sometimes as Ruby was preparing to leave they mentioned the weather; otherwise they didn't talk.

This was how it was, Esther thought, when you cared for people who invited you into their homes but not into their lives. This was how you might change.

Esther began spending most days and nights at her father's. She left only during Edwin's irregular visits, two or three times a week, for a night or for a few hours, during which she returned to Sarah's, visited Minah, or, more often, just slept in the spare room. During Ruby's night shifts, she tried to sleep so that she could be awake for her father during the day.

Sometimes when she was with her father, she could feel cruelty gripping his heart. She sensed its closeness; she felt herself at its threshold.

How was it that as her father was dying, there was a resurgence of life within him? He called Esther a whore, he accused her of sending Sue onto the streets; and she kept walking long distances to do the shopping, preparing meals served on a tray, picking up dirty clothes and towels and laundering them in the basement, guiding him back and forth to the bathroom, cleaning and replacing the mugs of mucus, emptying his urinal, setting him up on the sofa so she might launder the sheets as he watched TV. He wanted ice; he wanted not Coke but Sprite, or Fanta; he wanted another blanket; he wanted a heating pad, an ice bag, more ibuprofen. He wanted Edwin, not her; Sarah, not her; not her. She was living in his cruelty—it was atmospheric, the tension of his desire to inflict pain, mixing with his own pain.

When he was sleeping, she tried to read the books she borrowed from Sarah but often found it too difficult to focus. She wanted to be elsewhere and thought of the past. She longed to eat good food with Minah, forgetting the tears her sister had provoked. She dreamily recalled the time Sarah cut her hair, taking a long shower and feeling lighter and fresher than she had in a long time, as if she had not only washed but been watered. She dreamt she was traveling again, meeting strangers, driving through noisome cities and empty plains, past industrial farms and plots of asphalt exhaling heat back to the sun. Past cliffs and mountains ranges whose monumental lines, rolling with her through her window, were forever etched somewhere in her mind like the shape of a sensation.

Sometimes the thought of the past made her panic. The people she'd encountered during her aimless years, traveled with, lived with, nearly all of whom she would never contact or see again—they had mirrored back to her her own strangeness, her solitude, her thirst for sweetness, her taste for life. They had taught her more than she would have learned had she remained rooted in place. It was otherness that had brought her back to life. Only now she was starting to fear that they had not simply shown her who she was to herself, but embedded strangeness and solitude more deeply within her.

In the bathroom she noticed for the first time in a long time the blood vessel on her cheek that had burst between Sue's slender pinched fingers.

She yearned for a miracle: for her father to be cured so she could walk away.

When she saw Ruby, it was with simultaneous anguish and relief to have a respite from her father and to know that someone else, who bore no relation to him, who owed him nothing, should be subjected to his cruelty and his needs.

Ruby saw that caring for Eugene was growing painful. She began to give advice and words of encouragement.

She said, "I drink coffee at all hours, but most people can't handle that. No more coffee for you after five. Try ginger tea at night for your heartburn. Drink chamomile to calm your nerves. It'll help."

"When it's hard, I tell myself that God won't let me die alone if I do my job."

She asked Ruby if he treated her decently. Ruby replied with cool pride: "He's rude. He's weak. He's dying. I've seen dying patients throwing their own feces around, begging me to put them out of their pain. Screaming like they were burning alive. It was terrible. But I wasn't hurt. I don't take it personally." She gave Esther an awkward pat on the back and left.

Esther had wanted to be useful by caring for her father. What was more fruitful than the most elemental of human services, providing care? Let her sisters dispute the meanings of abstractions—of legal justice and personal fairness, of goodness and real love—while she performed these mysteries in her work and made them real. It was this feeling of reality that gave her courage and joy . . . She had wanted, too, to help her sisters by caring for him. She had been nourished with love under the care of her neighbors. She knew what it was to take care of someone in ways they did not; she had reserves of compassion and strength they lacked. She understood this now, that she had wanted to help Sarah and Minah as much as their father in caring for him. For, despite their avowals to the contrary, she knew her sisters found the thought of utterly abandoning their dying father as unbearable as his nearness.

So she volunteered to care for their father, and for weeks her father's cruelest insults and crudest gestures did not hurt or offend Esther. They were like white noise to the essential sound of his deeper life, the murmur growing into a hiss, the sea roaring in a shell, as he felt his time grow short, as he lay in bed with nothing but time to reflect, as he realized Sarah did not love him. She was drawn to it; it stirred her, tested her, made her strong. While it lasted, her own strength was mysterious and remarkable to her.

Was she wrong in thinking this was good work, to help him? She'd told Sarah she wanted to make their father's dying better—what had she even meant by that?

His dying self was stronger than her.

This week, Ruby gave notice abruptly. She had her own family emergency, the agency said.

She hadn't wanted to talk to Ruby simply to be kind. She still wanted to talk to Ruby for her own sake. She had never been more in need of a friend, a neighbor, a benevolent stranger.

Though the agency had initially insisted no aide was free to start until Monday, Sarah woke in her old bed on Friday morning to find a text from Esther saying the new aide would arrive that morning. She sat up, her spine straightened, her heart thumping, jolted by joy.

Gloria was surprisingly petite for someone who said she could lift a grown man onto a bed. She had muscular upper arms that Sarah could make out under her thin long sleeves, but was otherwise diminutive, roughly the same height as Sarah. The whites of her eyes were gleaming white, as were the rows of small teeth revealed with her cheerful smile. Sarah would have liked her even if she wasn't overjoyed and unspeakably grateful to be relieved of her duty. Gloria seemed to be alert with a happiness that was more like a ballast than a feeling. It would probably not be shaken or damaged by ongoing association with her father. Probably. Sarah panicked at the thought of another decent soul fleeing the household; she had no doubt Ruby had finally quit in disgust.

"Did the agency warn you about my father?"

"About Mr. Kim?" Gloria laughed lightly. "No. What's there to warn me about?"

Alarm burned away Sarah's short-lived confidence in Gloria's success. Gloria might be constitutionally hardy, but she was obviously not mentally prepared for her father.

"There's no easy way to say this. My father's a jerk. He's worse than a jerk, he's a brute. He's a monster with disgusting habits, like spitting into a cup all day, which he's done for decades. It's not something that started when he got cancer. He's also racist. I should warn you. I should have warned the last aide, too. He's racist against everyone, really, especially Black people and Latinos. Japanese and South Asians, too," she added hastily, as if, confronted up close by Gloria's complexion, she wanted to mitigate the racism she'd just denounced—with which she suddenly felt complicit—by pointing out her father's animosity toward those closer to herself ethnically. She felt a surge of self-loathing, but she kept talking. She let it propel an excessive honesty that ultimately seemed to sully herself.

Gloria did not flinch, though her eyes were wide with attentive wonder.

"We, I mean his children, are trying to arrange for good care for him because we want to do the right thing, but also because we really can't stand to be around him. He was abusive to us as children, and we can't bring ourselves to look after him. At least my older sister and I can't. My sister Esther, who's a kinder, better soul than the rest of us, she was doing the most for him, but even she can't bear it anymore. And he has the money for private care. I hope you know that we are very, very appreciative of anyone who will take care of him. And we want to make sure you can put up with it and won't quit suddenly like Ruby and leave us in the lurch. It's going to get even more difficult, since he's finally agreed to hormone therapy, which will make him really weak. Though that might actually make your job easier, if he's too weak to yell and complain all the time—" She halted abruptly. "He's actually been pretty calm since I got here yesterday," she concluded, bemused by this realization.

Even while speaking, Sarah knew she was saying too much, but an irresistible compulsion was pushing her to overshare. She would not have been able to forewarn Gloria properly if she hadn't embarrassed herself with her garrulous, unseemly, desperate manner.

Gloria's expression was sympathetic and tender. Sarah was wrong. Gloria not only didn't need to be warned; she was unfazed by emotional outpourings from her patient's family. Sarah wanted to clasp Gloria's hands and weep with gratitude.

"I get it. The agency didn't tell me everything you did. But I get it now. Thank you. We'll work it out."

She rested her hand on Sarah's shoulder.

Sarah showed her around the apartment, the sippy cups and protein drinks in the cupboards, the emergency numbers on the fridge, the spare room, the bathroom. She felt like a fraud, pretending to know firsthand the details of her father's care. Gloria pulled back the shower curtain to reveal a low-hanging handheld showerhead and a stool. "Don't worry," Sarah said. "He won't let any woman help him bathe. That's up to Edwin. My brother."

She knocked at the bedroom; there was no response. They entered the shaded room, where Eugene was huddled under two thick blankets. Sarah introduced Gloria. He muttered and turned away. His breathing quickly became heavy and regular.

Whispering, Sarah pointed out the crate of bottled water, tissue boxes, and spare linen in the closet. She went through the bottles of pills on the table by his bed: the prescription acetaminophen and ibuprofen that

Edwin, through Esther, said he took too liberally; the oxycodone he was starting to take; the marinol pills that seemed to help with his appetite.

"I don't know what this is." Sarah pointed to something that resembled a metal water pitcher on its side.

"That's a urinal."

Sarah froze. "I—I didn't know he needed it."

"Maybe he makes an effort when you're here."

Outside the room Gloria said, "He's only just starting to take oxycodone?"

"Yes, as far as I know. Esther told me he kept saying he was strong, he could handle the pain."

"At this stage most patients want more and more of the strong stuff. He must be strong indeed, to resist taking morphine."

"He is," Sarah said without thinking. She frowned, bemused once more by her own response.

"But it's good he's taking it now. You can't resist for too long. It's too hard."

Sarah would spend the night in the spare room in case Gloria needed anything. She had originally planned to call Esther once the new aide had arrived to tell her she was returning home. But she found herself hesitant to interrupt Esther's reprieve.

She sat on the bed not knowing what to do with herself. She had no interest in reading or watching a video. She realized she was hungry, but she was also reluctant to prepare a meal for herself in Gloria's presence.

She couldn't decide what to do. She felt her hunger slowly leaving her as her stomach relaxed and the pangs seemed to travel to her heart, which began to beat more quickly. What was wrong with her? She felt giddy and fragile; she could not think properly. The portable urinal in her father's room had been empty. Had he left his bed at all since her arrival yesterday afternoon to use the bathroom? Esther said he normally needed support if he wasn't using his walker. Sarah hadn't even noticed where his walker was.

Her phone pinged with a text from Esther. She promptly typed, He's fine. He's mostly been sleeping. Resting.

Her heart was pounding. She wasn't sure if he was fine. She tried to recall what she had done for him in the past day. And what had Edwin told her on his way out? When she got to the apartment she heard her father raising his voice, which was emphatic rather than angry. "*I am tired now.*" Edwin entered the living room with a look of such dazed consternation that she forgot the friction between them and asked him if he was all right. At that, he stared at her without seeing her. Then he blinked, shook his head, and cracked a grin. "I'm fine," he said. "I'm fine." He got his coat and added, "He'll need his medication when he gets up." Then he rushed out. But Esther had told her to give him oxycodone only if he requested it; perhaps Edwin meant the marinol? Was she supposed to administer the ibuprofen and acetaminophen herself; couldn't he be trusted to take generic painkillers on his own, even if they were at prescription concentrations? Yesterday she'd gone to his room every hour until midnight to ask if he wanted anything. She'd been thrilled to hear him snore or mumble he needed nothing. Edwin had left him a tray with two bottles of water, a chocolate-flavored protein drink, and a slice of chocolate cake, one of the few solid foods he was still eating. She remembered noting her father had inserted a straw into the box of the protein drink. Should she have reminded her father to drink and eat? Was he so lifeless he could go twenty-four hours without relieving himself?

She went to her father, who was sleeping. The cake was untouched.

She went to the living room. Gloria was on the sofa looking at her phone. "I'm afraid I forgot to give him his medication," she said in a voice that sounded pitiful to her own ears. "I'm not even sure which he needs now."

"That's all right. I just talked to Edwin about that. Your dad's getting a new pain medication next week. In the meantime Edwin tried doubling his dose, which looks like it's too strong. That's probably why he's been sleeping all day. But too little, and he's in too much pain." She looked Sarah up and down. "I'm here now. Why don't you go to bed? It'll be all right. Get some rest."

Sarah returned to her bed. She lay on her side and felt her heart slow.

❧

She woke to a knock on the bedroom door.

It was Gloria. "I'm heading out now," she called out from behind the door. "I'll be back on Monday morning."

"Monday?" Sarah said groggily. She scrambled out of bed to open the door and face her. "Monday?" she said again. Why did she sound so pathetic around Gloria? Panic began to tickle her throat.

"Yes. I'm not here on weekends. I'm here Monday through Saturday morning. It's all in the schedule. Edwin said you'd be here. Isn't that right?" Again, Gloria scrutinized Sarah. "If that's not right you should call him. Your dad's sleeping. He was up in the night a couple times to use the bathroom and eat a little. He's been an easy patient. You don't need to worry." She hesitated. "I'll be back Monday," she said again.

"Thank you," Sarah said feebly as Gloria receded down the hallway—too feebly, she realized, for Gloria to hear.

She checked her phone. She had a text from Esther.

How's Gloria? it read.

She began typing: She's fine. She's great. But I didn't know she wouldn't be here over the weekend. Will you be coming back? She nearly hit the send button. She could hear the obnoxious whine of her pitiful—self-pitying—tone with Gloria reproduced in text. She was supposed to be helping Esther. It was her second, relatively painless day with her father. He had not caused a scene or insulted her; she hadn't even been alone all this time. With Gloria's assistance, she had slept through the night. She could not ask Esther to return.

She composed a text to Edwin. Are you coming this weekend? Gloria just left. She mentioned a schedule. Not sure whether I'm expected to be here till Monday when she gets back. She deleted the last sentence and added, Let me know.

She waited.

She was breathing not air but something cloying and palpable. This was the room of her childhood, incarnated again within these walls. The dust of the fifteen years she had inhabited the original room was here: the sloughed skin of the three sisters, the tiny cotton fibers shed by these quilts and sheets, the grains of wood and flecks of paint, the dirt and pollen and insects from the teeming outside world ground into the powdery debris of their private life; and decomposing with it all, the dead cells of their father, along with traces of their mother. The dust was pervasive, suspended in the atmosphere he established wherever he planted himself, overpowering the elements of life with his suppression of life, curiosity, creativity, tenderness for otherness. She was inhaling it now; it was deadening her now.

Her heart leapt at the sound of Edwin's text.

I'm supposed to take him to radiation Mon and Wed and drop off meds this weekend probably tomorrow so I can't take any more time off work not this weekend. I talked to him a few hours ago he thinks you're staying with him this weekend. Don't forget his meds he needs a double dose until I see him.

"No," she said aloud. "No, no, no, no, no."

She consulted the list of phone numbers on the fridge. On the second page she found the information to access his insurance account online. She compiled a list of agencies other than Gloria and Ruby's covered by his insurance from the website. She called them all; all the offices were closed for the weekend. She spent the morning on her computer pursuing the results of variations on the search "private home aide new jersey." Eugene gave Esther cash for household expenses; she would draw upon every ounce of her influence over him to compel him to write a check to any private aide who didn't accept his insurance. With each click she could feel herself losing herself, pulling away from the solid, sane standards of decency she normally tried to uphold, until she reached a breaking point and called the local number of a woman looking for work on an obscure forum about long-term care. Marianna agreed to meet Sarah that afternoon.

When Marianna arrived she buzzed from below and asked Sarah to meet her outside. The request puzzled her, but she complied. In the parking lot

Sarah saw a young man and woman leaning against a car. The man was smoking, saying something to the woman. They looked South Asian; she guessed they might be Filipino. He glared at her as she approached. When she stood before them he turned away; he never met her eyes.

"Hi—Sarah? I'm Marianna. And this is my boyfriend." She spoke with the nasal inflections and elastic, singsong syllables of a woman who enjoyed behaving and being treated like a child. "He's very protective of me and just wanted to make sure this was all legit before I go in. But you look all right, doesn't she?" He didn't acknowledge Marianna, either. "So it's all good," she concluded cheerfully, snapping gum.

Upstairs, Marianna unzipped her oversized parka to reveal a tight-fitting V-neck shirt the pale blue color of most scrubs. Sarah could see the seams of Marianna's bra and the impression of her nipples. Marianna's drawstring pants, on the other hand, were loose and low; at her hips the red rim of her underwear stretched above the waistband.

Sarah hired Marianna to care for her father on weekends, starting now.

5
Medicine

The lights were out when Sarah got home. She brushed her teeth and fell into bed, sleeping deeply until Esther woke her up with a shake.

"What's going on? Who's with Dad now?"

Sarah rubbed her eyes. "He's fine," she said.

"I thought you were staying there over the weekend. That's what Edwin told me. I called him when you didn't reply to my messages."

Sarah gave a terse account of what she had done. She had judged the situation, especially for Esther, untenable. And so she had hired someone to work on weekends.

"You didn't think to consult me or Edwin or even our father, did you?" Esther's voice quavered with disbelief and chagrin. "I could have gone back if you couldn't handle it."

"I introduced her to him and he was fine with her." Sarah gulped. "I did this for all of us. Especially you."

"How can you lie to yourself like that?" Esther said softly.

Esther returned to their father's that hour.

∞

Sarah heard Esther shut the front door. She fell back asleep; she woke in the late morning and thought of getting up. She remained in bed, her mind as inert as her body.

The short day was growing dusky when she left her room. She was craving greasy food. She ordered a delivery of a burger and fries and started watching a period drama about salacious and sadistic court intrigue. It was a show she'd been saving for an occasion like this, a time she wanted urgently to sink into vegetal consciousness. It was moderately engaging, but she longed for something to swallow or smoke that would transport her elsewhere more effectively than any distraction could. She'd never had an appetite for strong drugs; perhaps this was yet another inheritance from her father. Now, though, she longed for something more potent than the vodka in her freezer, even if it made her vomit or see demons or shortened her life. She would give up a year of her life to be able to lose herself for a day.

Minah called; Sarah turned off her ringer. Minah called twice more. An hour later, Sarah saw a missed call and voicemail from her brother.

She stayed up smoking, sipping vodka, and bingeing the show, relishing the permission she'd given herself to disavow responsibility for her father, to give him and Minah and Edwin all a tacit middle finger. But when she remembered Esther, her spiteful joy turned to ash in her mouth. Esther had called her a liar. How dare Esther, whom Sarah so deeply envied, judge Sarah? Sarah admitted it to herself freely now. She envied Esther for being so different from her: graceful even in her odd, often ill-fitting clothes as she sat at their father's bedside; gracious in her commitment to reach you, even when some part of her—which Sarah barely sensed—demurred in the difficulty of the moment. Above all, Sarah envied Esther for whatever engine of patience and courage and strength purred perpetually within her to sustain her grace, even when she was worn down.

How could Esther judge her? Sarah could not forgive Esther for expecting her to be as good as her, she who was loved by her mother and sisters and the adoptive family of her childhood.

The characters on her laptop screen were denouncing betrayals and threatening revenge in the rain. Would Esther appreciate a show like this? The few times they'd watched TV together Esther had worn an alternately perplexed and bored expression, and Sarah had the impression of being with a foreigner on whom the cultural nuances were lost, or being seated next to the awkward dinner guest who didn't laugh like the rest of the table at the good-humored jokes and had a palate so painfully refined they struggled to swallow their meal. Esther was what Sarah, along with the other typically cruel children she knew in grade school, would have denounced as weird. Perhaps the pleasures of facile entertainment were lost on sensitive, ethically serious Esther, while Sarah, with her hard-heartedness and gracelessness and ineptness with people, was doomed to find her only consolation not in noble communal engagements but the isolation of mindlessly crass TV.

Even when Esther insisted that she wanted to keep watching, Sarah didn't feel at ease beside her. Perhaps Esther did, in fact, enjoy the show, or simply liked relaxing in silence beside her sister. Sarah didn't know, but she did know she couldn't lose herself in TV with Esther. If Esther was a discomfiting opacity to Sarah, didn't it follow that Sarah must be a puzzle to her?

Esther could not be allowed to judge someone as different from her as Sarah.

And yet, Sarah wanted her younger sister to console her for the wrong she had done. She knew she had done something wrong; she knew it was pathetic and detestable and absurd, this wish, but she held on to it like a broken woman to a child's toy. Only Esther could cure her of her guilt, which was spreading across her life, her one finite life, across her past and her future, like a stain.

I've never been forgiven for anything, even what I've done in all innocence, and I'll keep on being wrong and doing wrong, again and again, until someone who loves me forgives me and grants me grace . . .

She received two emails from Esther in the middle of the night while she was watching the third season.

Sarah, I tried calling you. So has Minah. I don't know what to do. Please call.

The second email was sent twenty minutes later.

You can call anytime, even now.

She decided to wait until morning to call. When she woke around noon, she found a third message in her inbox.

Gloria showed up this morning and Marianna, with Dad's permission, took away her key.

Minah says she's seduced him. He's attracted to her, that's true. But he also understands what Marianna represents. She was your message to him.

He laughs and jokes with her, then weeps and says you've broken his heart. He teases her and pinches her, and she squeals and slaps him. It's mostly playful, but a few times she's really gotten angry and called her boyfriend to complain. She says he's violent and jealous and is threatening to come over to beat him up. I'm afraid of what might happen if I leave.

Apparently he called Minah and Edwin to say he's done with us, none of us will ever have his money. He told me you're the only one who isn't after his money and broke down crying. Marianna was sitting on the bed patting his hand. He won't take his medicine. He's been crying and yelling and cursing for hours. He's started drinking again.

Minah says she and Edwin will come by later today. I don't know if that's a good idea. But I think you need to come. Please come as soon as you can. As soon as you read this.

Love,
Esther

To Sarah's surprise, instead of further aversion, she experienced a surge of inspired energy at the prospect of returning to her father's. She wanted a definitive conclusion to the ongoing farce of her father's dying.

The train ride, which normally was painfully long for her, passed in a trance. From the station she marched rapidly in the same trance, the paralysis of the past day having given way to the most turbulent restlessness. She had no plan to resolve the sordid domestic crisis with Marianna, no intention but to unburden herself before her father.

She found herself at the mostly empty parking lot of the office complex with dark windows. A man exited the building and headed toward one of the few cars under the sodium lights. He took out his keys and stared at her for a long moment before getting into his car. It occurred to her, as the sky was changing from indigo to black, that the area was probably not safe at night. She pressed on. She thought, Let me be robbed, raped, beaten, and let him know it was because of him. She sprinted down the darkened alley not far from the apartment.

Let him be robbed and beaten, she thought as she ran. She could not bring herself to wish rape upon anyone. Let him be robbed, she repeated to herself. She was not sure she could stomach seeing him beaten, though as a child she had often fantasized about beating him herself with a bat, a hairbrush, a pot. She saw herself standing by his bed, thundering: I want to be rid of you forever. If I had to risk death to efface you from my life, to cut you out like my liver from my body, I'd do it now. Die alone, with anyone you want, but die without me. Die without me. You say that the best part of you died with my mother. The best part of me died long before then, when you first claimed me as your own.

She heard the maddening retort of the real: He won't even understand me if I say everything I want, if it finally pours out of me. Even if I speak slowly and clearly, he won't understand anything but the command "Die alone." Commands are all that he understands. He won't even understand—

Her father's spoken English had always been stronger than his comprehension. He could talk and talk at length in broken English, but if he was interrupted with a question, he'd often fail to process what was being asked. He seemed unable to comprehend how anyone could justifiably ask him to explain himself.

Her heart pounded with fury. He won't even understand. He won't even understand why I hate him, even if I explain it to him with the simplest eloquence. She thought of how the tragic figures in Euripides's plays, restive with complex passion and conviction, and in Beckett's, those sieves of irrational pain, were not so tragic or ambiguous after all, because they could speak, and there would always be an audience who understood their bare words and grappled with their deeper meaning. Whereas she would not even have the chance to speak badly and be heard, because her father could not understand any complex sentence of consequence. He once told her he hadn't finished high school and wanted her to excel on his behalf. But that was not what he most wanted. He wanted her not to be a person. She could not imagine him absorbing, even attempting to grasp, the language of emotional logic and personal difference. It wasn't a matter of education or aptitude, or even a question of a native or non-native tongue. He took the complexity of others, which he saw as obfuscation, as an affront to himself—to the simplicity of his desire to be placated, to be obeyed.

He was incapable of understanding anything he didn't say himself. To be understood by him she would have to limit herself, to break herself down, to sink lower and lower, to think and talk like a dog gifted with speech and then degrade that miracle by barking only negations and commands.

She had slowed to a walk. Her shirt and scarf were damp with sweat. She picked up her pace; she had to hurry if she ever wanted to rest again. It was so cold out, her ears were aching from lobe to skull; she was so hot, she was dripping under her coat. She was falling through the abysses between sentences, between words, into the silence of a shame that could never be expressed.

She had never enjoyed the theater.

The true tragedy, the most unforgivable and tragic limitation of her situation, was this: though he might recognize the depth of her anger when she unleashed it in a fit, this very hour, he would never understand the nature of the long suffering that was its source.

Am I right? The question flashed purposelessly as she knocked at the front door. The answer didn't matter. She was committed to this final expression of her implacable anger, this final judgment.

Esther opened the door. Sarah walked past her into the living room.

They were united for the first time: her father, her sisters, her brother, and now herself. Her father was lying on the sofa, and Marianna was seated in front of his chest, his arm around her waist. Edwin and Minah were standing in front of the dining table, where Esther was now sitting with bowed head before a nearly empty bottle of soju. At the center of the room, on the coffee table, lay a slice of chocolate cake topped with a candied cherry.

Edwin was dressed in a dark suit, his hands in fists at his sides, his entire face clenched tight, looking to Sarah as if he'd arrived at the wake of his beloved father only to find this buffoon of a relative intoxicated and dribbling insults. Minah was at his side, her arms folded, her dark eyes flickering with intensity. Her face was powdered a shade too pale, her lips were blotted a crimson red. Through her makeup she seemed to be communicating that she was prepared to meet any conflict with vindictive focus and unnatural energy. Her fierce appearance and rigid comportment rhymed with his, his with hers. They look like a couple, Sarah thought. They've met and talked more than a few times, more than Minah has let on. Their closeness generated a particular magnetism. As with the many couples Sarah met who looked and moved and talked alike and could easily pass as siblings, if not fraternal twins, she intuited that the erotic appeal was in the golden taste of a nostalgic homecoming, a delicious shared dream of an original home. No one else in the family truly made sense to another member, not Sarah to Esther, who would never forgive her, nor Minah to Sarah, who had never dreamt of raising a child. Only Edwin and Minah belonged to the same world.

These were the impressions that crowded Sarah's mind when she entered the room. It was Marianna, however, who commanded the core of her attention. She consciously noted again that Marianna was South Asian: her rapid elevation in the unwholesome household suddenly made more sense. Eugene reviled other, darker-skinned Asians as trashy, dishonest, immoral, just as he did other collective bodies of color. When he maligned Mexicans and Black people, his judgment was more severe, not heated but cold and absolute because he deemed them wholly, inhumanly other. Yet he tended to be reticent and even timidly respectful when in close contact with Latinos and Black people, in offices and lines, in transactions behind or before the register. In parking lots he ceded a coveted space; on narrow sidewalks he smiled mildly and drew to the side, pulling Sarah beside him. Around these others he sensed most uncomfortably, even fearfully, his own hatred and confused it with their potential to inflict violence on him. And so Sarah was not surprised when she heard from Edwin, through Esther, that their father had apparently been polite, if cool, with Ruby in the beginning, until growing familiarity made Eugene feel entitled to treat his aide as he would any other woman under his roof.

Other Asians, on the other hand—they were like failed, fallen creations of the same maker of the Chinese and their offshoot on the Korean peninsula. Other Asians to the southwest roused in him the heat of excited disgust, the sickly-sweet allure of slumming and sliding down the standards of civilized Asia, the thrilling promise of denigration, baked into the very pigment of their skin. A hot wave of nausea roiled through Sarah. She was seeing Marianna from within her father's skull, and the family resemblance between him and herself roused disdain, even a desire to treat Marianna badly. The thought was devastating, sickening: though she might consciously reject all forms of bigotry, she'd been unable to disinherit her father's fear and judgment of otherness. It was difficult for her to be with people not because she was broken by her past. She, too, hated and feared contamination.

She would not be sullied any further.

Marianna made her precarious position on the edge of the sofa seem like a lofty perch. One moment she was derisively ignoring Eugene's children by exaggeratedly chewing her gum and examining her glossy nails; the next, she was sitting upright with subtly lifted chin, projecting noble superiority. She had exchanged her scrub-like outfit for black leggings and a red tube top under a ratty open cardigan.

Marianna's eyes alighted on Sarah but a second before she lowered her gaze to study her nails again. Her presence, Sarah realized, unnerved Marianna, and Marianna did not want to show it.

Minah was the first to break the silence. She addressed Sarah.

"This person you hired from God knows where has convinced our father to refuse radiation and hormone therapy. On her recommendation, he's asking for special herbs—do I have that right? Herbs that will cure metastatic cancer? Which she says she'll administer, because she knows a lot about alternative medicine. Did you know her uncle cured a cancerous mole with some black paste he got off the internet?"

Sarah felt her throat swelling. It was a lifelong somatic instinct to preclude any words that could be turned against her; to play dead. The courage of rage drained from her.

Marianna patted Eugene's arm and turned to whisper in his ear so that her breasts were hovering by his face. Sarah noticed that her father looked well, strangely well. Only then did she realize his face was sallow and drawn when she first saw him here months ago and Saturday morning, too, whereas now his complexion was tawny and bright. He was glowing, once more, as the indomitable patriarch of her youth. He wore an amused, noncommittal grin, as if the tension in the room had nothing to do with him, and he was waiting with all the patience in the world for it to die down so he could enjoy his chocolate cake in peace.

He clucked his tongue.

"You might be a lawyer in nice clothes, but you're no better than this Filipina girl here. At least she's honest with me. And why shouldn't I try the medicine she says will cure me?"

Sarah didn't know the precise meaning of what he said, but she understood its significance as it blustered through her like a hot, cindery wind. His Korean was like a searing hallucination. It was not her mind but her nerves that translated the phrases, the cadences, the overwrought tones that vibrated in the tortured dialect of her childhood.

"What do you care? What does he care?" He pointed his chin toward Edwin. "You want me to die. I know. I know you were pretending to care because you want my money. Now you want your revenge. For everything you did for me. You want revenge for doing what you freely chose to do. Fine. But at least be honest. This one here"—he pushed his index finger into Marianna's thigh—"tells me what she doesn't like about me. She says I smell bad and my teeth are yellow. My scarred hand is the hand of a monster. She says I'm a miserable creature. But she understands how much I've suffered. And she's going to help me enjoy the rest of my life. I'm not going to spend my last days vomiting and limping and going out of my mind from your medicine. I know that's what you want. No, I'm going to be with someone who can make me happy!"

He gave a guttural snarl. Its savagery jolted everyone: Minah's jaw dropped, Edwin's fists unclenched, Esther's breath caught in her chest as it rose. Sarah's throat closed tighter. The family had taken another step further into madness, into a terrible new dynamic in which anything was permitted.

He chuckled. "Edwin, my son, at least you did help take care of me. But that bitch there—I curse the day I met her mother, I curse the day she was born!"

"I've stayed away because you despise me, you insult me, you said you couldn't stand the sight of my face. And because I can't stand the sight of you. I came here to help, believe it or not. It makes me sick just to be in the same room with you, and I still came here to help! Despite everything you did to our mother. Despite everything you did to my mother. I know God will punish you for what you did. Knowing that gives me peace. That's why I can pity you. I pity you so much I'm even trying to help you by getting rid of this ignorant slut of a criminal who's the only one here trying to kill you for money."

It was, for all in the room, astonishing and even thrilling to see and hear Minah rising to meet her father in flawless Korean. Her siblings knew of her fluency, but none had ever witnessed it flood a room with such power.

"He's already punished me. You're here now, aren't you? I'm dying, and here I am, with you." He locked eyes with Minah. A leering smile spread across his face.

"Appah," Sarah said. *"That's enough."* The Korean words broke from her unexpectedly. She heard an echo of her mother in them. Stop, that's enough. That's enough, she would say in Korean when her daughters were fighting, crying, or complaining.

His grin faded.

"I have to talk to you," she said in English. Again, the words emerged without volition.

He pushed Marianna off the sofa. He was wearing a long hospital-style gown that tied at the side. As he kicked off his blanket, Sarah had a glimpse of his purplish hairless testicles. To her surprise, she did not react with horror, but took in the sight as a neutral, abstracted picture of human genitals.

They reminded her of newborn mice. An epithet from a poem she couldn't remember came to her: *Apollo, Lord of Light and Mice.*

She had spent too long alone in her room magnifying his awfulness, putting her father in a category outside the bearable, natural, salvable. He was another sick mind in a dying body. That was all he was now.

She thought, Maybe I wouldn't be so shocked by my fucked-up family if I got out more.

She would do what she hadn't intended to do. She would try to undo the chaos she had indirectly caused through Marianna. She would make a penitent effort for Esther's sake.

"Help me walk to the bedroom," he said, his voice mild, even cowed.

Wait a minute, she thought. That doesn't make sense. I have to remember to look up the poem. How is Apollo the Lord of Mice?

He leaned into her, and she smelled Marianna's perfume. It smelled amazing. It must have rubbed off Marianna—she balked at the thought— or Marianna had anointed him with it as a joke. She imagined it was the kind of play that had occupied them since she'd left her father in Marianna's hands only forty-eight hours ago.

She was acutely conscious of Marianna and her siblings watching her hoist her father up. She felt she could simultaneously see her hands before her and, from their perspective, see herself supporting him.

Say it, she said to herself, as she watched herself: You have an unseemly pervert and tyrant of a father.

You have an unseemly pervert and tyrant of a father.

It was not so hard. Didn't support groups also encourage you to articulate plainly what had happened to you? It was supposed to be therapeutic to say what was making you suffer and hurt yourself, but in language that was neutral and accurate. She told herself, Don't even call him a pervert or a tyrant. Just say, *He abused me.* But what if naming was not the problem? Just as with survivors, victims . . . She had grown up hearing and referring to those who suffered crimes as "victims." She was still training herself to substitute for the older term, with its fatalistic overtone, the more positive descriptor connoting resilience and evolution. She studied language, she paid attention to how people spoke, she was sensitive to the contrails of words. But surely the change in term made no substantial difference in the life of the person, even if it subtly altered public perception of the person who did or did not continue to suffer from the violation. She wanted, in theory, to espouse the more politically sensitive and humane language; and she wanted to lash out at those for whom a change in language was a substitute for the dirty work of care. She had flinched from this work all her life; she recoiled from the grotesquely upbeat thought of herself or others who suffered like her, worse than her, as benefiting materially from words that were so easy to change and choose, so ineffectual compared to what she was doing for her father now. She was holding him.

As they made their way down the hallway she heard Minah raising her voice: "Here, take my card! Look up my law firm! My family will sue you for elder abuse."

"Don't threaten me!" Marianna shrieked. The next moment she gave a forced laugh and said, "Take it easy! You need to relax!"

Once in the bedroom Eugene asked Sarah to close the door and set him down in the chair. He motioned for her to sit on the bed.

On the mattress her feet hovered inches above the floor. He, in the chair, appeared formidable, unmovable. His presence had the brute facticity of a slab of meat on marble.

The thought was a whisper: I am not going to say anything I wanted to say.

"It's good to sit in a chair," he said with a sigh. "I feel more like myself. Your father's feeling better now."

He reached for her hand, but she did not offer it. He could not take it without bestirring himself and gave up.

"That's okay. I understand. Your *daddy* is acting shamefully. I know that. I'm sorry."

His impudent smile revealed his teeth. They were no longer merely yellow but brownish, with white mossy spots here and there.

She thought, It's only a symptom of his treatments. That's what it has to be.

When a response did not come, he grew annoyed. "Well? You had something to say to me?"

"Yes."

"What did you want to say?"

"I should have"—she remembered he didn't use past conditionals in English—"I wish I came to see you before. I wish I came to see you more often."

Because I was not fair to Esther.

His face lit up like a jack-o'-lantern's.

She said, "If you want to keep Marianna, that's okay." *If you—want to— keep—Mari—anna*. She was laboriously reproducing the stilted rhythm of his English, the ugly spondaic hammering of syllables unnaturally isolated or joined.

When she tried to scan poetry she nearly always got the meter wrong. If poetry was based on breath and human rhythms, she had the wrong body. In the body that she had—in the body that she was—she couldn't hear its meter or feel its music.

"That's okay," she repeated. "But she's not helping you. She is not helpful. She does not care about you." He tended not to use contractions, as if they rendered too supple the hard meaning of his words. "She cares about herself. She is not trying, she does not try"—he didn't use the present progressive; the eternal, simple present was his world—"to make you better."

"What are you saying?" he asked in Korean, suspicion edging into his voice. She wasn't sure whether he was questioning her sincerity or rightness, or simply uncomprehending of what she was saying.

"I say, she is bad for you. She is not good. She wants only money. She does not care if you die. We care. We care if you are healthy or not. If you are sick or not. We want you to see the doctor and take real medicine."

"*Say again?*" he said in English, his expression hostile with frustration.

"I say, we want you to see the doctor and listen to the doctor. The doctor tries to help you. The doctor wants to help you. We try to help you. We want to help you."

"*You want help me?*"

"Yes. Me and Esther and Minah and Edwin."

How had she gone from preparing her tragic excoriation to this insipid recitation of what her siblings no doubt wanted her to say?

I am playing a role. The role of a decent person. I am playing a role for my sisters' sake. If now I say what's in my heart, I will privilege my unhappiness over theirs. The curtain will close over me, and I will be alone.

"*You, you come here, you do help?*" he said, still eyeing her with suspicion.

"Yes."

"*You come every day, like Mari?*"

"I'll try. To come. Every day. It depends."

"*Depends?*" His face darkened.

"It depends on how much work I have." She stopped conforming to his brutally emphatic English, though she was still speaking slowly. "I cannot come all the time. I have too much work. But the others can help. Esther will come, and Minah will come. She should come. You should let her come. Minah cares about you, too. Edwin will come and also take you to your doctors' appointments. We will all take care of you."

He grunted. "*You come, or you do not come?*"

"I come," she said with obvious exasperation. "But not every day."

He grimaced. "*You do not come every day, why I fire Mari-anna?*"

"Don't fire her then. *I said I come. But not every day.* I can't. *I cannot.* You can ask Marianna to stay sometimes. Some nights. And we come during the day. *Daytime I come, Esther and Edwin and maybe Minah come. Okay?*"

"Okay," he said gruffly.

"Don't fight with Minah. She's not bad. Minah is not bad. She helps you and she helps me, too. She wants to help. Okay?" She could already hear herself explaining to her sister that she'd persuaded him to let her visit so she might further her mercenary plan herself.

"Okay," he said, still glum.

"Okay," she said, and exhaled. She got off the bed.

"*Okay. Daddy tired now. You help me.*" He got up and sat where she had just been and pointed to his feet. She was confused at first, then helped him lift his legs onto the bed.

"*Okay, okay,*" he said, sighing. "*You go.*"

She went to the bathroom and washed her hands.

Sarah found all three of her siblings seated around the dining table. Marianna was gone.

"I think she got scared. She got scared when she found out I was a lawyer," Minah informed her matter-of-factly, without evincing any relief.

"I told him I'd come by more often. I said all of you wanted to help, and he agreed. He even agreed to have you, Minah, help him."

Minah raised her brow in surprise, which then fell as she brooded over the implications. "Okay," she said. "I'll do that."

"And Marianna?" Esther said.

"He won't fire Marianna. But he's agreed to reduce her shifts. Mostly to nights." She thought, This is not a lie. It's a consequence. I'm not coming here every day. I won't spend a night here again.

"All right, then," Minah said with a low exhalation of disgust. "Have her crawl out of whatever hole she lives in and look after him some nights this week until we can find someone else."

"He says it's either us or Marianna."

This, she confessed to herself, was a lie. But she could not bear to have yet another well-meaning woman enter their circle to endure their father.

"Fine." Minah turned to address Sarah forcefully. "You have to look after him tonight. Okay?"

"But I don't have any of my things, my toothbrush. I—okay."

"Okay."

Edwin cleared his throat. "I have his new prescription. I'm gonna go in and talk to him now. The directions are on the bottle, as always. Give him just one pill as needed. It might help with his mood, too."

The hard shine of his hubris was gone. He had complained to his sisters of being sleep-deprived without ever looking less than eager and vigorous, until now. His cheekbones appeared sharper; his eyes were sunken and filmed with fatigue. He pulled the stapled paper bag of Eugene's medication out of his backpack and disappeared down the hall.

Minah, too, appeared deflated, her shoulders slumped, her expression mildly bewildered, as if she was trying to remember why she thought her cause was worth this battle. Only Esther remained visibly agitated by the scene that had just taken place. Her eyes were glittering. Her chest was still rising and falling visibly, though more steadily.

As Sarah lowered herself onto the sofa, she felt she was sinking into the reigning silence.

After a minute, Minah said, "I'm going to get a ride back to the city with Edwin. Esther, why don't you come with us? And spend the night with me."

"I—I don't know."

"Just come. You need a break. And I'll finally be able to help you. Help out. Sarah, are you sure he'll really let me come by sometimes? Are you sure he'll accept that?" Minah asked quietly, almost meekly.

Sarah was moved by her tone. "That's what he said. Whether he actually will or not, I don't know. But I think he will. I'll ask him again."

"I should ask him myself. I want to make sure he will. I don't . . . want any more scenes. I'm going to ask him. I'll talk to him before I leave."

"If you want."

They fell silent again until Edwin reappeared. "He just asked to see you," he said in a low voice.

"Who?" Minah asked.

"You."

Minah got up with slow, almost ceremonious deliberateness.

Sarah, too, got up. She wanted to extract herself from the dazed atmosphere. "I need to catch up on some emails. I'll call you later, Esther. Bye, Edwin." She addressed him particularly with conciliatory mildness.

Esther was brooding over the bottle of soju.

Sarah left for the other bedroom. She opened her laptop with the intention of carrying through with her excuse and responding to a couple of students protesting their grades. She didn't hear Esther enter.

"I'm not going to stay with Minah. I think I'll stay here with you."

Sarah didn't know why she was so vexed by the way Esther had slipped into the room, but she allowed her irritation to carry her. "Why?" The question emerged as a challenge.

"Because Dad is acting strangely."

"Of course he's acting strangely. That's who he is. Though I'm not sure 'strange' is the word."

"That's not what I mean. He's been sleeping or half asleep all week, then suddenly he's all excitable. That's strange even for him."

"He has metastatic cancer. This excitable phase is just him getting worked up over Marianna and shaking off a totally normal lethargy for his condition. He's dying. Whatever you think about her, she's actually making him happy. What's wrong with that?"

"Marianna's letting him drink. He can't drink on his painkillers. I don't care if Marianna stays as long as he's getting the right care," Esther said defiantly.

"What makes you think he isn't? Because I'm here and you don't trust me?"

After a moment of reflection, she said, "I don't know."

"Esther, stop taking care of everyone!" Sarah said with vicious exasperation. "Please, just go back with Minah or to my place. Whatever you want. I want to be here alone."

Sarah expected to see her sister wounded, her eyes watering and lip trembling. But Esther was eerily stony, almost impassive, with the exception of her eyes, which were focused intently on Sarah.

"I'll be fine," Sarah said more equably. "We'll be fine. I won't let him drink. I promise." She looked up timidly, hoping to see Esther returned to her usual even temper, but her sister's face was still intent and hard.

Sarah knew Esther could be tough when toughness was called for. She saw now Esther also possessed the rarer ability to invest her insights with power. Had she inherited it from Anna? The first she admired in her sister; the latter now disturbed her as she felt Esther's illuminated consciousness burning through her, seeking to uncover and lay waste to everything within her that made her weak, that might push her to betray her family again. If Esther stayed the night, she would be hollowed out.

"Please, leave us," Sarah said gently, trying to conceal her desperation and then her sadness. Had this exchange never taken place, she would have been glad of Esther's company.

Esther shut the door behind her. Sarah got up to leave it ajar, to signal to her siblings that she was surveilling their father.

She'd heard Minah enter their father's bedroom and close the door, and could hear her speaking to him now. She thought she heard her father grunt, "All right, all right," and Minah's words continuing to flow unimpeded. She kept straining her ears to catch something of what Minah was saying. It didn't sound to Sarah as if Minah were distraught; if she wasn't clashing with him again, she must be repeating more or less what Sarah had said before her. She gave up trying to understand but kept listening. The steady susurrations in Korean sent her into a reverie. She imagined Minah delivering the speech with which Sarah herself had wanted to confront their father. In this fantasy, Minah was translating Sarah's message so perfectly that her words surpassed Sarah's English in their accuracy. It was a miracle by which all that Sarah wanted to say was so wholly, ideally expressed that the translation transcended language. It was the truth imparted with such purity that her father would suffer not only her judgment, but all that she had suffered under him, once the words flowed into the cup of his ear.

She was roused from her daydream when Minah left her father's room.

Bustling in the living room indicated that Minah and Edwin, at least, were leaving. She waited a few minutes and crept down the hallway. Esther had left with them. She was, indeed, alone with her father.

She knocked on her father's door and entered. He was sleeping.

She returned to the other bedroom, stretching out once more on her old bed. She felt empty; time passed.

She stared at the bookcase for a long time before she realized she recognized one of the spines. It was a notebook with a drawing of a cat sleeping in a flower bed on the cover. She had asked her father to buy it for her when she was eight or nine. For a year or more she'd kept it concealed in her underwear drawer, taking it out to write diary entries or stories. She vaguely remembered neglecting it, then losing it. He must have found it and held on to it.

She sat kneeling on the floor as she turned the pages as circumspectly as if they belonged to a medieval manuscript.

Dear diary, Esther is a spoiled brat and Minah is stupid and mean. It's not fair. Emily has such a nice big sister and her little sister is so cute. I wish I could babysit her. Emily is so pretty too. She's so lucky. I really want a skirt like the one she wore this week.

I hate him I hate him I hate him. I'm going to run away. I'm sick of everyone.

We went on a field trip. I need a new backpack to carry everything for when I leave.

Minah came home with a goldfish yesterday and it's already dead. Minah said I fed it too much and killed it but it wasn't me. Esther is a brat she thinks everything is hers so I know she fed it.

Emily lived in a sad small house with her sisters and her father, who was cruel. One day in her backyard she heard a voice. It was someone talking to her on the other side of the fence.

"I am a witch," the voice said. "Come with me and I will make you a powerful witch like me."

Emily didn't know what to do. She wanted to leave and be powerful but she didn't want to be a witch.

I WISH HE WAS DEAD TOO

Europe sounds so beautiful. I'll go there and everything will change. Everything will be beautiful.

Sarah shut the book.

"Hey! Help!" her father called out. *"Hello! Help me.* Is anyone there? *Hey, hey!"*

Sarah was still sitting on the floor with her notebook in her lap. She pulled herself up, entered his bedroom, and switched on the light.

"What's wrong?" she said tonelessly.

"Ah, it's you." His voice was gentle with relief. His eyes were still closed and he was breathing heavily.

"Do you need something?"

"I'm thirsty. Get me some Coke."

She remembered to pour it into a tall glass with ice and add a straw, as he liked. Back in the bedroom, her father was sitting up.

"My back is hurting again," he groaned, rubbing his side. "Help me get to the bathroom." He carefully swiveled his legs off the bed.

She didn't know where to leave the drink. The nightstand was littered with used tissues hard with dried mucus, used straws, an open can of Coke, the odious mug of sputum, his phone. She guessed he or Marianna had recently spilled Coke on the carpet where a brown stain had set in.

She noticed a greasy impression of his head on his pillow. When was the last time Edwin washed his hair? When had anyone last washed the sheets?

She moved to the other side of the bed, where the table held various prescription bottles, pamphlets about medications, printouts from the hospital, opened and unopened mail, his laptop, and a legal pad with notes and phone numbers in her father's familiar slanted hand. The numbers, most with LA area codes, had a corresponding list of names and identifiers in English and Korean. In English she read: *Doctor LA. Edwin. Lawyer. Sarah. Insurance. Doctor Uro. Edwin Work. Attorney. Esther. Mari.*

"Hey! I need bathroom!"

She left the drink at the edge of the table and turned and realized the walker was behind her. She started pulling it toward him when he said, "*No, you come here.*" He leaned on her with what seemed like more than his full weight. He felt heavier than he had that afternoon; she thought she would topple. He stooped lower, and she thought he would pull her through the floor.

"You have to stand straighter," she said with a gasp.

He didn't. He would not. He did not acknowledge that she'd spoken, any more than if she'd been a mule. She repeated herself more loudly.

He repeated, more vehemently, *"I need bathroom!"*

With her next breath, strength seemed to return to her. She dragged her father, step by step. He moved his legs with nearly spastic jerks, as if he was, not weak, but not entirely in possession of his body because it was half flesh, half stone.

She stopped at the bathroom threshold.

"Toilet! I—need—sit!"

It had been a long time since she heard him explode with such rage. Adrenaline lit up every filament of nerve in her. The cracks and tiny pores in the beige paint of the walls shot into focus. The skin on her nape tingled and grew hot, burning as it did when she was young and he raised his voice. The surfaces around her were rendered vivid and exact as if by the electrical power of her nerves. At the same time she felt herself receding within herself: she was there, glimpsing her environs with these shots of brightness, but her mind was withdrawing. She nearly tripped on the door sill as he drooped once more. A scene from the past infused with the same quality of apocalyptic rage flashed before her. He was holding her hand, confronting a white man outside the man's place of business. Her father said he was owed three months' rent. With an air of snide indifference the man said he didn't understand. Her father repeated himself; the man said he didn't understand. The blast of rage vibrated through her body: *"My English is not good goddamn it! You talk to my lawyer, goddamn it!"*

He was still leaning against her as she lifted the lid of the toilet. The back of the seat was sprayed with yellow-brown shit.

"Okay. You go now," he said wearily.

She ran into the kitchen and washed her hands, soaping and rinsing once, twice. A voice told her: Leave. You have to leave. She would rush home and shower in the hottest water she could stand. Another memory blazed into her consciousness with the same hallucinatory immediacy of the confrontation with the white mustached man indebted to her father. She was about seven or eight, at home with Minah, who was taking a bath. Their father had left on what he said was a business trip the day before; Carla was supposed to come by after school to look after them but hadn't shown up. They felt an effervescent sense of freedom without him. So Minah had decided to take a bath. From the bathroom she called out for Sarah to get her *Teen* magazine from her backpack. The sight of the cloud banks of bubbles, the sophisticated luxury of reading in a steaming tub, filled Sarah with envy, and she declared, "I want to take a bath, too." "It's too hot for you," Minah said. She took Sarah's hand and plunged it into the scalding water. Sarah screamed in pain; she forgot her pain at the shock of Eugene bursting into the confined space. He banged his fist on Minah's head, crying, "What did you do? What did you do, you worthless bitch?" As Minah thrashed and screamed, he grabbed her hair and pounded her head, shoulders, neck, breasts, again and again. Sarah would never hear a scream like that again. It was a horrifying screech, like that of a rat, a monkey, being rent alive by a predator. It only riled Eugene further.

She could hear Minah scream again. She would help him back into his bed. Then she would leave. She didn't care if he was alone, if he died in the night alone. She had to save herself.

She would go mad if he touched her again. She remembered the first time he had locked her out of the house at night when she was a young child, how he'd shouted from behind the front door: "I give you up, let anyone who wants you take you. Let any stranger come and do whatever he wants with you." As she pounded on the door she knew she would lose her mind if she felt even the slightest touch at that moment. She felt now as she did then, but now it was not a stranger, it was her father whose contact would maim her forever.

She would die if she had to touch him again.

She would have to touch him again to help him back into his bed.

He was still in the bathroom when she got her phone and called Marianna.

"Hi," Marianna said brightly. "What can I do for you?"

"I want you to come back for the night. We agreed after you left that we'd still like you to come over some nights. I'm sorry if my sister was harsh with you, but we do need you, and she agreed."

"Mr. Kim still hasn't paid me for the last weekend," she said with saccharine sweetness. "Can I get paid tonight? He said he'd pay me every Monday."

"Sure, I'll make sure he pays you." She could hear him farting, grunting, cursing. She had no intention of involving herself in any other of her father's matters. A lie didn't deserve judgment if it was told in utter panic.

The alacrity and ease with which Marianna agreed to return told Sarah that she was unfazed by melodrama, even comfortable with it. Sarah envied her then. Marianna had a fluency in human affairs that she doubted she'd ever possess.

"Come as soon as you can."

"Well, I'm sorry to bring this up, but I didn't know I'd be returning this evening and I don't have a ride. I'll have to take an Uber, and from where I live it'll be about fifteen dollars. That's more than I make an hour. So, is it—"

"Fine, I'll pay for your ride and for overtime today."

"Great! Thanks so much! It's very generous of you. You know, your father told me you're his favorite."

"Just get the fuck over here as soon as you can!" She caught her breath. "I'm so sorry, I'm really sorry, I didn't mean to swear like that. I'm under a lot of stress. It's not personal." She heard herself adopting the same mincing, cloying tone as Marianna. "I didn't mean it. I'm sorry. Will you come soon?"

"Of course," Marianna said with a laugh.

Sarah's place was empty. So Esther was with Minah.

She took a hot shower, washed down potato chips with vodka, and went to bed. As she was falling asleep she wondered whether she was sensitive to heat or whether Minah was literally thick-skinned and exceptionally receptive to it. How could Minah have tolerated the temperature of that water? Sarah's hand was tender for hours.

Sarah's phone buzzed and rattled on her nightstand. She heard her phone but found it nearly impossible to rouse herself. "I'm coming," she said weakly.

She opened her eyes, remembered she was at home, and reached for her phone. It was Marianna.

"Please, please, come, come now!" Between words, Marianna was gasping and sobbing.

"What's happened? What's going on?"

"He's dead, I called 911, the ambulance is coming, I have to go, I can't be here. Please come, come now, please!"

"What?"

"I told you! He's dead! I called 911. I don't want to be here. You have to come now! I can't be here!" She hung up.

Sarah put the phone down and lay back in bed. She breathed steadily for several seconds before her chest began rising rapidly. The news hit her heart before it reached her brain. She sat up with a feeling of something like savage anticipation, like a hound pawing and howling to begin the hunt.

She called Esther and reached her voicemail.

She called Minah, who answered after just a couple of rings.

"What happened?" she demanded anxiously. Sarah had an image of Minah spending this night and many before this in semi-wakefulness, waiting for death.

"I think he's dead."

"Did you call the ambulance? The hospital?"

"Yes. No. Marianna did. I'm heading there now."

"You mean you're not there? You were supposed to be there! Why aren't you there?"

"That doesn't matter now. What matters is that she's totally panicked and says she's going to leave. I'm headed there now. I can't wait for a train, I'm going to call a car, but if you do the same you'll get there before me."

"Okay. Okay." Minah hung up.

≈

Sarah found Marianna weeping on the sofa with Minah and Esther on either side of her.

The paramedics had arrived and pronounced Eugene dead on the scene. They had already taken his body away.

"They said it's not my fault," Marianna said to Esther.

"What was happening that made you call 911?" Esther asked.

"He was dead. He wasn't breathing."

"Did this happen in his sleep?"

"No," she said with a powerful sob. "I don't know. They said it's not my fault. They said it happens," she went on with terrible, needy urgency, appealing to each sister in turn. "They said they've seen it before."

"Seen what before?"

She shook her head and continued sobbing.

"Tell us now," Minah said coldly.

Marianna looked pleadingly to Sarah. She looked so unhappy, so pathetic, that Sarah felt a tug at her heart, but she said nothing.

"Tell me," Esther said gently.

"Okay . . . Okay. When I got here, he was sleeping. After you left"—she looked to Sarah—"I checked on him. Around ten or eleven I heard him shouting for Sarah. He thought she was still here, and he was really angry she was gone, and that maybe set off his back pain. He was so angry and kept yelling that he was in a lot of pain. So I did what you told me, I remembered everything you told me. I even double-checked the bottle and the instructions you left in the kitchen. I gave him a pill of the new stuff. But he kept complaining and a half hour later he was still in pain. He said he wanted more, so I gave him another pill around midnight. But he wouldn't stop complaining. It was awful. It was awful, he kept groaning and complaining, he even started to cry. It was so awful. I held his hand and told him I wasn't supposed to give him more. So I . . . I gave him some soju. I couldn't say no, he was in so much pain, and it seemed to help. I was about to call you, but the soju calmed him down and I thought I could wait till tomorrow. He seemed better, and I was so tired, you know. I had such a long day and I went to lie down. You have to understand, I had such a long day. I was so tired from worrying and crying after meeting all of you. So I fell asleep and didn't wake up until around six. That's when I went to his room. He wasn't in his bed. I checked everywhere. I thought I was going crazy. I went back to his room and didn't know what to do. That's when I noticed lots of pills on the floor, in the back of the room, on the other side of the bed. And I went there and he was on the floor. There were pills everywhere. He was lying on the floor, and he had a plastic bag on his head."

Part 5

—Hypocrite lecteur,—mon semblable,—mon frère!

—Charles Baudelaire, *Les fleurs du mal*

1
After hell

M inah felt she'd been waiting all this time to brush her hapless sisters aside and take over.

When Minah learned the EMTs had taken their father's body to his hospital, which was also Edwin's hospital, she left at once for the morgue, identified the body, and arranged its transfer to the funeral home she knew through clients.

She contacted the pastor at her church to organize a humble funeral, which she attended with her sisters. No one else was there. Edwin had already called Esther to say he had an emergency with a patient.

She charged Esther with deciding what to do with the ashes, to find a plot or scatter them as she chose. She directed Sarah to either take for herself or get rid of everything in his apartment. Either she or Sarah was also to fly to California in the near future to meet with an estate liquidator whom Minah had already hired for the family home. And she took it upon herself to call the numbers for the lawyer and attorney noted in Eugene's papers.

The lawyer was a man based in Koreatown whose receptionist answered the phone in Korean: "You have reached the law office of Joseph Cheong."

When she heard Eugene's name, her voice grew cold. "He's no longer a client with us," she said.

"But he was your client, and I need to know if he wrote a will with you," Minah said.

The receptionist hesitated, then repeated, with stupid helplessness, "He's no longer a client with us."

"Will you at least leave my number for Mr. Cheong?"

Minah's phone rang ten minutes later.

"Your father has some nerve asking you to call me. I represented him for twenty-two years. Twenty-two years of my life I slaved over all his suits. I funneled heaps of cash his way. And he drops me? He's a criminal, that's what. Tell him I said that. He's a common criminal and a cheat who still owes me money. If he wants another favor from me he's going to have to settle his debts and then some."

"Mr. Cheong, my father is dead. I need to know if you have a copy of his will."

"Oh. Oh. I'm sorry for your loss. But I don't know anything about a will." He received the news like an athlete clearing a hurdle, accelerating, stoking himself to anger again. "He left us three, four years ago. He still owes me money. It was a debt of honor. As his daughter, it's your responsibility to pay his debts. The things I did for him—it's your filial duty."

"Dear Mr. Cheong, I don't know what kind of favors you granted him in the past, but I'm sure that you, too, are no better than a common criminal if you could represent a man like my father for that long. Goodbye."

After hanging up she promptly dialed the number for the "attorney."

"Hello" boomed through the receiver in a thick, meaty, masculine voice. "This is Jeffrey Miner, attorney-at-law."

Minah explained the reason for her call. She wondered if her father had discovered this lawyer, who didn't even have a receptionist, on a billboard or in a hospital waiting room.

"Well, yeah, I have the will. So he's deceased then? Too bad. I'm sorry to hear that. He was a good guy. He was funny. He did want to make another change in the will, and I told him we had to work through some details together and he'd have to approve it and sign, and he told me to do it myself. So it's the same will he made in September, which updated the one he made in the spring. Everything goes to you. But I'm telling you now, he told me he wanted to give a quarter of his estate to that son of his. I just thought you should know his wishes. It's the least I can do for him now. He kept telling me to figure it out. He was funny that way. Let's see, yes, I'm pulling it up now. I have it all saved on my computer. Don't worry, I have a copy he signed, too. Everything goes to Sarah Kim."

"Sarah Kim." She drew the name out softly. "I'm Minah."

"Oops, sorry about that. I'm not good with foreign names. But it's here. It's in black and white. Everything to his daughter Sarah. Every cent and stock. Sorry again about that, and for your loss."

Minah gathered the sisters in her apartment to tell them what she'd learned about the will. "I don't want to talk about it over the phone," she'd told Sarah.

At the moment Minah was forking her deli salad and avoiding the subject. She was wearing a soft gray woolen robe over luminously pale silk pajamas. Esther was across from her, breaking crackers into her fragrant chicken soup. She had evidently borrowed a light blue sweater of visible cloudlike softness and dark jeans, which fit her seamlessly; she was closer in height and shape to Minah than Sarah, her figure fuller with more obvious curves. She was transformed in Minah's fashionable clothing, changed to the point of appearing to Sarah, to one who knew her, as diminished or lost. With appropriate touches, Esther could blend into any situation because she never dominated a scene, either visually or by dint of charisma. She was easy to forget until you needed her.

Before Sarah's arrival, Esther had expressed her desire to return to school, possibly at CUNY. Now Minah was talking on and on with sententious effusion about how proud she was of Esther; how hard it had been for her to earn her own degree and then defy all expectations to go on and receive an advanced law degree; how she would support Esther in any way as she pursued her dreams.

Sarah was watching Minah bubble with encouragement, trying her best to remain seated upright on Minah's sofa. On her left lay the enticingly plump down pillow Esther had used last night. She longed to sink her head into it and wrap its sides over her ears. Minah is so transparent, Sarah said to herself. He didn't leave her anything, did he? That's no surprise. But with that thought, her heart fluttered.

I'll be free.

She was jolted back to the scene when Minah raised her voice: "Sarah, can't you help Esther apply to CUNY?" To Esther, she added, "Then you could stay in the city with me."

"Minah," Esther said, putting down her spoon, "what did you want to tell me and Sarah?"

Minah's already wan face seemed to grow thinner. She pushed her chair back and gathered up the remnants of her meal. "I talked to Dad's attorney," she said from the kitchen. She returned with a small glass of water, which she poured into a leafy potted plant by the window. "And I wanted to tell you about the will. But I got so excited when you told me you were going to stay, I got carried away."

"I'm not sure I'm going to stay. It depends."

"On what?"

"I don't know yet. On how I feel about staying here."

"Well, you don't have to decide now. Now we have to discuss the will," Minah said coolly, seated at the windowsill with folded arms, abruptly adopting the formal attitude she presented to her clients. "Sarah, you get everything."

All three lifted their gazes to survey the other two, like dancers meeting to attempt a complex choreography.

Minah was darkened against the afternoon light. Though her expression was obscured, Esther, at the table across the studio, and Sarah, between them on the sofa, could feel her studying them.

"Sarah, you made a promise to me, remember, the day we first talked about his will. You promised you would share anything with us equally. Will you keep your promise?"

"Yes," Sarah said, the word falling from her mouth in a stutter.

"Minah," Esther said. "Did you talk to the lawyer? Did he send you an official copy of the will?"

"Yes. It's here. I'll show you."

"When was it dated?"

"It's dated from September of this year. So it's recent."

"I know he called his lawyer just a few weeks ago," Esther said. "I heard him. I heard him saying he wanted to change his will to benefit Edwin. He said it in front of me, deliberately. He said, '*I change it for Edwin, not you,*' and told me to leave the room."

"Are you sure he was actually talking to his lawyer?" Minah asked.

The muscles in Esther's face did not move as she fixed on her sister a gaze of piercing lucidity.

"I don't know, he often does things for show!" Minah said in self-defense, rising and throwing up her arms before glancing down to her left and right, as if looking for the response she should have offered her sister.

She sat down onto the sofa, seemingly unaware of Sarah a couple of feet away at her side as she leaned forward to stare at Esther with equal intensity. "He often did," she said emphatically. But there was in her eyes a mere semblance of opposition that melted into a protestation of love, a plea for sympathy.

Esther turned to her sisters. Every lineament in her face, the very movement of her shoulders, bespoke an almost brutal self-certainty.

Minah swallowed. "The lawyer did tell me Dad said he wanted to leave something for Edwin. But he never bothered to finalize it even after his lawyer kept reminding him. It was an idea he deliberately never carried through. The lawyer emphasized that." She cleared her throat. "Saying that in front of you, saying that to his lawyer and not following through—that's just the kind of teasing game he likes to play." She paused. "That he liked to play."

Sarah was still reeling from the news of her inheritance—the whole of it, the millions, bursting into her life like a flood of fresh oxygen. Yes, she'd promised to share it, but she never said how. Her thoughts were racing. She could live off the interest of her millions and wait until she got settled before transferring two-thirds of the estate to her sisters. What she meant by "settled," she couldn't say. She'd be happy to pay for Esther's education, of course, and maybe Minah's credit card bills. That she could settle now, while promising the final disbursement later on. These are just fantasies, she told herself. Of course I'll share with them as soon as I get the money. I'm having fantasies because I'm free.

"Maybe," Esther said with a trace of impatience. "I don't think he would have cared if you didn't share with us"—at this Esther focused on Sarah, who suddenly felt deeply embarrassed to be looked at—"because he wanted you to do whatever you want to do with it. He imagined that you would probably share it with us. You say you will. If you do, it's up to us to decide whether to share with Edwin. That—that does seem like a test of the kind he wanted to leave us."

"*If* she does? She just agreed," Minah said severely, glancing at Sarah, challenging her, as if she'd read her mind.

Sarah's heart fluttered. The embarrassment of exposure turned to resentment. She thought, Okay, I'll share with Esther, and maybe even with Edwin, but to Minah I'll offer dribbles of cash now and then if she's in dire straits. She doesn't even need the money the way Esther and I do. She's going to marry Paul. In that same moment, she realized Minah hadn't mentioned Paul for a while. In the negative space between Minah's communications, Sarah made out Paul's absence.

"I said I would share, and I'll keep my promise," Sarah said with such anger that she surprised herself. Because a part of her was already suppressing the qualms of conscience, which murmured that Minah had spoken as she did because she'd intuited Sarah's fantasies of betrayal. Sarah had power over Minah. She felt this power clearing a space for itself within her, working to scrub away any remaining compunction. She would succumb to it if it paved a path of ease before her.

This is how it starts, she thought. I'm ready to stop scrambling and second-guessing myself. I want to rest.

Esther spoke, softly now. "Sarah, you say you'll split the inheritance with us. If you do, then we'll each be in a position to share with Edwin. That's a decision for each of us to make alone."

Minah raised her voice in ready response, shaking off the meekness that had momentarily overcome her before Esther. "No. I'm not going to share with Edwin. Neither will you, Esther."

"I would have thought that you'd want to share," Sarah said.

"Why?"

"Because you seem to like him a lot."

Minah glared savagely at Sarah. Sarah tried to return the searing look of fury and felt the beginning of tears. She thought, I've never wept from anger before. The next moment she sensed another emotion behind the tears she effectively suppressed, but she didn't have the time, not now, to identify it.

"I have been meeting with him now and then lately. I wanted to know what he was up to. I thought we agreed he's untrustworthy."

"Are you serious? That's why you've obviously been seeing him without telling me?"

"Stop it," Esther said wearily, as if she had already sat through a long hearing of the recriminations rapidly ramifying in her sisters' minds. "I know I want to share with Edwin. Whatever his motive, he did a lot for our father. He did. I think you're probably right, Minah. He might have encouraged Dad to come over to the East Coast with a false promise of better doctors. But I also think Dad knew Edwin was misrepresenting things or just lying. He played along because he didn't want to be alone during his

296 / MAUREEN SUN

treatment. You say Edwin's untrustworthy, and here we are, already arguing over Dad's money."

"No! I won't agree to it! I won't give him anything! And I won't let you give him anything, Esther. I won't let you!" Minah shouted imperiously. She leapt up; the next moment she willed herself to cool down and sank back into her place next to Sarah. She spoke almost softly; her words, however, remained equally vehement. "We deserve it, not him. Edwin may be our father's biological child. But he's not the child of his nurture. He didn't have to endure his nature at home for endless years. Endless days, hours, and years. We had to suffer it, you, me, and Sarah. That's what makes us his children. Not love, not even blood, but time. The time we lost suffering under him. Our brother is not his child."

"Suffering is a bond, but it's not the only one. It's not the only thing that ties you to me," Esther said passionately. "Our dad did feel bound to Edwin. I know he visited Edwin often when you and Sarah were gone. He'd often leave me at home for a few days or even a week. Maybe he came here or traveled somewhere we don't know. But he also went to see him. I've talked to Edwin about Dad's visits to him and his mom. He knew Dad was his father."

Sarah was sitting very still. She hoped her sisters wouldn't notice her. All anger, frustration, and embarrassment had drained from her, leaving only a distillate of fear. Minah shouted her outrage at Esther. Esther, too, was aflame. Sarah was appalled that Minah did not recognize the rarity of Esther's anger, nor its undeniable lucidity, which struck Sarah almost violently and frightened her. It felt violent to be asked to recognize anything but the demands and the suffering of the sufferer—the suffering of the three sisters. To do so was both heartless and lucid, righteous and obscene. Sarah did not want to agree with Esther, but she wanted Minah to stop defending herself. She did not want to hear any more of Esther's heartless illuminations.

Minah cried out, "No. No! Why don't you see? Edwin was trying to manipulate you. He knows you're the softest of the three of us. You're doing

UNCORRECTED REVIEW COPY — NOT FOR SALE

exactly what he wants you to do—argue on his behalf in the case he wasn't named in the will. You think I was spending time with him for his company?" She flashed a look of contempt at Sarah. "I found out he knew that if he could prove our dad recognized him officially or informally as his son he could easily claim at least a quarter of the estate. He made it clear that was why he was doing so much for him. But neither of us knew if Dad even had a will until recently. That's when he told me Dad was going to change the will to give everything to him and to Esther. He claimed Dad said he'd given up on me long ago and was now giving up on Sarah, too. God, he tried hard to hide that shit-eating grin when he told me. That was more or less what you told me, too, Sarah." She pronounced her sister's name with a hiss. "The whole time he was trying to manipulate all of us, to get away with our father's money by doing next to nothing. Because what he did for him was nothing, nothing compared to what you and Sarah and I have suffered! And he can never have suffered in the same way as us." She jerked back toward Esther. "Even if you and he spent an equal amount of time looking after our father, it couldn't have been as bad for him as it was for you. Don't you understand?"

Esther met Minah's eyes with calm dignity. She looked to Sarah like a cat staring upward with fearless curiosity at a person capable of starving or beating it. "I don't understand. Why was it worse for me?"

"Because he's not a girl. He's not a woman! He just can't have suffered in the same way as us. No. He wasn't a girl living under a domineering father, an abusive pervert, a leering misogynist. No. No!"

A sob throbbed through Minah's protest. She was sitting on the edge of the sofa, leaning closer to Esther, when she folded her chest over her lap. Her posture was essentially that of a mourner, a supplicant, but she gave the impression not of relinquishing power, but of focusing it, pressing it into the very core of her.

She sat up again. "He's not our brother. And he's not our father's son. He doesn't deserve any of our money. It was thanks to my mother—not

Jeonghee, but my mother, the woman who gave birth to me—that Dad made his first investments. The money he stole from her is the real root of his fortune." She began speaking and breathing more steadily. "My mother inherited from her father, my grandfather, in Korea, after marrying him. He forced her to transfer it to their joint bank account and wouldn't return it after she ran away. She couldn't do anything about it because she was in Korea. And she couldn't risk seeing him again. He would have murdered her. Maybe the money was legally his, but legal in this case doesn't mean right." Her voice began to rise with passion once more. "He stole from her. He stole from my mother, and I won't let him take my money from me again."

She unraveled with this final utterance. She moved back to the window, facing outward. She turned and began raging again. "The money was stolen from her, and from me, and I'm not giving up on it! I accept that I can't claim everything of his. But I'll never agree to splitting my share with Edwin. And you will be robbing me—you will be betraying me—if you don't keep the money for yourselves."

She glanced wildly from Esther to Sarah and back again.

"Minah—" Esther said. Tenderness was returning to her attitude.

"What?" Minah cried, stepping into the center of the room. Consciously or not, she was affirming her role as the host, the eldest, the schemer, and the leader. For a fleeting moment, Sarah thought she recognized herself in her sister: the sob trembling in her voice, the simultaneous suppression of tears. It was not so much emotion, not rage or frustration or desperation, that made both of them want to cry, but the fact of vulnerability coming to consciousness, throbbing through the bodies that felt so dense, so dark to them now.

"Why didn't you tell us this before?"

"Because—I nearly went crazy when I found out. I didn't want it to be true. I didn't want to have another reason to hate him. The man who was so cheap with me all my life. Who said if I wanted any clothes, Sarah, who was just a kid, would choose them for me. The man wouldn't give me a penny to spend on birthday presents for friends, who stopped inviting me to parties . . . I couldn't take it, it was too much, I thought I would combust. I confronted him about it. I called him from Seoul. That's where I found out. I met my aunt, my mother's sister, and she told me. I was ready for him to deny it. I told myself, If he denies it I'll accept his answer, even if it's obvious he's lying. I can't live like this, hating him so much. I wanted him to deny it. But he didn't. He wouldn't even do that for me. He laughed at first, like it was a joke on me. Then he got angry and said my mother owed him more, much more, for forcing him to raise me." She wiped her eyes and nose on her sleeve. "I couldn't stand to think about it for a long time. I thought if I told anyone else, it would make it true. Now you know. It's true. It's why I know I have more right to say what we do with the money than either of you"—she faced Sarah now—"even if you have the legal right to keep all the money for yourself. I know I'm right. I know I am."

She looked to Esther with febrile longing for her sister's compassionate conversion to her own point of view. She sat down again at the table.

"Minah. Minah," Esther said, as if calling out to a figure about to step into a crowd. "I know you had reasons to hate him. Hate him, hate what he has done to you. But you have to stop calculating what can't be calculated. It'll kill you. You've seen people ruin themselves fighting for what they think they're owed. You say you can't stand your work anymore, you can't stand serving the entitled who have power just because they have money. You know money is never clean. You know this. We are talking about the money of a man who abused you—and killed himself to end his pain. This person who caused us all so much anguish was in so much pain he tied a plastic bag on his head and choked to death on his own vomit—"

Sarah was thinking, I thought the money came from his lawsuits.

Minah erupted. "What's your point? I'm alive, Esther. So are you. I talked to the coroners at the hospital. They regularly get terminally ill suicides. I know he was in pain. He was terminally ill and in chronic pain. Like most people, he was weak. He was basically a weak and cowardly little man who hurt women and children and killed himself to end his pain. He was weak. I'm not." Her chest was heaving.

"Yes, I'm alive," Esther said. The quality of her intensity was now less hot than hard. "And I once took a check for fifteen thousand that Dad gave me for college and spent it to live in a way he thought was demeaning and dirty. Was that right or wrong of me? You said he had millions. Maybe over ten million. I want to go back to school with whatever Sarah gives me. But I don't need three million. Why should we keep what we don't need? You want to give your children the best. Edwin does, too. He does. But you don't need a third of the inheritance or even a quarter to do that. Unless your ambition is just to raise a millionaire. You're a lawyer and he's a doctor. You can make a living. Why do you need so much? What do you want to teach your children—generosity, or miserliness and greed?"

"You don't understand anything about money," Minah said, defensive, scornful. "You don't understand estate taxes. You don't know what it costs to raise a child today. You don't know."

Sarah had never seen Minah address Esther with anything approaching contempt before.

"Maybe you've convinced yourself that you need more than you do." Esther inhaled deeply; a shudder seemed to pass through her. "Whatever money there is, I hope Sarah will share with us, because there are things I want, too. But whatever I receive I will share with Edwin, whether or not you do. Because we're each our father's children. I don't know what Edwin did or didn't suffer under our father, but he *knew* him. He knew him as his father. He knows what he is. That is enough for me."

"No," Minah said, shaking her head. "No."

"Are Edwin and his son really entitled to nothing? Am I entitled to more than you for being all alone with him and Sue while you were in Korea and Sarah was at school? What are you entitled to for being the focus of his cruelty? What about Sarah, for the way he's convinced her she's the only child after his heart? You're holding on to your suffering as if it's currency you're saving for your children. How can we live with what we've suffered if we can't let go of it for once, to try to be fair? The only thing we can calculate is equality. Only equality will let us survive our father. Only equality will let us forget him."

Sarah could not, moments ago, understand how Minah would not recognize the force of Esther's veracity; now she was appalled that Esther did not see the danger she was risking. Sarah was scared of Minah. She could sense her desperate fury coiled endlessly within her depths. If Esther didn't stop, Minah might lunge. Stop, stop, stop! she called out to Esther in her mind. Don't speak of justice, equality, suffering—this last, especially, sounded less like pain than a mere idea when compared to its resonance in Minah's mouth. Those words, at once abstract and visceral, immaterial and vulnerable, could not stand up to Minah's fury. Whatever they meant would ultimately crumble and feed into it.

And there would be nothing left to recuperate, nothing to imagine or to cultivate: nothing surviving between the three sisters any longer.

Esther said quietly, "That's what I wanted to say. If I haven't convinced you, I can accept that. But I can't accept—I won't accept—that I will have betrayed you if I do what I want to do with Dad's money."

Minah continued to face Esther but said nothing. To Sarah's small relief, Minah's hair had fallen from behind her ear in a dark curtain to hide her profile from Sarah.

"I also want to be free of him," Esther said.

Esther wasn't shaken; she did not seem aware of the precipice. Sarah could not tell whether Esther was brave or oblivious, emboldened by her courage or uninhibited by her sensitivity. Or was this the wrong question, the wrong distinction? Was the meaningful distinction, here and elsewhere, between ignorance, which spoke fearlessly because it did not know suffering, and innocence, which felt and explored widely and still saw no reason to fear the pursuit of what glimmered as good?

Minah folded her arms around her robe. "You're right. I can't tell you what to do with your share. We'll each get a third. I'll respect your decision to give it away to someone who knows nothing of our family, or not. I agree to be respectful. And to take on myself this task of actually getting the money into our hands. I know how to deal with paperwork and bureaucracy. It's less hellish when you're trained to do it well, as I've been." She spoke calmly, but her tone was no less imposing, her words no longer molten but hard and glazed with intensity, like freshly fired clay.

She walked briskly into the kitchenette. Sarah and Esther looked at each other as they heard her loudly gulping down a glass of water, refilling it, and gulping that down, too.

Sarah opened her mouth. Esther shook her head, which Sarah didn't know how to interpret.

She didn't know whether Minah would ever forgive Esther for the things she'd said.

Minah returned to the living room. "If you don't mind, I have a lot of work to do."

Sarah and Esther got up and put on their coats. Minah went to the bathroom; they heard her lock the door. Esther tapped at it softly.

"What? I'm peeing."

"I love you, Minah," Esther said. There was no response.

In the elevator Sarah had a sudden inspiration.

"You go home first," she said. "I have to finish some paperwork on campus."

"All right."

Esther's face was brittle with desolation. Sarah felt sorry for her sister then. After her bitter argument with Minah, Sarah offered her no consolation, only a lie.

Sarah called a car to take her all the way to her father's apartment. The ride was expensive, and she was now in credit card debt, but she would dissolve it soon enough.

They had forgotten to draw the blinds. Ordinary light filled her father's bedroom, although her father had died in it days ago.

The dark textured vomit that still weighed down the sodden plastic bag untied by the EMTs, now chalky and dry, was recognizably his chocolate-flavored protein drink and the chocolate cake he ate the evening of his death. Some of the vomit had spilled from the bag and dried and crusted over the carpet. Two bottles were lying on their side by the stain. The dozens of scattered pills, some round, others oblong, glowed white on the floor, mysterious and sinister, as if all the die the gods had cast for him over the course of his life had materialized in them at the moment of his death.

She got two plastic storage bags from the kitchen. She scooped up all the pills on the floor and poured them into one. She decanted the dozen or so remaining pills in the two bottles of oxycodone lying on the floor into the other. She looked under the bed for any other bottle of pills but found only empty water bottles. The four bottles on the table contained prescription-strength acetaminophen, the same combined with morphine, prescription-strength ibuprofen, and marinol. She got more storage bags from the kitchen and emptied the pills laced with morphine and marijuana into them separately. She didn't want anyone, namely Esther, to discover the bottles in her possession, and knew she could always identify the pills by looking up the numbers and letters engraved on them online.

She checked once more below the bed and noticed something under the nightstand. There, beneath a soiled undershirt, she discovered an open box of transdermal fentanyl patches. There was one of three refills left.

He'd vaunted his masculine stoicism before his children, claiming to be tough enough to resist the temptation of narcotics and get by on high doses of common painkillers alone. This was why he never asked for oxycodone pills often; he'd been receiving a steady, stealthy dose of a particularly potent opioid under his clothing. It was a lie he must have shared with at least one other—probably Edwin, maybe Esther or even Ruby—whoever it was who brought him his prescription.

They hadn't been strong enough for him toward the end. They might be dosed just right for her.

She gathered the empty pill bottles and the bottles of straight ibuprofen and acetaminophen in the wastebasket. She dropped the fentanyl patches and the storage bags into her tote and, with her lips curving into a smile, zipped it shut.

She wanted the drugs to intervene in the postmortem numbness, which was interrupted at times by random fleeting flights of elation and even bursts of rollicking laughter. She needed the drugs to dissolve her mind's punitive bent, its determination to indict her for the ghastly death, the suicide, the murder; to repeat its judgment, again and again, like a caged animal obsessively licking its skin raw.

She told herself she wasn't responsible. She replayed her last hours with him; they unfolded with a kind of inevitability, like a series of actions and reactions in which psychology and physiology were bound by laws of causality as ironclad as those that governed the orbit of the planets around the sun.

How could she have stayed with him that night and not perished? She protested to herself that she was guiltless, she'd been helpless to do otherwise but leave her father with Marianna. Marianna was obviously inexperienced with terminal illness and home care, but Sarah could not have survived the night on her own. She had abandoned her father to save her life. She was rejecting her guilt now for the same reason. Her guilt haunted her more like an invasive specter than an inborn feeling. She could get rid of it.

He killed himself because she rejected him.

With her father's medication, she would align her body with her wish to be free—because she understood herself, without him, to be free.

She cast a backward glance at the bedroom. She planned to put the apartment and the rest of the building on the market in as-is condition once it devolved to her. Minah had tasked her with readying the property for sale, but she knew Minah wouldn't blame her for getting rid of it as soon as she could with as little effort as possible. Besides, she could do as she would; all that he owned was now hers.

She shut the door to his bedroom. She would not return to this room, this building, or this town again.

But there was one more thing she wanted to keep. In the other room she retrieved her old notebook. She cast her eyes over the rest—the furniture, the bedding—then left the room and closed the door. All the rest could go.

She threw the contents of the wastebasket into the kitchen trash, tied up the trash bag, and dropped it in the hallway. She locked up the apartment for the last time. Outside, she threw the bag into the dumpster in the parking lot.

She inhaled the cold air deep into her nostrils. An immense wave of euphoric relief washed through her.

She broke into a quiet laugh, smiling at the irony of her spoils. Never in his life had her father offered anything that promised a feeling of contentment, a sensation of peace.

At home, Sarah knocked at Esther's door, which was ajar. She heard rustling and throat-clearing before Esther called for her to come in.

Esther was sitting up in bed with a book on her lap. "I think I fell asleep."

"Go to sleep. I'm going to bed, too. Don't forget to turn on the space heater."

Esther got up as if to go to the bathroom; Sarah stepped aside to let her pass. But Esther wanted to embrace her sister and hung her head on Sarah's shoulder.

"I'm still so tired," she said. She projected the miserable, profound puzzlement of one who cannot accept that their body was not made to adapt to their life.

"It's all right. It'll be all right." Sarah held her sister close, feeling something like hope knowing that she had enough opioids to ferry her across the long nights ahead. She pictured her spirit floating above her body, temporarily released from the guilt that she struggled against, day and night, as if it were a foreign contagion.

"Why didn't you say anything this afternoon?"

She was about to lie, to say simply she didn't know why. But their closeness confused her; the freedom from Esther's gaze and the granular immediacy of the damp black hair brushing against her face, almost indistinguishable from her own, pushed her to speak as if to herself: "I believed you and what you said. But I agree with Minah."

She held Esther for a moment longer until her sister lifted her head. She kissed Esther's cheek, a thing she had never done, even when Esther was very young. She wished her good night. She knew Esther would not come to her again until morning.

Behind the closed door to her room she rummaged in her tote for the storage bag with the oxycodone from the bottles on the floor, which she remembered held about a dozen pills. She took one. She recalled her experience with Vicodin after a root canal years ago, how it had wiped away the ongoing stress of fighting with her roommates and finding the money for the treatment. The following morning she calmly corresponded with her insurance company, which reimbursed most of the cost of the procedure, and came to an understanding with the rest of her household. The medicine was magic; it was like grace. How else could she have escaped the laws of her character?

She got in bed with her laptop and saw that *Fanny and Alexander* was now streaming for free. She'd once shared a few moments of small talk at a conference with a young Iranian scholar who told her that seeing Bergman as an adolescent for the first time had been a revelation: he realized other people in the world were unhappy, too. They laughed quietly, and she wanted to talk to him again, but he left the room with friends in the audience before she had a chance.

She watched half the first episode, then checked the time. She finished the first and started the second; nearly two hours passed without her feeling the creeping warmth and soothing waves of euphoria she was expecting. She thought it might be too soon to take another pill and decided to spike her seltzer with vodka. The alcohol, she hoped, would jump-start the more powerful narcotic.

She was concentrating on her physical condition so intently that she was barely taking in what the characters were saying. It was late; she was getting drowsy. That was all.

She took another pill from the bag of oxycodone and examined it. It was an oblong white tablet, its center engraved with the identifying code I 7.

She paused the show and opened another window on her computer, where she googled "I 7 pill identification."

The top result read: "I 7 (Ibuprofen 600 mg)." Beside it was a photograph of the very pill in her hand.

Had she really been so careless as to mix the contents of the bottle of oxycodone with another? Or had she mistakenly taken a pill from the bag of mixed round and oblong pills amassed from the floor, the only one that might contain ibuprofen? She wasn't one to lose her keys, to forget a date, to mistake a roommate's black sock for her own. She was sure she'd thrown out the bottle of prescription-strength ibuprofen. She held the bag of what she'd thought was oxycodone up to the light. All the pills looked identical, like six hundred milligrams of ibuprofen. She panicked; she might be losing her mind.

She could hear Esther saying, *Sarah, for the way he's convinced her she's the only child after his heart.*

She poured out the contents of the bag and examined the engravings more closely. She did the same for the other bags and looked up their engravings online. She had trouble believing what she saw; she took photographs of the pills and magnified them to confirm what she saw with her own unmediated eye.

If her father had fallen out of bed on the side where he was found, and been unable to lift himself up, he wouldn't have been able to reach the box of fentanyl patches, even if he had known it was covered by laundry.

He died after swallowing a fistful of acetaminophen, aspirin, and ibuprofen to manage the pain of a tumor growing into his spine. He couldn't find the patches, he found no relief in his pills; his brain was unhinged. He called out weakly, and no one came, and nothing he swallowed assuaged his pain. He took more and more pills, gulping them down with his chocolate-flavored drink, and the pain was flaming, raging, crowding his mind out of his body. He was obeying his body when he grabbed a plastic bag from the floor and tied its handles under his chin to extinguish the conflagration of pain.

He died in far greater agony than she had imagined.

2

The song

"Thank you so much," Minah said to the server reaching over the counter with her ice-cream cone. "Have a wonderful day, thank you . . ."

Sarah followed her outside into the pale flooding light of the winter sun. The metal bars of the playground across the street, the sidewalks, and the bodies of passing cars were glittering white, as if everything hard had been polished with fine, powdery ash.

"It feels so good to be out," Minah said. She lapped greedily at her cone in a way that sickened Sarah.

But it did feel good to be out in the sun. The shape of real things was clear. She glimpsed gleaming teeth between lips parted in chatter; she noticed the rusted trash cans that were so real they were trembling, just a little, like Platonic forms tuning in and out of the world. What Sarah knew was real.

She was going to contribute something to this world of truth.

She knew her terminally ill father was deprived of essential pain medication. She was nearly certain Edwin had done it and Minah was complicit. She was going to learn their roles in his death.

She had barely slept, but when she woke she felt unusually refreshed, like a bird that had molted all its old, tired feathers, with strange sensations ruffling through the new. She checked on Esther before leaving; her sister was still sleeping. It was probably the first time Esther hadn't headed out before Sarah to do the unhappy work she'd felt compelled to do. She was the only one Sarah assumed was innocent.

Minah wanted to walk on the High Line. "I live close by," she'd said querulously, "and I never get to it." She kept talking. She needed to buy vacuum bags and light bulbs and chicken breasts. She wanted to work out more, cook more, take a trip in the spring.

Sarah nodded. What had they done to their father? If she never knew the truth, all her thoughts and ideas would become mere verbiage, wood shavings blowing in the wind, with nothing enduring to put in their place. She understood how people could listen hungrily for a revelation that would hurt them indelibly. Knowledge was vaster than her small life, as beautiful and logical as the sun. She could aim for nothing higher than to be its medium.

If this clarity of purpose could suffuse her consciousness forever, she would have the purity and self-sustaining power of a saint. She would be a person whose every thought and action, fart and fit of laughter, even error and flaw, would cohere into something perfectly luminous and true.

But she was far from being a saint. The light was already sputtering. She didn't even believe in saints. She believed in entropy, in impurity, in the mystery of sleep that provided no relief.

This shining clarity would not last forever. Once it was gone, it would cast only shadows onto the future.

Their father was dead. He tied a plastic bag around his head, as a mother would a bonnet on an infant's head to protect it from the sun. They were already out of time.

"This is so beautiful," Minah said of the tall fine-stemmed flowers by the entrance to the High Line fanning tiny white, fuchsia, and periwinkle petals around yolk-yellow centers. "That reminds me. I want to get some flowers for my apartment. Maybe tulips or irises. Which do you prefer?"

"I don't know."

"Have you talked to Paul recently?" she asked, as if the question were not unusual.

"Me? No. Why? Haven't you?"

Minah pressed her lips together moodily, then relaxed her features with a sigh. "No. He's been writing and calling, but I don't feel like talking to him now. I can't deal with it now."

"With it?"

"With him, with our relationship. You know," she said, suddenly acid, "I know you think I'm a liar. That if I wasn't telling lies, then I was lying to him through omission. Well, guess what—I told him the whole truth about our father. I told him everything. I was afraid he'd dump me if he knew about our wretched origins, and you know what?" Her laughter glittered.

"He didn't dump you."

"Right. Instead, he kept calling and telling me he still cared about me. He even said he forgave me. He's just like you," she said, acid once more. "He thinks I lied to him, that I'm a poor lost soul, and he has the right to forgive me because I wasn't raised as politely as him. Prick. I never lied to him—you were both wrong about that—but you, Sarah, were right about him being a self-satisfied prick."

"I don't remember ever saying that about him. Did I?"

"You might have said that about another boyfriend, but they've all been the same," she said wearily.

"For what it's worth, I like Paul. I like him better than any other guy you've dated before."

"Oh my god, I don't believe I'm hearing this." Minah lifted her head to address the sky, ironic and extravagant. "You like him? You like him because he has the nerve to forgive me for trying to become the good woman he wanted. I should have told him about my debts. All my student loans *and* my credit card debt. He might be able to *forgive* me for my debts, but he wouldn't marry me. He's not that good."

"He can be smug and obnoxious, but he's not a bad person."

"What do you mean by that anyway? Good person, bad person. You're making me tired."

"You brought him up."

"I did," she said faintly, and swerved to sit down on a just vacated bench. Her expression was at once imperious and troubled. "I do miss him, a little," she added, so casually the sentiment was ironic.

"I went back to the apartment yesterday."

"That reminds me, I don't think anyone's deposited the rent checks from the tenants this month. Dad's lawyer is really a piece of work, I don't think he knows what he's doing. You'll need someone else." Her voice grew gentle. "I can help you find someone. You'll probably also want someone who isn't me to help you through the whole probate process. I don't think I can manage it on my own right now, and there's an obvious conflict of interest. It turns out yet another lawyer is making some claim, saying Dad never paid him. I'll try to . . ." She fell silent and stared blankly ahead.

Sarah began in a neutral tone, as if she were describing the distant past. "I went back to the apartment yesterday because I wanted to take Dad's pills. I wanted to take his drugs. To help me sleep, to help me get over his suicide. That's why I went. I admit it. So I gathered up all the pills I could find. I threw out the stuff that can't get you high. At least I thought I did. When I got home I realized that the pills I'd taken from the bottles labeled as opioids were in fact just high-dose ibuprofen or generic store-bought painkillers."

"And?" Minah didn't flinch. She continued to gaze ahead.

"That means that someone switched out the opioids he needed with much weaker pills that wouldn't have made a dent in his"—her voice caught in her throat—"level of pain."

Minah looked at her sister with a raised eyebrow.

"That means he killed himself because he was in too much pain."

"You promised me you would stay with him that night," Minah said with quiet severity.

"I didn't, and he died alone. That's my fault. But what happened to those pills?" A gentle plea for acknowledgment entered Sarah's voice.

Minah turned to look her squarely in the face. "Sarah. You are not guilty. And I'm not guilty, either. He killed himself. I don't know what he did with the bottles I gave him. And he had his fentanyl patches. Did you know about them? He tried to keep them a secret, but Edwin told me about them. If he was in such pain he could have used one of them. I am guilty, you could say, of not throwing away the plastic bag I saw on the floor. I imagine that was the bag he used. But I'm not guilty of his death. His room was always a mess, even with Esther and that other aide around, because he was such a pig. It's entirely possible, in fact I'm sure, that those unopened bottles are still in the room somewhere you haven't discovered."

For a second, Sarah believed her. In that second, she was her former passive, hypocritical self. She shut her eyes. Her old self was a lucid nightmare to her now. "What did you say to him, when you were in his room? Why did you go in to see him?"

Minah stared at Sarah with outrage, trying to decide whether to eviscerate her. She sighed; it wasn't worth it. "He asked to see me, remember? When I went in he complained on and on about you and me and Esther. That's all."

"I heard you talking."

Minah's expression changed; Sarah thought she had caught her in a lie. But the thing that was making Minah's features quiver did not seem to be confusion or panic, but sorrow.

"I wanted to make sure he wouldn't hurt Esther anymore," she said at last. Sarah heard faint contempt, not for their father, but for her.

"They're not there," Sarah said with calm insistence.

"Check again."

Minah parted her lips and hesitated. Sarah wondered if to the passersby they looked sad and somewhat unseemly, as she often felt of people who chose to talk of intensely private, difficult affairs in public spaces; who, even when she couldn't overhear their words, emitted troubling fumes around themselves.

Minah said, "My first year in Korea I hired a private investigator to find my mom. He specialized in tracking down bio families for Koreans who were adopted abroad. I thought my situation was similar enough. I paid him a lot of money. Dad's money. He only paid for those years in Seoul because I said if he didn't support me there I'd report him for abuse. You and Esther were still living with him. He didn't want to lose you especially. So that's what I did, and I don't regret it. The PI didn't find my mother because she was dead. She died very poor, of a simple asthma attack because she didn't have the wherewithal for an inhaler. But he did find her sister, my *eemo*. She's a miserable shrew, but she told me what I wanted to know. She's the one who told me Dad took my mom's money. My aunt didn't like my mom. She hated her. She was a mean and bitter woman totally eaten up with envy. She was so much uglier than her little sister and she never married. You could see how beautiful my mom was from the one photograph she showed me. She cheered up when she talked about how awful our father is and why my mom married him. Everyone thought it was strange such a beautiful woman was marrying him. But they didn't know she was already pregnant with me. Eemo said my mom wasn't even sure if Dad was the father. Eemo really loved that. She said my mom was basically a whore. She also said Dad nearly killed her. My mother. When she said that, I remembered opening the door to their bedroom a long time ago when I could barely walk and seeing him choking her. I can see it now. What's strange is that when she said that, that my father nearly killed my mother, she was outraged on her sister's behalf, like she felt protective of her. Up until then she was just oozing hate and bitterness. You wouldn't think she'd ever had a single noble impulse in her life. When my mom returned to Korea she stayed with her sister for a few months until she got picked up by another man. My aunt said she didn't deserve him, he was a decent man who deserved better than a whore. Just like that, she switched back to hate. Sometime after moving in with that man, my mom died.

"I seemed to learn Korean at lightning speed after that. I learned it so well I was confident enough to visit our uncle, Dad's brother. The one who took me in for a short time. They invited me to some gathering where they wanted to push me into a corner. But they couldn't. I started making them uncomfortable, and they realized they couldn't do that to me. I could feel it. Somehow I scared them. So instead of ignoring me or joking about how difficult I was as a toddler, they started telling the truth. They said, 'You know your father never even graduated from high school, though he tells people he went to Seoul National?' He was in the army, and after the army he drifted for some years before going to America. At one point he lived in Germany for a year, working in a mental hospital. He was an orderly restraining violent psychotics. When I heard that . . . Why is it called 'poetic justice'? What's so poetic about justice? I didn't really think about it until then."

It startled Sarah to hear Minah raise a question that had privately exercised her not long ago. Thoughts were not always personal, psychological; they were more like charged particles hanging in the air. She should know what happened; she should have known what was going to happen. If she'd paid more attention to her sister, her brother, her father, she would have known.

No. She couldn't have known. Even if she knew what Minah was thinking, she wouldn't know.

"Minah. Edwin picked up the prescriptions and took them to Dad in his room. Do you remember if the staples were intact on the paper bags they came in when you went in to see him?"

"Yes," she said simply.

"You're sure?"

"No. They might have been open. I don't know. I didn't check. Does it matter? For God's sake, who do you think you are? Agatha Christie? In real life murders are never mysterious. They sometimes become mysteries because cops and prosecutors are stupid and biased and misread or fuck up the evidence, but ninety-nine percent of the time if you do any poking around it's one hundred percent clear who did it. He had terminal cancer, he was in pain, he killed himself. Only one thing is bothering me. I'm telling you so you'll get off my back, though I don't think it'll amount to anything. I saw Marianna's boyfriend in the parking lot when I left that day we were all there at Dad's apartment. He's a very sketchy, very unsavory character. There was something wrong with him. Something really off. You think human nature is so mysterious, but it's really simple. Addicts and criminals and sketchy people who wait in parking lots for no good reason are more likely to steal pain meds than other people. If something unlawful happened I'd bet good money—I'd bet your inheritance, if it was mine—" she said, smirking, "that he was behind it. But proving even that would be hard. Because no one, no lawyer or investigator, will be interested in proving that a man with metastasized cancer might not have killed himself because he knocked his painkillers off his nightstand after alienating everyone close to him."

"But that's not what might have happened. I'm telling you there was no oxycodone there."

Minah riffled through her purse as if Sarah hadn't spoken. After checking her phone she said evenly, "And I'm telling you they were there. Maybe, just maybe, the pharmacist made a mistake. That's possible, too. But it's too late to matter. He's already been cremated."

The traffic rose from below and enveloped them, the cacophony, the fumes.

It's how she's been trained to think, Sarah assured herself. Minah didn't see the relevance of Sarah's questions without the literal body of evidence. It's because of her job. That's why.

Again, Sarah had the impression Minah had absorbed her thoughts when she said, "It's not easy juggling my job with everything I'm doing for *us*. And it's not going well. It's not going well at all."

"What isn't?"

"Trying to figure out his estate. I wish I could hand it all over to you, but you wouldn't know the first thing about straightening it all out," Minah said bitterly, rising from the bench. "What good is all your superior education if you can't handle what I'm handling for you?"

On its face the question was rhetorical. Yet there was an echo of despair in it, a strangled howl. If Minah managed in the future to raise her children in considerable privilege, what purpose would her sacrifices have served if they turned out as helpless as her sister?

At home, Esther's light was off and her door closed.

Sarah sank into bed.

She dreamt of the priest she'd heard at Paul's church. When she woke, the memory of the dream was like a slap on the face: she hadn't realized until then that she was attracted to him from the moment he opened his mouth. Her desire for him made up the lurid atmosphere of the dream. He smiled at her pleasantly, and she followed him to the back of the church, quickening her step, until he disappeared. She found herself facing Edwin in a purple house robe. She kneeled before him, inexplicably, reflexively, despising him and herself as she did so. She resolved to get rid of him, one way or another, so that she could find the real priest.

He said he forgave her and told her to rise.

A sudden access of gleeful cynicism inspired her to remain on her knees. She said, "You're no better than me. You, too, should be kneeling." She gestured to the floor at his feet. He looked down upon her with dismay and pity, with a quality of tenderness that pinched her heart and reminded her, then and there, of Paul. That was how it ended.

◦∞◦

If there was an answer to the riddle of the dream, she didn't uncover it when she met with Edwin in the flesh.

They met at the same spot they had at their very first meeting, perhaps even the same table. The outsized red and blue geometric sculptures were still there, their surreality this time deriving not from their style but their unchanging stasis.

This time Edwin stood up as she approached. When she was close he raised his arms to embrace her. She recoiled automatically. In the moment, she wasn't sure why. Then she processed the doubt that had pulled her back. What had he wanted from her sister? What did he want with Minah?

He snickered softly. "I'm sorry you feel that way," he said with an affected ironic detachment that brought back to her the way Minah spoke of Paul on the High Line.

She saw his chest begin to puff up with grandiloquence.

"I don't know why I'm being—"

She cut him off as he was leaning toward her. "Did you pick up the prescription from the pharmacy yourself, the one you dropped off the day before he died?"

"What?" he said indignantly.

She repeated herself calmly.

"Why are you asking me?"

"This is important. Please answer."

He remained frozen, hanging over the table with his face close to hers. She thought she detected a glimmer of alarm concealed behind the half-hearted attempt to intimidate by scrutinizing her.

"I got them from the hospital pharmacy, like I always do. Now tell me why you're asking. Is this the reason why you wanted to meet? I actually thought you might be here to apologize for the shitty way I've been shut out ever since our father—yes, *our father*—died. Minah deliberately scheduled the service for a time I couldn't get away, and then—"

"If that's the case I'm sorry, but that's not why I wanted to meet," she said hastily. "But I know Esther's kept you informed about everything you need to know."

"Why are you asking about the prescription?" His face assumed once more the ironic, calculating expression she knew better than his ill temper. As had their father, he slid in and out of these two aspects seamlessly, like an amphibian sunning and slipping into water, and back again.

"Did you give him any pills from the new prescription when you were there?"

"Yes, I gave him a single pill to take for his pain. It wasn't a new medication, it was just a higher dose. Why are you asking?"

She could hear Minah demanding that she stop: *Don't tell him, he still wants our money.* Then she remembered: But it's too late to matter. He's already been cremated. "When I went back to the apartment yesterday I gathered up all the pills and pill bottles. I discovered there wasn't any oxycodone in the bottles labeled oxycodone. There was nothing stronger than six-hundred-milligram ibuprofen mixed up with over-the-counter painkillers."

His eyes flitted from her face to her waist, her knees, her hand resting on the arm of her chair, and back to her face, as if the parts of her body were puzzle parts to the mystery.

It occurred to her then that Minah couldn't have remembered seeing their father choke her mother. She was too young.

"You discovered there wasn't any oxycodone," he finally said with grim satisfaction.

She must have seen him choking their mother, her adoptive mother. She was like the tongueless woman of myth who cannot say what violence has been done to her and transforms into a songbird, able to express her story only indirectly. She must have repressed the memory, displaced it and projected it onto the mother she did not, could not, know. This most graphic memory of violence was rendered just bearable by being displaced from woman known to woman unknown.

And now she hated their father so much she told herself her biological mother's money had given rise to his fortune—a lie contradicting the truth she'd claimed not long ago, that the money came from the disfiguring burn on his hand. Her hatred was cleaving reality in two.

"Yes. Not in any of the old bottles on the table or new bottles on the floor."

They shared a silence. She sensed that he wanted to abandon his exhausting defenses.

She said quietly, gently, hoping that he would understand, that he might even feel pity for her burning need to know what was real: "I found an open box of fentanyl patches in another corner of the room. The prescription for it had already been filled twice. I know he was using the patches, and I think he wanted to use one right before he died, but he couldn't find the box. It was hidden under some clothes. And so he tried all the pills he could find."

"What are you getting at?" he snapped. "I didn't hide those patches. I gave them to him, I'd get them for him. I don't know what they were doing under some clothes. I'm the only one who knew about them because he made me swear I wouldn't tell anyone. I kept them on the top shelf of the closet, but maybe he told Marianna to get them down for him and she knocked them over. But he didn't want a patch when I saw him. He said the combination of pills and patch was too much and he wanted more control over timing and dosage, which you don't get with a patch. He said the combination was making him sleep all day, so he just wanted a stronger pill. That's all I know."

Her heart sank, but she was still committed to her purpose. "The room was a mess when he died. I don't know if he or Marianna knocked the box of fentanyl under the nightstand or if someone deliberately hid it from view. But I'm sure someone tampered with the pill bottles. Someone removed the medicine he needed most."

Someone—she said it at last, she gave agency to the actor, the torturer.

He glanced at her again as if studying her, then said, "Not too long ago, Minah told me about two doctors she saw during an emergency room visit last year. She arrived between two shifts with really bad abdominal pain. She told the first the pain was extreme. When the doctor found out she was menstruating at the time, he told her to go home and make an appointment with a gynecologist and gave her a prescription for antianxiety medication. Thankfully she got the attention of the doctor on the next shift. He said, 'On a scale from one to ten, how much pain are you in?' And she said seven. And he said, 'Then you mean a nine or ten. Women tend to underrate their own pain.' He said she had appendicitis.

"She told me this story and asked me, 'Which is it? Do women exaggerate their pain or underestimate it?' I said, 'Obviously the first doctor was wrong to dismiss you so quickly.' She said the diagnosis was obviously wrong, but the first doctor wasn't wrong to think her anxiety had something to do with her pain, or that her pain had something to do with her anxiety or even her period. Because she's so often in pain of some kind. That's what she said. 'Because I'm so often in pain of some kind.' Then she asked me about our father's pain levels. She asked if most people suffering through terminal cancer managed without opioids. I didn't know what to say because he'd made me promise not to tell anyone about the fentanyl. I didn't even tell Esther. I changed the patch when I was there after helping him bathe, and he changed it himself when she was there. I felt sorry for Esther, you know, because I think he was in worse pain when she was around and more . . . difficult." His tone grew gentler, sympathetic; Sarah was hopeful once more that they could speak to each other frankly, with a shared sense of duty and decency. "But like I said, I promised. I wanted to tell Minah the truth, but I couldn't. So I told her that most people with a tumor on their spine couldn't do it. And she seemed to mull that over very seriously."

He regarded Sarah with what seemed at first like the gleam of gentle mockery. She was confused, then frightened, when it became the happy glint of a malign accuser.

"Why were you going through the pills? Those are strictly the property of the patient."

Her lips parted without a sound. She saw him relish her muteness. It was aversion to his pleasure that forced the words from her.

"I went through them," she said slowly, "because I wanted to take them. But I didn't take any, because the pills weren't his prescription. Except for maybe the ibuprofen, and that's not a controlled substance. I might not have the right to take his medicine, but I have the right to take whatever was in his possession." Her heart began to climb higher and higher in her throat until what she said next sounded like a weak croak. "He left everything to me."

He wasn't like her. He didn't miss a beat. His face blanched like a sheet of paper, but he didn't falter.

"I suppose that's why Minah's been avoiding my calls," he said with a forced laugh. In the next breath, he erupted. "But that can't be right. He said he changed the will to give me and Esther everything. He fucking told me that. He told me he didn't care if all four of us were his children, only Esther and I took care of him. You didn't do a damn thing for him. So how did he leave everything to you when you did the least of any of us? I fucking bathed his filthy ass twice a week. I did that. I took him to his fucking appointments. I watched his goddamn shows with him. I did. You did less than Esther, less than even Minah, who tried to make things easier for Esther. Everything to you. Everything to you. I don't fucking believe it."

Sarah followed only the first half of his rant. "All four of us were his children": she remembered what their father had said to her. "*I change it.*" She remembered Minah's interpretation of what Sarah repeated to her. Minah claimed he wanted Sarah to prove her love, or at least earn her inheritance, by taking care of him. Edwin was echoing Minah's understanding. So they had met to talk about the will. But neither had understood his direct or secondhand statement accurately.

Sarah hadn't either until now. When her father said "*I change it*," he'd meant "*I changed it.*" Unlike Minah, Edwin was right in interpreting it as the past tense. But if their father had more or less repeated what he'd said to her to Edwin, as Sarah assumed, then no one at the time had understood what he meant to say.

She spoke quietly, faltering a little, as her thinking groped its way into utterance. "He said to you, 'You are all my children, but you are not the same. You are not the same, Esther is not the same. You aren't like Sarah. You aren't Sarah. So I change it. I change the will.' He said something like that to you. He said, 'Who care?' He didn't care if you or anyone else judged or hated him for not leaving anything to you or Esther. You and Esther did so much more than me for him, but he didn't care. He'd planned to leave everything equally to the three of us, maybe the four of us. That was the original will, and he changed it before he died. He got closer to death and he didn't care about being fair. He still loved me the most," Sarah said in a near whisper, in the throes of her lonely revelation.

He was barely educated and cruel. He spent his life speaking so crudely in both Korean and English, it was finally too difficult to express his last wish lucidly. Having so blunted the capacious human mind he was born with, over a lifetime, with every cruel word, every lie of bad faith, every depraved gesture toward those who shared his life, he died believing in his lucidity.

He died believing he had made himself clear. This last thought was even lonelier than the love—the attachment he called love that Sarah did not recognize as such—that his daughter could not bear to receive.

Edwin breathed hard through his flared nostrils. "This is bullshit. Pure bullshit. Let me guess—you breathed a sigh of relief when they saw no point in an autopsy. And you've already cremated him. Because you tortured him to death. You and Minah, together. I despised him, too, but I'm not sick like you. Like my dear sisters. If anything, I would've had him overdose on morphine. But you fucking fucked-up murderers—you tortured him to death. Now I know. That's sickness of another caliber. And you're going to have everything now?" His eyes were glittering with pure, mad hatred. "He promised me he'd leave me half of everything. Half. He promised me. He told me himself. He promised me. I deserve half. For everything I did. And for more."

"For more?"

"I guess it makes sense. Of the three of you and the four of us, you're the only one who doesn't care about anyone else. You have no one to care about, you care only about yourself. That's why you're his favorite. You're more like him than any of us."

He grunted and pushed his chair back and was about to get up when Sarah started to speak.

Minor tremors were still erupting throughout her body. She was beginning to feel the winter cold in her hands and feet. He had insisted on their meeting once more in the cold, which he didn't seem to feel. She could feel the cold stoking her anger, and she wanted her anger to have shape in the world. She wanted what she said not to spin through air but hit something hard, even at the risk of being hurt herself.

"I wouldn't have murdered my father even if I'd had the chance to do it without being caught. It wouldn't have been worth it. I would have had to squeeze my hands around the disgusting flesh of his neck as he watched me. I would have had to stab him in the chest or batter his brains with a frying pan and feel his blood splatter on my face. It wouldn't have been worth it if a single drop of his blood touched me. I'd be covered in his blood, and with each blow I'd be closer to him than I'd ever been. Of course I also imagined poisoning him. Killing him from the inside out, without touching him. How much better our lives would have been if I'd just poisoned him before leaving home so Esther wouldn't have been left alone with him . . ." She cleared her throat. "But when I imagined it, really thought hard about it, it became too much. I imagined the poison corroding his throat and burning through his guts and melting his liver. It began to disgust me, and not because he didn't deserve punishment and pain. He did. What I really wanted more than anything was to have him disappear from my life and my thoughts completely. I was imagining him dying, and even that was too much. I was imagining the life inside him, inside me. I couldn't kill him because I didn't want to do anything that would bring him closer to me. I know Minah feels the same. You think you know me, you think you know Minah. You don't understand anything. It's true, we were happy to learn he was dying. We were relieved. But we didn't kill him. We just let him die."

She caught her breath. What was it that was giving her the power to deliver her triumphant, twisted discourse so forcefully that Edwin knew, as she looked into his shocked face, he'd not only lost, but was vulnerable?

She knew what he had wanted from her sister.

She went on. He knew not to say another word.

"I found out just yesterday that I inherit everything. It wasn't such a surprise. Anyone who ever knew our family could tell you I was always the favorite. You entered our lives just months ago, and you received nothing. Do you really think anyone will believe you if you tell them Minah and I murdered him?"

As she felt herself channeling Minah's argument about the futility of any investigation, she had the feeling of stepping into her sister's body. Minah was right: she could occupy Minah's position because they had suffered together, and he had not.

"You thought he'd already made a new will to leave everything to you and Esther. And you were afraid he was going to change it again, to favor me. And so you instructed Esther to give him extra oxycodone so he wouldn't have the presence of mind to contact his lawyer and make another will. The new prescription, the stronger prescription—you didn't give it to him for his pain."

When he met her eyes, it was with the face of a stranger. His face reflected their final estrangement: the truth of her final word, as well as his confusion over her transformation, his total astonishment at this demonstration of her power. He got up and left.

3
Poetry

Sarah's apartment was silent and dark. She fell into bed and woke up in the middle of the night.

The door to Esther's room was open. She entered and turned on the desk lamp. She didn't know what she was looking for. She found a few receipts and a half dozen flyers for discounted sunglasses and sushi, the kind of ads dispirited-looking workers handed out on crowded streets.

On top of a small stack of books borrowed from her, she found two cards. The first featured an elephant perched on a ball under a spotlight. Inside the card, printed as if in colorful crayon, was the line "You always steal the show!" In her father's large, severely slanted handwriting she read: *SARAH. You must be good or I am not proud.* The other card had an illustration of a boy with spiky red hair waving from a hot-air balloon. Birds were chirping the black notes floating across the sky. Arching above all was the wish: "May your dreams take you high!" Both cards were faded; she guessed they were several years old. Esther must have found the unsent cards in their father's apartment. She didn't open the second card.

She stored them in a box under her bed, where she'd also put her childhood notebook.

He was wicked and sentimental. He understood rage as the legitimate demand of love, self-pity as the tragic longing of love. There was no hell where he would be forced to suffer what he had inflicted on his children. He would never suffer from knowing himself.

He died in pain greater than she'd wanted to imagine for him. When he tortured her as if she were a slave, stared at her as if she were an insect, raised his hand as he would to a dog, she wanted to push him headfirst into the doorknob, she wanted the lid of the grand piano to slam down on his neck. But her imagination died with his death.

She wanted to weep, not for him, but for what she had become—for what Minah and she had become. For how the years of hating him, suffering under him, hating him and then hating herself, had deformed her, beginning when she was only a child.

I was innocent, she thought. I was powerless. I was just a child, and this is what she and I have become.

I am innocent. And I am wrong; and I have been wrong.

In the cupboard the only food was a stack of canned sardines. Esther liked to eat them on toast. She texted Esther to ask where she was and went back to bed.

She remembered what she'd said to Edwin and felt weak and nauseated. She reached for her computer, conscious of an urgent purpose that would express itself as soon as she began typing.

> Edwin,
>
> You took care of him because you wanted money. But you did take care of him. And you hated every minute of it. I did little for him, and I hated it, I hated it too.
>
> You couldn't wait for him to die. I don't know whether I would have done what you did. But I know I might have.
>
> This brings me closer to you.

She kept it as a draft in her inbox.

She ate sardines on stale crackers, then returned to Esther's room and lay on her bed. She slipped in and out of sleep until the darkness lifted and the room turned gray.

She was certain Esther was safe, though she couldn't say why.

She fell asleep again. When she woke it was nearly one in the afternoon. She saw a text from Esther sent that morning: I'm at Minah's apartment. I stayed at Paul's last night. He gave me the key to Minah's.

She watched the ellipsis blinking below her texts. Fear rose dimly within her.

I met him last night at his church. We were supposed to meet Minah there. She never came. We went to her apartment afterward. She was there but she wouldn't let us in. So I stayed with Paul. I went back this morning and she wasn't there. Her office says she hasn't showed up. I'm going to wait for her here. I'm not sure where else to go. Do you know where she might be?

I don't know. Sarah found herself adding: I'm leaving now to join you. I'll be there by evening.

She felt she was floating on the walk to the station. The disaster was imminent but still abstract. On the train yellow rays of sun flashed through her reflection in the window and warmed her face. Heaps of dirty snow were sparkling under a cold blue sky. The steel smokestacks were shining, and splinters of light were flashing on chain-link fences and the river coiling and uncoiling around the city in the distance.

A familiar, unexpected smell was hanging in the corridor of Minah's apartment. When Esther opened the door Sarah realized it was emanating from Minah's kitchenette.

It was a mild but unmistakable mixture of odors. She encountered it most often at some Asian grocery stores, where the smell of enormous sacks of rice mingled with those of freshly hosed produce, wet cement, and the sweat of the workers. It evoked the smell of their mother's unwashed body during the last months of her illness and the rice porridge she made and often left curdling on the stove. She ate little else during her last days.

Esther had shadows under her eyes. After letting Sarah in she sat at the dining table, which bore a lone pot at her usual place.

"I'm waiting," she said. "I don't know what else to do."

Sarah watched her peel and slowly chew clumps of burnt rice out of the pot.

Sarah sat on the sofa, staring at her hands. She didn't want to explain to Esther what she knew. She was still doubtful of what one part of her, the heart of her, acknowledged as true. All that mattered now was finding Minah.

Her phone rang.

"Sarah. Sarah, hello. It's me. It's Marianna."

"Yes?" She could hear, like an engine in the distance, her heartrate beginning to climb.

"I—I'm sorry I didn't call you before. I was—I was traumatized, really. I haven't been an aide that long, and I'd never seen a dead body before." Marianna choked up, then exhaled forcefully, almost whistling. "Anyway. I'm sorry I didn't tell you before that I have a check for you. Mr. Kim asked me to give it to you. I can drive to Princeton to give it to you there, if you want."

"That's all right. Why don't you mail it to me?"

"I don't mind," Marianna said genially. "Princeton is such a pretty town. It would be a nice trip for me. Anyways, he told me to put it directly in your hands. That's what he said. Put it in Sarah's hands and only her hands."

When Sarah said she was in the city and didn't know when she'd be back, Marianna brightly insisted she could drop it off in the city today. Sarah gave her Minah's address.

"That's a great neighborhood!" Marianna said. "You're lucky. I'll be there soon."

330 / MAUREEN SUN

Sarah looked up to find Esther watching her, having clearly followed the call. "Marianna's stopping by with something for me. Something Dad left behind."

Esther shook her head as if to revive herself and said she was going to take a bath.

Sarah walked to the window. It was twilight. Lights were shining through the dusk on the High Line. She turned to face Minah's studio. Shadows draped over the furniture like worn-out garments. The apartment didn't feel merely empty. It was hollowed out. Minah would not live here much longer.

She closed the blinds and turned on all the lights. Fatigue and ferment sloshed around inside her like thick paints that wouldn't mix. She made herself coffee and sat with crossed legs on the sofa drinking slowly. Caffeine began branching through her brain; the tug of panic was growing more insistent. Or perhaps it wasn't dread mounting in her, an urge to withdraw, but its opposite: a sense of readiness, of ripeness; a hope for release.

She needed to void her bowels. She knocked at the bathroom door and Esther called out for her to come in.

It was stifling. The water was still steaming. Sarah expected her sister to have her back toward her or to have the shower curtain drawn. But Esther was exposed, her face vivid and flushed, her knees drawn up halfway without concealing her breasts, which, Sarah thought in a flash, were broad and round like her own, but fuller. The skin on Esther's body looked much softer and smoother than on her face.

Sarah was more embarrassed now than she ever was with half-naked roommates or completely nude classmates in the gym. She herself never wanted to be undressed before others, even lovers, with whom she insisted on the dark. She was thrown into confusion at the sight of what seemed to be her own nakedness before her, presented without shame.

She was turning away when she saw a white scar curving two or three inches between her sister's ribs and her back. Concern and curiosity, in equal measure, penetrated her embarrassment.

UNCORRECTED REVIEW COPY — NOT FOR SALE

"Where did you get that?"

She didn't point, but Esther knew what she was talking about. "I was running and I fell on a tree branch. It was surprisingly sharp."

"Why were you running?"

"I was hiking alone in the woods. I met two hunters who were drunk. I walked away, then ran."

"I have to—"

"Go ahead," Esther said simply.

Sarah had the sense that, after asking Esther about her body, she was expected to reciprocate intimacy by pulling her pants down without hesitation. Then Esther drew the curtain.

"No—I have to shit," she said urgently.

Esther pulled the curtain back, got out of the bath, wrapped herself in a towel, and left the bathroom.

When Sarah came out, Esther was rummaging through one of Minah's drawers. She pulled out a set of flannel pajamas for herself. As she changed, Sarah stared out the window at the gibbous moon. She could just make out, beyond the dark plains and white patches, the textured surface of craters and furrows like dry streambeds. It was a mistake to make of the moon—solid, grainy, scarred—a symbol of dreams and unreality. It was more like the bedrock of dreamless everyday life, laid bare.

Esther joined her on the sofa. She was still flushed and radiant. Her dark eyes were like velvet; the lines of her face were indelible and pure. "The check Marianna's dropping off," she said quietly. "I'm not so sure it's made out to you. But we'll see."

Sarah felt the beginning of panic again. She had consciously avoided saying Marianna was bringing a check. "If she says she's supposed to give it to me, why wouldn't it be made out to me? Do you know something I don't?"

"Yes. I saw him fill out the check that Marianna's bringing tonight. A few days before he died. He did it because I kept asking him for money. I told him I didn't want an inheritance. I wanted money to pay for the next step in life. For college, and for the in-between months before I actually started classes. And money for you. I know you wanted money from him but you didn't want to say you were broke. I thought he'd probably leave you money, but I couldn't be sure. And I didn't know how long it would take for that money to reach you."

"So the check is made out to you. And you said it was for us." Sarah's voice trembled. She felt deceived, but why, or by whom, she didn't know.

"Probably. But I'm not sure. I didn't lie, I said I wanted money for myself. That's true. But I thought we might live off it together if you didn't have a job or a place to stay." Esther continued, cautiously: "For a long time he said he didn't trust me. You know he kept saying I was a whore. I'd been a whore and was a whore using him for money. He also kept saying he had more money than he knew what to do with. He was furious at first, that I would even ask. But he changed his mind, around the time we all had dinner with him. I'd been trying to explain to him that I would take care of him whether or not he agreed to give me money—but that wouldn't stop me from asking him to change his mind if he didn't want to. I wasn't always sure how much of my English he understood. I'm not sure he knew, either. I told him I wanted to go back to college. I could do it without his help, like so many others have. But if it was in his power to help me, why shouldn't he?"

Sarah understood Esther's subtext: Esther, too, was his daughter, with material needs and wishes of her own. She wasn't the saintly caregiver to which her sisters reduced her in their minds, preoccupied as they were with the complications of their worldliness.

"How much did you ask for?"

"I said thirty thousand would cover tuition, room, and board for me for two years, with in-state tuition at a public school. I think that was right."

"That's not enough. Not nearly. Room and board, too?"

Esther knit her brow. "I wanted to ask for the minimum. I can get a job, too. It would be harder, but I can do it. And . . . if you wanted to, we could live together and save money that way. I know you want to be alone, and you can stay at your place for a few more months. But it's a thought. You don't have to tell me now."

Sarah thought, I don't want to live with you or anyone. I want to be alone. She thought, with tenderness filling her heart like liquid warmth, She was thinking of me when she asked for money. But help was contingent on living with Esther. She didn't want Esther. She wanted to be on her own, not dependent. What she wanted most was freedom.

She said, with a slight stammer, "That might work. We'll see."

"We'll see," Esther echoed mournfully.

Tenderness was confusing Sarah's thoughts like hot liquor. She wanted a future of perfect autonomy. But right now, she wanted to talk to Esther.

"What do you want to study?" She hoped Esther would understand the meekness in her voice as she intended it: as gratitude.

"Did I tell you I sat in on a poetry class yesterday?" Esther produced a frail smile. "I showed up really early at the church to meet Paul and Minah. I was wandering around and someone asked me if I was there for the class and said I was welcome to wait for them in the classroom. Sometimes I think I'd like to study what you do, even try writing. So I was curious." Esther's kindness was a soothing sensation: she was talking in a low voice as a parent would a child in bed at night, talking about an experience that did not make sense of the darkness, but diminished its strangeness. "I liked listening to the others reading their poems. Of course, they weren't all very good. But it felt good to be there. The women—they were all women—just liked being there. The woman next to me kept writing in her notepad. She was about my age. I think her first language is Spanish. When I glanced over at her I saw her writing was filled with spelling errors. 'Light' was *l-i-t-e*. I saw the word *m-a-h-n-a*. She read a poem about the manna of angels. It was very simple. I might go back next week."

"That's why people like you. You're a good listener. And you like people."

Don't cry, Sarah told herself, though she could not remember the last time she'd cried when she was upset. At such times her eyes might burn, but they always remained dry.

"Maybe. People often talk to me. I don't know whether they're talking because of me or because they want so badly to talk, they would have talked to anyone that didn't walk away."

"It's you, Esther. It's because you don't walk away. And because of who you are. They want you to listen to them and see them for who they are. Because if you do, they'll feel closer to you. And then they'll see themselves in you."

Esther gazed at Sarah intensely before uttering, "You've never talked to me like that before."

Don't cry.

"I want to talk," Sarah said, half desperate, half mournful. "To other people, people I know, people I don't know. I want to have people in my life. I've always been too ashamed to talk to you. Really talk to you. I'm not sure I've talked openly to anyone before. I was never ready. I didn't want to talk to you till I knew I was different. In this fantasy I've changed, I'm good, I'm not mean and bitter. I'm a different person. I lived with this fantasy for a long time without knowing it. But I had no intention of changing. I have no illusions that I can. What I'm always imagining for myself is something else."

"What? What do you imagine?"

Sarah told herself to stop, but she knew she was going to give in to the craving to keep talking about herself. Her heart was pounding with rare vigor; she knew this craving; she wanted always to suppress it. She admired in herself the drive to acquire knowledge, to discover the truth for herself. She scorned as narcissism, as a distinctly feminine weakness, her equally strong impulse to divulge details about herself that no one asked for. To indulge in this impulse was to be like someone compulsively peeling off her clothes while every other, decent person chose to sweat in tacit comity. Over and over, she resisted this lust to share what was private.

She wanted and did not want Esther to stay with her; she enjoyed her dinners with Minah despite herself. She longed for friends for whom she was transparent, lovers for whom every aspect of herself was both a mystery and revelation. This evening she would allow this craving to take hold of her.

"I always see myself in people I don't want to be. I see myself everywhere I shouldn't be. I read and watch TV and I never identify with the hero. I can't be the good character who learns and changes for the better. I'm the one you want to forget. The bad one." In her mind's eye, she saw her face in a seething, malevolent crowd, some blurred amalgam of hate-fueled mobs from history books and the news. "I'm not the one I should want to be. I want to talk to you. I want to want to live with you. At least I can admit that now. But I can't do much else. I can't pretend I would be glad to live with you."

"I feel something similar all the time. 'There but for the grace of God go I.' I see myself in others, too. Others worse off than me, and worse than me."

"No, no, that's not what I mean."

"Then explain to me." The command in Esther's tone said, *It's about time.*

"You can't see. You're too good. Once, years ago, on a TV show, I saw a man, a father and a drunk, beating his children. I thought he should die and go to hell. I remember feeling almost—an almost intoxicating indignation. I watched him whaling on his shrieking children and I wanted to savage him, to murder him. But I felt something else, too—I also wanted to beat the whining children, and the dog that dares to beg for food when the man's already pissed off from working his shit job and being spat on all day. I wanted to beat the children and kick the dog, again and again. The children finally escape the room with the dog. The camera stays with the father for a second before following them. But even after it leaves, I'm still in the room with him. I'm still there. I feel myself there . . ." Her voice grew faint. "Instead of just hating him, I'm ashamed of being him. I don't just see myself in others. And I don't mean I feel like I'm wearing a mask. I'm not caught in a mask, I'm caught in a membrane containing my real desires, my real worthlessness. And it keeps expanding. It contains everyone, everything I shouldn't be, that I don't want to be, but I'm caught in it, because it's my own skin."

Esther's eyes glinted. "It's your shame—and your pride—that makes you think you're so different from me. That makes you think you can't talk to me. You are talking to me now."

"I'm sorry, but I can't stand when people compare themselves to me. I hate it. I hate when people think I can be like them, do something because they can do it. I'm sorry," she said with mounting passion, "but when you compare yourself to me like that, you sound like one of those evil teachers and parents and men of God who say, 'Suffering has been good for me—and it will be good for you, under my hand. I'll make you suffer, and it will be good for you.'"

"You're comparing me to a sadist because I think you're not cut off from me the way you feel you are?" Esther said this without betraying any offense, only bewilderment.

Sarah laughed with pain. "I guess I am. I—I could never see myself in you."

Esther parted her lips, then closed them. She looked pale now. Sarah's face felt warm; she was sweating heavily under her arms. She had the impression she'd siphoned her sister's heated glow for herself. She waited a beat for Esther to speak, then felt an urge to flood the silence herself, with herself, once more.

"I am what I've become, and I know I'm not like you," she said, plaintively forceful. "Minah was talking to me about justice yesterday. Poetic justice. She knows what it means. What it really means. It means revenge. But maybe I'm wrong. I don't know. What I'm talking about is poetry. I think you believe in poetry. I don't. Poetry is wrong because it thinks something can be other than what it is. You compare two things, two people, like you and me. You bring them together and move beyond likeness to some kind of perfect language that makes everything equal and just. Or you take one thing, and you say, as you do, it's not alone, it's also poetry. Poetry isn't real. I'm not like you, and I'll never be like you, even though we're sisters. Even though I do love you. But I still read poetry." She was beginning to sound pathetic to herself, but she wanted her patheticness to be known, too. "I even love some of it. I feel like I need it when I go without it for a long time. I need some of its touchstones, even though I don't believe in them, either."

"What touchstones?"

Fleeting recollections of her students scrambled through Sarah. She was so often frustrated by the way they thought they could see beyond the limits of their experience. Now it seemed to her the essential questions had the shape of time, and she was groping in the dark as earnestly, as blinkered, as they. Still, it was resentment that powered her speech, an unkillable sense of grievance for which she wanted an answer, not only for herself, but for Minah.

They were nearing the end point. Sarah could feel them approaching it. She still felt the last remnants of protest in her. She would empty herself completely before they reached the end. She would delay it a little longer.

"Love. Love and fire and light. Love, and milk, and the soul. I love the words, and I resent them. I can't stand poems about love and beauty that say we need poetry because we need love and beauty. It shuts out all the rest, what has nothing to do with love or light. The unpoetic. The lonely. What I am. Love isn't like fruit on a low-hanging branch. It's something inside you, or not."

"Why do you have to think that way? I do compare myself to you. But not as a judgment. I don't know about poetry. But I know life is good. People may not be good, but life is. I believe that." Esther added, in a pressing whisper, "The way you're talking to me now is good. You love me, but you're misreading your own love. The way that we're waiting together, and not alone—that's also good."

"Minah wanted justice," Sarah stated simply. "And she'll never have it."

"Sarah, tell me what she did. What did Minah do?"

"I—she—she wanted to make him suffer. She wanted him to suffer in one night, in one hour, what he'd made us suffer all our lives. She didn't want him to die. She wanted me to save him and for him to be so grateful he'd be sure to leave me all his money. Or—I don't know what she was thinking. All she wanted was for him to suffer."

Esther was breathing hard. "You have no idea where she is now?"

"None."

"That's how he died." She opened her mouth and choked on air.

"You, at least, have nothing to blame yourself for."

"I'm not sure of that." She wiped her nose on her sleeve. A few tears caught the light as they fell. "I knew and I didn't know. I wanted so badly not to know. I came here and knocked on the door. I said, 'It's me. I missed you at the church.' She could hear everything in my voice. And Paul said he missed her. He was also getting scared. We tried the door, but the chain was locked. I asked Paul to leave, and he did. I told Minah he was gone. It was just the two of us. She could talk to me. I knew she was sitting on the other side of the door. I sat there, too. I said, 'Do you know how lonely it is to be out here? Don't leave me alone now. Please.' I waited for a quarter of an hour maybe. She promised me she would see me tomorrow—today— and begged me to leave her. One night alone. She needed one night alone. I left."

Sarah had wanted so badly not to know she had lied to herself; she'd told herself Edwin alone was responsible for their father's suicide, even when she knew she was trying to protect Minah from Edwin. He was a doctor, and he must have advised Minah on how much medication would be too much for their father's heart to take. That was the crime, she'd told herself, whereas what Minah did was no more than substitute one painkiller for another, which did not rise to the level of a crime. She told herself these lies the same hour that she believed she wanted nothing more than the truth.

"That's how he died," Esther said again.

Esther was weeping silently and staring at her hands. Sarah drew closer to her and touched her shoulder. She had a flashback to another lifetime, when her elementary school class took a trip to a farm. She was very timid then, but an uncharacteristic boldness came upon her when they reached the barn. Touching Esther at that moment was like touching a species of animal you'd never touched before, a lamb, a hog, a mare. Esther's great kindness was to care for the animal part of you, the humanity that wasn't personal and ached more deeply. She let you rest, she helped you breathe, she made your body feel whole. And so she tried to protect the deep tissue of innocence in her sisters and in her father, the fundamental innocence that could never stop believing that you should know care and not harm. Sarah had never appreciated this more about Esther than she did as she tried to reciprocate, stroking her sister's back gingerly, holding her breath as that strange, warm life rippled under her palm.

4
Minah's prayer

My Father, who art in heaven.

What part of me will survive the resurrection?

Will I be again the unmarked child, or the body and the fullness I am now?

Will I know my body?

Will I want it forever?

The pain that tears through me. The happiness that revives me. Will you preserve these with my body?

Will you preserve my loathing and my fury in the heaven of your mind?

Will you resurrect the horror of his being in your kingdom to come?

Did his body come from you, as my body did from him?

My Father, you are in heaven.

My mother, whom you never touched, whom you would not touch, was in this world.

You did not raise me.

Lift up my body in the end. Let me know what I know now. At last.

5
The law of the mother

The last time Sarah saw Marianna while her father was alive, he was laid out on the sofa with Marianna perched beside him, looking less like a terminally ill patient than a sybarite, grinning with lascivious defiance at his daughters.

When she appeared at Minah's apartment she looked very different. She wasn't wearing any makeup. At first glance the monochrome of her smooth, untinctured complexion, and especially the absence of dark eyeliner and smoky eyeshadow, gave the paradoxical impression that she was bruised into colorlessness.

Sarah invited her to enter, and Esther offered her tea. To Sarah's surprise, Marianna accepted.

While Esther was in the kitchen she took off her coat and sat down beside Sarah. In place of the cherry-red tube top and skintight leggings, she had on an ivory sweater with a high crewneck collar and black slacks. If before today Sarah had been asked Marianna's age, she would have said her father's aide was in her late twenties. She realized now Marianna was more likely in her early twenties, twenty-three, maybe twenty-four. She realized she'd judged her for looking vulgar, and so wanted to see her as a mature, fully responsible adult. Marianna looked now like one of her students dressed for a job interview.

"What a beautiful apartment," Marianna said cheerfully.

Something was beginning to bother Sarah. She wondered whether it was guilt over leaving Marianna with her father. But it didn't quite feel like guilt.

"Yes. It's Minah's," Sarah said.

"She has good taste. I could tell when I met her. She's very elegant. Very classy."

Esther came out with a steaming mug. Her eyes and nose were still red from weeping.

"It's so nice to warm your hands in weather like this," Marianna said holding her mug, beaming now at Esther.

There was a silence during which Sarah seemed to be the only one who felt impatient or ill at ease. She wasn't sure how many minutes passed before Marianna said, "I have the check."

"Thank you," Sarah said, her tone even and formal.

Marianna kept sipping her tea until she registered Sarah's look. She put down her mug and reached for her bag.

"I didn't open it. He just never sealed the envelope."

"Thank you," Sarah said again as she reached for it.

She pulled out a cashier's check made out to Esther in the amount of $30,000. She turned the envelope over. Her own name was written on the back in her father's hand.

She wanted to wrap up this business as quickly as possible. "Thank you so much, Marianna," she said coolly. "We realize how upsetting it must have been for you to be there, with our father. Then. Thank you for passing this on. And for coming all this way. We appreciate it. I'm sorry it ended this way."

"Yes," Esther said. "I'm sorry."

Marianna dabbed at her eye. "It was so horrible, to see him like that. It was traumatic. Really traumatic."

Sarah's blood pressure rose at the sudden thought that Marianna might try to sue or otherwise take financial advantage of her family. Yes, that was the suspicion that had been nagging at her. She gave Marianna another look of cold impatience and hoped it was more piercing this time. She was not going to feign grief or parrot platitudes about death while waiting for Marianna to ask for money.

"Do you want money?" Sarah said abruptly. She was in no mood to mince words.

Marianna's glance chilled her heart. It was far more piercing, no doubt, than what Sarah had achieved, because its tenor was not irritation but steely courage. She felt its intensity and intuited unplumbed depths to Marianna, a past and a mind like the hidden rooms discovered in dreams.

"Well, yes," she said plainly. "I was never paid for any of my work. I wouldn't ask, but I'm in a bad way now, financially. So I would like to settle that now if possible. Or you can send me a check. Either way. I don't want to trouble you anymore."

Esther said, "I don't think either of us has a checkbook right now, or any cash. We'll send you a check. After I deposit this." She smiled faintly at Marianna. "Did you want more than that? More than what we owe you?"

Marianna lifted her chin in a gesture of pride intended to counterbalance her humbling request. "Yes," she said firmly.

Esther received the answer as if Marianna had asked for another cup of tea. "I still couldn't offer you anything till I deposit this. How much do you want?"

"I wanted to ask for one thousand. To be able to move. I found a room in the city." She leaned forward, away from Sarah, to supplicate Esther, less humbly than passionately. "One thousand two hundred, if you can spare that much. Which would include what I'm owed for my work. For a deposit on the room. I can't live with my boyfriend anymore. I never wanted to, but I wasn't getting any work and he pressured me to. I can't be around him anymore. I tried to explain to him what it was like for me to find your dad. It was the worst thing I've ever seen in my life. I'm still not over it. And he's mad at me for not getting more cash out of him. That's all he kept saying when I was falling apart. I was traumatized. I was also so scared you'd blame me. But you don't, do you? You can't blame me. You shouldn't, I mean. I never wanted to hurt him. I really tried, I did, in my own way, to help him. I'm being honest with you. I'm not a thief. I could have cashed your check if I'd wanted. My boyfriend knows how to do things like that. But I didn't. I'm asking you honestly for money. I don't know who else to ask. There's no one else I can ask who won't make me do shit or feel like shit for asking. If you don't want to give me anything, I'll walk away. I won't bother you again. But I didn't just come to give you money or ask for money. I don't know anyone else to talk to. I know your dad wasn't easy. I know. But I wanted to talk to someone who would understand why I'm still having nightmares about him. You understand, don't you? And you understand why I have to get away from my boyfriend. I hid your check from him because he would have made me steal it. If he found out I was giving it to you now, he'd kill me. I can't live with him anymore. Will you help me?"

"Yes," Esther said. "I'll call you when we have the money ready. We can talk more then."

"Thank you," Marianna said. A tear rolled down her face, which looked more emphatically denuded and vulnerable than before.

"What do you mean, get more cash out of him?" Sarah said.

Marianna flushed. "It was nothing. It was petty cash. Your dad gave me cash a couple times to pay for takeout for both of us and said I could keep the change. It couldn't have been more than fifty dollars. I'm trying to save money every way I can. I haven't always made the best choices." She was addressing Sarah now, no longer coldly, but with the same ardent conviction with which she'd spoken to Esther. "But I shared what I had with my boyfriend because I lived with him. There's nothing wrong with that. He pays the rent. I owed him what I could give him."

"You're not wrong," Esther said, as dispassionate as Marianna was emboldened.

Sarah went to the bathroom, pulled down the toilet lid, and sat down, hanging her head. She couldn't bear to be around Marianna anymore. She heard her say, "You understand. You understand me. Thank you. I'll be in touch."

The front door shut. Marianna had appealed to Sarah with her naked face to tell her: I know what I've done and what I should do now. I do.

When Sarah stepped out of the bathroom there was a knock at the door. From the hall Marianna called out, "I forgot one more thing. Sorry, can you open?"

Esther was washing Marianna's mug in the kitchen. She gestured to Sarah to get the door.

"So sorry," Marianna said sweetly. "I forgot to ask if you would mail me my earrings if you find them. My gold hoop earrings. I left them at your dad's place. They're not valuable, but they're special to me. If you find them can you hold on to them for me?"

"Yes. Of course," Sarah said dully.

"I wanted to ask Minah, but she didn't give me a chance. I don't blame her. The way I acted last time—"

Sarah revived. "You talked to Minah?"

"Yeah. This morning. I met her outside the building for just a minute to give her the keys."

"She asked you for the keys," Esther said.

"Yeah. I hope that was okay?"

"It's fine," Sarah said. "It's fine. I'll look for your earrings."

"Oh, thanks so much. Thank you. And please tell Minah I hope there are no hard feelings."

"Yes, of course. Of course."

Marianna looked to Esther and then to Sarah. "Thank you," she said, and left.

Sarah and Esther were largely silent in the car service to Englewood.

Sarah found herself asking, "Do you plan on keeping in touch with Marianna?"

"I might."

"You really trust her with that money? Is she going to pay you back?"

"I don't know."

"You're going to hand over twelve hundred dollars to someone you don't trust. We're not alike, Esther. Not at all."

"I didn't say I didn't trust her. Besides, we have money, a lot of it. And others don't." She spoke slowly and heavily. "What else is money for?" A brave spirit was quivering through her despondency like a tiny blue flame.

"It's for food and shelter. It's for college. It's for you."

"Yes. And for gambling." She turned to the window.

"I'll give you money, Esther," Sarah said. "But please take care of yourself first. I mean it."

Esther didn't reply and squeezed Sarah's hand and continued to stare out the window.

Sarah knew she was thinking of their father's last hour alive.

They were crossing the bridge. They would be at the apartment soon.

Sarah's heart was beating hard again. She felt almost breathless; she felt fear twining with something approaching joy, joy that begins as panic. She wanted the silence to break once and for all: the silence she suffered when the bathroom door was shut and she looked in the mirror and her inheritance stared back; the subterranean silence of the moments before sleep, of her commute, of her time on the toilet, of dishwashing, of online browsing, of waiting rooms, of her life. She needed to share the words locked in her head and make them flesh.

"Would it have been better if we'd never returned to him?" Esther asked, still facing the window. A strange tremor in her voice, like a metallic twang, made her sound both delicate and unbreakable.

Sarah didn't know. She longed for cold air and lowered the window a little. The dirty black night roared around them.

She thought of their mother. Would she be riding in this car now if their mother had not died young? She had no memory of feeling love for her mother. She remembered only a terrible longing for Jeonghee to want her and to save her from her father. She gave up when she was eight or nine. "That one is your child," Jeonghee used to say to Eugene of Sarah. Eugene's blood in Sarah was an ineradicable taint, whereas in Esther it had no valence at all. Jeonghee cherished Esther, and so Eugene refrained from hurting her in an obvious way, as his one concession to his wife. She grew indifferent to Eugene's abuse of Minah. She enjoyed seeing Sarah punished by her husband.

Yet there was a time when she would not tolerate the sisters hurting one another. Whether it was Minah pushing and teasing Sarah, Sarah pinching Esther, or Esther tattling on either, their conflicts seemed to represent for her the final limit of evil and decay. It was as if she could not bear to think her own misery was branching out into the world; that it would outlast her. It was brief, the period when she was able-bodied and responsive to her three children, so brief that Sarah barely remembered it. At the sight of them inflicting their unhappiness on one another, Jeonghee would assert her maternal integrity in a flash of indignation that might be expressed as a threat of punishment, for Sarah or Minah, or a scold, for Esther. And for once, her daughters trusted their parent to establish justice at home.

Sarah could hear her mother in the afterlife. I will forgive you for forgetting me as I was when I was good, her mother said. For judging me. For letting me die. For killing your father. What woman—what person—has never wanted an end to their father's law? And so they say there is no greater crime. But I will forgive you for his death as long as you don't let your sisters die.

She closed the window so that her sister could hear her.

"No, Esther," she said. "No."

Minah was kneeling on the floor of the spare bedroom. Torn pages of *Gray's Anatomy* were curled all around her.

"Minah," Esther said. "Minah."

"I'm so sorry," she said. "I'll clean this up. I'm sorry."

She started gathering the loose pages, then stopped.

"Sarah, I don't know what to do. There doesn't seem to be anything I can do. There is no estate. There are two suits against him. One by a former lawyer, not even the one I talked to, who says he was never paid. The other suit claims he sold land with polluted wells. And—and the IRS is claiming he owes a fortune in back taxes. They've put a lien on the estate. It'll be in probate for ages. There won't be much left at all. There could be as little as one million, half a million left. Probably less. And after inheritance taxes—" She laughed weakly. "He didn't—he didn't even have as much as I thought. I thought there was more than ten million. I thought there was because I wanted to believe it. I heard him say it on the phone—but of course he would say something like that." She fell silent. Her long hair hid her face. She said with fearful vehemence, "Everything I did, I did according to my conscience. And for you two. I did. I might be guilty before you, Esther—even you, Sarah—but never before him. Never. But I did it for nothing."

She got up slowly and smoothed out her dress.

In the corner of her eye, Sarah caught Esther's lip quivering.

With Minah, she watched in horror as Esther crumpled on the floor, amid the wasteland of ripped pages, gripping her skull in her hands. The pitch of her pain caused both her sisters to take a step back.

"And all that I did for him? That I did for him—for him and for you—for you—thinking of you?"

Her voice was a terrible spirit released into the air, but what it performed was a reverse exorcism: it was a spirit expressed before descending upon the three of them, to possess them all together.

Minah lowered herself again to lay her trembling hand on Esther's back.

"The way he died—the way you let him die," Esther sobbed. "All that I did—all my work—was all my work for nothing?"

Part 6

Some people have to fight every moment of their lives
which God has lined with a burning animal—
I think because

God wants that animal kept alive.

—Anne Carson, "Teresa of God"

1

The faithful

A fine layer of snow was gleaming on the streets. Though clouds were insulating the sunless dome of the sky, the snow seemed to generate its own light, like the mineral glimmer of an underground cave.

Paul's apartment, too, was like a grotto when Sarah arrived. None of the lights was on, and the second-floor windows seemed to block rather than transmit the radiant grayness outside.

He greeted her with the same openness she'd experienced with him before. It was a quality he exuded effortlessly, and it hit her like a familiar smell, a smell like cinnamon that seemed to carry warmth itself. She was relieved—and moved—to feel his openness to her the moment he opened the door. The next moment she was moved, and pained, to feel his undercurrent of depression, the weary aftermath of shock.

The first tug of pain on her heart was surprisingly sharp. The pain grew dimmer, diffuse like a mood, as she took in his apartment.

She hadn't expected the modesty of the place. The kitchen appliances had the polish of the newest models, the wooden floorboards were gleaming and straight, but it was smaller than Minah's, with a low ceiling, bare walls, and sparse furniture. She recalled a stray remark he made to Minah the evening she met him about boxes lost during his move. Even as a new residence, the place was awkwardly bare. The single item that signaled taste or pleasure, and not merely function, was a long leather sofa with cushions so taut with stuffing, Sarah imagined one would slide off or the leather crack if they sat down. She sensed that the sofa, lonely in its luxuriousness, was a recent purchase, the first major furnishing Paul acquired for the place before giving up.

He sat down on the sofa and invited her to take the facing armchair, which looked grimy in the dimness of the room.

Sarah paused before sitting, caught in the movement of perception arcing to insight. Paul was not a materialist; possessions didn't give him comfort. For him, homes were not showcases of style or repositories of life's material overflow. They were supposed to capture love. He lost things during his move and did not replace them; he did not treat his apartment as a permanent dwelling, because he'd wanted to make one with Minah that conveyed her taste, her touch, his happy approval, their love. And he was able to tolerate the dreariness of the place because he had known loneliness and lack before. He had even savored it, because it whetted his anticipation of marriage.

Sarah wanted to know if he had been very lonely before, in such a way as to be permanently changed by it. She wanted to know if her impressions corresponded to the truth.

Or was this confusion of impression with truth the beginning of a deeper response; was it the beginning of compassion for him?

Maybe he just had no taste, no sensitivity to his surroundings, at all.

"I wanted—I didn't know who else—I hope my email—" Paul stammered.

"What did Minah tell you?" She spoke with a directness that, like her pang for him, like this space, surprised her.

"Everything." He cleared his throat. "I don't want—I didn't plan—to impose myself, or burden you. But there's no one else."

"Yes."

"And maybe you feel the same? I mean, I know you have Esther. I just—"

"Yes. And now you."

She thought, I am, I am feeling compassion for him.

"Yes," he said gratefully. "What I want to know—maybe she didn't. I want to know if she really did tell me everything. She came by to return my things. She said she was leaving her apartment."

"She is. We all are. I mean the three of us. She's moving somewhere with Esther."

"She told me that."

"She lost her job. Or she quit. I'm not sure which. But she can't afford her apartment anymore."

"She told me that, too. She said goodbye to me as if it were the last time. She assumed it was the last time."

He swallowed hard.

"I forgot to offer you something. Would you like something to drink? I'm going to get myself some water."

She declined and stared at the sofa, waiting in the room where he had been waiting alone for something else for a long time. She heard him gulping loudly and blow his nose.

When he returned he appeared more alert and self-possessed. After a moment he said, "She poisoned him."

"No. Not quite."

"Then tell me what she didn't. Please."

"She deprived him of his painkillers. And so he killed himself."

He swallowed again; the pang throbbed again in Sarah.

"She thought I would be with him through the night. She didn't want him to die. She wanted him to suffer during the time it took for me to realize something was wrong. She thought I'd take him to the hospital. Or call my brother, who'd tell me where to find the fentanyl patches. But that didn't happen."

"She didn't tell me all that." A new light entered his eyes. "And you?"

"Me?"

"Why would she do that to you?"

She thought, He feels compassion for me.

"She wanted him to feel grateful to me. I'd done so little for him. Only Esther really took care of him. Esther and my brother. She was afraid he'd leave them all his money. She wanted the money to stay with the three of us. Not him."

"She did it for money. She did that to him, and to you."

His outrage was beginning to burn through the fog of his lamentations. She felt unsettlingly vulnerable to Paul. He wanted something from her—a judgment—that she instinctively didn't want to give. He believed in his right to extract it from Sarah and would pursue it aggressively, this precious gold nugget, even at the cost of blackening the stream.

"It wasn't just for money," she said.

"There was Esther."

She started. How much had Minah told him, and how much had he guessed on his own?

"Yes," she said. "Minah wanted to protect Esther. And there was you. She said you wouldn't want to marry her if you knew about her debts."

He sniffled. "I wouldn't have given a damn about her debts," he nearly spat.

Sarah thought she detected resentment rather than disgust. The resentment at discovery—at having to exert the energy to lie to himself. When his tone sank into sorrowful outrage, she believed him again.

"I was shocked, I was sickened. I was horrified by what she did. I've never felt such despair before—can you believe that? Do you believe me? But I could understand it. Her wish to make your father suffer. When she told me—I could see, in her face, that he'd hurt her in ways I could never imagine. It made me want to protect her. To hold her. The feeling didn't last. Because it wasn't just revenge. It was something more—"

"Cruel?"

"Evil. And horrifying. And . . . sick. Unspeakable, and horrifying. And yes, evil. I never met your father. I know he hurt her. But the thought of anyone dying like that—I could never see her again. But it wasn't just him,

I thought of you. It was you, too. I know she wanted to hurt you, too. Otherwise she would have done it herself. Why did she need you to be a part of it? And what kind of evil would she do to me if I married her?"

She hated the word "evil" on his tongue. When he uttered it, he drew a line between himself and her sister. The stirrings of compassion dissipated. She was supposed to tell him he was released from any duty to Minah. He saw his heart sullied by loving intimacy with the transgressor, and he was anxious to be told he was innocent, he was clean. His love had been pure. He wanted to be told it insulated him, not only from the taint of Minah's love, but from any responsibility to the one who was once beloved.

"Paul."

"Yes?"

"Don't."

"Don't..."

"I don't want to hear you cast your rejection of Minah as God's judgment."

"Is that what I'm doing? Is it wrong of me to judge that torture unto death is wrong? She tortured her own father to death. I don't care what he did to her. That is evil. In God's eyes what she did—" He tried to soften his voice in an appeal to the tenderness he knew existed between them. "Sarah," he said, "how can I marry and have children with her now? How? You can't expect that of me. That isn't mercy, or justice, for her or for me."

"I'd never want you or anyone in the world to be told who to love or be forced to touch anyone they didn't want."

It was as she articulated this tenet of human decency for the first time, out loud, to another person that she became sensible of something in herself, and in the person before her, that might be described as a soul. She was not convinced the soul existed, but she perceived then the paradox that might describe it. Though it was inviolable, it was connoted by the part of you that could be violated. It was impossible to say where it ended and the rest of your perishable self began.

Perhaps even more than the instinct to honor this tenet, more than the intuition of its justice, her rage at the uncountable transgressions of this basic law—the pain coiled within this intuition, like a chicken in an egg—told her that she had a soul.

She had seen Paul at church irradiated with faith in his own goodness. He was unfamiliar with soul-killing injury; he knew evil only in theory, as acts he would condemn and never commit. He was innocent of suffering as an evil in itself.

Was this the truth, or was she being grossly ungenerous to him? These were judgments she'd made of most people she knew. Whether or not they were true, she understood now she made them to protect herself. Unlike Esther, she shielded herself as best she could from the suffering of others—and so, though she recognized in theory that many others suffered like her, and many suffered greater harm than her, she could not believe that she could touch the suffering heart of another person.

She wanted to try now.

"You want me to do what then?" he asked.

"You know better than me. I know you do." Her tone was not gentle. She wanted clarity to hurt him. "I've read more books than you, but you're more generous than me. The books I've read say that Christ is the savior because he came for the noble and the pure of heart—and for the murderers, the torturers, the child abusers and outcasts and common criminals. Aren't you supposed to try to imitate him?"

"I'm not her family. You are. What am I supposed to do? If you know better than me, then tell me."

"I'm telling you what you already know."

"Tell me then. Tell me," he said, his voice quavering between aggression and helplessness.

"I'm not Christian. I'll never believe like you. But I believe, like Christians, you can choose your brothers and sisters. They aren't defined by blood. You are born to think for yourself, to choose what's just and good. Isn't water more powerful than blood? I don't believe in God, and I definitely don't believe he had a son in the world. But you say you do. What is your Christ worth if he can't redeem a scarred woman who wanted to avenge herself and protect her sisters? Forget Christ then. What are you worth if you turn away from the woman you once wanted to marry? Don't marry her. Don't be her lover. Be her brother then, and her friend. Your heart is better than mine, Paul. I've always known that. I'm cold. My heart is cold. I can't reach her as you can. She told me once she didn't know whether she loved you. It was a lie, but I know why she said that. She's been waiting for something else from you. She's been waiting for you to see her for who she is and still not flinch when she reaches for you."

Her own rhetoric was inflaming her. For whom was she feeling compassion now? For Minah or Paul? For anyone? Was this compassion—confused about its object and its source, confusing her about her own desires—making her heartless?

I wanted the truth to feel real. It was the most convincing explanation that Minah had offered her. Until that moment, she had mentioned once, twice, only money and revenge.

Sarah could just make out his nostrils flaring as he breathed hard. He was driving his nails into his thighs.

"You want me to save her because you can't. Because you don't want to."

"Both."

"Because I can. And I don't want to."

"No. Not because you don't want to. And I didn't say you have to save her . . ." It was so draining, trying to change a person. "She has to save herself. She tried to, and it didn't work. She'll try again."

"Do you really believe that?" he said, his cynicism twanging with a crudeness that took her aback. He peered at her in the shadows. The vulgar meanness of his expression made her catch her breath. She rallied herself again.

"Yes. She'll try again. Isn't that why you loved her—because she was someone who tried?"

"I loved her because she's attractive and smart and looks good on paper and on a man's arm. That's why. That was my sin. Thinking I loved her. It was just vanity. Vanity and lust. For that I've been punished."

"You've been punished? You? You're fucking kidding me. You." She forced a hard, contemptuous laugh.

"I'm being punished," he said again. His features were no longer distorted with vulgar belligerence but awash with self-pity.

"You're teaching me something today about a story I sometimes teach. A Greek myth about the goddess of the harvest and fertility. Her daughter was abducted, dragged down to hell to be raped by the god of the underworld. Others thought this was a good idea, a good marriage, including her father, who was like your god, the god of all the gods. Anyway, this kind of thing happened all the time, back then. But instead of accepting it, the goddess unleashed plague and famine and made the whole world cold and barren. She created winter. She was prepared to destroy everything in the world the gods depended on to save her daughter. You have your own myth of goodness and redemption. Your god gave up his son. This goddess wanted to save her daughter. I guess this is the story I believe in. It's a story of what happens when people lie to themselves to live heartlessly ever after. The only thing left to do is to take everything away."

She couldn't read his face, the parted lips and bright eyes that might have been hints of shock preceding revulsion or fear—she sounded threatening and unhinged, even to herself. Why had she told this story?

"Give everything up," he said, returning her gaze.

She got up. She realized she was still in her coat, and she was sweating. A rivulet of sweat trickled down between her breasts.

"Yes," she said, without quite knowing what she was affirming.

2

The notebook

For days after her sisters discovered her in their father's apartment, Minah insisted she deserved punishment.

Justice demanded that she report herself to the authorities. In the next breath she would laugh and say, as she had already explained to Sarah, that no prosecutor would take up the case of the manslaughter of an obscure elderly man with metastatic cancer who had already been cremated.

Minah laughed and lay catatonic, cried and slept. She said nothing; she shouted furiously at her sisters, as if they were the transgressors, that her crime deserved punishment. In response, with bitterest frustration, Esther snapped that if Minah turned herself in, she would intervene and claim Minah suffered delusions of guilt. What good would it do Minah, or anyone, to live in a cage? She was offering to punish herself for her revenge by submitting to another form of revenge. She wanted punishment when she should want to do things that were difficult, fruitful, and good.

Esther was offended by this melodramatic, masochistic call for punishment, which she claimed Minah didn't believe in herself. Sarah was not sure that Minah didn't believe in it. She knew her sister had believed in it for others before. But contemplating the possibility for herself, did she still believe?

"This is what you know, in your heart, so please try to spare me more pain," Esther said bitterly.

Prison was a symbolic hell. Minah deserved purgatory. What form it would take, Esther did not know. But she believed her sister would not escape it in this world, not as long as she received a modicum of care.

At the end of three days, in a moment of meek clarity, Minah conceded.

The next moment she laughed again and continued laughing. She felt a cynical thrill of relief that there was nothing more to dread. The inner voice she wanted to believe was dominant said she would have surrendered herself to the police if Esther had asked her to. Another voice murmured she would have first accepted, then lied, then refused, and lost her sister forever.

Esther was perhaps the only thread that tied her to life. She was otherwise untethered, unpunished, free. And at this, she couldn't stop laughing.

In the weeks after her confession to her sisters, Minah slept at least twelve hours a day. Sarah, too, slept unusually long hours. Adrenaline had helped Minah enact her plan and guard herself from the truth; Sarah, to push herself to discover it.

Esther had already moved in with Minah. She began the search for an apartment for herself and Minah—they had come to this agreement with little discussion—and cooked, packed, and cleaned. She took long walks, which she said were more restorative for her than naps, and read at night before falling asleep on the sofa, sometimes letting the book close as she lost herself in thought. She listened to music on her headphones while tapping messages on her phone or pacing between the dining table and the window, humming. She stared out the window. She attended the poetry class at Paul's church, where she began to volunteer in the soup kitchen, and walked into businesses where she saw HELP WANTED signs. She applied to be a restaurant hostess and a groomer at a pet store. Neither came through, and so she began asking contacts at the church for help.

The hours, days, and nights of work Esther undertook for their father stretched behind her like a salted field.

She continued to wake in the morning and lose herself in the work that would make her future with her sister.

In a quiet moment preparing dinner together in the kitchen, Sarah told Esther there was a history to the very idea of hell, which did not appear in the Bible as a fiery pit in the center of the earth. Esther wanted to know more, but Sarah didn't know more.

"Maybe that's something I can study," Esther said.

Sarah, at first, made attempts to help Esther with her errands, chores, and searches, until Esther said that for the time being, providing company for Minah was the greatest help she could tender. And so Sarah visited nearly every day, walking briskly to the morning train with the same commitment with which she used to commute to teach in the city. To her surprise, Sarah found herself enjoying her long day with Minah. They sat on her bed for hours as they streamed shows and movies, chuckling and sharing opinions and funny asides.

Briefly, Sarah and Minah were lulled into relief, like children at home on a sick day attended upon by a devoted parent. The more they watched Esther, the more her resilience mystified and unnerved them. They wondered whom she was writing to, what she was thinking. They absorbed her presence from the corner of the studio, with the creeping understanding that theirs was the calm at the eye of a storm. They had not been spared, but were suspended in an illusion of security. They had passed through the storm into the center, this stillness, and they realized they were watching their younger sister walk tenaciously outward, back into the tempest—with a brave readiness to be touched, weathered, warped by all the tempers of the world.

They told themselves the worst was over. They watched their sister, and they understood that they had the rest of their lives.

As they streamed their entertainment on the bed, Sarah and Minah fell into a rhythm of silent watching and glib commentary. From time to time, the lively notes faded, and in that caesura they took turns asking personal questions.

"Will you two stay in New York?"

"For now, probably."

The questions grew more probing.

"Do you have any money saved up?" Sarah asked.

"Yes."

"Much? Enough?"

"Enough for now. What about you?"

"Almost nothing."

"Where are you going to live?"

"I don't know."

"What are you going to do?"

"I don't know."

"I've heard about other people in your situation. Like my friend's brother-in-law. He couldn't get a job at a college so he's teaching high school now."

"Maybe."

"It's something to think about."

A handsome actor they recognized but could not place was playing a hospital intern, the love interest of the ward's top pediatric surgeon.

"I heard he's half Korean," Minah said.

"Maybe . . . Yes. Look at his eyes. There's something to them."

"Paul wanted to set you up with someone, you know."

Sarah said nothing. She had not told her sister about her visit to Paul's apartment. They kept their eyes on the screen.

"But I knew you'd say no. The guy's smart and cultured and very sweet. And Korean. I told Paul to forget it."

She, the top pediatric surgeon, was devastated by the death of a little boy whom she had assured would survive. She decided to swear off dating until she could trust her judgment again.

"Why do you only date white guys? Aren't there any Asian guys who study art or philosophy or whatever Victor does?"

"I don't know. I hardly date, you know."

"You're worse than me."

"How?" she asked indifferently, as if Minah were talking about one of the characters in the drama.

"You're ashamed of being Korean."

"Hmm."

"Do you still talk to Victor?"

"Not if I can help it. He—he cheated on me."

She'd concealed the reason for her breakup from Minah out of pride, and out of shame: her jealousy had crippled her for months.

"Oh. What a bastard," Minah said softly.

Twenty minutes later, Sarah said, "This is your chance not to make things harder on Esther."

"Oh, fuck off" was the response, but it was produced without passion.

"Fine."

"It's nice not to lie all the time," Minah said abstractly.

"Did you give him the ibuprofen from your own surgery? Your appendicitis?"

"Yes." Minah paused. "Did Edwin tell you about that?"

It was Sarah's turn to pause. "Yeah."

"I didn't hide the patches. I didn't know where they were. I thought"— she unstuck her voice—"you'd find them. I thought maybe—"

They returned to watching in silence.

❧

The door shut. Minah picked up her phone.

She'd anxiously awaited Sarah to return to Princeton and Esther to leave on one of her walks, worrying she'd miss once again the chance to talk to Edwin in private during his break. She had on her lap a notepad where she'd prepared some responses to what she expected Edwin to say.

"Minah," he said softly. She said nothing. "Minah," he said with a hint of insistence.

"I'm here."

"Minah," he said, tenderly now. "Why have you waited so long to call me?"

Again, she said nothing.

"Why did you wait so long? Do you know what it's been like, waiting to hear from you?" His tenderness evaporated in a hiss of resentment. "I'm sick of trying to talk to your sisters. I have nothing to say to them. I wanted to talk to you. Were you too busy to toss out a message? No, you couldn't have been busy. I know because I called your office and they said you weren't employed there anymore. What the hell is going on? Are you quitting because of his millions? Is that it? Sarah's sharing the largesse with you and not her brother? Have you all decided to leave me in the dark after everything I've done? Answer me. Please. Tell me now."

Minah glanced at her lap. Her whole body trembled.

He said, "I know what you've been keeping from me. I know about New Jersey law. I have a lawyer now. I can still contest his will. He told me he was giving me half. He wanted to give me half."

"You could have contested it," she said sharply, "if he hadn't decided to leave everything to Sarah."

His silence told her he was bluffing. He already knew.

"You know Sarah inherits everything. I couldn't give you anything even if I wanted to. Besides, the money's still tied up in property and stocks." She found herself eliding the estate's considerable diminishment. "If your lawyer told you his drug-addled promises of wealth will hold in court, you should have paid more to find someone else. Your lawyer hasn't even tried to contact me. I'm guessing it's because he knows he can't compete with my old firm. Since our father chose to leave everything to a single descendant, it'll be very hard for you to argue that he wanted his estate shared equally by all his natural children."

"You talk about the law like it isn't man-made. You have agency. Will you honor his wishes? You know he wanted to give me half his estate. You and Sarah and Esther. You all know."

Minah consulted her notes again, then threw the pad to the floor. Her heart was pounding. "No, I don't know. Because that's another lie. You thought he made a new will to leave everything to you and Esther. But you told me something else. You told me he said he was going to change an existing will that divided the estate equally between me and Esther and Sarah, and write a new one to favor you and Esther. You lied to me, and I believed you. You knew what I would do when you lied to me." She paused, and he said nothing. "You were afraid, too. Part of you knew he would never cut Sarah out entirely. You . . . you even said I should try talking to him alone, one last time, right after you dosed him. You said—you said it would make him gentle. I might find closure . . ."

"We tried to manipulate each other," he said at last with unexpected mildness. "I did it for my son, and you did it for the children you're going to have. Yes, I said those things to you. I was offering you revenge. And you told me to make sure he'd be falling asleep when you went in to him. You used me, too. I didn't know what you were actually planning. I thought you were going to give him another patch. I didn't know what you were going to do. I told you he didn't have much time left. I don't know why you did it. I never wanted you to do that."

Minah's heart pounded more violently. It was breaking. The love that girded her heart was crumbling to dust—but love for whom, she didn't know. "I know I'm guilty. Guiltier than you. But to use me like that, to lie like that—" She gasped.

"Minah, it doesn't matter anymore. Would you believe me if I said since the moment I met you I've felt a stronger connection to you, Minah, than to either of your sisters or our father, maybe even more than my mother?"

"Your mother."

"Yes. Even my mother, whom I love and respect."

Lies and clichés she'd heard from men glowed in her mind like dim lights across dark water. "I care about you, but this isn't working." "I've been busy." "Of course I do, but not now." In her mind she said to Edwin, I believe you believe in your love, that it is love. She wondered, with rising anguish: Is his lie stronger than me? Is his idea of love stronger than mine?

"Minah? Are you there?"

"Would you ever introduce me to your son?"

She heard him hesitate and hung up.

Esther had intended to take an aimless walk. When she found herself at Madison Square Garden, she decided she should visit Sarah in Princeton.

"You should try to give people more notice before stopping by," Sarah said on opening the door. She added quietly, "I don't mind. Other people might. Nothing's wrong, right?"

"No. Can I have a glass of water?" Esther asked. She sank into the sofa and closed her eyes. She opened them when Sarah returned with the glass and sat down in Esther's chair.

"What do you want to do now?" Esther said.

"I want to leave."

For a long moment, Esther felt herself caught in her sister's yearning. She longed to travel. Zoya's aunt had just sent her a message from Mexico. She wanted to lose herself again, in unpeopled landscapes, in unknown lives.

She cleared her throat and pulled an envelope out of her backpack.

"This is for you. I forgot to give it to you when you were over."

Sarah knew at once what it was. She was even certain of its amount. A glance within confirmed a banker's check for $15,000. She had not expected the estimated two or three hundred in cash.

"It should last you long enough to go where you want to go and live for a little while."

Sarah put the envelope down on the table and contemplated its white blankness as if it were a pool of water.

Esther said, "I want to live with Minah now, but I don't want to live with her forever. But you'll come back, right? When you're ready."

"Come back?"

"From wherever you go with the money. Come back to see us. To see her if she needs it and I'm not there. Emails and calls are good, but being with someone is better. Or maybe you'll stay here. But if you go away you'll come back one day, right? To wherever we are?"

"I don't know what I'm going to do," she said.

She wanted to cry. But the necessary glands in her had long been deadened, trained to remain dormant unless shocked into sobs by bad physical pain. At such moments, the tears were a purely physiological response, flowing like blood from a cut. There were times when intense emotion gripped her, and she felt an inchoate sob between her chest and her throat, the faintest tingling behind her eyes. The sob would clear, and the tingling stop, as if the inciting emotion had never applied its hot pressure to her chest, her throat, her eyes; as if it were a hallucination, a dream of emotion. She would blink and find that she was as she had been, that she was unchanged.

What a strange longing this was—wanting to cry from emotion but finding herself incapable. It was like so many of her failures: wanting to eat better but feeling too tired to cook the vegetables wilting in her fridge; wanting to be friendly to someone but finding her jaw rigid, her tongue heavy, so that she couldn't say the simple words that would have changed the very air between them. Wanting to be loved for what she was and not being loved; wanting to love and feeling herself unmoved, unmoved, unmovable forever.

She placed her hand on the envelope. She thought that if she did not cry now and release her pain, this time it would not dissolve into the chemistry of the lifeless blood coursing through her hard, constricted heart. It would split her heart.

"I feel old," she said, gazing again at the envelope. She looked up at Esther. "Why are you smiling?" she asked defensively.

"Because—I don't know, when you said that, I suddenly got so excited—and hopeful—because you don't know what you're going to do."

"I'm not excited. I'm depressed. And scared."

"I remember after I left school I was scared all the time. But when I look back, I remember the fear but I don't feel it. I feel almost happy. It's like I'm excited now about what I didn't know then, what I've learned since then. Does that make sense?"

"Maybe," Sarah said with gentle skepticism.

"I've met people who want to be alone with their thoughts. Who want to be left alone. I get the feeling you want to be like them," she said tentatively. "But I'm not sure you'd be fulfilled that way. And I don't think you, or anyone, can know the value of your thoughts if you can't talk about them or teach them. You don't know what they really mean. I know it's the hardest thing. It takes up your whole life."

"You lost me."

"You can get another, better job. Teaching, or something else that makes you think with other people."

"Maybe," Sarah said with a sense of moodily brushing away the subject. Then, seeing Esther's face knit in self-critical frustration, she said more clearly, "I think you're right. I hope you are."

"Maybe somewhere else, not around here. You might like that better."

"Maybe. Actually, probably."

Esther was still nonplussed. She tried again. "I went to confession once. This was a long time ago. I was very lonely at the time. I kept thinking, Who will listen to me? Who can I talk to? I looked up the local church and walked an hour there in scorching heat. It was nearly empty. There was just one woman in the back kneeling and praying. When she got up I asked her where to go to talk to the priest. She led me to the confessional and knocked for me. I got in the box and closed the door, and for a minute I felt too shy to say anything. Finally, I said, 'I've come here because I'm lonely.' I tried to say more, but I started crying. I was crying, and he was mumbling. I stopped crying and tried to listen. Everything he mumbled was rote. I couldn't see his face, of course, but I could tell he was either bored or tired. He said, 'God doesn't test us beyond our ability,' and I thought that was cruel and untrue. I know it's possible to be broken. To be murdered. He said, 'It's hard to understand why a perfect God would allow us to suffer so much.' I thought, No, it's impossible, because I don't believe your god is perfect. But when he said, 'God's love has brought you here,' the words touched me. It wasn't him but that single line he recited mindlessly. The priest kept mumbling and the rest faded away.

"I don't understand anything. I don't believe in anything in this life but grace. I don't know what will bring you back to me. But something, I hope, will."

Sarah folded her arms tightly and leaned forward, hanging her face above the particleboard floor. She saw crumbs mixed with dust and cigarette ashes, a long hair trapped in the sealant. Her eyes were burning; she could not squeeze out any tears. She had to leave this place. The money would allow her to leave—to go far—but leave and do what? It wasn't enough to last long, not at all. Why was she as she was? Why could she not stay and live with and love her sisters? Her shame was greater than her love. She could not cry; she wanted to disappear.

"I want to be alone now. Thank you. For the money," she said.

She felt her sister kiss her on her head. She heard her shut the door and listened to her footsteps out of the housing complex toward the train station. She kept listening until she realized she must be imagining the footfalls; it did not take long to reach the main road, beyond which they were surely too far to hear.

She panicked and rushed out to the end of her block. She did not see Esther.

She returned home, wincing at the cold of the snow seeping into her socks. She sat on the sofa where Esther had been. She peeled off her socks.

I'll miss her. I miss her already.

She was going to leave. She wanted to travel; she had seen other countries and she wanted to see more. She wanted to fall in love. She was a small, unextraordinary person. *God's love has brought you here. God's love will take you there.* She wanted a home to return to, people to return to again and again.

What was it she had written as a child? She rushed to her room, where she kneeled to retrieve the box under the bed with her old notebook. Had her father discovered it rummaging through her and Minah's underwear drawers for anything unexpected? Had he read it and wanted to return it to her? He probably hadn't known what it was—he could barely read English—and simply packed it together with the other things he'd shipped to the other side of the country. She realized she still did not understand why he had done so.

> *I hate him I hate him I hate him. I'm going to run away. I'm sick of everyone.*

She glanced at the rest of the familiar page.

> *Europe sounds so beautiful. I'll go there and everything will change. Everything will be beautiful.*

No, she said to herself fiercely. I want to go somewhere else. But I don't want to run away anymore. But that's what I do.

She saw the two cards she'd found in Esther's room in the box. She remembered the message from her father in one: *You must be good or I am not proud.* She opened the second for the first time. He was dead; she was prepared to read it now.

> *Hi Sarah,*
> *How are you? Do you like your new school? I bet your school is a lot more fun than mine. Are you having lots of adventures? Anna says hi study hard and stay healthy. That's what she always says. Anyway I hope you're having fun. We miss you.*
> *Love,*
> *Esther*

Esther had acquired two cards to send to Sarah at boarding school and given one to their father. She must have asked him to post them, and he never did.

So overpowering and unexpected was the impulse to which Sarah submitted that it seemed meaningful and pure. She stuffed the two cards into the notebook and ran out of the house, still barefoot, stopping once more at the end of the block. The streetlight turned green, and cars passed her. The first time, she'd run out with the urgent desire to see Esther. This time, she'd felt a need to see the street into which her sister had disappeared.

She turned back and headed not home but to the center of the housing complex. She wanted to die, to disappear. She passed the laundromat, where a neighbor opening a dryer glanced her way. He doesn't know I've gone crazy, she thought. She was nearly running. She remembered seeing Minah again for the first time after they'd both left home. Minah looked so graceful, so beautiful. In that first glimpse after many years, she'd had a foretaste of old age, the richness of years that would teach difference, difficulty, tenderness. As she'd drawn closer, she thought Minah looked anxious. Sarah was anxious, too. The pang of tenderness was swallowed up in their mutual fear of the past.

How could Minah have saved the child that she was before she saw her mother being hurt and before she was hurt, time and again—the child so terrified and loving and blind, innocent in her anguished amazement at any injury, at her own power to harm? How could her sister save herself now?

But that wasn't the question Sarah had to face.

How will I save myself—and how will I save the child?

Her feet were aflame with the pain of the cold. I can't forgive anything, either. In her mind she was talking to her sister as she was then, at that tense reunion. I don't want to forgive, and I can't forget. But everything we are, we can redeem.

She reached the dumpsters. She pulled out Esther's card from the notebook and gripped it so tightly she felt it crumple in her fist. She raised the lid of the dumpster and dropped her notebook and her father's card inside.

She headed home.

When Victor told her he was sleeping with someone else, someone he loved, she thought she would never survive her jealousy. In her last hour with her father, she thought she would die of loathing. The pain of this moment was new. It was a revelation. Something clotted in her throat and made it clench. Her eyes burned, and tears fell down her face.

3

The message

I want to come visit you. I hope you'll let me stay with you.

And I hope you will forgive me for my silence. I haven't been in touch, but I've wanted to talk to you for a long time.

I still don't know what you suffered when we were together or what you're going through now. But I want to know. I want to know what I didn't know when I was living with you and since we've been apart. I still ask myself: How could I not know what was a part of my life—and continue not to know?

It's true—I was rejecting you when I disappeared so many years ago. I didn't just want to be alone. I didn't want to remember anything. I was sick to death of everything.

But I thought of you and Minah all the time. Even when I thought I was thinking of something else, or not thinking about anything at all.

I told myself your life was better without me, you didn't really want to hear from me, and got angry and felt sorry for myself. There are times when bitterness eats away at me.

I know your own life asks enough of you to fill your days.

I also imagined you thinking about me. I imagined you wondering about me while reading, worrying about me when you closed the curtains in the evening, saying something to me when you woke in the middle of the night. I imagined these things to console myself. The more I imagined them, the more I needed to reach you. Then I found myself praying in the middle of the night.

Please never let her feel alone.

Maybe you won't write back. I hope at least, if you ever feel weak, remembering this message will give you life. And if you are lonely, my love will bring you peace.

PHOTO BY KOBI WOLF

MAUREEN SUN is a writer and scholar. Her work has been recognized in *The Best American Essays 2021* and received support from the Elizabeth George Foundation and the MacDowell Foundation. She has taught at Princeton, Barnard, NYU, and the University of Hong Kong, and is currently based in New Haven, Connecticut. She is at work on a second novel.

Printed in the USA
CPSIA information can be obtained
at www.ICGtesting.com
JSHW021028301123
52886JS00004B/66